By Dawn's Early Light

Max Anderson Mysteries, Volume 2

Hayden Trenholm

Published by House of Straw Press, 2021.

This is a work of fiction. Similarities to real people, places, or events are entirely coincidental.

BY DAWN'S EARLY LIGHT

First edition. November 6, 2021.

ISBN: 978-1927881644

Written by Hayden Trenholm.

This book is dedicated to my great friend and political mentor, Mike Whittington.

One – Monday, May 17, 1920

Max Anderson looked up from reading *Les Temps* to find Captain Gereau of the Sûreté filling the doorway of his narrow office. Gereau had lost weight in the last few months but he was still a big man by anyone's standards. Max nodded and Gereau entered the office, closing the door behind him. He looked dubiously at the wooden chair in front of Max's desk before lowering his bulk into it.

"Nice place," said Gereau. "Though how you get anything done with all that noise downstairs is beyond me."

Max smiled. Gereau was a good cop but a little old-fashioned. Unlike many of his Parisian compatriots, he didn't yet appreciate the pleasures of jazz. The office above Chez Jake was small but the kitchen was always open and, if he was bored, Max could wander downstairs to watch the players rehearse.

"I like it," said Max. "The music helps me think. If I need peace and quiet, I come in before noon or go to the National Library."

"Every fish has to swim in its own stream," said Gereau.

"You didn't come here to criticize my taste in music."

"No." Gereau paused. The silence stretched. Max was in no hurry to break it. Even after more than a year, Gereau was a bit of a mystery. He still held himself erect but his age had begun to show; the lines around his eyes had deepened and his close-shorn hair and thick mustache had gone from grizzled to grey.

"There has been a murder."

"I don't deal in things like that," Max said. Paris had its share of murders. Guns were readily available in the wake of the war and plenty of desperate men and some desperate women were willing to use them. Several killings had occurred in the last week but Max knew which one Gereau was here to see him about. It had been splashed across the more popular Paris newspapers for several days, ever since the body was found the previous Thursday morning.

"You did once."

"That was a special case," said Max. "I dealt with his death because no-one else, including you, was willing to do it."

Gereau reddened and for a moment, Max thought he would leave. "This may be a special case, too."

Max waited. He had avoided reading past the headlines. He wasn't sure he wanted to know the details. But he wasn't quite ready to ask Gereau to go.

"There is a woman," said Gereau.

"Isn't there always?" said Max with a lightness he didn't feel. "Is she the victim or the killer?"

"Maybe neither; maybe both. It's complicated."

"Murder is usually complicated."

"No, murder is usually simple. Two men fight in a bar; one is stabbed. A man finds his wife in bed with another man and gets his gun. Neighbours argue over a fence; it escalates. Nine times out of ten, murder is like that. An obvious motive, a ready opportunity, the means to hand and an almost certain culprit. This one is a puzzle."

"Is that the official position of the Prefecture?"

"The prefecture has not taken an official position. Yet."

Max leaned back in his chair. His stomach grumbled; he had not eaten, other than a small brioche and coffee taken at a café near his new apartment. He was having lunch with Henri and Yesim at Le Coq Bleu but that wasn't for another hour. He opened a desk drawer and removed a bottle of amontillado and a pair of tulip-shaped glasses. Gereau nodded and Max poured them each a measure. Gereau took a small sip, raised his brows in surprise, and took another one.

"It's very fine."

"I brought back a case the last time I was in Spain. I can spare a bottle if you like."

"Only if you take on the case," said Gereau. "Then it will look like a finder's fee instead of a bribe."

Max laughed. He didn't imagine Gereau was incorruptible but he was so close that it didn't matter. "Tell me about this murder."

"The body was found in the Luxembourg gardens when the watchman opened the gates. A man, Caucasian, early-forties, perhaps, shot in the back of the head. The police surgeon said he had been killed somewhere else and then moved sometime around dawn. Between five and six, say."

"A gang killing? Or a political one?" Though given the nature of extreme French politics, it was sometimes difficult to distinguish the two.

"The investigating officer suspected the latter. But then there was the matter of his clothing." Gereau paused. "He wasn't wearing any."

Max's bile rose in his throat. He had found Havel Barzani's body, naked and mutilated in a bath house. The memory still haunted him. He finished his sherry and poured another.

"We kept that out of the papers so I'd appreciate it if you didn't spread it around. Nor was he simply dumped over the fence into the bushes. He was sitting on a park bench, his legs crossed and his face turned toward the statue of Henri Murger. You know who I mean?"

Max nodded. Murger had been part of Henri's course of studies, designed to make Max into "un vrai Parisian." He was a writer best known for his Sketches from a Bohemian Life, a study of poverty in Paris that had inspired at least two operas.

"It seemed like a statement. The usual suspects were rounded up but no-one knew anything about it. It didn't help that his face was damaged beyond recognition. There were no fingerprints on file, nor did any of his measurements match our files."

The French police relied on the Bertillion system that used body measurements to supplement photographic records of known criminals. Fingerprints had only recently become standard. Max suspected the French police resented the intrusion of British methods into their procedures.

"Fortunately, the victim was an American," said Gereau.

"I know everyone blames the Yanks for the devaluation of the franc but that seems a bit harsh."

Gereau didn't laugh. "We made routine inquiries at all the major embassies. The Americans sent someone over the same day and identified the man as Mark St. John."

"An American diplomat?"

"Yes and no. He was an attaché to the American embassy – but in Canada, not France. He was here on personal business. Apparently to visit his mistress, a Russian émigré, named Irina Pavlovna."

"The woman you mentioned. St. John was mixed up in Russian politics."

"No. And probably yes."

"Now you're starting to confuse me," said Max. "There's another woman."

"Precisely. St. John's wife, Sarah, is also in Paris. She arrived a week ago, three days after her husband."

"You think she killed her husband because he was having an affair?"

"Not in the least," said Gereau. "But it doesn't matter what I think. I am in the political wing of the Prefecture. Murder is outside my jurisdiction."

"So I've heard."

Gereau shrugged broadly. "You need to move beyond past injuries. Sarah St. John has been interviewed several times. I was present because of the diplomatic ramifications but I was not in charge. She claimed not to know her husband was in Paris but refused to say why she was. She was shocked by Mr. St. John's murder but she didn't seem grief-stricken. Perhaps, that is the Canadian way."

"Mrs. St. John is Canadian?"

"Didn't I mention that? St. John was from one of the border states." Gereau consulted a small leather-bound notebook. "Michigan. They met while he was on business in Ontario. Whirlwind courtship, love at first sight. You know how that works."

"It usually doesn't turn out well," said Max. The sherry was making him feel warm. He opened the small window that looked into a green inner courtyard. The cooing of pigeons competed with the faint sound of the musicians. The air provided little relief. For all the talk of springtime in Paris, it was always either raining or too hot. Today it was both. "Did Mrs. St. John tell you all this?"

"She seems remarkably reticent. What little we know of the state of their relationship comes from the new political attaché at the American embassy. I think you know him. Ginger Buchan."

Buchan had been part of the American delegation during the treaty negotiations the year before. He wasn't exactly a friend but he was considerably more than an acquaintance. *I'll have to have a talk with him*, Max thought. *If I take this on*. "You think she'll be more open with a fellow national?"

"It's possible. People do tell you things."

Max had to acknowledge they did. Maybe it was because, as Yesim claimed, he had an open face and an easy manner, though he supposed it had to be more than that. He had done everything he could to become Parisian, living and working in French, adopting the latest fashions, lingering in cafés and strolling the wide boulevards in the evenings like a proper *flaneur*. Yet, despite that, he was still an outsider, a stranger among a city of strangers. That, according to Henri, encouraged trust. It didn't make sense to Max but it seemed to be true.

"Look, Gereau, I appreciate your faith in me. But I really don't deal with this sort of thing. I find things for people. I look into shady business dealings or questionable relationships. I help mediate disputes. I stay away from apaches and criminals. And I don't investigate murders. I'm sure the prefecture has a record of my activities since I returned to Paris last June"

"Without question. We have a file as thick as this." Gereau gestured with thumb and forefinger.

"Then you know what I'm telling you is true. Why did you think I would make an exception?"

"The romantic in me hoped you would come to the rescue of a damsel in distress – a pretty one at that. The patriot dreamed you would rush to help a fellow citizen. The realist? The officer in charge, the one who most certainly will arrest Mrs. St. John in the next few days, is your old friend, Captain Marcel Fontaine."

Fontaine was everything Gereau was not. Short, weasel-faced and sallow, he viewed his commission as a path to greater wealth and power. He was a venal little man of limited wit but great animal cunning with close ties to the anti-parliamentary forces on the right. Most importantly, he had arrested Max twice on suspicion of murder and never missed a chance to cause difficulties for Max and his friends.

Max grinned. "I'll see what I can do."

Two – Monday, May 17 to Tuesday May 18, 1920

It had stopped raining by the time Max had finished recording his conversation with Gereau. He sent a brief message to Sarah St. John at the address Gereau had provided, then walked across the west side of Montmartre, past the Le Consulat restaurant and down the stairs to Le Coq Bleu on Rue Gabriel. Henri had just finished his shift at Le Gare Nord and was still wearing his dark blue porter's uniform with its carefully polished brass buttons. He was perched in his usual place at the end of the bar, his first beer already half gone, talking while Yesim made baguette sandwiches from charcuterie and chevre. He was laughing at one of Henri's remarks and Max stood at the open door and watched them for a moment.

They made an odd pairing. Henri was over seventy now, though no-one would think so if they saw his short compact body hauling bags from the train station to the many hotels that surrounded it. His hair was mostly white but still thick and his round pink face unseamed except for laugh lines around his mouth and eyes. Only the paleness of his watery blue eyes suggested the years and hardships he had seen. Yesim was several decades younger, lanky and several inches taller than the old porter. His coloring was Mediterranean, his features hawk-like. His dark hair was receding at the temples and his beard, when he neglected to shave, was flecked with grey. The two men couldn't look more different.

Henri was a Parisian born and bred; Yesim was a relative newcomer, arriving in Paris from Marseilles in 1909, just in time to experience the great flood of the following January.

Yesim had fallen from one of the makeshift wooden sidewalks and broken his leg. Henri had found him and, without hesitation, hoisted him on his back and carried him all the way to his little cottage on the backside of Montmartre, where he insisted on keeping him until his leg was healed. They had been strangers brought together by a flood; now they were friends that nothing could separate. Max felt lucky to know them both.

Max didn't discuss the death of St. John and changed the subject when Henri brought it up. He still wasn't sure he wanted to be involved in another murder investigation. He had made an appointment to see Sarah St. John the next day; he would make up his mind then, or have it made up for him. There was no guarantee St. John's wife would say anything more to him than to the police.

After lunch, Yesim's thick sandwiches and a plate of dark olives and pickled onion washed down with a hearty burgundy, Max made his way to the morgue on the edge of Île de la Cité. As usual there was a crowd of gawkers lined three deep around the plate windows where unidentified bodies – pulled from the Seine or from the rubbish of a back alley – were displayed in the hopes some relative might happen by. It was a part of Paris that most baffled Max; everything, even death, was viewed as entertainment.

Gereau had provided a letter of introduction and the coroner inspected it closely as if he thought people might forge permissions to view a corpse or read his report. Given the lineups outside, perhaps he had reason to be suspicious.

Max had seen dead men before, more than he cared to remember. The fields and trenches had been full after every battle, bodies stacked for burial. He could still smell the cloying odour of decay from bodies unearthed by the constant churning of the ground during artillery attacks. Even now, two years removed, the memories sometimes came back to him, paralyzing him until he could shake them off. He pulled the sheet down.

Mark St. John might have been a handsome man, based on the symmetry of the lower half of his face. His jaw was square, his mouth, wide and sensuous. His eyes had been blue, or at least, the left one was. The other was covered by a modesty cloth that stretched from the left side of his brow across his ruined nose to just below his right ear. The single bullet had entered his head a few centimetres behind the left ear and was sufficient caliber to tear away much of the right side of his face when it exited. A .45 caliber or perhaps a .445 – like Max's own Webley revolver – both common these days in the streets of Paris. The muzzle had been close enough to the man's head that the flash had singed his hair. It seemed an unlikely wound to have been administered by a jealous wife, who, if the papers were to be believed, would more likely empty her small caliber pistol into the guilty husband and anyone else who was unlucky enough to be standing nearby. Max knew better than to believe what the papers said about women who killed. He had seen what evil could hide behind a pretty face.

He forced himself to examine the body but it told him little else. There were bruises on the right shoulder and bicep, faint now from age. In either case, the marks were too vague to tell him anything of their cause. No jewelry had been found on the body but Max saw the pale band where a ring had circled the third finger of his left hand and another on the index finger of the right. Another pale band circled his left wrist, a bracelet perhaps or one of the new wristwatches more fashionable men had begun to wear since the war ended. There were a few faint scars on his abdomen and his right leg but they were from ancient injuries. He was uncircumcised.

The doctor could add little to what Gereau had already said. St. John had been killed between two and four in the morning and moved a few hours later to the park bench in the Luxembourg gardens. He had been wrapped in a wool blanket—some fibers had clung to his skin—which had not been found. He had eaten a heavy meal with wine several hours before he died. There had been nothing unusual about the food; it could have come from any of a hundred restaurants in the city. If he had known what was about to happen to him, the body showed no sign of it. There were no ligature marks to indicate he had been bound, no trauma to the hands or fingers as a result of a struggle. He had been sitting, or perhaps standing given the angle of the wound, when someone pressed a revolver to his head and shot him.

"We'd know more if they could have examined the room where it occurred," said the attendant with a ghoulish grin. "There must have been blood and brains scattered everywhere. All cleaned up by now, of course."

Maybe, thought Max, *but not without a trace.* Someone had to have cleaned it up and, if it wasn't the killer himself, that someone might be willing to talk. Jean-Marc, the manager at L'Aquilon, the hotel that had been his home until just a few weeks before, knew half the cleaners in Paris. He might be able to help. Max made a few notes in his journal, tipped the attendant, and made his way back to Chez Jake eager to wash the stench of death away with a cold beer and cool music.

§

Sarah St. John was staying at a small private hotel a few blocks from the Garnier Opera house. The concierge examined Max's business card and checked the hotel's book before ushering Max up a narrow set of stairs to the third floor. The room was small even by Parisian standards, habitable only because the bed folded up into the wall. The rest of the furnishings were sparse: two chairs in the Art Nouveau style, a matching writing desk, a small bedside table with a ceramic wash basin and pitcher.

Sarah St. John was younger than her husband, no more than thirty-five, probably younger. Her pale skin, even in the harsh morning sunlight, was unlined, though faint circles underlined her large grey eyes. Her dark brown hair was tied back in a severe bun and her green brocade dress was conservative by Paris standards and a little old-fashioned. *Probably all the rage in Ottawa*, thought Max. She gestured him to one of the chairs but she remained standing, looking out the window at the street below. She was an inch or two over five feet and slim, though not unfeminine.

"Your note said you could be of assistance," she said. "What makes you think I need any?"

"You are about to be arrested for the murder of your husband."

"I didn't do it."

"Nonetheless." It was warm in the room. Max regretted wearing a wool suit. It was his best but he suspected Sarah St. John cared little about such things. "You had a motive. And the opportunity."

"I didn't know my husband was in Paris." She turned to face Max. Her expression was calm.

"It is remarkably difficult to prove a negative. Look at it from the police's point of view. Your husband comes to Paris to visit his mistress. You arrive a few days later. Shortly after that, your husband is shot. Motive and opportunity."

"Do you think I did it?"

"No."

"Why not? Because a woman couldn't commit such a brutality?"

Max snorted. "The war showed that women can do almost anything a man can do. Why not murder? My reasons are simpler. The body was moved. You couldn't have done it alone. The police haven't identified an accomplice. Do you know someone in Paris who would help you move a body?"

"Don't be ridiculous," St. John said, turning back to the window. "The police will surely come to the same conclusion."

"Perhaps. Or maybe they'll find someone who fits the bill. You must have come to Paris for a reason. Your husband had a reason."

"Yes, his mistress. My husband may have had a mistress in Paris. I know he had one in Ottawa. If infidelity was my motive, I could have killed him there."

"Did you tell the police that?"

"I don't even know why I told you. A rehearsal, perhaps, for when I need to say it in a public courtroom. My husband was not a moral man, not in the conventional sense. If he came to Paris, it was to pursue his political agenda or advance his business interests."

Maybe, thought Max, *you are making one confession to avoid making another.* "What business interests?"

"He has a business partner. Pierre Armand. I've met him a few times. An extraordinarily polite man. He and my husband have a long relationship – from our time in Paris before the war. Pierre is some sort of international banker. As with most of my husband's life, I don't know the details. He has offices here in Paris, though I understand he is as often found in London or New York. I mentioned this to, what was his name, Captain Fontaine, but he didn't seem too interested."

Which is interesting in itself.

"Speak of the devil," said St. John, gaze directed at the street. "Captain Fontaine has arrived."

"It would be better if I weren't here. Do you want me to investigate your husband's murder?"

She was silent for several seconds, staring down at the approaching detective. She turned to Max with a faint smile on her lips. "I did love my husband. Once. I owe him some measure of justice." She gestured at the sparseness of her room. "I can't afford to pay you much."

"I'm not doing this for money," said Max. Barzani had left him a considerable sum in his will; the recent devaluation of the franc had further increased his fortunes. He stuck out her hand and Sarah St. John took it.

"There is a back stair at the end of the hall," she said.

"I'll be in touch."

§

Max drifted down Boulevard de L'Opéra, wondering exactly why he had agreed to take this investigation on. He disliked Fontaine but embarrassing a powerful police captain was not the soundest of reasons to get involved in a murder. Barzani had been different. He had been a friend and a good decent man. Mark St. John was a stranger and, in some respects at least, far from decent.

It was the rush to judgement that bothered him, the willingness of people like Fontaine to do what was expedient rather than what was right. Why had he been uninterested in Pierre Armand? Why was he so willing to convict Sarah St. John when the evidence was so weak? Max suspected the answers to those two questions were related.

He turned on Rue de Rivoli and walked for a few blocks before settling into a café not far from the Pont au Change to write up his notes. He would need fortification before he faced the bureaucracy at the commercial registry. No trip to the Île de la Cité seemed to take less than an afternoon to complete. He ordered a small beer and the plat du jour, a sandwich of country ham with patates gratinées, and spent a pleasant hour watching the crowds flow by and trying not to think of the task ahead.

Several hours later, after filling out the necessary forms and paying several fees, both official and unofficial, Max had what he was looking for: a list of Pierre Armand's business interests and an office address. They had even provided a telephone number, a relative rarity in Paris. *Perhaps I should see about getting one installed at Chez Jake,* thought Max. *It might prove useful someday.*

Afterward, he walked through the enormous glass and iron pavilions of Les Halles, looking for furniture for his new apartment on Rue Lepic. He selected a small table with leaves and four chairs for his kitchen and a miniature roll-top desk that would fit into one corner of his bedroom. He arranged to have them delivered the next morning. Satisfied with his day's labours, he took the Metro to Pigalle and climbed the long hill to Le Coq Bleu.

The place was surprisingly full for a Tuesday evening and Max took a seat at the zinc bar rather than at his usual table under the neon rooster that gave the place its name. Yesim put a plate of olives and bread in front of him.

"The usual?" he asked. For Max, the usual, at least to start the night, was a pale lager from the Alsace.

"Not tonight. Open a bottle of Clicquot."

Yesim frowned but took a bottle of champagne from the ice chest beneath the bar. "Something to celebrate?"

"I have a new case."

"Must be pretty special." Yesim filled a flute for Max and another for himself.

"Help yourself," said Max.

"Thanks. If you can drink up your share of the profits, I can drink up mine."

"Since when does this place show any profits?" The truth was Max had no reason to regret his investment in Yesim's business, or in Jake Sullivan's new place on Caulaincourt. He ate and drank for free most days and received a small monthly income as well. These days he plowed most of the money back into the bars, which had allowed the move of Chez Jake from St. Denis to a more trendy, and profitable, location.

"So, what's this new case of yours?" asked Yesim, as he poured them each a second flute.

"I'm looking into the St. John murder."

"For whom?"

"His widow."

Yesim pushed the late edition of *Le Petit Parisien* across the bar. The headline proclaimed the murder of the American had been solved. A picture of Captain Fontaine, his hand gripping the upper arm of Sarah St. John appeared beside a short article. She was staring straight into the camera and smiling slightly.

"You better hurry. The trial begins next week. I think Fontaine wants her convicted and out of the country by the end of the month. Anyway, what makes you think she didn't do it?"

"Fontaine arrested her, didn't he?"

Yesim laughed. There was nothing he liked better than hearing police officers mocked.

"Have you ever heard of a businessman named Pierre Armand?"

"There is an Armand family in Marseilles that's big in shipping. I think they have a couple of chemical factories, too."

"This one lives in Paris, at least, part of the time. He does a lot of business in London and New York. A banker of some kind."

"I don't exactly run in those circles," said Yesim.

"Which circles are those?" asked Henri, slipping onto the stool beside Max.

"Tell him about your new case, Max. I've got to tend to customers."

Max gave Henri a brief rundown of the day's events.

"I don't believe you took the case simply to discredit Fontaine – though he certainly deserves it."

"I suppose I think she's innocent," said Max.

"You've thought that about people before," replied Henri.

"It's not like that."

"Why did she come to Paris if not to kill her husband?" asked Henri.

"She wouldn't tell me. She may be trying to protect someone."

Henri went behind the bar and poured himself a small brandy, dropping a couple of francs in the cash box. "Women like to keep secrets. Sometimes for no other reason than they can."

Max didn't know about that. His experience with women was limited. He had been in love once but it had not worked out well. *It could hardly have worked out worse*, he thought ruefully. *Well, let Sarah St. John keep her secrets for now. They would be revealed when she, or someone else, grew desperate enough.*

Three – Wednesday, May 19 to Thursday, May 20, 1920

Early the next morning, Max took the first Metro train to St-Germain-des Prés, a few blocks from the Luxembourg Gardens. It was clear and cool, perfect for walking, and Max took his time, enjoying the sights of early morning Paris: the landladies sweeping debris from their stoops; the horses, snorting and blowing, as they pulled delivery wagons to the cafés and markets that seemed to occupy every corner; students staggering their way home to the cheap flats near the Sorbonne after a night of philosophizing in the local bars.

The gates to the Gardens were still locked so Max walked along the high fence, wondering how a body could be delivered from some unknown place, lifted over the fence, and propped, naked, on a park bench without anyone witnessing it. He met a gendarme coming from the opposite direction. From Gereau's description, he was the one who had been the first on scene.

"Constable Lepêcheur?"

"I am he," said Lepêcheur. He rested his hand on the white baton strapped to his side.

Max handed him Gereau's letter of introduction. Lepêcheur glanced at it and gave it back.

"You found the body of the American?" asked Max.

"No," said Lepêcheur. "The groundskeeper found him. He called for help and I came running. I told him to lock the gates again and go to the local station for a detective. I watched the body to make sure no one interfered with it."

"Was there anyone else nearby?"

"Only the types you usually see at that time of day – delivery men, drunks, a few bakers or cooks getting a start on the day. There was no one in the park and I doubt if anyone could see the body. The bushes are quite high along the fence there, though if you peered in at the gate, his legs might have been visible. No one else gave an alarm, though."

Max was impressed. Lepêcheur was more observant and thoughtful than most of the gendarmes he had met in the last year. He would mention him to Captain Gereau; Lepêcheur would be an asset.

"Any idea how the body was brought to the bench?"

"Not through the gate, in any case," said Lepêcheur. "There are only three keys and they were all accounted for. The groundskeeper and his chief assistant both had solid alibis. The bushes nearby weren't disturbed, so they used something other than brute force."

He hesitated before adding, "I saw some marks in a tree about fifteen metres from the bench. Captain Fontaine seemed to think it was nothing, but the area there is dark. A car or a truck could pull up without being seen. A ladder to mount the fence and then a block and tackle attached to the tree to hoist the body. It's only a theory, of course. And I, as Captain Fontaine pointed out, am not paid to think."

The more Max learned of Captain Fontaine, the less he liked him. "Can you show me the spot?"

"You see," said Lepêcheur. "The trees block the streetlights here and a car could park there for a while with little risk of being seen."

"Let me hoist you up," said Max. Lepêcheur looked dubious but stepped into Max's cupped hands. The officer was heavier than he looked and for the first time in a long time, Max felt a twinge in his injured leg. He braced himself so Lepêcheur could stand on his shoulders.

"There are scrapes on the paint, where a ladder might have rested."

After he lowered Lepêcheur back to the ground, Max thanked him and headed back to the main gate, which was now standing open. He stood in the gap and tried to see the bench where the body had rested. As the gendarme had speculated, part of it could be seen through the bushes, from the far side of the gate, but it would take an effort.

He walked past the bench to the large tree Lepêcheur had indicated. There were small abrasions on the trunk just above the top of the fence, but it was unclear what might have made them. The ground around the base of the tree was surrounded by low bushes. A few twigs had snapped off but, after more than a week with several heavy rainfalls, there was little other indication the constable's theory was correct. In the absence of an alternate one, Max decided to adopt it anyway.

Even with an accomplice, Sarah St. John couldn't have been involved, except perhaps as a witness. Two men, at the least, had moved the body. Max returned to the bench and looked at it from several angles. The gravel path, of course, was well trampled and, in any case, the bench had been cleaned to remove any traces that it had ever held a dead body. He took out his journal and recorded his conversation with Lepêcheur and his observations of the area around the tree.

The verdigris-covered bust of Henri Murger rested on a stone plinth a dozen paces away, his gaze almost directly at the bench where Max was sitting. Bronze roses draped the statue and trailed down the pedestal in a permanent memorial. Murger had only been thirty-nine when he died though the face on the statue looked older. *Perhaps people aged faster a hundred years ago*, thought Max, or perhaps the sculptor felt an artist of such magnitude needed the greater gravitas.

Murger's stories had chronicled the lives of people who lived in desperate poverty. The want of money had often led them to desperate actions. Money, its love or its lack, was not the root of all evil but it certainly had its place in the pantheon of motives that lead to murder, right beside love gone wrong.

The police thought Sarah St. John killed her husband out of jealousy. Yet, she had seemed strangely blasé about her husband's amorous activities. Was it a sham or did she really not care? And even if his love affairs didn't bother her, she might have another motive for murder. Freedom from a loveless marriage? Money?

If money was the motive, did that point to other suspects? Pierre Armand seemed a likely candidate – why had Fontaine been so uninterested in him? And what about the Russian woman – Max checked his notes – Irina Pavlovna? Could she have a reason for killing her lover?

Three potential suspects, then – Armand, Pavlovna, and, of course, Sarah St. John. Were there any others, perhaps driven by more obscure motives? In Paris, one could never rule politics out of anything. But to answer those questions, he needed to know more about the victim. It was time to visit the American Embassy.

§

Ginger Buchan had changed little in the year since Max had last seen him. His red hair was a little longer but his green eyes retained their mischievous twinkle. He greeted Max with a broad, gleaming smile and a warm handshake.

"Gereau told me you might drop by," said Buchan after they were comfortably seated in brocaded wingback chairs. "You're here about the St. John affair. Dreadful business."

"Did you know him?"

"We'd met in Washington a few times but we weren't friends. I met his wife once but she didn't make an impression. I understand they've arrested her."

"That's why I'm here. I've agreed to look into it."

"I'd have thought you'd had enough of that for one life."

"I thought so, too. But one should never say never. What can you tell me about St. John?"

"Officially?"

"That's a start."

"St. John was a senior consular representative at our embassy in Ottawa. He'd been there since right before the start of the war. It was his second foreign posting – he had spent two years in Paris as a junior in '11-'13."

"He started late – what did he do before that?"

"St. John followed in his father's footsteps, first in business and then to the U.S. Congress. He was defeated in the 1910 election and appointed to the diplomatic corps the following year, the same year he married Sarah Carmichael. He proved surprisingly good at it, diplomacy, not marriage, and was kept on when Wilson became President."

"Is that when he met Pierre Armand?"

"Probably. The first record we have was the partnership formed a few months after St. John returned home, an investment house with offices in New York. Armand spent much of the war there before coming back to France in 1917."

"What do you know about him?"

Buchan looked uncomfortable. "Officially what I just told you. A French businessman with financial interests in New York and an

American partner. Strictly on the up and up. His politics are on the right but not extreme by French standards."

"And unofficially?"

Buchan went to his office door and peered into the hall before closing it. He poured another cup of coffee and perched on the edge of the broad mahogany desk, which along with the wingback chairs and several low bookcases, made up the furnishings of his office.

"Unofficially, he's a well-known anti-Semite."

Max knew, that despite Buchan's red hair and southern accent, he was a card-carrying member of the Zionist Organization of America.

"As you say, not extreme by French standards," said Max.

"Sadly true," said Buchan. "He's written a few inflammatory articles – under a penname – for the Action Française."

Max had read a few copies of the paper as part of his Parisian education. It was the official journal of a political movement of the same name, sometimes referred to simply as the AF, a movement that was both anti-Semitic and anti-democratic, calling for a restoration of a Catholic monarchy. He was always surprised at how respected and influential such views were in France, especially since the end of the war.

"However, it is not his ties to the right that are of concern to America – we take a strictly hands-off approach to the internal affairs of foreign states."

American politics continually oscillated between openness and isolationism, even more so since the failure of Wilson to obtain ratification for American membership in the League of Nations. Some said that was what had led to his final stroke and premature death.

"No," Buchan continued, "there are concerns that some of Armand's business associates are not as on the up and up as he appears to be. Black marketeers from the war years. And worse."

"Then St. John may have been involved with gangsters – once removed."

"No evidence, of course. But plenty of rumours. It certainly puts a different light on his murder, don't you think?"

Max nodded. *Money, crime and politics*, he thought. *What were you doing in Paris, Mark St. John?*

"What about the Russian woman?"

"Irina Pavlovna? Not a lot to tell you there, I'm afraid. Between you and me, St. John had a reputation as a womanizer. He might have met this Pavlovna woman during his time in Paris. Russian aristocrats – she's the grandniece of some Duchess – have been drifting between Moscow and Paris since the Napoleonic wars. When the Bolshies grabbed control in Russia, most of them took up permanent residence. The rich ones, Pavlovna included, live mostly in the Monceau quarter in the 17th arrondissement; the rest in the 15th. Go into almost any café in that part of Paris and you'll probably be served by a Russian count."

Buchan put down his cup and stood up. Max recognized the signs and stood as well, extending his hand.

"I thought you'd need to be able to speak French to be posted to Paris," Max said.

"I've been studying," said Buchan, switching languages. "It helps but I don't use it much. You may recall – my expertise is in eastern Europe. Paris is the hub of Europe. Whenever people get in trouble at home they come here if they can. When the tide changes, they go home. I keep my eye on the flotsam and jetsam."

Including, Max thought, *the flood of Russians coming into Paris. Buchan knows more than he's willing to tell me here – even in the security of his own office.* Max shivered. Nothing in Paris ever changed.

Four – Friday, May 21st to Sunday, May 23rd, 1920

Max dropped by Pierre Armand's offices first thing in the morning. The office, behind a door bearing the plaque "Entre-Océan Financiers," was located on the second floor of the Banque Lyonnaise on the Boulevard de L'Opéra. The dark-haired woman at reception smiled at him brightly and took his card before informing him Mr. Armand was in Marseilles for the weekend but had an opening at 10 a.m. on Monday.

Irina Pavlovna's apartment was on rue Daru, not far from the Russian Orthodox Cathedral. She had agreed to meet him at a small restaurant across from the church but their appointment was more than an hour off. Max strolled the twenty or so blocks and stopped for thirty minutes in Parc Monceau. The gardens were in full bloom, splashes of red and yellow amidst the green, and young couples meandered the shady paths to the accompanying music of birdsong. Baron Haussmann's urban renovations of the previous century had somehow left the mansions of the rich, which ringed the park like battlements, untouched.

Max arrived at the Restaurant Petrograd a few minutes early and chose a table where he could watch the front door as well as that leading to the kitchen. The waiter plunked a small glass of what turned out to be vodka in front of him and left him to peruse the menu, written in both French and what he presumed to be Russian. He was engrossed in deciphering the oddly worded French descriptions when he was startled by a surprisingly deep female voice.

"Mr. Anderson?"

Max looked up into the bluest eyes he had ever seen. Irina Pavlovna was not quite beautiful – her face was slightly too wide, her jaw too square – but she was striking. She was tall with a full figure, accentuated by a calf-length sheath of brocaded pale-yellow silk, nothing like the loose-fitting dresses that most women were wearing in Paris these days. He supposed she was nearly forty but in the dim light inside the restaurant she looked at least ten years younger. A white fur stole draped her neck and her blonde hair was piled high on her head and topped with an elaborate feather hat.

She stood with her hand held out, palm down. Max stood and reached to shake it, only realizing at the last moment that something else was expected of him. He raised her gloved fingers and brushed them briefly with his lips. He pulled out her chair and she floated into it. The waiter appeared, at once, with a second glass of vodka, took the fur and placed it into a nearby cupboard. Pavlovna removed her gloves, placing them in her lap.

"Za Vas!" Pavlovna raised her glass and downed it. Max followed suit, trying not to cough as the harsh liquor burned the back of his throat.

"Let's order," she said. "Then we can talk in peace." She made a complicated gesture with her hand. The waiter hurried over with two more glasses of vodka. Fortunately, Pavlovna merely sipped at the fresh drink.

With Pavlovna's guidance, Max decided on a bowl of borscht, a thick beet soup filled with chunks of beef and shredded cabbage and served with sour cream, to start, followed by an order of pirozhki, dumplings stuffed with onions, mushrooms and rice. His companion selected a cold vegetable soup and shashlyk, a skewer of beef and onions. A carafe of red wine rounded out the order.

When the waiter departed, Pavlovna leaned back in her chair and regarded Max critically.

"You are police agent," said Pavlovna, in lightly accented French.

"I'm a detective."

"There is a difference?"

"I sometimes work with the police, but I don't report to them. Or take their orders."

"Interesting arrangement. What is your interest in Mark St. John?"

"I have none, except that I've offered to investigate his death on behalf of his wife."

"And what interest do you have in her?" Pavlova leaned forward, her elbows on the narrow table, her hands cupping her chin. It seemed strangely intimate.

"She's paying me," said Max. It wasn't exactly true but it seemed to satisfy Pavlovna.

"Good. A business arrangement. I can understand that."

"And what was your interest in Mr. St. John?"

"Mark was my friend."

"The police seem to think it was more than that."

She smiled wistfully, as if remembering something pleasant. The silence stretched. The waiter brought their soup and the carafe of wine. Pavlovna nodded at him and Max tried the soup. It was thick and hot and heavily flavored with paprika.

"Do you like Russian food?"

"So far," said Max.

Pavlovna had barely touched her own soup. She pushed the bowl away.

"It is for peasants. What do you want from me? Mark is dead. Whatever relationship we had is now over. The Cossacks have chosen their victim. There is nothing I can do about it."

"Do you think Sarah St. John killed her husband over you?"

Pavlovna again leaned back in her chair, the silk of her dress stretching over her bosom. Max looked down at his food. He could suddenly smell her perfume, the faint odour of lilacs wafting across the table.

"Do you think it impossible? That a young woman would fear to lose her husband to me?"

No," said Max. "But you haven't answered my question."

Pavlovna poured another glass of wine and, without asking, re-filled Max's as well.

"Do you know what it is like – to be an exile?"

Max's own exile was self-imposed. Nothing stopped him from returning to Canada except the memory of things lost. Still, he felt he knew what she meant.

"Why don't you tell me?"

She smiled again. "You remind me of him. Of Mark. He always wanted to know things. He was a good listener."

"I've heard that," said Max.

"For me, it is easy. I have money. Money papers over most tragedies. But the tragedy remains. The Communists took our country. Stole it from us. Still, it is not enough. They hunt us down. Even here in Paris agents of the secret police – the Cheka – circulate among us. Watching, waiting for their chance. The Prefecture knows all about it but does nothing."

Civil war still raged in Russia but the White army, a combination of old Tsarist forces and foreign troops from over a dozen countries including Britain, France and America, had suffered defeat after defeat and had been driven into the far south and east of the country. Most countries had now withdrawn their soldiers, though money and guns continued to flow. According to most of the French papers, the end was inevitable. Only a few, like the Alliance Française that Armand supported, still held out hope for a Tsarist return.

"It must be difficult," said Max. "Was Mark interested in the problems of the exiles?"

"I don't think I trust you enough to tell you that."

"Then why are you still talking to me?"

"Because you are buying my lunch." On cue, the waiter came out of the kitchen with their entrees. He frowned at Pavlovna's still full soup bowl. She flicked her fingers and he whisked it away.

"Another carafe," she said.

Max wasn't sure he wanted more wine but, he thought, *it might loosen her tongue.* Pavlovna did become more talkative as the carafe emptied. Max sipped his own wine, determined to remain alert to any clues the woman might provide into the murder of Mark St. John. Yet, each time he tried to steer the conversation towards the death, Pavlovna deftly changed the subject to a safer topic.

By the time the third carafe was half-empty, Max's head was swirling with the countless details of the Russian émigrés' long history in Paris and their intricate family connections with each other and with the noble families of half of Europe. When Pavlovna suggested they switch to vodka, Max held up his hand.

"I really must be going," he said, surprised at the slight slur in his speech.

"Must you, Max?" She reached across the table and rested her hand on his. Her fingers were warm and soft.

He pulled his hand away and stood up. A wave of dizziness threatened to topple him and he grasped the back of his chair for support.

"Perhaps you should lie down. You don't look well." Pavlovna was smiling up at him and Max realized she was toying with him, treating him like the boy she clearly thought he was.

"No," he said. "You have avoided answering every question I put to you. You are a clever woman. I grant you that. But the truth will come out. It always does."

"You only believe that because you have never dealt with Russians before. Even the truth is a lie in Saint Petersburg." Pavlovna chuckled deep in her throat. "I like you Max. You do remind me of Mark, though I expect you have that spark of decency he always lacked. He was flawed but not truly bad. I shall miss him."

§

Afterward, Max walked back through the park, hoping to recover some peace of mind. He stopped at the same bench as before but he had little to add to his journal. If he had some natural charm that encouraged people to tell him things, it had failed spectacularly to move Irina Pavlovna.

She was hiding something – she was hiding everything – but he suspected that her relationship with St. John had been deeper than a mere friendship; more complex than a love affair. They had some common purpose, though what it was he had no way of guessing.

She had pretended to be afraid of the police, but she had no more to fear than any other of the tens of thousands of resident foreigners in Paris. Probably far less than most. Money did paper over a myriad of troubles. Was she afraid of someone else? Pierre Armand or his shadowy partners?

The food, wine and frustration served up at the Petrograd had left him with a sour stomach. Max decided to make an early night of it. If he needed to eat again there was bread, hard cheese and a few winter apples in his cupboard.

There was a burly gendarme standing in the hall outside his third-floor apartment. The door was open; inside Captain Marcel Fontaine was sitting on one of Max's newly-purchased chairs, smoking a cigarette.

“I’d prefer if you didn’t do that,” said Max, opening a window. “It’s hard to get the smell out.”

Fontaine looked at the cigarette in his hand as if he didn’t know how it had gotten there. He stubbed it out in a makeshift ashtray: one of Max’s new plates appropriated for the purpose.

“Filthy habit, I know,” said Fontaine.

“I wondered when I might have a call from you,” said Max. As a foreign citizen, Max had been required to register his change of address with the Prefecture.

Fontaine gestured to the gendarme in the hall and he closed the door.

“You have a filthy habit, too, Mr. Anderson. Interfering in police business.”

“Not all your colleagues see it that way.”

“Gereau. He should tend to his own onions. I’m in charge of the American’s murder.”

“Have you made any progress?”

“You know very well we’ve arrested the culprit.” Fontaine’s face was flushed and he fumbled for a cigarette from the pack on the table. Max took the ash-filled plate and dumped it in the wash basin. Fontaine grimaced and put the pack in his jacket pocket.

“My client,” said Max, sitting across the table from Fontaine, “is innocent.” *Of killing her husband at any rate*, he thought.

“You’ll have to prove that.”

While it wasn’t true the French legal system considered an accused guilty until proven innocent, the burden of proof was less onerous for prosecutors than under the common law. It would take more than a reasonable doubt to free Sarah St. John.

“Have you figured out how she did it?”

“Don’t be foolish; she shot him.”

“Yes, he was shot,” said Max, “but how was the body moved?”

"What?" Fontaine frowned, as if the thought had never occurred to him. "In a car, I suppose."

"But how did she get the body into the car and, more importantly, how did she get it through a locked gate or over a three-meter fence?"

"Details!" Fontaine drummed his fingers on the table. "I'm not an idiot no matter what you think. We know she had help."

"But who?" Max didn't think Fontaine was an idiot; one didn't rise to the rank of Captain without a modicum of cunning. But he was no genius either. He had come to warn Max off the case, thinking his mere uninvited presence would be enough. When that didn't happen, he had no backup plan. So, he kept talking.

"We are already questioning people who knew her before the war. One of them will crack sooner or later."

That seemed like a good idea. Max wondered if Fontaine had thought of it himself. He should talk to Sarah's friends, too, if only to find out more about Mark St. John. Or to discover if one of them had a motive for murder.

"Then you've ruled out Pierre Armand as a suspect. Or Irina Pavlovna?"

"Sarah St. James, aided by persons unknown, killed her husband. I will find them soon enough. They don't call me The Bulldog, for nothing. You would be wise to leave it like that."

"Undoubtedly. But it is a free country." Though not, he supposed, if men like Fontaine and the politicians they supported had their way.

"I can make things difficult for you."

Max shrugged. If Fontaine could do more, it would likely have been done.

"Look, Fontaine, you're most likely right. Jealousy is a powerful motive. But look at it my way. Mrs. St. John is a fellow Canadian. And she is a very attractive woman."

Fontaine's grin wasn't pretty. "I understand you completely. Go ahead and make your inquiries. I'm sure Mrs. St. John will be very... grateful... for your efforts. As long as you don't cause trouble for me, I won't cause trouble for you."

Max forced himself to reach across the table to shake Fontaine's hand. If his deception gave him a few days grace to investigate without Fontaine or his men running interference, it was worth besmirching Sarah St. John's reputation. Given what the worst of the papers were already calling her, he was sure she'd find it in her heart to forgive him.

§

Chez Jake was packed but there was always a table available for Max, Jake Sullivan's silent partner. He ordered a bowl of the spicy seafood gumbo that had become the bar's signature dish. It came with a sweet coconut cornbread and a pitcher of cold lager to offset the tang of the broth. Jake delivered the food himself and slid into the chair opposite. He poured a small glass of beer "just to be sociable."

After Max had taken the leading edge off his hunger, he nodded at Jake. "What's up?"

"This and that," said Jake. "Trying out a new band tonight. From New Orleans. They go with the gumbo." When Max didn't laugh, he added, "Police came around before opening. Looking for you. You aren't in any trouble, are you?"

"No more than usual. Captain Fontaine dropped by my place for a chat."

"I heard you were looking into that American's murder."

"News travels fast."

"Yesim came by to look at our new digs. He mentioned it."

Probably wanted to compare notes, thought Max. Yesim was happy enough to have Max as an investor – a considerable improvement over the late unlamented Eduard Lachance – but he always bristled at any suggestion Max made about improving Le Coq Bleu.

"Have you ever heard of Pierre Armand?" asked Max. "Some kind of banker." It wasn't an unreasonable question. Chez Jake was popular with the growing American population of Paris. If Armand did a lot of business with Americans, it was possible he might have brought them here.

"The name doesn't ring a bell," said Jake. "But I'll ask Smitty." Smitty was a broad-shouldered black man who doubled as maitre d' and bouncer for the jazz club. He made it a point to learn the name of any customer who came more than twice. "Got a description?"

Max realized he had no idea what Armand looked like. For all he knew, the man could be sitting at the next table. "I'm told he's exceptionally polite."

"Doesn't sound like any of our clientele," said Jake, smiling. "Tall, short, anything."

"No," said Max. "I haven't met him. His politics are right wing."

"That covers a lot of ground," said Jake.

"He sometimes writes for Action Française."

"I've read that a time or two," said Jake. "Don't care much for foreigners, do they?"

"Some less than others."

Jake nodded knowingly and finished his beer. "More like to find that sort in a church than a place like this."

"A church. Of course. That's what I'll do – look for him in a church."

"There's an awful lot of churches in Paris," said Jake. "And I think services are done for the day."

"Even if they aren't, I've never heard New Orleans jazz before." Several musicians had wandered onto the small stage at the rear of the restaurant and begun to tune their instruments. "Church can wait until Sunday."

§

Max waited in the back of Saint-Germain-l'Auxerrois, the ancient church across from the Louvre, for mass to end. André Bucard was seated in the front row and would be the first to leave after communion. If anyone could tell him about Armand, it would be the charismatic head of the Black Cross, the most influential of the many para-military groups that had sprung up in France after the war. With his connections to every right-wing movement in the country, not to mention deep within the Prefecture of Police, he would undoubtedly know all there was to know about Pierre Armand, banker and part-time journalist. The question was: would he share that knowledge? The right in France was notoriously competitive, attacking each other as often as they did those in the centre or on the left. If Bucard viewed Armand as a rival, he might well tell tales out of school.

Bucard, flanked by his ever-present bodyguards, spotted Max as he came down the aisle and gestured for Max to join him outside.

"I wasn't sure if you'd remember me," said Max, as they waited for Bucard's car to be brought around.

"I never forget people who accuse me of murder." Bucard's smile took the sting out of his words.

"That's why I'm here."

"To accuse me of murder? Who is it this time?"

"I'm looking into the death of Mark St. John. I thought you might know his business partner, the banker Pierre Armand."

"The one who writes for Action Française? I know him but we're not close."

"Is there anything you can tell me about him?"

"I was told by my good friend, Fontaine, that an arrest has already been made," said Bucard. "His wife."

"My client," said Max.

"Of course, a damsel in distress. The lovely Dulcinea, I suppose."

"Her name is Sarah and her cause isn't lost. At least, not yet."

Bucard's car, a gleaming black Delage CO, drew up in front of the church. Michel, the smaller of the two bodyguards, hurried to open the door. Bucard paused with his foot on the running board.

"Armand has provided funds to a number of organizations, the Action Française, of course, and select cadres of their Camelots. There have been other, less respectable, recipients of his largess, as well. I don't need his money and wouldn't take it if I did. He's not particular with whom he associates."

Bucard was a dangerous man but, so he claimed, one with moral standards.

"I had heard he had connections to criminal elements," said Max.

"Then there is little I can tell you that you don't already know. Be careful, Mr. Anderson. Pierre Armand may seem harmless, almost innocuous. But don't let his slight stature or his polished veneer fool you. He would give himself blessing without confession. Don't trust him. And don't get in the way of his associates."

Five – Monday, May 24, 1920

"Keep your head up! Up!" As if to punctuate his words, Kid O'Brien tapped the top of Max's head with his glove. "You can't see a punch coming if you're looking at your feet."

Max looked up in time to see the O'Brien's jab aiming for his left cheek. He slipped to the right, the rough leather scrapping his face and stinging his ear, and countered with a left hook to his trainer's ribs. The older man made a satisfying whoof and wrapped his arms around Max, pushing him against the ropes.

"Okay, okay, that's enough for today." Kid O'Brien released Max and held out his gloves. Max tapped them with his own and turned away. O'Brien snapped his right hand against the side of Max's face. "Never lower your guard until you're sure your opponent is finished."

Max worked his jaw from side to side and grunted his acknowledgement. He waited for O'Brien to step out of reach before he tried to leave the ring again.

"You're still too much of an officer and gentleman, Max," said Henri, who served as Max's corner man in his thrice-weekly lessons from O'Brien. "Hasn't six months with the Kid taught you anything?"

"That I should stay out of fights," replied Max, as Henri cut his gloves away.

In fact, O'Brien had taught him plenty. He'd been a middle weight before the war and had lost to both Al McCoy and Mike

O'Dowd, both of whom later became world champion. He was hardly a Kid anymore. At thirty-seven, his thinning red hair was already going grey and the lines around his eyes and mouth came as much from age as from scarring. But he still could find his way around a ring and he'd taught Max plenty about The Marquis of Queensbury's rules and how to break them. Max was never going to win any titles in the ring but he wasn't going to be the helpless victim of another beating either.

After a quick rubdown and a shower, Max joined Henri for a coffee and a brioche at a café a few doors down from the gym. At 9:30, they parted company, Henri heading to La Gare du Nord for his shift; Max, to Armand's office on Boulevard de L'Opéra. The same dark-haired woman greeted him and then ushered him into Armand's office.

The room was small, panelled in dark wood, with a well-stocked library along one wall. Armand was sitting behind a moderately sized desk of similarly dark wood. The desktop was tidy, a green blotter pad flanked by a brass lamp on one side and a telephone on the other. Armand had been writing a note on a small pad but he looked up when Max entered, replaced his pen in its holder at the top of the blotter. He stood and came around the desk to greet his guest.

"It is with greatest pleasure that I make your acquaintance,' said Armand, extending his hand.

Bucard had said the banker was slight and he hadn't been exaggerating. Armand was barely more than five feet in height, with a slim build and a small well-formed head. His black hair was short and plastered to his head with hair cream. A dark mustache drew a line across his upper lip. His pale features were delicate, his lips and nose, thin. Only his eyes were large: luminous dark orbs under long lashes and thin pointed brows. He was dressed in a black suit of conservative, even old-fashioned, style.

Despite his size, Armand had a firm grip and he held Max's hand firmly for several seconds without shaking it. He was clearly used to dealing with Americans, as he neither offered not expected the perfunctory kiss on the cheek that the French used to greet each other.

"Please sit. Would you do me the honour of accepting a cup of American coffee? Or perhaps an espresso and a meringue?"

"An espresso, if it's not too much trouble."

"No trouble at all, I have my own machine." He picked up the receiver of the phone. "Gerta, two espressos and a small plate of meringues. The good ones from Kaysers."

Armand would talk of nothing but the weather and the upcoming bicycle races until Gerta had deposited their refreshments and closed the office door behind her.

"I understand you wished to speak to me of the unfortunate, no, tragic, death of Mark St. John," said Armand. "What is your interest in the matter?"

"I'm acting on behalf of his wife, Sarah."

"I see," said Armand, coolly.

"You were in business with Mr. St. John?"

"We had worked together on a number of deals, yes. Mark was very well connected. In New York, where I do most of my business, but also in Detroit and Chicago. I was hoping to expand my operations there but, alas, it is not to be."

"Did he have any enemies?"

"I understand his wife has been arrested for the crime."

"Did that surprise you?"

"Yes and, yet, no. On the few occasions I met her, she seemed pleasant, almost placid. Not someone given to strong emotions. Still, Mark had confided in me that their relationship was strained. There was some talk of a divorce but... Mark was a devout Catholic."

"I didn't know that."

"He kept it private. For political reasons. I understand Americans are touchy about religion."

So are the French, thought Max, *though in a different way*. There had been a strong strain of anti-clericism in French society and politics since the days of the revolution. However, most conservatives, even those who supported the Republic, were resolutely Catholic. Those of the left were, at the very least, secular, if not openly opposed to the Church. The official separation of church and state had only become law in 1905 and fifteen years later the wounds were still fresh. Max wondered what connection, if any, St. John's Catholicism had to do with his relationship to Armand, or, more importantly, to his death.

"Can you tell me anything about the nature of your business dealings with Mr. St. John?"

"I don't see the relevance," said Armand. He paused to sip his coffee. "But I have nothing to hide. Won't you have a meringue, they really are superb."

Max smiled and nibbled one of the small cookies. Armand hadn't exaggerated. Even by French standards, it was superb, like a vanilla cloud.

"There is a shortage of ready cash in France," said Armand. "The Germans have not yet begun to pay war reparations, yet the Americans insist on receiving theirs. The recent devaluation of the franc is a direct result of that. I'm sure your own remittance is going farther these days."

Most of Max's money wasn't held in francs, though only a small portion of it was in American dollars. Still, there was no question the devaluation had changed his status from comfortable to well-off. "I do okay. Your company is called Entre-Océan Financiers. What does it do?"

"Industry is trying to re-tool for peacetime production but much of the local capital is tied up in gold or government bonds. No one quite trusts the peace. Americans love a bargain. If you doubt that, go to the antique shops and art dealers – you can't swing a cat without hitting an American millionaire. France has bargains galore; America has millionaires. Mark and I put them together. Some loans but mostly stock purchases, some partnerships, a few mergers."

"Selling France one factory at a time."

"You make it sound unpatriotic," said Armand. "Dormant capital accomplishes nothing. In fact, it leads to moral decay. We put money to work for the good of both our countries. Jobs are created, profits are made. Everyone benefits."

"Where did Irina Pavlovna fit into this miracle of modern capitalism?"

"I told you Mark was unhappy in his marriage. Irina provided some relief."

"I thought St. John was a devout Catholic."

"We're all born sinners," said Armand.

"I got the sense there was more to it than a simple dalliance."

"I can't imagine who might have given you that idea. Madame Pavlovna comes from a good, if minor, branch of the Russian aristocracy. She has good looks – if you like that type – but little money, though you would never know that from the way she cavorts around Paris. No, I'm sure you've misunderstood."

Maybe I have, thought Max. Certainly nothing either Ginger Buchan or Irina Pavlovna had said pointed to anything more than a love affair. But he knew there was something there, the same way he knew that Pierre Armand was much more than he seemed to be.

§

After leaving Armand's office, Max walked down to the Tuileries gardens. He found a shady bench to write up his notes while watching love-struck couples stroll along the wide gravel paths. After, he fed the fat pigeons and then walked along the Seine for an hour. Usually, the river, blue green at this time of year, helped him think, but nothing came to him so eventually he made his way back up to Montmartre for an early supper at Le Coq Bleu.

There were only a few men playing dominoes in the back room and Max took his usual spot under the neon rooster and ordered the plat du jour – mushrooms fried in butter and garlic and served with small cubes of heavily smoked ham and goat cheese. Yesim suggested a white Rhone wine and Max ordered half a bottle. When Max had finished eating, Yesim joined him at the table with two small glasses of eau de vie.

"Have you seen the Petit Parisian tonight?" asked Yesim.

"The usual round of criminal outrages and political scandals, I suppose."

"Both at the same time! Look." Yesim pulled the folded paper from his back pocket and spread it across the table. The headline blared – Notorious thug pulled from river! There was a photograph of a sedan being hoisted over the Pont Neuf at the end of a chain. The story was told in three columns of dense text.

"What's the short version?" asked Max.

"The usual mix of half-truths, suppositions and outright lies," said Yesim. His opinion of journalists was only slightly better than his views on the police and politicians of the city. "There was a man behind the wheel. Shot in the back of the head."

"Like Mark St. John."

"I thought you might see the connection. They say the body has been in the Seine for more than a week, but less than two. Hard to be exact because of the water. The car was dumped somewhere up stream and the current carried it down the river until it wedged against one of the abutments and was forced to the surface."

"St. John's body was found eleven days ago. It had been moved – probably by two men in a car."

"Now there's only one left," said Yesim.

"There is no evidence the two killings are connected. Was the guy in the car naked?"

"I don't think I want to know why you're interested. According to the papers, he was dressed like a bit of *un gandin*."

"I don't know that word," said Max. His grasp of French slang had improved over the past year but he still found the occasional new expression.

"You know, swanky – like an aristocrat. They say he was a *Camelot* – a hawker for the king's party."

"I take it from your expression you doubt it."

Yesim grabbed the paper and pointed to one of the columns. "It says here: his papers listed him as Paul Ponant, thirty-seven, from Marseilles. I know a man of that age and name; there is no way he was a soldier for the Action Française."

"A communist?"

"Better yet," said Yesim, with a hint of pride in his voice. "An anarchist."

Six – Wednesday, May 26th, 1920

Max had spent most of the previous day dealing with several minor matters for other clients. None of them were important but they couldn't wait, either. Besides, he had been uncertain how to proceed in the St. John case. He'd met with all the principals but wasn't any farther ahead than when he started. He was certain that each of them was withholding vital information, either because they were themselves guilty of the American's death or had something else to hide about their relationship to the dead man.

It was as if he was trying to put together a puzzle with several of the pieces missing. He was almost certain there were others involved in the case – the other man in the car, for example, or one of Armand's associates. He wasn't ruling out a Russian connection either. Things had grown desperate in the East and Buchan, at the very least, was wary of some of the refugees from the on-going civil war. Pavlovna, too, had seemed wary of something, though Max knew too little of Russian politics to know exactly what and she had been too cautious in her remarks to enlighten him.

Then there was the matter of the dead man in the car. He had asked Yesim to try to reach his former contacts in the anarchist movement. He was reluctant – he had burned a few bridges with them the previous winter – but he promised to try.

Despite the tumult of conflicting ideas, he had slept well and woke refreshed. He would obtain a list of Sarah St. John's friends and begin there. He doubted his client would be very cooperative; she seemed to value her privacy. Perhaps Gereau could help.

He was finishing breakfast – a day old strawberry tart and black coffee, the best he could do until he found time to stock his larder – when a sharp rap at his apartment door interrupted him. A boy in the blue jacket and pillbox hat of a bicycle courier handed him a white linen envelope, with "Max Anderson" typed in upper case letters across the front.

"The gentleman asked me to wait for a response."

"Did this gentleman have a name?"

"I think he said his name was Minerva," said the boy, smirking. That was the picture on the ten franc note. More than enough to pay for both delivery and silence. Max was tempted to try a bribe of his own, but he doubted the boy had much to tell him.

Max opened the envelope and carefully removed the folded paper inside. It was of equal quality, unscented with a linen thread running through it and a faint watermark.

The message was also typed in upper case letters.

Sarah St. John is innocent of the crime of which she is accused. I can provide proof if you will meet me privately. Your utmost discretion is requested. If you agree, I will send details. Please return this note with your answer.

The letter was unsigned. The V's in the note were slightly elevated while the P's dipped. The lower bar of every E was slightly faded. Max found his pen and scribbled that he would be pleased to meet, provided it was not until at least Friday and if he could be assured of his own safety.

He wanted time to further his own inquiries. Besides, Thursday was his birthday and he had other plans.

As soon as the boy departed, Max wrote down the words of the note as well as he could from memory. The French had been impeccable and sophisticated in its structure, even if the machine it had been typed on was somewhat shabby.

The unexpected note was exactly the break for which he'd been waiting. Someone cared what happened to Sarah St. John. Max had no doubt that someone was why she had come to Paris in the first place.

§

He had not been mistaken about Mrs. St. John's reticence.

"I'd rather you didn't bother my friends," she said, when they had been escorted to the interview room. She kept her voice low, as if she was worried the policeman standing outside the open door would overhear her telling him nothing.

"What about Mark's friends? I need to find out more about your husband's activities if I'm to have any chance of finding his killer."

"Pierre Armand killed him. Or had him killed."

"Do you have any proof of that?"

"Mark didn't trust him," said Sarah.

"Did he tell you that?"

"Not in so many words," she said. "Mark and I ceased to be confidants some time ago. Still, a wife can tell. Mark was a naturally cautious man when it came to money; with Mr. Armand he seemed especially vigilant. Before agreeing to anything he would double-check with his sources in New York or Chicago. The Western Union man practically lived at our house in Ottawa."

"Were there people here in Paris he consulted?"

"Not that I know of," she said, glancing to the door. She mimed writing and Max slipped her pen and paper. She scribbled a couple of names. Max shoved the note in his jacket pocket. "I really wish I could help you."

"What about this?" He put the copied message in front of her. "Any idea who might have written this?"

"It looks like your handwriting."

Max resisted the urge to snap. "It's a copy. The original was typed. All capitals. The machine was probably old. The V, P and E keys were misaligned."

"I really can't say."

"Can't or won't?" asked Max.

"You place me in a difficult position."

"How am I supposed to help you if you won't tell me anything?"

"I told you all that matters. I didn't kill my husband. I suspect Pierre Armand is somehow involved. I have no proof. Nothing but my women's intuition. I doubt that will stand up in court. But I doubt if any of Captain Fontaine's suppositions will either."

"Don't be too certain. I've seen people convicted on less."

"Then I'll have to throw myself on the mercy of the court."

"It's France. It might work." Max recalled that in 1914 Henriette Calliaux, the wife of a well-known politician had shot and killed the editor of *Le Figaro* in his own office. Caught red-handed and freely admitting her guilt, Mme. Calliaux claimed it was a "crime of passion" brought on by fear that the editor, Calmette, would publish scandalous letters she had sent her husband, while he was still married to another woman. After a brief but sensational trial, a jury found her not guilty after less than an hour's deliberations. French law was nothing if not unpredictable.

St. John pushed the note back across the table. Her finger rested briefly on the line: 'meet me privately.' "You'll have to do the best you can," she said. "I have confidence in your abilities."

It was more than Max could say for himself.

§

At least Yesim had good news for him. Jacques Grand had agreed to meet with him. The larger of the two anarchists, Jacques Court, had left Paris. Apparently, the political division of the Prefecture, the one to which Gereau was assigned, had made it too hot for him after he was implicated in several anarchist-inspired bombings. Max didn't mind. One Jacques was more than enough to deal with.

At least the meeting didn't involve the usual convoluted process of passwords and secret rendezvous. Yesim told him to be at La Rotonde in Montparnasse at two that afternoon and Grand would contact him there.

The café occupied one end of a narrow building, its curved red awning providing cover against showers. Sketches and paintings were tacked haphazardly to the inside walls and several artists were hunched over tables producing more drawings. However, the exterior seats offered good views of both Boulevard Montparnasse and Raspail so Max took a table near the front entrance. He was early so he ordered a pain bagnat and a glass of Chablis and scanned the passing crowd for the anarchist. He didn't recognize her until she sat down opposite him.

No longer dressed in men's clothes, Jacques Grand looked younger and less serious than he remembered. She was still remarkably short, well under five feet, but her calf-length dress complimented a slim but shapely figure. With her pixie-like face, Max wondered how he had ever mistaken her for a man, however briefly.

"Good afternoon, Max," she said, smiling sweetly. "I understand you had some questions."

"Will you have lunch...? I'm sorry. I can't bring myself to call you Jacques."

"Try Jacqueline. Still not my real name, but perhaps more fitting. I'll have a glass of that wine."

Max signalled the waiter who quickly appeared with another glass and the open bottle, which he left in a bucket of ice on the table.

"The usual rates apply," said Jacqueline.

Fifty francs for every useful piece of information with Max to be the arbiter of its value.

"It is sad but everything in Paris these days, for good or ill, revolves around money. And even revolutionaries have to eat."

Max nodded his agreement. "And are you still working for the revolution?"

"Not so much these days. A few articles in *Les Temps Nouveaux,* that sort of thing." Jacqueline looked at him over the edge of her glass. "You've filled out since I saw you last. It looks good on you."

Max blushed. Since he'd been going to the gym, he'd had to increase his jacket by two sizes, though his pants were no longer snug. He still hadn't got used to the way it made some women look at him.

"What can you tell me about Paul Ponant?"

"The dead man in the car. He was a Camelot."

"Yesim said he was an anarchist."

"He was, but that was before Yesim became... respectable. The war changed a lot of people. Ponant was one of them. It's not an uncommon story. Look at Georges Valois. He was an anarchist as a young man and now he's a big shot in the AF. Some people become reactionary as they age. Hardening of the arteries or hardening of the heart, I'm not sure which."

"I don't have strong views one way or the other."

"I suppose that is a good quality in a detective."

"So Ponant switched allegiances?"

"Some might say so. Anarchism isn't so much a side as a point of view, a belief that any state is naturally oppressive. That men – and women – are better off in self-organizing collectives, without masters or servants. We try to tear down the state and all its apparatus. Some believe it can be done through peaceful means, others, only through violence. And once violence is involved, there are those who are less interested in theory than in practice. Ponant always struck me as one of those. And with the Camelots, he got to wear nice clothes and hang around with people pretending to be of a superior class. Some people are meant to be willing slaves."

"But Ponant might have been a double agent?"

"It could explain why he was killed in such a dramatic fashion, but I have no way of confirming that. Anarchists operate in cells. Communication between them can be sporadic. There are other reasons why he could have been killed like that."

Max nodded. If Ponant was a witness to the murder of Mark St. John, he might have been considered unreliable, given his history, and therefore disposable. Dumping the car in the Seine would also ensure that any evidence linking it to the first murder was washed away.

"You know I'm working on the Mark St. John murder case."

"Yesim told me that, yes. St. John was an interesting character. He was attached to the American embassy as an economic advisor but it was well known that he was mostly there to spy on the French and Germans in the lead-up to the war. He had links across the political spectrum – royalists, radicals, socialists, even anarchists. I met him once. I was only a girl of sixteen, just being brought into the movement by my brother, but I remember St. John. He was a very charming and attractive man."

"What about his wife?"

"She was a diplomat's wife – social but largely invisible. But later I heard rumours. That she and her husband had an arrangement."

"What sort of an arrangement?"

"You are so young," said Jacqueline. She took another sip of her white wine.

"I'll be twenty-seven tomorrow." Max tried not to sound defensive.

"Really? Anyway, that's not what I meant. The St. Johns were a modern couple. They turned away from each other's indiscretions."

"So, Sarah St. John did have a..." he hesitated.

"Lover?" Jacqueline seemed to be enjoying his embarrassment. "One might have thought they were French and not stodgy old Americans."

"Did the rumours contain any names?" Max wasn't sure he approved. But, then again, why not? The war had shattered everyone's idea of right and wrong. What was the point of morality if supposedly good men could do such monstrous things? He shook his head as if that might clear the growing fog.

"One. Denis Jourdain, a newly minted deputy from the socialist ranks."

"Jourdain? I think I've seen his name in the papers."

"I'm sure. Labelled a hero or a devil, depending on which papers you read. A bit of both, I suspect. Some say he'll be Prime Minister someday, if the socialists can stop fighting with each other long enough to defeat the Bloc National."

"And is he still her... lover?"

"They were linked before the war. Who can say if it survived – except Jourdain and St. John. You should ask them."

"I suppose I should." He gestured to her empty glass, but she declined a re-fill.

"You have to learn to treat affairs of the heart as you treat affairs of state – with impartiality."

"Yes." He took three fifty-franc notes from his billfold and slid them across the table. Three notes for three useful facts – Ponant was a man of violence who little cared who was at the receiving end; that Mark St. John was a spy who operated across the political spectrum; that Sarah St. John was once romantically involved with a prominent left-wing politician. He wondered who else knew these things and which, if any, had led to the American's execution.

Seven – Thursday, May 27th, 1920

Max had spent the rest of the previous day visiting newspaper offices and gathering clippings on Denis Jourdain's political career. He had been elected in 1910 at the age of thirty-four, recruited from the Sorbonne by Jean Jaurès, the charismatic leader of the socialist French Section of the Workers International. Jaurès had been assassinated on the eve of the Great War, crushing the hopes of the French socialists, and, some said, extinguishing Europe's last hope for peace, but Jourdain had carried on. Through the war he had walked a fine line between supporting French troops while denouncing the conduct of the conflict by the Clemenceau government. He had not only survived the crushing victory of the Bloc National in 1919 but increased his plurality in his own *département*.

He had been raised a Catholic but was an avowed secularist, a champion of the separation of church and state and a frequent critic of Catholic conservatives, whom he often denounced as puppets of Rome. He was a staunch republican as well and as a junior deputy had even introduced a bill to ban the use of titles in public affairs. His private life was less well documented, unusual for a French politician of his stature. He had married his childhood sweetheart and they had two young children. However, Jourdain seldom appeared with them at public events and never at political ones. There was no breath of scandal to be found, even in the most virulently right-wing accounts.

Max knew he should spend the day following up some of the leads Jacqueline had provided. He especially wanted to track down the gang of Camelots with whom Ponant had associated. He knew he should also confront his client with the name of her purported lover. And there were still loose ends from his other cases that needed attention.

But Max had other plans.

Between visits to newspaper offices on Wednesday, he had bought cookware and curtains for his windows and Max spent the morning unpacking dishes and re-arranging his furniture.

His apartment, on the third floor above a café, had been recently renovated to add modern conveniences – plumbing, electricity and gas – and was small but well-designed. The bedroom, large enough to accommodate a matrimonial, had two built-in closets and space for a chest of drawers and his small rolltop desk. It was at the back of the unit, away from the street, with a small window overlooking a tiny green courtyard.

The other room had a small chesterfield and matching chair at one end, near a large window that looked down on Rue Lepic, while at the other end was an efficient kitchen, with a miniature stove, a small icebox and a sink. A cupboard for dishes stood next to the sink with a railing above it to hang pots and pans. His folding table was pushed against the wall but could be expanded to accommodate several guests. The water closet had a toilet and a sink and vanity. A tiny shower he could barely wedge into was sufficient for most days but if he wanted anything better, he could use the public baths or the showers at the gymnasium.

It had been expensive – though much less so with the recent forty percent devaluation of the franc – but as he looked around at his new furniture and crisp linen curtains over the window, he decided it had been well worth it. The Hotel Aquilon had served him well for over a year but now he felt he had come home.

At noon, he walked up Lepic almost to the end, then cut across to Rue Gabrielle to Le Coq Bleu, where Henri, Yesim and a few of the regulars had gathered to drink champagne and toast his birthday. Yesim had even bought a chocolate marble cake with a thin layer of chocolate icing, and they ate cake and drank champagne and sang their wishes to him.

After he walked back to his apartment, stopping at shops along the way for fresh baked bread, rich creamy cheese, black and green olives and a fresh killed duck. He stuffed the duck with the dark olives and herbs and put it in the ice box until it was time to go in the oven to roast. He read for a while from the book of French poetry Henri had given him at the bar. While the duck cooked, he walked along Clichy to his favorite vintner and bought two bottles of Bordeaux and a small flask of pear liquor. On the way home, he spotted strawberries newly arrived from the Loire valley and bought half a kilo for dessert.

To Max, home was the place you brought your friends and hid from your enemies. It was a place of warmth and shelter. He had had such a home until illness took his mother and a suspicious accident, his father. After, he stayed in his Uncle George's house until he was old enough to leave, first for university and then for war. But it had never been a home. Tonight, his best friends in Paris; his best in all the world, Henri and Yesim, would come and turn this house into a home.

At six, Max lifted the lid of the gift he bought for himself and wound the crank of the phonograph until the spring was tight. When he heard his friends at his door, he lowered the needle onto the thick wax recording and welcomed them with the sweet sound of Irving Berlin's "A Pretty Girl is like a Melody."

Yesim handed him a bottle of Armagnac and a small painting he had bought from one of the artists who hung out at Le Lapin

Agile. Henri had a parcel wrapped in red paper – more books – and a basket of Anjou pears.

"I'll give you a tour," said Max, laughing and gesturing from the doorway. "There is the kitchen. And the dining room. And there, the music room and salon. And past that folding screen, you can see my bedchamber and study. And if nature calls, you can answer through that door."

"It's magnificent, Max," said Henri. "The perfect place for a young bachelor – though a wife might fill it to its limits."

"Small chance of that," murmured Max.

Yesim clapped him on the shoulder. "All wounds heal, my friend.".

They ate hunks of bread covered in brie with slices of pear and green olives on the side and sipped the pear-flavoured eau de vie. When the duck was ready Max served it with rice and a small salad. The Bordeaux was fruity and rich, but not overpowering. He frowned as he tried his meal; he had followed the recipe the chef at Chez Jake had given him to the letter, but it didn't taste as good as when he had eaten it at the restaurant.

"It is one of the miracles of food," Henri said when Max apologized. "It always tastes better when someone else does the cooking."

"It's better than I could make," said Yesim. "I don't bother anymore." He looked so sad for a moment that Max wondered what he was thinking. Then Yesim smiled and raised his glass. "To Max. Twenty-seven on the twenty-seventh."

"My lucky year," said Max. "That's what they used to say at home."

"Let's hope so," said Henri, lifting his wine.

Max served the strawberries in a blue bowl he had found in the weekly flea market held in the park across from the art nouveau church, Saint-Jean de Montmartre. He poured them each a small glass of Armagnac and they ate berries until their mouths were red and the fumes of the brandy gave the light from the window a rich golden glow.

"It's like being in a nightclub," said Henri, as Max cranked the phonograph again.

"It's nice," said Yesim. "But the singer only knows four songs."

"True enough," said Max. "I'll buy some more when I get the chance."

"You know," said Yesim. "There's a club up the street. They have a girl there who sings like a nightingale. It's always crowded but the owner owes me a favour."

"Why not?" said Max. "You only turn twenty-seven once."

The last of the day's light still painted the few clouds that hung in the dark blue sky like tattered shreds of cotton. Flaneurs, out to enjoy one of the first evenings of real summer, spilled off the sidewalks onto the cobbled street, weaving around the chairs of the dozen cafés and clubs strewn along Rue Lepic as it wound up the hill to Sacré-Coeur. Occasionally, the pedestrians were forced to give way as open cars, horns blaring, bulled their way up the crowded street.

The trio stopped at the café on the first floor of Max's apartment building to quaff an espresso, fortification for the drinking to come. The bar with the singer was crowded but Yesim gave the high sign to the owner, a stout florid faced man with a greasy black mustache, and he led them to a narrow spot at the bar where they could see the tiny stage. They ordered a round of the house wine and had barely managed a sip when a small circle of light illuminated the stage and the singer stepped into it.

The girl was quite lovely, slim and dark with large sad eyes. She was dressed in a floor-length green gown and her bobbed hair cupped her face like hands. She stood straight, looking out at the crowd before her without seeming to see any of them. She waited and the men and few women in the bar grew silent. Then she sang;

soft wavering notes that seemed to hover in the air and then fall like rain on the audience. She sang two songs like that, sad haunting melodies without accompaniment, the only sound in the still air. Then a piano started playing and the spell was broken. The girl smiled and sang a popular love song as the crowd roared its approval.

They finished their wine and had another glass while the singer finished her set. The crowd thinned and they found a table and ordered a third round.

"I won't open until noon," said Yesim. His voice was slightly slurred as he stared blearily at the remains of his wine.

"My shift doesn't start until three in the afternoon," said Henri, his voice as steady as his hand. "What about you Max? Do you want to make a real night of it?"

Max knew he was beyond making a rational decision. He knew he should go home now, or he would regret it in the morning. But he also knew he was in Paris on a warm summer night with his two closest friends. The morning would take care of itself.

"Why not?" he said. "But let's see what other places have to offer."

"Onward and upward," intoned Yesim. He lurched to his feet and had to steady himself on the back of his chair. "I'm fine," he said to no-one in particular.

Henri took Yesim's elbow and guided him out on to the sidewalk, Max following on. He was surprised how solid he felt on his feet. It was darker now, but the crowds on Lepic hadn't thinned, groups of young men in suits streaming up the hill past couples who strolled sedately, the men chatting with passersby while their companions window-shopped. Only a few stores were still open, but the cafés were doing a brisk trade.

Yesim shook off Henri's hand and drew a deep breath through his large nose. It seemed to steady him. "I know a little place on Durantin that has a cabaret."

The club was several blocks away and they stopped for another drink before they got there, sitting at an outdoor table where they could watch the flow of people. There were more of the well-dressed young men now, many carrying canes that tapped rhythmically on the cobbles as they walked.

"I don't like the looks of this," said Henri, as he watched them over the rim of his glass.

"What is it?" asked Max. He had learned to trust Henri's instincts.

"Camelots," said Henri. "Too many for a simple meeting. There'll be a march."

Yesim's head came up at that, his mouth twisted in a sneer. "Pity help the socialist who gets in their way."

Max had seen his share of marches since he came to Paris. It was a national pastime. Monarchists or anarchists, veterans or socialists – they all had their own favorite routes and districts and their particular flags and songs, but in the end they all seemed the same to Max, angry mobs of red-faced men demanding justice from an uncaring city, while the police looked on, white sticks propped on their shoulders, ready to intervene at the first sign of riot.

But the Camelots du roi were different. They were the foot soldiers of the right and, somehow, they were given greater leeway than all the rest.

"They're heading for Sacré-Coeur," said Henri.

The cathedral had been nearly fifty years in the making, commissioned by the City council, though paid for by private subscriptions, after the outrages of the Commune and its destruction. Its construction had become a cause célèbre for the Catholic right that dominated conservative politics in Paris. For secular republicans and the supporters of the left, Sacré-Coeur was nothing but a curse.

"Let's go," said Max. "I've never seen this crowd in action."

Yesim shook his head. "It's not a good idea. The AF is big in Marseilles – maybe it's a hangover from Napoleonic times. It doesn't pay to get in their way."

"I don't intend to get in their way," said Max. He felt alert, almost eager to see the Camelots in action. There were rumours out of Italy, that similar gangs were gaining greater and greater sway. "What could go wrong?"

"Plenty," grumbled Yesim, "so I'll come along to keep you out of trouble. I'd feel better with something more in my pocket than a handful of keys. Say, a revolver."

"Guns are illegal in Paris," said Henri, glancing at Max. "Everyone knows that."

Max had two revolvers, a .445 Webley and a 5-shot .32 – both with the tacit permission of Gereau – but he seldom took either out of the safe in his office. He had had his fill of guns in the war, though he knew their value when things got rough.

"We'll be fine," said Max, clapping Yesim on the shoulder.

They walked to the top of the hill through the winding streets of Montmartre to reach the broad courtyard that fronted the ornate church. The whole of Paris was spread out beneath them, the lights of the boulevards stretching out from the Île de la Cité like the spokes of a wheel. To the southwest, the massive steel tower of the Tour Eiffel reached for the night sky like a glittering spike.

The Camelots milled at the foot of the stairs leading to the basilica, their faces gleaming in the light of a gibbous moon, their canes tapping a nervous rhythm on the cobbles. Max estimated their numbers at more than two hundred and others were trickling in. An equal number of curious onlookers filled the fringes of the plaza.

"This is for show," said Henri. "If they wanted to cause real trouble, they'd be over in the Latin Quarter."

At the top of the church steps were a half-dozen older men clustered in a semi-circle, gazing approvingly at the swelling crowd.

Max recognized a few from the newspapers, all important figures in the Action Française, including several newly elected deputies in the French Chamber. At the end of the line, Pierre Armand, his diminutive figure conspicuous among his larger companions, was talking animatedly.

One of the leaders, not Armand, called out a command and the Camelots shuffled into an orderly column. Many had the bearing of ex-soldiers; a few carried the marks of the war on their faces or a pinned-up sleeve. All shared the same expression, a mixture of anger and glee that would have been comical if it were not so frightening.

The men organized themselves for the march, distributing batons or simple clubs to those without canes, raising carefully printed banners, denouncing unions and socialists with equal vigor. At one point, a group burst into song, the words of the "Marseillaise" echoing from the walls of the basilica. A few in the watching crowd picked up in the refrain, others looked on sourly, perhaps angered at seeing France's anthem being used so cynically.

A few dozen gendarmes, some afoot, others on bicycles, were scattered strategically along the entrances to the square or standing in clusters at the top of the broad stairs leading down the hill. Max spotted one he knew – Lepêcheur from the Luxembourg Gardens. He left Henri and Yesim discussing the best way to break up a parade and crossed to where the constable stood by himself, writing in a small notebook. He looked up as Max approached.

"Mr. Anderson," he said. "Come to see politics in action."

"Is that what this is?"

Lepêcheur shrugged. "It has its political purposes."

"I thought you were assigned to the 7th arrondissement."

"I go where I'm told." Lepêcheur laughed. "And when Captain Fontaine got sick of my useful suggestions, he told me where to go. Besides, I've had experience with these fellows before. How is your investigation coming?"

"Not that well. Everything I've learned so far seems to make my client look more guilty, not less. Though perhaps things will change soon. See the short well-dressed man at the top of the stairs? He was the dead man's business partner."

"You think it was a political killing?"

"Isn't everything in Paris political?"

"Without doubt, the same way everything is about art, food and sex. Usually all at the same time."

"It's a wonder anything ever gets solved," said Max.

"I often feel the same way myself. Fortunately, criminals make mistakes. Sometimes we're smart enough or lucky enough to discover them."

The man in command, whom Lepêcheur identified as Charles Maurras, was speaking now. His voice was high but it carried well and he accentuated his phrases with swift chopping gestures. His face was narrow, with large eyes glaring from beneath dark brows. His hair, worn long and swept across his brow, was dark with streaks of grey also visible in his mustache and goatee. His large ears and nose made him look a bit clownish but there was nothing funny about the intensity of his expression, obvious even from a distance.

"We are here to serve the fatherland," he said. "All our efforts must be expended in that direction. Demonstrate order and reason in all you do. Those who oppose you are less than human. Nothing but filthy socialists and Dreyfusards. France awaits a leader who will restore the Church and the monarchy. You are the forerunners. Strike down any who oppose you. Avoid violence when you can but use it well in the service of reason and of the fatherland. God bless you all. Long live France!"

He finished the short speech by saluting his troops. They responded by raising their canes and clubs. The captains of each squad barked a command and the Camelots turned as one and began their march out of the plaza, their canes pounding a steady rhythm on the cobbles. It appeared for a moment that some of the crowd would block their way and Max felt Lepêcheur tense beside him. But at the last moment, they lost their nerve and faded into the side streets and small parks that surrounded the church.

Lepêcheur nodded to Max and then followed his fellow officers, keeping a discreet distance but with their white batons at the ready should trouble arise.

Max watched them go and then rejoined Henri and Yesim where they were sitting on the steps, overlooking the city below. They had obtained a bottle of wine from somewhere and were passing it back and forth. Henri offered the bottle to Max as he approached and he took a healthy swig, more to wash the sour taste out of his mouth than anything else.

"That cabaret is still open," said Yesim.

Max could hear the chanting of the Camelots in the distance. "Why not?" he said. "The night's young."

"Even if we're not," said Henri, helping Yesim to his feet. "But as you say, you only turn twenty-seven once."

Eight – Friday, May 28th to Saturday, May 29th, 1920

The single thing Max had accomplished on Thursday to advance his investigation, arranging a lunch meeting with Denis Jourdain, now seemed an insurmountable challenge. The sound of his alarm, which he didn't remember setting, couldn't have been louder if it had been the bells of Notre Dame ringing in his bedroom. The light, filtering through the crack in the drapes, throbbed against his eyes. He stumbled the few steps from his bed to the tiny bathroom, cupped water in his hand, to wet his lips and mouth, before splashing the rest across his fevered cheeks. He ran a cold cloth over his chest and arms until his skin tingled.

The remains of last night's meal were scattered on the table; the sink was piled with greasy dishes. The aromas of food and wine that had seemed so delectable the night before now threatened to empty his stomach.

Max wanted nothing more than to crawl back into bed and pull the covers over his head. He could remember going to Yesim's cabaret, but he had no recollection of leaving it. Henri, a professional drinker if there ever was one, must have seen him safely home. *If Henri can do his duty*, thought Max, *then so can I.*

He found and pressed a white shirt from his closet and pulled it on. The collar was a struggle but at last he managed to get it attached and straightened around his neck. His black suit was a bit formal for lunch, but he wanted to make a good impression. Besides, Jourdain's club was one of the better ones in the city and Max wouldn't look out of place. The matching shoes were tight but he could ride the Metro most of the way so they wouldn't pinch too much.

Max ran a comb through his hair; the image staring back from the mirror appeared much better than he felt. It was only a few steps to the station at Blanche and he had time to stop for an espresso and a sweet roll at the café across from his apartment. He couldn't face lunch on an empty stomach. The coffee seemed to help so he had a second, before climbing down the short flight of stairs to the train.

Jourdain's club was on the second floor of a building not far from the Place de la Concorde, where the Chamber of Deputies met. He was seated at a table beside a high window that overlooked the Seine. Jourdain looked up from his paper – *L'Humanité* – when the maître d' led Max to his seat.

"Mr. Anderson," said Jourdain, standing and offering Max his hand. The politician was tall, well over six feet, and looked fit, despite the reputed hazards of his profession. His thick straight hair was still dark, save for a streak of grey at the temples and his clean-shaven face was handsome in a chiseled way. His eyes were blue and intelligent, his smile, warm and sincere. Unlike many politicians Max had met, Jourdain smiled with his whole face.

"Thank you for seeing me," said Max.

"I appreciate your coming into the city," said Jourdain. "There are some important bills being debated this week. I apologize in advance if I happen to be called away. Please sit."

Jourdain waited until Max was seated and had ordered a light lunch – leek and potato soup and a small tomato salad – before speaking again.

"You said you wanted to talk to me about French-American relations. I have little influence in that regard, but I am happy to talk to you. I have a fondness for Americans, and," he said, smiling, "Canadians, too."

Max smiled back. Most Europeans didn't make the distinction. "I'm afraid my note was a trifle misleading. I'm only interested in the relations between one Frenchman and one American woman."

Jordain's smile disappeared and a faint flush reached his cheeks. "I see."

"I know of your relationship with Sarah St. John," said Max. "At least, the one you had before the war."

"And where did you hear this ridiculous rumour?" Jourdain was smiling again but it looked forced.

"I have my sources. I also have places and dates. Would you like to hear them?" Max tried to keep his expression neutral. Jacqueline had supplied few details. He tried a guess. "And I have the letter you sent in Mrs. St. John's defence."

Jourdain paused to compose his features, as the waiter delivered their salads. When they were alone, he said: "She warned me you were clever. Your sources must be very good. I've worked hard to keep my relations with Sarah discreet. Both before the war and since."

"So, you are still Mrs. St. John's lover." It got easier to say each time he said it.

"Surprisingly, yes. I saw her only twice in the years after she and Mark left in 1913, yet the passion remained for both of us. When she wrote me last Christmas, saying how unhappy she was in her marriage, I invited her to Paris. My wife hates it in the city and is seldom here when the Chamber is sitting. It was unfortunate that Sarah's husband decided to visit at the same time."

"Particularly for him."

"Sarah had nothing to do with her husband's death."

"Can you provide her with a firm alibi?" asked Max.

"I can. Though obviously I would prefer not to do so publicly. My career is at a turning point and I cannot afford a scandal."

"I thought the French expected their politicians to have mistresses."

"Well, yes, but not with the wives of American diplomats. It would appear disrespectful to French women, perhaps even treasonous to France."

"I see," said Max though he really didn't. Morality, despite his experiences in the war or maybe because of them, was black and white to him, not painted in shades of grey.

"Nonetheless, I've done what I can," said Jourdain. "The conservatives control the prefecture but I still have friends in the judiciary. I've arranged for Sarah to be put under house arrest and have had the trial delayed for several weeks."

"I've seen her rooms," said Max. "It's not a large improvement over the cells."

"She's been moved to the Grand. I may be a socialist, but I take care of my friends."

The Grand wasn't the best hotel in Paris but it ranked near the top. Max knew it well; Havel Barzani had made it his headquarters during the negotiations of the Treaty of Versailles.

"It is up to you, Max, to make certain Sarah never comes to trial. Find the men who murdered her husband. I will make it worth your while."

Max was sure that he would. Jourdain had come from a modest background but his wife had not; her father had made a fortune in the colonies and had left it all to his only child. Of course, Max wasn't sure he would ever collect. Jourdain, despite his seeming desire to see justice done, remained one of the key suspects.

"Do you have any suggestions where I should start?"

"You know of Pierre Armand?" asked Jourdain.

"Mark St. John's business partner. I've met him. I also saw him last night with Charles Maurras."

"The Camelots' march?"

"Yes. A peaceful one for a change."

"They're only warming up," said Jourdain. "Armand has other so-called business partners. From the ports of Marseille and Sète. And from Italy. Not everything they deal in is strictly legal."

"Are you suggesting that St. John was mixed up in criminal activities?"

"I'm certain he wasn't. But what if he found out? What if he threatened to go to the police with his discoveries? Do you think men like that would stand idly by?"

"No," said Max. "I've met that type. They don't tend to greet betrayal with a pleasant smile."

The waiter brought their second course: Max's soup and a Croque Monsieur for Jourdain. The politician pushed the plate to one side, his appetite apparently gone.

"Still," said Max. "I need some sort of evidence. Or at least a clue where to begin."

Jourdain nodded. "Of course. You are not the only one with sources of information, Mr. Anderson. I can provide some letters – incriminating letters – as well as some bills of lading that will point you to certain people, certain warehouses on the south side of Paris. I'm sure you could take it from there."

"I don't suppose you have them with you."

Jourdain looked around the half-filled restaurant. "I didn't know for sure you had made the connection. But I always prepare for the worst." He slipped a thin beige envelope from his jacket pocket and passed it to Max.

"Why don't you take these to the police?" asked Max. "You could have done so anonymously."

"The police have made their decision. Why would they change their mind because of a few letters?"

"You said they incriminate Armand in criminal activities. At the very least it would make them take a closer look."

Jourdain flushed. "The letters have a certain ambiguity. I know their meaning but others less motivated to see the truth could still discount them. It is what I have; the rest, as I say, is up to you."

"I'll look into it," said Max, tucking the envelope into his own jacket pocket.

"Be careful. These men are dangerous. If they killed Mark, they would not hesitate to do the same to you." Jourdain glanced at his watch. "I should go. I'm scheduled to speak today in the Chamber and should prepare. Finish your soup, the sandwich, too, if you like. Don't worry about paying; I have an account."

Max stood and shook Jourdain's hand, then watched him across the restaurant, his back straight and his shoulders square. He had the elegance of a dancer, gliding past tables as if his feet never touched the ground. Max sat down and ordered a coffee. The sandwich was cool, but the bread was still crisp and buttery; the ham sweet and salty. Just what he needed to calm his seething stomach.

§

It was raining when Max left the club and he bought an umbrella from a street vendor, choosing to walk for a while along the banks of the Seine rather than grab the Metro or a cab. The flowing water always soothed him and helped him compose his thoughts.

It had been ten days since Gereau had come to his office, but it seemed he had made little progress. He had discovered the reason Sarah St. John had come to Paris, but the addition of a lover did little to clear her of her husband's murder. The police already suspected her of seeking revenge for her husband's infidelities; now they might accuse her of covering up her own. True, there was no doubt that Sarah couldn't have killed her husband alone. She might have pulled the trigger, but she would have needed help – one or, more likely, two men – to move the body. Ponant, a volatile man enamoured of violence and the upper classes, could have been one of them, used and then disposed of by his accomplice. Another Camelot or one of Armand's criminal confederates? Or Sarah's lover, Jordain?

If she was involved, he almost certainly was, too. But if she was indeed innocent, did that take the politician out of the picture? Not necessarily. But would someone of Jourdain's stature and reputation for subtlety risk his career, his very life, for a lover that he had seen twice in nearly a decade? Anything was possible, but it seemed flimsy to him. First impressions were only that, but Jourdain struck Max as a man of infinite calculation, a man who used passion but was never used by it.

If Sarah, and therefore Jordain, were eliminated, who did that leave? On the one hand there was Pierre Armand, the business partner with political ambitions and criminal connections. He might have been threatened if Mark found out about the latter. If he found out... that didn't ring true. St. John had a reputation both for political acumen and for sharp business dealings. Jacqueline said he was a spy. Would he have entered into a partnership with Armand without learning everything he could about the man? But if he had foreknowledge, why risk it?

The American government was growing more and more distrustful of foreign interests or even engagement. They had rejected President Wilson's proposed League of Nations and largely withdrawn from the world stage except where their interests were directly affected. Moral rectitude had become the order of the day – the passage of the 18th amendment banning the sale of alcohol only five months before was only the most obvious symbol – and a man like Mark St. John would certainly understand the risks he was taking in associating with foreign criminals.

The rain was heavier now, splashing on the stone walkway, soaking his good shoes and pant legs. Max was surprised to find he had walked all the way to Pont Alexandre. To the left, the Tour Eiffel gleamed wetly, its highest segments shrouded in low cloud, to the right, the long climb to the Trocadero to reach the Champs Elysée and the road home. He was cold, his wounds throbbing as they always did in this weather. His head still ached slightly from his birthday indulgences; the thought of his warm little apartment was appealing and a Metro station was only a few streets away.

Instead, he ducked into a nearby bistro, ordering a café au lait instead of his usual espresso. The creamy texture of the hot drink calmed his stomach, and the coffee eased the pain in his head. He took out his journal and summarized his thoughts on the case. He looked though the documents Jourdain had given him. They suggested certain unnamed goods had been brought into into the country without proper licenses. Bribery of port officials was hinted at but it was hardly sufficient to convict Armand of serious criminal activity, let alone murder. Max would need to visit the warehouses Jourdain mentioned if he were to find anything more substantial.

That left the Russians. Irina Pavlovna had been far less frank with him than Denis Jourdain. She had not denied a love affair with Mark St. John but she hadn't admitted it either. A friend, she had called him, but what did that friendship entail? And did it extend to others within the Russian community? Or even beyond the Paris enclave to Russia itself? Pavlovna hinted at communist persecution of the exiles, perhaps even threats of violence. Could Mark St. John have been the victim of an assassin's bullet?

Max shuddered and resisted the urge to look around. What did a member of the secret police look like? Max supposed they could look like anyone. Better to stick to the facts. He'd deal with the Cheka when he had proof it was more than the paranoid fears of a Russian aristocrat.

Regardless, he needed to know more about Pavlovna and her friendship with St. John. And that meant another visit to the Petrograd. "Even the truth was a lie in Saint Petersburg," Pavlovna had said. Max ordered an espresso to fortify him against the ordeal of deciphering Russian intrigue. When it arrived, he drank it in a single gulp before venturing into the rain to find a taxi.

§

Half the tables at the small restaurant were occupied when Max arrived. Yesim had always said rain was good for business, as long as it didn't last too long. It appeared the same was true for Russians as for Frenchmen. The same waiter was serving tumblers of vodka and plates of steaming dumplings. He nodded at Max when he entered – in greeting or recognition wasn't clear. He certainly was in no hurry to come to the table Max chose near the back where he could observe the other patrons and see the ornate Russian cathedral across the street.

The other diners seemed to share little than the same dour expression and a hunched posture that precluded sociability. They concentrated on the food and drink in front of them or engaged in whispered conversations with their companions, looking up only to glance furtively at the street entrance or at those sitting at neighbouring tables; suspicion had become a way of life, it seemed.

When the waiter finally arrived, he dropped a glass of vodka in front of Max before he could protest. He hadn't brought a menu, so Max asked for the plat du jour and an espresso. The waiter returned a few minutes later with a bowl of consommé and a plate of the white cheese-filled dumplings, smothered in chopped tomatoes and served with a healthy dollop of sour cream. They tasted better than they looked and settled in his stomach like a warm lump. The espresso had miraculously transformed into a glass of red wine, which Max sipped hesitantly.

"You should drink the vodka, Max," said the lone occupant of a neighbouring table, his voice vaguely familiar. "It helps dissolve the dumpling before it can get stuck in your liver."

Max looked up and then looked again. Joseph Asper had changed in the fifteen months since Max had last seen him. He had gained thirty pounds, softening his angular features. His hair was longer, drooping over his collar and lying across his forehead in lank bangs. His features were further transformed by the heavy beard that covered the lower half of his face. Its grey streaks and the lines around his eyes added a dozen years to his appearance.

"Joseph, I'm..." Max sought for the right thing to say. "Surprised to see you."

Asper laughed. "I'm glad Paris hasn't yet taught you to lie. But surprise is a good word. I'm surprised to see you here, too. I thought you preferred more sophisticated cuisine."

"I'm working."

"And working men must eat when they can. Yes, it's a good philosophy. May I join you?" He was already moving before Max nodded his agreement. He glanced at the untouched glass on the table. "Are you drinking that?"

"Help yourself," said Max. He waited until Asper had downed the vodka in a single gulp. "Another?"

"I'd prefer wine. If you're buying." He struggled to keep his eyes off Max's food.

Why not, thought Max. Asper has been useful in the past. And he speaks Russian. He waved the waiter over. "A carafe of this and another glass."

"Big or small?"

Max shrugged. "Big. And a plate of the dumplings for my friend."

Asper grinned in gratitude, fidgeting until the waiter returned a few minutes later with the food and drink.

"I thought you'd be back in Croatia, now that everything's settled."

"Typical American. If it doesn't affect you, it doesn't count."

"Canadian, remember?"

Asper looked up from his food, a puzzled expression on his face. "Yes. I seem to have lost my ability to make fine distinctions. But the war in the east isn't settled yet, though they say a final treaty with the Ottomans will be signed in a few months. Which will be the end of the Ottomans, of course. What the Turks will do after is anyone's guess."

Max had indeed lost interest after the treaty with the Germans had been signed the previous June. His war, the one that had nearly cost him his leg, had ended that day. Though sometimes, when he awoke in the dark, sweating, with the echo of shells in his head, it felt as if it were merely a truce.

"Still, the fighting's done. But here you are, still in Paris."

"Croatia is beautiful but it's not Paris," said Asper. "In any case, it was made very clear by my new government there was no place in Greater Serbia for a 'troublesome' Croat. So, here I am, without a country, without proper papers, without prospects, reduced to begging from friends and running errands for Russian aristocrats."

"What kind of errands?"

"Same old Max. A man can't even grouse about his sorry circumstances without being interrogated."

"I'm willing to pay for information. And, if you're having trouble with your papers, I have friends in the political branch."

"Gereau? I don't think he likes me. But money is good. Do you pay in francs or dollars?"

"Whatever you like. The going rate is fifty francs per useful item. I get to determine what is useful."

Asper pushed the last dumpling around his plate to capture the few remaining tomatoes and cream and popped it in his mouth, chewing thoughtfully. He emptied his glass and reached for the carafe. Max rested his palm on its mouth.

"Before you drink your first payment, why don't you answer a question or two?"

"Fire away. But show me the money first."

Why is it, thought Max, that people never trust me about money? He took his billfold out and slipped out five fifty-franc notes. He doubted he would have to spend it all. Asper didn't look like he travelled in elevated circles.

"Do you know Irina Pavlovna?"

"Great grandniece to Emperor Nicholas, connected to the Royal House of Netherlands and half of the Duchies of Germany. She first came to Paris in 1899 as a young woman and has lived here permanently since the early days of the war. Never married, though she is rumoured to take after her distant ancestor, Catherine, if you catch my meaning."

Max was no expert on Russian history but even he had heard of the notorious Catherine the Great. Whatever St. John had been to Irina Pavlovna, it was more than merely a friend.

"What does she do – besides being an aristocrat?"

"What they all do. Plot and scheme and live beyond their means."

"Schemes?"

"The usual. They're all supporters of Denikin and Wrangel and still hope to take Russia back from the Bolsheviks. A lost cause if you ask me. The Russians here are always trying to raise money for the fight back home.

"Does she have money?"

"Not enough to win a war but some, enough for a spacious place here in the 17th and all the champagne she can drink. Though she's remarkably cheap when she wants something done. In my experience, at least."

Buchan had claimed she was wealthy, Armand, nearly penniless. Asper seemed to come down somewhere in the middle.

"Did you know Mark St. John?"

"The dead American? I've seen him around. Here. At the cathedral across the street. With Pavlovna, if that's what you're waiting to hear. More than a few times. They seemed to have fun together."

"Was that all it was?" asked Max.

Asper stared into his wineglass for several long moments before answering. "I'd say no. I don't have any proof. A hunch, that's all. There was something else there, but I don't know what it was."

"Was St. John giving her money?"

"I don't think she was... oh, you mean for the boys back home. That's a thought. It certainly would make him a target of the Cheka. Though the method seems a trifle flashy for those Cossacks. A knife between the ribs in a dark alley or poison in your soup is more their style."

"You speak from experience?"

Asper shrugged. "The secret police is much the same wherever you go."

Asper's information was interesting, but Max wasn't sure it was exactly useful. If St. John was involved in one of the Russian plots, especially if he was providing money to fund it, it seemed to take Pavlovna off the hook. But not Sarah St. John. Or Armand. The money had to come from somewhere, either the household accounts or his business with Armand. In Paris, love might be the main motive for murder, but when Americans were involved, money took the prize.

Max peeled off a pair of notes and handed them to Asper. The waiter was nowhere to be seen so Max dropped another fifty on the table.

"For the bill. You can keep the change. Think of it as an advance on our next conversation."

"You figure we'll have one."

"I figure you like to eat. Get me the names of Pavlovna's closest associates. Find out if there is anything more to their schemes than talk. Find out if St. John was bank rolling the counter-revolution. That kind of information I'd pay real money for."

"What makes you think I can find out any of that?"

"You fit in and you speak the language, which gives you two advantages over me. Besides, I've seen you at work. I have faith in your abilities."

Asper smiled, a soft quirk to his lips, like the expression of a whipped dog that had been given a treat. Max almost felt bad using the man like that. But not so bad he was about to stop.

"And watch out for the Cheka."

§

Max felt almost happy as he climbed the stairs on Rue Drevet to Le Coq Bleu. Meeting Asper had been fortuitous, almost too much so. Had someone known they were acquainted and sent Asper to spy on him? Nonsense, how could they know he would be at the Petrograd? Still...

Paranoia is as contagious as the flu, he thought, *and as dangerous to your health*. The Russians seemed to exude it from their pores, along with the smell of onions and grim pessimism.

Max stopped a dozen paces from the entrance of the bar and took a deep breath to clear his head. The sky had started to clear though water still ran between the cobblestones. Already a few customers had taken advantage of the empty seats on either side of the Le Coq Bleu's doors, quiet conversation occasionally punctuated by bursts of laughter.

The air was fresher here on the hill, the rain having washed it clean of the usual odours of cooking and the pervasive stench of urine from the public pissoirs. Bright red and yellow flowers cascaded down the retaining wall on the opposite side of the street and Max watched small birds flicker among the vines under the watchful gaze of a lazy orange cat perched on a second-floor windowsill. Farther off, someone was singing, perhaps rehearsing for an evening performance; the voice was high and sweet, the words in a language neither English nor French.

In these pauses between moments, when Paris seemed to hover between its languorous and casual beauty and the urgent demands of modern life, Max sometimes wondered what he was doing here. Why had he, a farm boy from Nova Scotia, chosen this ancient city to create a new life for himself? Was he like the artists and musicians who flocked here from every corner of the world, to create something new out of the bones and ashes of a wounded land?

A truck turned the corner from Lepic onto Gabriel, its tires rumbling on the cobbled road, its engine growling from the steep incline. Max filed his questions for another day. He had no more answer to them than he did to those surrounding the death of Mark St. John. At least there was a chance the latter might have an answer he could discover.

Le Coq Bleu's interior was crowded with workers pausing for a drink before trundling home to their families, students looking for a cheap drink and a few elegant couples who were clearly lost. Max's head hurt, the remnants of last night's overindulgences, exacerbated by drinking red wine at lunch. The dumplings were still sitting in his stomach like lumps of clay. He wedged against the zinc bar and ordered a blanche from Alice, the young woman Yesim had hired to help him out during the busy part of the evening. Despite the recent devaluation of the franc, or perhaps because of it, trade had improved as the city's café season got into full swing. The streets and the bars that lined them would be busy now until the city emptied during the sweltering heat of August. Max had already booked a hotel on the coast for his own retreat. He hoped by then the matter of St. John's murder would be resolved one way or another.

The crisp hoppy beer settled his stomach, and he knew that the pain in his head would soon recede. It was a temporary, and somewhat dangerous, cure but, if he were careful, it would keep him going until it was time for bed. He could almost feel the soft pillow beneath his head; he would need a diversion if he were to remain upright until a reasonable hour.

Roget – Pierre David Roget, though no one used anything but his last name – had become a regular at Le Coq Bleu and Chez Jake since Les Coquettes had closed down the previous winter. They seldom spoke, since the two things they had in common were not subjects either of them felt comfortable discussing, at least with each other. Mostly he drank alone at a table in the corner, the permanent scowl on his face discouraging company. If he had friends, he didn't bring them here. Tonight, however, his mood seemed lighter and he smiled at Max and waved him over. Seeing no better options – Yesim was busy in the kitchen and Henri was working nights this week – Max took his beer and a plate of olives to join him.

The older man – Roget was in his early thirties – was not Max's friend. At one time, they had been active and violent enemies, but they had both been soldiers and, in the spirit of the age, had reached an accord, less peace than a cessation of hostilities. Roget stood as he approached and they shook hands, testing each other's grip for several seconds before declaring a draw. Roget had grown a thin black moustache, which, with his well-tanned skin and aquiline features, made him look like one of the Spanish toreadors Max had seen during his months in Spain the previous year. He was dressed in a tight blue jersey that showed off the sinewy muscles of a practiced brawler. On one sleeve was an armband in the colors of the French socialist party.

"I hear you are up to your old tricks," Roget said by way of greeting. He had the remains of a ham sandwich in front of him and he kept picking at as they spoke, as if he were no longer hungry but couldn't resist the sweet saltiness of the meat or the freshness of the croquette it was served in. Max was tempted to order one himself but resisted. Three trips a week to the gym were barely enough to keep his weight down as it was. The olives and the beer would more than suffice until it was time for dinner.

Max shrugged. "News travels fast. You have connections... in certain circles. Have you heard any rumours?"

"I try to avoid that crowd." He pointed to the armband. "I've given up one gang of crooks for another." He laughed to show he wasn't serious.

"I never took you for a socialist."

"Life changes people, Max. In case you hadn't noticed." Roget paused, gazing off at something only he could see. "It gives me a sense of purpose, a sense that all that merde we slogged through had some meaning."

Max had known lots of men who had given up one vice for another. Religion or politics weren't the worst choices they could make, though they were seldom the best either. At least Roget had picked a democratic movement, unlike so many of his former comrades at arms, who were flocking to regiments of the far right and left.

"Do you know Denis Jourdain?"

"I've met him," said Roget, "but we're not bosom buddies. I admire him – a future prime minister, I think."

"That seems to be a common opinion," said Max. He wondered what Roget would think if he knew of Jourdain's relationship with Sarah St. John. Would he consider it an insult to French womanhood that his hero had a foreign mistress?

"I could introduce you if you like," said Roget. He seemed eager to perform the service.

"As it happens, we met recently."

Roget looked crestfallen so Max added. "But it was outside the political sphere. I know nothing of his views except what I read in the papers. And who can trust that? I'd appreciate the insights of an adherent."

Roget finished his white wine and gestured Alice for another. Max made a circling gesture with his hand and she brought him another blanche as well, along with a fresh plate of olives and small baguette to soak up the oil. Max gave in and ordered charcuterie, spicy deli meats and an assortment of cheeses. As part owner of the bar, he had an obligation to maintain custom. Besides, the food would keep the beer from going to his head.

"He's strictly middle of the road," said Roget. "Which is why he'll head the government someday. The French love their barricades and treasure memories of the revolution but, in their hearts, they are all bourgeois. I don't say that as an insult, the way the Bolsheviks do. I'm bourgeois myself. Steady work, good food and drink, a bit of fun on the side, and a reliable pension at the end of it all. Jourdain believes in all that, too, but, unlike the conservatives, he doesn't trust the industrialists to provide it out of the goodness of their hearts. Workers have to fight for everything they get, and the syndicates and the party are the weapons they use. We will win in the end."

"The elections last year seem to prove you wrong." The conservative parties had won a huge victory and those on the left seemed in permanent disarray.

"The people have a right to be wrong. The pendulum has already started to swing now the government has shown itself unable to recover the war debts or maintain the currency."

"They blame it on the Americans."

"They blame it on everyone but themselves. The Yanks deserve their share of the fault but, in the end, Frenchmen have to solve their own problems." Roget took the last bite of his sandwich and chewed it slowly, savouring the last bits of flavour. "Look, there's a rally tomorrow night. Jourdain will be speaking, you can hear for yourself what kind of man he is."

"That would be... interesting."

They arranged to meet at the Blanche metro stop early the next evening. Roget made his excuses shortly after. Max took out his journal and made notes on the day's events, nursing a third beer until it was time to go home to the comforts of his bed.

§

Sleep being the cure for most things, Max stayed in bed until noon, breaking his fast with brioche and coffee at a nearby café, while perusing several of the morning papers. *L'Humanité* had a front-page article about the planned rally which would take place in front of the monument to La Bastille, a traditional meeting place of the Parisian left. Jordain was featured prominently in the story although he was only one of several deputies who would be in attendance. The man's star was rising, of that there could be little doubt. A single line caught Max's attention. "Madame Jordain will make a rare appearance on the platform to introduce her husband 'so all France can know him as I do.'" *That*, thought Max, *could mean a lot of things*.

Max dropped into the gym to sweat off the last of his hangover under the careful tutelage of Kid O'Brien who taught him the effects of a kidney punch and how to guard against it. He spent several hours preparing an affidavit for one of his clients in a libel case before changing into an evening jacket and heading down the hill to the metro.

Roget was already there, dressed in a dark suit over a collarless white shirt. He had added a lapel badge to the armband and had a small flag furled around a stick which appeared stout enough to double as a club. He handed Max an armband, but he demurred.

"I'm not a citizen – best I don't get involved in politics."

Roget grinned. "Your French has gotten so good; I forgot you're not one of us."

Fifteen minutes later they emerged from the Bastille Metro and joined a rapidly growing throng who had already filled the space around the monument and begun to spill out onto the surrounding streets, much to the annoyance of taxi-drivers and the watching police. The forty or fifty swallows did nothing to interfere, though Max had no doubt they would, if things got out of hand. It was one thing for workers to rally around the red flag out in the banlieues or even the poorer arrondissements to the south and west of the city, but the authorities always grew restless when the left invaded the city centre.

Despite their numbers, the crowd was surprisingly orderly, arraying themselves around the hastily constructed platform in front of the monument, under the banner of some of the larger labour syndicates in the city. The carpenters and trolley-drivers were well represented, though both were reputed to favour the more extreme branches of the socialist movement. Perhaps, Jourdain was not as middle of the road as Roget claimed.

The festival atmosphere had attracted a number of food vendors and Max bought them each a steaming meat pie and a quart bottle of beer to share. The pastry was buttery and the meat spiced with onions and pepper, and almost as much fell to the ground to feed the fat pigeons as got into their mouths. The pale ale had been kept on ice – cold beer had become a vogue in Paris since the recent influx of Americans, attracted by cheap lodgings and legal alcohol – and the flavour of barley and hops was sharp and cut away the greasy aftertaste of the meat. When they had finished it, Max was full and satisfied and thought he could endure any number of boring speeches.

Shortly after seven, a ten-piece brass band played the Internationale and the crowd sang with one voice, many of the workers holding their hats to their hearts as if they were Americans singing their national anthem. Several speakers followed, adequate though not rousing, calling on the government to provide benefits to widows and orphans of the war or to improve working conditions in the factories that surrounded the city.

As dusk fell, the city lamplighters made the rounds; faces gleamed in the light of the burning gas. The last light of the sun painted the west side of the Bastille monument, and the more distant Basilica atop Montmartre, blood red.

A dozen people, including Denis Jourdain and his wife, mounted the platform and saluted the crowd as the band played another round of the Internationale. Madame Jourdain was not the only member of her sex in the group – woman had made great political progress during the war and were determined not to be pushed back into the shadows, as the current conservative government preferred. The socialists had not quite extended the principles of liberty, equality and fraternity to the other sex but they had done more than most. They had led the campaign to grant women the vote the year before only to see the will of the majority thwarted by the conservative-led Senate.

Roget knew them all by name and pointed from one to another, describing their role in the party and their public positions on a variety of issues. Frossard and Cachin were still in Moscow, observing the new Bolshevik government in action, but the stage held many lesser and rising lights in the movement.

The crowd waited patiently through several more speeches but Max could sense their growing excitement. Jourdain was reputed to be eloquent and passionate, the proper mix of reason and outrage designed to fire a crowd while avoiding a riot. Given the willingness of Parisian crowds to riot over the least thing – an avant-garde opera or a cycling race – it was no small talent.

Madame Jourdain stepped up to the podium and the crowd grew silent. Her voice was thin and even speaking through a megaphone, she was difficult to hear. She stammered slightly though whether from nerves or due to a more permanent defect, Max couldn't tell. She often glanced toward her husband as she spoke, her voice dropping away as she turned from the mouthpiece. Even from the back of the crowd, Max could see that her affection for Jourdain was genuine and deeply felt. He wondered if the man had kept his affair from her as well or if some people's love could bear any burden.

"You know m-m-my husband as an orator and a defender of the working m-m-man," she said, "but only I know the depth of his feelings for you. I have often said to him – show the people your love and they will show it back to you – but Denis is, by nature, a m-m-modest man and he detests those politicians who win a crowd by the force of their personality rather than the strength of their arguments. He is proud to serve you and to serve your party. His only aspiration is your victory. I give you my husband, Denis Jourdain." She paused for effect. "I only ask that you return him to me when the night is done."

The crowd laughed gently and then cheered when Jourdain kissed his wife.

"Now you know my secrets," he said. He held out his hand to her. "Camile – my greatest strength and only weakness."

Max knew that, at least, wasn't true but the audience cheered again and then settled in for Jourdain's speech. He squared himself in front of the podium and took in the crowd with a steady gaze, sweeping from one side to the other and back again in complete silence.

"Friends, Countrymen, brothers and sisters.... Comrades," he began, his booming voice reaching the back of the crowd without the need for artificial amplification. The men and women roared their approval at his choice of words. Flags were unfurled and banners waggled up and down. Jourdain let the volume build before holding out his hands for quiet. It was as if a light switch had been thrown; silence fell like darkness.

Max's heart was pounding in his chest; a shiver ran up his spine and across his scalp. At the edges of the crowd, the police stirred, removing their white riot sticks from the holsters at their sides. Their numbers appeared inadequate, yet they showed no fear, not even the slightest nervousness. Did they have reinforcements hiding in the neighbouring streets, Max wondered, cavalry, perhaps, ready to use clubs and steel and the bodies of their steeds to bully the crowd into submission?

Jourdain was in full flight now, his rhythmic cadences listing the injustices faced by veterans and their families, by workers and small shop owners, by everyone who had to slave while the rich played and decided the fate of nations. The answers, he said, didn't lie in petty nationalism or ethnic hatred but in the unity of the working class. "If we had kept to our beliefs," he said, "been true to our martyrs, we would not have suffered eight million dead and wounded, their blood soaking the fields of our homeland like a rain of tears." He didn't need to mention Jaurès's name, everyone knew Jourdain's inspiration and mentor; everyone knew the story of the assassination and of the conservative judges who had let the killer walk free. The crowd moaned and growled its indignation. Max could almost hear the tinkle of breaking windows beneath their cries.

But Jourdain wasn't simply a man outraged by the injustices of history; he had solutions, a program that would restore France to its rightful place at the forefront to the future. He had barely begun to enumerate its points when a sudden blare of music – the Marseilles –

burst from the southern edge of the crowd. There was a roar of anger and a shot was fired. The crowd surged away as police whistles started to blow.

More shouts and another shot. Jourdain and the others were hustled from the stage. The mob surged again, this time toward the disturbance. Roget grabbed Max by the arm and tried to pull him south.

"Come on, come on, I've been expecting this." He had stripped the flag from its pole and was now brandishing it like a club. "The Camelots de Roi! Come on – this is going to be fun."

Max pulled away and Roget disappeared into the milling throng. The sounds of battle raged around him – sticks striking sticks and heads – though no more shots were fired. More police poured from the buildings surrounding the square, but they hung back, only darting in to scoop up fallen warriors and bundle them into waiting vans, careful not to mix leftists with their rivals on the right.

Cavalry, too, had appeared but they were content to guard the exits to the square, letting those who wished to flee the scene depart while keeping the willing combatants confined. Property had to be protected even at the cost of a few broken heads.

Max inched away from the fighting. He couldn't see Roget but knew he would be in the middle of it, dealing out far more blows than he received, before slipping through police lines to safety. He was a warrior if nothing else. Max didn't fear a fight but he didn't relish it either. He had seen what he had come to see – though what it meant was best left for another day.

Nine – Sunday, May 30th, 1920

The Sunday papers were full of news of the "modern battle of the Bastille," as *L'Humanité* called it. Those who favoured the left praised Jourdain's impassioned speech and cursed the "reactionary scum" who had tried to disrupt it, only to be driven off by "the heroes of the working class." Those on the right decried Jourdain (though they resolutely refused to mention him by name) as a Bolshevik rabble-rouser who showed himself "hapless" in the face of the defenders of French freedom, who scattered the socialist hordes while singing the national anthem.

Those of the middle shrugged their collective shoulders and wondered when the madness would end – these radicals, left and right, were not a reflection of "real" French values.

Max didn't know. After a year and a half he had yet to ascertain what real French values were – beyond cynicism and a love of croissants. The mystery for him was Jourdain. It was as if he had met two different men: the quiet rationalist in his gentleman's club and the fervent demagogue who could play a crowd's emotions like a well-tuned guitar. He wondered which was the real man, the private or the public. Perhaps both were masks for yet another Jourdain, the one only his wife and perhaps Sarah St. John knew.

He needed to speak to his client again. It should be easier now she was living in the Grand, no need to seek permission or to carry out his questioning under the eyes of a police guard. She might even be eager to see him, eager for news of her lover. Jourdain wouldn't risk a visit himself; Fontaine would have the hotel watched and would be happy to discover the involvement of a prominent socialist in his case.

Other leads were more pressing. He had still not contacted the two people Sarah St. John had identified as friends of her husband, though he had researched their backgrounds during his visits to the newspaper archives.

Erich Harvey was an American who had been living in Paris since before the turn of the century. Nearly sixty now, he worked as a freelance journalist, writing articles on French business and politics for a number of big city American papers. He had a small apartment in the 7th not far from the Sorbonne and generally, could be found taking a leisurely lunch at one of the cafés along St. Germaine, observing flaneurs and writing notes for future stories. A grainy picture of Harvey had accompanied an article on the art collectors Gertrude Stein and her brother, Leo. It should be sufficient to identify the man himself.

Information on Dominic Ledux was sketchy, confined to a few articles that appeared in *Action Française* and other conservative papers in 1917 when Ledux was promoted to Colonel and awarded the Legion of Honour. The articles didn't mention St. John of course, but it was easy to figure out the connection. Born to one of the old aristocratic families of the Loire valley, Ledux had worked for the French foreign service in Washington for ten years, during which time he must have met St. John. Ledux had returned home in 1912 and had worked closely with the American embassy, before joining the army as a Captain at the outbreak of the war. He had served gallantly and reached the rank of Major by the time he had been assigned to a section of the Noyon line. During the battle for Verdun, he had thwarted a German attack, holding a forward outpost against overwhelming odds. He had lost ninety percent of his unit but fought on, despite several wounds, until relief arrived. Ledux now lived in a private convalescent home in the 17th, not far from the apartment of Irina Pavlovna. Max wondered if there was any connection other than proximity between the two.

Max was reluctant to intrude on Ledux. If he required care after nearly three years, his wounds must have been severe, though presumably if St. John still consulted him on matters of business or state, he was of sound mind if not body.

Even now, reminders of the war were everywhere in Paris, if one were inclined to look. Despite the efforts of many to hide recent events behind bright lights and gaudy posters advertising the wonders of the modern age, it was impossible to miss the black-clad widows or the numerous amputees begging for sou on any busy street corner. Max had learned like so many others to avert his gaze from unpleasant realities, assuaging his guilt with the occasional handful of change. His war was always with him – he didn't need to be reminded of it. He knew he would have to see Ledux eventually as the man might hold the secret to the whole affair, but for now there were other, less painful, leads to follow.

The weather of the previous day held and the sun was bright in a nearly cloudless sky. The air was cool for late May but that did little to deter the diners who flocked to the cafés on St. Germain, especially those on the sunny side of the street.

Erich Harvey occupied a table for two at the far end of the Café de Flor, his papers and notebooks scattered across its surface so there was barely room for his coffee cup and the plate of scrambled eggs that was his current focus of attention. He was thinner than his photograph, which was nearly ten years old, but still recognizable. His face was lined and leathery from frequent exposure to the sun and thin with a high brow and long chin that gave him an equine appearance. His hair, which looked in need of a barber, was still mostly dark except for a hint of grey at the temples and a single streak of white that ran through his long bangs like a badge. His shoulders were narrow and had the hunch of a man who spent most of his life bent over a notebook or typewriter.

He looked up when Max approached the table, his skin around his dark eyes crinkling against the glare of the sky.

"Do I know you?" he asked. His voice was deep, almost a rumble, and carried the flat twang of his mid-western origins.

"I'm... a friend of Sarah St. John," said Max. He supposed he was – why else was he persisting in what seemed like an increasingly hopeless case?

Harvey grunted noncommittally and nodded at the chair opposite.

"You had breakfast yet? This is one of the few places in Paris where they know how to feed an American." He gestured and a waiter appeared out of one of the numerous entrances that connected the sidewalk to the restaurant. Max ordered a café au lait and a portion of meat pie. Harvey frowned.

"You should never eat meat before the sun goes down," he said. "It fouls the liver. How's Sarah? I heard some fool at the Prefecture had her arrested for Mark's murder."

"She's been released on bail. She's at the Grand. I'm sure she'd appreciate a visit from an old friend."

"I was Mark's friend." Harvey's tone was clipped, almost angry. His relationship to Sarah St. John was unspoken but clear.

"Mrs. St. John didn't approve of your friendship with her husband."

"Sarah couldn't give a damn what Mark did. She certainly didn't give a damn who his friends were.'

"Then she had no reason to kill him."

Harvey snorted and scooped another forkful of eggs into his mouth. He washed them down with the last of his coffee. The waiter arrived with Max's order and Harvey sent him away for another espresso and a fruit tart.

"Sarah St. John is as capable of committing murder as I am of playing Yankee Doodle Dandy on the bells at Notre Dame. Not impossible but damn unlikely."

"How can you be so sure?"

"That's a good question. Not sure if I have a good answer, not one that would stand up in court. I've been a journalist for forty years. I've met all kinds of people, seen them do all kinds of things. Most people are capable of most actions given the right circumstances. Some aren't. Sarah St. John is a lot of things, not all of them real nice, but killer isn't one of them."

The café au lait had been made properly, the milk steamed almost to boiling, and the heat warmed Max against the chill of the air. The meat pie was less satisfying and after a few bites Max pushed it to one side.

"Do you have a theory?"

"I've got four or five. Mark and I go back a long way. I started my career working for the Tribune in Chicago. I knew Mark's father – most reporters did – and we developed as much of a friendship as an honest newsman can ever have with a politician. Mark was a good kid, smart, ambitious and only a little devious, and it was no surprise when he followed his father's footsteps into politics. I met him again when he came to Paris. I found him interesting and he found me useful, and we had a common interest in bourbon and a certain kind of woman. Not much basis for a deep friendship but we built one all the same. I'd be happy to see his killer lose his head in the guillotine."

"You mentioned theories?" prompted Max.

"Mark had a lot of dangerous friends and his hands were none too clean, for all of his high principals."

"I've heard rumours about some of his dealings with Pierre Armand."

"I bet you have. Armand is the key to this whole business if you ask me," said Harvey. "I'm not saying he had Mark killed but I would be surprised if he didn't know who did."

"He's connected to the Action Française."

"Sure, and the Federation Republican and Poincaré's DRA as well. The man likes to hedge his bets. He has lots of money and he intends to keep it, no matter how many politicians he has to fund."

"That's not illegal."

"No," said Harvey, "though maybe it should be. Armand is pretty careful not to break any laws himself though he has been known to bend a few. Not all his business partners are quite that scrupulous."

"Including Mark St. John?"

"I asked him that once. We'd been drinking in a private club over in the 17th arrondissement. It was late and we were the last men standing. Despite the alcoholic haze, I remember exactly what he said to me. 'Morality is neither black and white nor a perfectly shaded scale; it exists in gradations. A minor sin committed for a higher cause is no sin at all. Saintly acts are shameful if they contribute to the advancement of evil. History, and history alone, will judge me saint or sinner.'"

"Sounds like a fancy way of saying: the ends justify the means." Max's coffee had grown cold and he ordered another.

"Maybe, though I don't think that was what Mark was driving at. He did believe in certain things, liberty maybe most of all. I suspect he'd do most anything to promote the cause of freedom."

"Including criminal acts?"

"To a point. But it wasn't Mark I had in mind. Armand's international connections aren't only with America; his interests stretch across southern Europe and into Africa. Spain, Italy, Greece, even Turkey, though he was careful to keep that hidden during the war. His family owns a lot of land in Algeria, too."

"What kinds of interest?"

"Shipping, textiles, machine parts. Guns. A lot of guns. Drugs, too, according to some. Though Armand mostly plays the role of banker. Bankers can always claim they don't know what their money was used for."

"How does that work?"

"Some of it is fairly aboveboard. People put up collateral, real or fake, and Armand raises the money from investors by selling bonds. I bought a few myself. The rates were good and they always paid off. Other transactions happen in the dead of night and involve suitcases full of cash. Higher risk, I guess, but higher returns, too. That's where Armand puts his own money."

"I don't suppose you have proof."

"I'd be living in a better neighbourhood than this if I did." Harvey gestured at the shabby tenements that lined the side streets off St. Germaine. He laughed. "Or I'd be dead."

"You said you had theories? If not Armand, then who?"

"Like I said, Mark had a lot of dangerous friends. Gun runners and drug dealers weren't the worst. Before the war, he dealt with people of every political stripe. He was officially the trade officer but I'm pretty sure he mainly spied on Europeans for Colonel House, who was President Wilson's unofficial foreign secretary. He made alliances with anyone who opposed the far left. Mark was prescient in that regard. He had met Lenin when he was living in exile in Paris for a few months in 1912 and took an immediate dislike to him. After that, he'd work with anyone who opposed the Bolshevik agenda. He made deals with conservatives of any stripe, even the virulently anti-Semitic – the leftovers of the anti-Dreyfusard movement. I think he liked the anarchists best; he once expressed a certain admiration for the audacity of Jules Bonnot."

Max had heard that name before, as Henri loved to regale him with true crime stories. Bonnot had led a gang of anarchists of the *illégalisme* who believed any action, no matter how violent, was justified to support the anarchist cause. Bonnot's specialty was car theft, though robbery, kidnapping and the shooting of police inspectors were also in his repertoire. He and his gang had staged a year-long reign of terror before finally being killed in a hail of gunfire on April 28, 1912. "And it took over a hundred flics to take him down," Yesim had added, gleefully.

"Bonnot and his gang were all shot or guillotined before the war. That rules them out as suspects," said Max.

Harvey laughed again. "True enough. But anarchists are like the mythical hydra – chop one down and two more rise up to take their place. It has a certain cachet for the young and violent."

"So do the Camelots du roi."

"True enough. But it does provide a rich palette of possibilities," said Harvey. "Anarchists, unhappy with his association with the Action Française or Bolsheviks unhappy with his campaign against them."

"Or his close friendship with White Russians."

"I wondered if you knew about Irina."

"What can you tell me about her?"

"Not a lot. The Russians don't come over to this part of town much. She has money – not rich but more than comfortable. You won't see her tending bar or driving cabs like half her compatriots. Or entertaining gentlemen for money. She does it because she likes it."

Max blushed. His own experiences were limited in that regard – the idea that women liked "it" was not new to him but he remained uncertain.

"I don't suspect her in any case," said Harvey, "but that may be my bias toward the gentler sex. Still, I'll ask around about her, and about Armand, too. Like I said, Mark was a friend of mine and I want to see his killers punished."

He stood up and patted his pockets absently. “Seem to have forgotten my wallet.”

“It’s there, under your notebook,” said Max, smiling. “But I’ll get breakfast. I appreciate your help.” It was cheaper than his deal with Jacqueline Grand or Joseph Asper.

“I’m here most mornings.” Harvey still hesitated. “Um, I may incur a few expenses.”

So much for cheap. Max removed a hundred francs from his billfold and handed it over. Harvey shoved it his shirt pocket, nodded and left without another word. Max sipped his once again cold coffee, took his journal from his satchel and recorded what he had learned from Harvey.

§

One of the letters Jourdain had given him had an address that was neither Armand’s office on Boulevard de L’Opéra, nor in the southern part of the 15th arrondissement – an area of factories, warehouses and working-class tenements – but instead in the middle of the Marais district, one of the more expensive neighbourhoods of old Paris.

The day had continued cool and, as the afternoon progressed, heavy clouds began to roll in from the west, threatening rain. Max was glad of the excuse to wear a billed cap pulled low over his eyes and a thin wool scarf that masked his lower face. He strolled along the cobbled street with small shops and cafés to one side and gated stone mansions on the other until he reached the address on the letter. The courtyard gate had been recently painted bright green; the wicket door was open, suggesting the resident was at home and expecting guests.

Max glanced through into the well-swept courtyard at the three-story stone building beyond. Tall double doors, painted a darker green and framed by narrow latticed windows, stood directly opposite the gate. The doorstep was flanked by flowering shrubs in elaborate stone pots, and similarly well-tended plants filled low containers beneath the windows. The third floor had cast iron balconies accessed by French doors; through one open set a delicate white curtain waved listlessly in the light breeze.

The brass plate affixed to the wall beside the gate only held the street number, but Max had little doubt that the mansion was the residence of Pierre Armand when he was in Paris. While relatively modest compared to some of the private hotels a few blocks away, it was well situated for a financier and conservative activist – within walking distance of key government offices and not far from several large Catholic churches, key gathering places for the deeply Catholic right.

Max circled the block and slipped into a small café a few doors down from his target. A table by the window offered a view of the entrance while the dimness of the interior shielded him from casual observation. He ordered the plat du jour and a glass of Chablis and pretended to occupy himself with a newspaper while keeping a close watch on Armand's house.

The standard lunch consisted of a small bowl of beef and lentil soup, hot and salty though largely lacking beef, and a melange of country sausages and steamed potatoes. The meat was firm and spicy; the potatoes, tender and buttery. The Chablis had a delicate green-apple bouquet and a sharp flinty taste, drifted with honey. It was surprisingly good and Max determined he would buy a bottle to take home.

Max had switched to coffee by the time his patience was rewarded. Two men walked briskly along the cobbles, the hobnails of their heavy boots audible through the thin glass of the café window, and stopped in front of the open wicket door. The taller of the two glanced up and down the street before leading the way through the door, closing it behind them. They were the expected visitors.

Both men had had their lower faces wrapped in scarves. The shorter of the two had a cloth cap on his head though strands of curly black hair stuck from beneath it. The taller was bald and beefy. He seemed vaguely familiar, though Max was unable to place from where he knew him.

He paid his bill and shoved the bottle of Chablis in his satchel, leaning back in his chair so he could still watch the door without risk of being seen. He had a hunch the business taking place in Armand's house would not take long. Less than ten minutes later the two men emerged, both carrying small black attaché cases. Max let them almost reach the corner before sliding out of the café and following them. When they turned left onto Temple, he hurried to catch up, slowing as he came around the corner.

The men were in a hurry and were already a half a block away. They seemed intent on their destination or eager to put distance between themselves and Armand. Max closed the distance as best he could without drawing attention to himself. After several blocks, the men separated, the shorter one turning right on Bretange, the other continuing along Temple.

Max followed the shorter one, having finally remembered that he'd seen the taller of the two in the role of bodyguard to Andre Bucard. That would make him easier to find again. His quarry slowed and soon Max was less than a dozen paces behind him. When he turned into a hotel, Max closed the gap and was able to enter the small lobby in time to see the concierge hand over a key. The number seven was clearly visible on the substantial brass fob.

Max examined the hotel's rate card, then shook his head and exited. There was little point in asking the concierge who occupied room seven. He would undoubtedly tell him, for a substantial bribe, but couldn't be relied on not to immediately inform the guest of the inquiry. Waiters or bellhops were more reliable informants. He made his way to the back of the hotel. A young man in a slightly stained red jacket was lounging near the kitchen entrance, a thick Gaulloise cigarette hanging from his lower lip.

"You're not supposed to be back here," the waiter snarled, gesturing rudely with his left hand.

"I've a note from the government that says it's okay," said Max, holding up ten francs. He pulled it back when the younger men reached for it. "Who's in room seven?"

"How should I know?"

"Maybe someone in the kitchen knows." Max stepped toward the open door. The waiter glanced at the width of Max's shoulders and decided not to block his way.

"Merde, what do I care? It's some Italian."

"Got a name?"

"Jacques or something like that."

"Jacopo?"

"That's it. Jacopo... Gee-a..." The young man's brow furled as he tried to recover the unfamiliar sounding name. He grinned in triumph. "Giamatti!"

Max handed over the ten-franc note and the waiter tucked it into his jacket pocket.

"Would you like more of that?" he asked.

"Sure." He looked around furtively; Max doubted management approved of the staff spying on their guests.

"I won't ask you to do anything illegal," Max glanced at the small nametag on the jacket, "Alain."

"That's okay. Are you with the Prefecture?"

"I'm connected to the political division." Not exactly a lie since he and Captain Gereau were friends.

Alain nodded sagely. "Unofficially."

"You're clever. I'd like to know if Mr. Giamatti has any visitors in the next few days. But I don't want him to know he's being watched."

"I can do that. How do I reach you?"

"When do you get off shift on Tuesday? I'll meet you in a bar near here. There's another twenty in it for you, no matter what you have to tell me, more if I think it's useful." There was always the risk that Alain would make something up to gain the reward but Max doubted he was bright enough to prepare a convincing lie. They agreed on a time and a place and Max headed for home, satisfied he had finally made some progress.

§

Max had planned to take the rest of the day off – it was Sunday after all – but the Metro was full of veterans returning from some demonstration or rally. Their pinned-up sleeves and pant legs nagged at him. He had pushed Colonel Ledux out of his mind, not wanting to be reminded of the war, but it seemed fate had other plans for him. He switched trains and continued to the 17th arrondissement.

The private hospital occupied the second and third floors of a Haussmann style building along Avenue de Villiers. A nurse in a pale grey uniform and peaked cap examined his card and then led him into a well-appointed room where she asked him to wait while she informed Colonel Ledux of his presence. The furnishings had been expensive once, but their Belle Epoque opulence had faded and the ornate curlicues and decorative flourishes seemed unsuited to modern times. Max much preferred the straight lines and angles and the simple colours of the pieces that had begun to fill the show windows on the Grand Magasins along Boulevard Haussmann. Several minutes passed and Max shifted uneasily on the edge of his seat, fearing that his presence was an unwarranted intrusion on a man whose wounds still kept him confined three years after he had received them.

A tall, erect man entered the room, his dark suit neatly pressed, if slightly out of date, and his high-collared shirt sparkling white. Max at first thought it was a doctor, come to tell him that Colonel Ledux was indisposed. This was no cripple, his limbs whole and his posture exuding grace and confidence. His ascetic face was largely unlined and his close-cropped hair dark, but Max guessed he might be fifty.

"Mr. Anderson. I am Colonel Ledux."

Max stood up and, when Ledux extended his hand, crossed the several paces to grasp it. Ledux smiled warmly but his eyes did not meet Max's. Still, it was only when Ledux stepped into the room, his hand slightly extended until it made contact with the back of a chair, that he realized Ledux was blind. Max rocked on his heels, caught between the urge to help and the desire not to embarrass the man. Ledux moved easily through the room and took a seat in a large wingback chair near the window.

"I'm fine, Mr. Anderson. I know this room. Staff are under strict orders not to move anything or, if they must, to replace everything exactly as they found it." As if to prove his point, he leaned forward, opened a brass case and extracted a cigarette and lighter. "Help yourself, Mr. Anderson."

"I don't smoke, thanks." Max found a chair close enough that they could converse easily. Ledux lit his cigarette, leaned back in his seat and crossed his legs. Now they were seated opposite each other, Max could see the bar of ribbons that decorated the pocket of Ledux's jacket. The red stripe of a commander in the Legion of Honour was worn separately and above the rest.

"There are no scars."

"What?" said Max.

"The injury was internal. So my doctors tell me." Ledux frowned as if remembering an unpleasant exchange. "What can I do for you, Mister Anderson?"

"Call me Max if you like," said Max, gently. He knew too well what doctors meant when they claimed an injury was internal. Even now, few of them understood what caused "shell shock," let alone what could cure it.

"No. It implies a familiarity I don't feel."

"Very well, Colonel. You know Mark St, John?"

"Knew him, don't you mean? I may have lost the power of sight but not that of observation. And three years haven't made me forget the importance of reconnaissance. I may be confined but I'm hardly isolated. Mark was murdered, his wife suspected and you were hired to prove her innocent. For the record, I have no doubt Sarah had the capability of arranging her husband's death but I doubt her motive. Theirs was a marriage of convenience, though that wasn't always the case. I liked Mark a great deal but I was not... blind to his flaws. He tended to use people up. Though he was always immensely charming in the process."

Whatever injury had robbed Ledux of his sight had left his intellect unimpaired. And his tongue sharp.

"You're not the first to tell me that."

"And I will not be the last. Few of his friends – and none of his enemies – had any illusions about Mark St. John."

"And he had enemies."

"What man of action does not? Mark was likeable but not impossible to hate. Though I'm not convinced hate had anything to do with his death. You have heard of the Great Game?"

The Great Game was a term coined in the nineteenth century to describe the clandestine competition between England and Russia for influence in the sub-continent. It had come to refer to secret wars that all countries fought when real war was undesired or impracticable. Max had learned all he wanted of the Great Game during the treaty negotiations in Paris the previous year.

He nodded and then realized that was a useless gesture to Ledux. "I know what you mean."

"I wonder. We don't hate our opponents. Not in the usual sense of the word. No more than a footballer hates the opposing team. As a sportsman may change teams, we may change allegiances. The opponent of yesterday may be the teammate of tomorrow."

"St. John had left the employ of the American government."

Ledux barked his amusement and took a long drag on his cigarette. He leaned back in his chair and blew the smoke up at the ceiling. When he straightened, his face was composed, like that of a teacher gazing at a particularly slow pupil.

"He may not have received his pay from Washington. Not directly, at least, but I assure you he took his orders from there. Go to the embassy and ask them. I'm sure they'd be more than willing to confirm it."

"I have contacts in the American embassy, none of whom..." Max felt Ledux was mocking him. His earlier sympathy for the man had evaporated.

Ledux laughed again, softer this time. "Please, Mr. Anderson, we've gotten off on the wrong foot. You may know *of* the Great Game but you can't possibly *know it*, unless you've been a player. Mark operated on his own. He had orders yes, but also a great deal of latitude as to how he carried them out. Men like Mark, like me in my day, operate on the edge of patriotism. Sometimes it is not clear, even to us, when we may have crossed it."

"Are you suggesting Mark may have been killed by his own people, by the Americans, because he had crossed some sort of line?"

"It's possible. If I were investigating his murder, I'd take a cold hard look at those who most claimed to be his friends, whether his fellow Americans or those he did business with in France."

"Armand and his associates."

Ledux shrugged expansively. He took another puff on his cigarette and then stubbed it out in the center of a large glass ashtray.

"Then you think Armand is the killer," said Max.

"No."

"But you said..."

"I said that Mark's murder was not a crime of passion. It was cold and calculated."

"For gain?"

"Yes, money was central to it, in my view, but only as a proxy for something else. Power, perhaps, or national advantage. It *feels* like that to me."

"The way he was killed suggests some sort of execution."

"That troubles me. Spies, by their nature, hate publicity. A naked body in the Luxembourg Gardens – it's like something out of a popular novel. Cheap and gaudy. Not professional. Not sporting, the British would say. No, that was a cover, designed to make us look somewhere else."

"Who then?"

"The Russians."

"You think Irina Pavlovna had something to do with it?"

"Something, yes, though perhaps not directly. How well do you know her?"

"We've met."

"You should meet again. Irina is not what she seems. She is not even what she seems not to seem. A player, though for what side, I've never been sure. Hell, I'm not even sure if there are two sides in the Russian equation. Or twenty. Irina, or, at least, Irina's business, is at the heart of this crime. Mark my words on that, Mr. Anderson."

"Everyone seems to have a different take on Mark St. John's murder. You can't all be right."

"Why not? Mark took pleasure in being all things to all people; why should he be any different in death? Now if you'll excuse me, I have some correspondence to dictate. Please ask the nurse to send in my secretary when you leave."

Ten – Monday, June 1st, 1920

Early the next day, Max sent a messenger to the prefecture to arrange a meeting with Gereau "at his earliest possible convenience," then headed over to his office above Chez Jake. A small stack of mail had accumulated and he knew it couldn't wait much longer if he was to retain his reputation as a man who got things done.

Vice never takes a holiday. Half the correspondence came from suspicious wives or, in one case, a suspicious husband. Max hated that kind of work and, since he didn't need the money, posted his standard response, thanking them for their interest and suggesting a couple of detectives who specialized in domestic matters. A missing grandson, who was due an inheritance, and a brother seeking his long-estranged sibling were of more interest, and Max telegraphed his willingness along with his rates. He judged they would accept and began filling out the necessary police inquiries in expectation of their agreement. A particularly happy client had sent a cheque for six hundred francs, a hundred more than the amount billed, along with an effusive letter describing the successful results of the lawsuit against the crooked accountant Max had investigated.

Gereau had still not responded when Jake poked his head in the office. They had been partners for over a year. Jake handled the day-to-day operations of the restaurant and nightclub while Max dealt with the French bureaucracy and the vagaries of police enforcement of Paris's flexible liquor and obscenity laws. Some of the acts Jake booked were risqué, even by the City of Light's standards and, lately, Jake had taken to checking with Max before finalizing the contracts.

"Got a few minutes, boss?" Jake drawled. Jake spoke impeccable French but reverted to his Louisiana roots whenever he talked to Max about business. He had once told Max he worried about the nearby clubs spying on them and stealing his acts. "They can understand your English, boss, but not my Cajun accent."

"I'm not your boss, Jake, I'm your partner. Did you bring croissants?"

Jake produced a tray from behind his back that contained croissants, small buttery brioche and several sugary tarts as well as an assortment of jams and two steaming café lattes.

"You look like you've been losing weight," he said as he placed the tray on Max's desk and pulled up a chair.

"It's a testament to my tailor more than my will power," said Max, smearing raspberry comfit across one of the brioche. "What can I do for you, Jake?"

"Oh, I've got a few contracts for you to look over to see if I need to send them to a notary. But I was more concerned with what I might be able to do for you. Remember I told you I'd have Smitty look into that Armand fellow for you?"

Max didn't but he nodded anyway. It would be interesting to hear what the doorman at Chez Jake had to say about a French banker.

"This Armand is not only very polite but he's very short, right?"

"That's the one," said Max.

"Maybe he's tall in all the right places. Smitty says he has been in the club a few times with a different woman on his arm every time. The only thing they have in common is they're all young, pretty and six inches taller than him."

"He's also very rich."

"That could explain it. Funny thing is, he doesn't spend more than five minutes with them. Pretty soon he's at another table, talking to this guy or that. Then out he goes, sometimes alone, sometimes with two or three other men."

"Who pays the bar bills?"

"They get paid, that's all I care about."

"Does Smitty know who he leaves with?"

"No. None of them are regulars, but Smitty says most of them aren't Frenchmen, either. Italians, mostly, but Russians, too. Rich ones if their clothes are any judge."

Armand had given no indication he had any relations with Russians; indeed, this was the first Max had heard about it from anyone. What was his business with rich Russians and did it have anything to do with Irina Pavlovna's mysterious relationship with Mark St. John?

Max was still pondering those links when the messenger arrived saying Gereau would see him in his office in the Prefecture when he returned from lunch at fourteen hundred.

§

No matter how often Max passed through the huge oak doors of the Prefecture of Police on Île de la Cité, he always felt a faint frisson of dread. It had been over a year since he had been held in one of its small cold cells on suspicion of murder, yet the experience – the sour smell of sweat and urine, the dim grey light pouring through the high grey-glassed windows, the itchy coarseness of the bed and the nearly inedible food – still haunted him.

Now, of course, he was a familiar sight in its halls. His relationship with Gereau didn't quite classify as friendship but they were more than casual colleagues. While not everyone welcomed his involvement in police matters to the extent of Gereau, few resented it as much as Captain Fontaine. *Perhaps*, thought Max, *few feel as threatened by it as Fontaine.*

Gereau was hunched over his desk, a stack of thick files to one side and two open in front of him. He gestured Max to the worn leather seat opposite his desk and continued studying the open files, absently chewing at the ends of his thick mustache as he did. Finally, he grunted and placed the now-closed files on top of the pile.

"I've got a meeting on the half-hour, so be brief," said Gereau, gruffer than usual.

"I'll try," said Max. Gereau claimed to be "almost retired" but always seemed to be on the verge of rushing off somewhere. "Before I forget, if you're looking for a good young constable to promote, I've met one by the name of LePêcheur you might consider."

"Ferdinand LaPêcheur has been in my sights for some time."

Trust Gereau, thought Max, *to keep an eye out for talent.*

"But I'm sure you didn't come all this way to provide a reference."

"No," said Max. "I'm looking for information about two men, associates of Pierre Armand, Jacopo Giamatti and a man named Michel, who used to work for Andre Bucard, and perhaps still does."

"No. Michel Tourangeau had a falling out with Bucard earlier this year, personal or political, I can't say. He now operates as a free agent, though I understand he has been closely aligned with Jean Martel for several months."

"I've heard that name somewhere. Is he with the Action Française or one of their affiliates?"

"Hardly, which makes Tourangeau's adherence so odd. Martel is a conservative but hardly extreme in his views. He's a deputy with the Bloc National, not a Minister but close to several who are. I'm told he keeps his options open and often serves as a go-between for the government and the more extreme extra-parliamentary elements like the AF. I expect money comes into it. It usually does when politicians are involved."

"Is that the 'official position' of the Prefecture?"

Gereau didn't find the joke funny and Max wondered for a moment what was in the files on his desk that had made him so sour.

"What about Giamatti?" Max asked before Gereau could terminate the interview.

"He's known to us." Gereau bit at his mustache again, his eyes drifting to the pile of folders.

Something's up, Max thought. Gereau was clearly worried about something, although whether it was connected to Giamatti or to Mark St. John's death was unclear. Gereau was with the political branch, charged with monitoring those people whom the Prefect of Police had decided might be a threat to the state. That might well include foreign nationals; it certainly included the type of people St. John was rumoured to deal with on a regular basis.

Gereau came to a decision. "Giamatti is an Italian citizen, though you'd never know from the time he spends in Paris. He's been implicated in several criminal conspiracies though never actually charged. My colleagues on the domestic side suspect he may be a member of the Italian syndicate, the Cosa Nostra as the yellow journalists like to call them."

The popular press was full of stories of organized criminal gangs infiltrating French cities. The Italians were often singled out as a particular danger.

"I thought they were bogeymen designed to whip up resentment against foreign workers."

"You never see smoke without fire," said Gereau. "Not my concern in any case. I find it interesting that he's associated with Armand."

"Armand is rumoured to have lots of dubious associates. I've been told he often fronts business deals that are, well, between us, criminal."

Gereau grunted and stood up, pacing behind his desk beneath the high narrow windows in the back wall. The sky had grown dark and Max regretted not bringing his overcoat.

"Have you heard the name Mussolini?"

Max shook his head. He had few dealings with Italians.

"He's a bit like our friend Maurras, the leader of the Action Française, only, I'm told, a much more charismatic speaker. They say he can put five thousand troops on the ground at a moment's notice."

"Five thousand is quite a mob."

"If it were a mob like the Camelots, no-one would take notice. My colleagues in Rome say he's nothing but a two-bit demagogue, but they always have a tremor in their voice when they say it. There have been 'conversations' between this Mussolini and his counterparts here in France. Nothing open, of course, nothing like Frossard and Cachin trotting off to Moscow to be schooled in international socialism."

"It's difficult to stay true to the teachings of Chauvin while holding talks with foreigners."

Gereau laughed this time. "Henri has expanded his curriculum from literature to philosophy, I see. Yes, ardent nationalism does seem to stand in the way of any real partnerships, though necessity often finds a way. The right has a morbid fear of Bolsheviks."

"Are you suggesting Giamatti has been acting as an envoy for these conversations?"

"There's no proof of that." Gereau frowned. "Sometimes I wish these people would simply do what they are constantly threatening. Storm the Palais Bourbon and overthrow the Republic."

"They couldn't actually do that, could they?"

"Why not?" said Gereau. "It's not without precedent. Déroulède and the League of Patriots tried exactly that in '99. I was a mere Sergeant then but I did my bit to stop them."

"Times have changed."

"Maybe," said Gereau. He subsided in his chair with a sigh and went back to chewing his mustache. "I hear you still have contact with anarchists."

"I have contact with a lot of people. It's my job."

"Your job is to help the Prefecture to make sure criminals are brought to justice, not to involve yourself in French politics. You should tend to your onions."

Max could feel his face flush. He had been told often enough by Parisian police officers to mind his own business, but he hadn't expected it from Gereau.

"You're the one who put me onto the St. John case. You must have known where it would lead. And I work for my clients, not the Prefecture. And a good thing, too. Someone has to care about justice."

"Don't lecture me!" It was Gereau's face that was red now. "You have no idea what you're getting involved in."

"Then why don't you tell me?"

"I am telling you." Gereau slammed his hand on the desk. "You need to tread carefully."

"Are you under pressure? Has someone told you to warn me off?"

"I'm always under pressure," said Gereau, waving his hand at the stack of files. "From the left, the right, from the government and my fellow Captains. I'm telling you to be careful who you confide in, who you befriend."

Max stiffened. "My friends are my friends."

"Don't succumb to the pig-headedness of youth. You think there isn't a file here about you?"

"Let me see it."

"Don't compound your stupidity. I'm trying to help you here."

"Then stop threatening me and tell me something I can use."

"Oh, get out, I've got work to do. Real work."

Max glared at Gereau but the man had turned back to his desk as if Max had already left the room. Max's stomach roiled and his wounded leg trembled. A dozen retorts sprang to his mind and he had to clench his jaw to keep from shouting. He felt frozen, almost afraid to move, the old fear that had haunted him since 1916, and it was only with an effort of will that he turned his body and walked stiffly to the office door.

"Max," said Gereau.

But Max didn't look back. He never looked back.

§

His encounter with Gereau left Max feeling angry and confused. Something was bothering the man; something he was unable or unwilling to confide in Max. Had there been pressure from his superiors to warn Max off certain lines of inquiry? Or, was something else troubling him? Max had always thought Gereau's obsession with anarchists to be misplaced.

Certainly, a single man, or woman, even lightly armed, could prove a danger to the state. It had been just over a year since the anarchist Emile Cottin had tried to assassinate the French Prime Minister, an impulsive act that may have checked an even larger plot. Cottin had been sentenced to death but pressure from the left-wing and anarchist press had forced the government to commute his sentence and now there was even talk of his early release. Anarchists themselves might lack power but they had a certain cachet, especially among the Parisian intellectuals.

Had a new plot been hatched? Certainly, Jacques Court, Jacqueline's enormously fat partner, had abandoned Paris to escape "police persecution." Was he back, stirring up trouble? And what about Jacqueline? She claimed to have given up on the revolution but how well did he really know her? His friend, Yesim, had old ties to the black flag, though he, too, seemed content to fight the oppressors from the comfort of a barstool. Still, Max had no desire to get either of them in trouble. Besides, there were greater threats to French society than a few bomb-throwing radicals.

There was no way to investigate St. John's death without digging into French politics; the man had been up to his hips in the morass of double dealing and backroom plots. And there was no way he could simply walk away. He remained convinced that Sarah St. John was innocent of her husband's murder, despite the fact he had found no evidence to exonerate her. Though French law didn't exactly presume she was guilty until proven innocent, the burden of proof was lighter on French prosecutors than their English or Canadian counterparts. She had motive and opportunity. Right now, it was only the lack of a clear method, and the friendship of a rising political star, that was keeping her confined to the Grand Hotel rather than a cell in the Prefecture.

The heavy skies now delivered their promised rain; a few fat droplets quickly turned into a steady downpour. Max ducked into a café before his suit could be ruined. He ordered the soup du jour and a café americain. Newspapers hung from a rack along one wall and Max gathered several of them and carried them to a table near the back. There was a copy of *Les Temps Nouveaux* from the previous week and Max read that first, trying in vain to determine if it contained an article by Jacqueline. He had never read an anarchist newspaper before and he was surprised to find he had a certain sympathy with their arguments. Certainly, he found their emphasis on equality and the rights and responsibilities of individual men and women appealing, even if he didn't agree with their methods. However, nothing gave a hint as to what Gereau might be worrying about. He supposed it would be surprising if it did.

Les Temps and *L'Humanité* offered little of interest, although the latter had a short opinion piece by Jourdain commenting on the current discussions between Socialist leaders and the Bolshevik government in Moscow, the new Russian capital. Though he encouraged dialogue, he warned that the party's leaders must be careful not to compromise the good of French workers in the interest of international solidarity.

The waiter arrived with the soup, which was served with a small baguette. The broth was thickened with grated potatoes and cream, with shreds of chicken mixed in with carrots and rice. The seasoning was light – some crushed basil and oregano – and Max added a dash of salt and a generous sprinkle of coarse ground pepper. The baguette was light and still warm from the oven and Max alternated spoonfuls of hot soup with bites of broth-soaked bread.

The rain showed no sign of letting up, so Max ordered a plate of cheese and olives and a glass of white wine, returning to the newspaper rack for more reading material. The Herald Tribune reported that the American Ambassador expected to sign the final treaty with Austria-Hungary in a few, days, putting the end to another empire and creating a raft of new countries in central Europe. Concerns were raised about the continuing threats of Bolshevik expansion.

By the time he had finished the remaining papers, which contained much of interest but nothing of relevance, the rain had slowed to a bare drizzle and Max decided to risk walking the few blocks to the nearest Metro. It was only a half-dozen stops to L'Opéra and the Grand Hotel but the skies were still dark and the suit had been expensive.

§

Sarah St. John agreed to receive Max in the sitting room of her suite while her police "companion" waited outside. The female auxiliary looked at Max suspiciously before granting him access. Clearly, she didn't approve of modern social behavior.

Sarah rose to greet him from the wingback chair by the window but didn't offer her hand. She was clad in a pale blue dress that reached to the middle of her calf. A matching demi-jacket covered her shoulders; a scoop neckline showed off a string of small blue stones in a line across her pale throat. There was a matching bracelet on her left wrist. She was no longer wearing her wedding ring. She gestured to the chair opposite hers, a straight back affair in the ornate Art nouveau style.

"I ordered some coffee and pastilles," she said. "They're quite good."

Max poured them both a cup from a silver urn and offered her the plate of small cookies. She took a rose-coloured one and nibbled it delicately.

Sarah appeared younger than Max remembered her. Perhaps the atmosphere of a five-star hotel had certain rejuvenating qualities. Her skin had lost its pallor and her cheeks had a faint rosy glow. It might have been make-up but, if so, it had been expertly applied. She had loosened her hair so that it fell in ringlets around her face. *She's nearly forty*, thought Max, feeling the heat rise at his collar. He looked away and cleared his throat.

"They're treating you well?"

"Splendidly," she smiled. "I have everything I could want except my freedom."

"I'm working on that," said Max. "I've spoken to both of the men you suggested. If it's any consolation, neither think you were involved in your husband's death, though they don't agree on who was."

"Unlikely character references but I'll take what I can get. Captain Fontaine seems quite determined to send me to the guillotine."

"Your friend, Jourdain, seems equally determined to save you."

"Denis is a good friend."

"More than a friend, I think. From what he said."

The colour in her cheeks intensified and she glanced down at her lap. Max felt oddly relieved that she would display some shame at her behavior. He supposed it was a remnant of his Baptist upbringing.

"I see," she said. "Then we have no secrets between us."

"I think that's for the best, don't you?"

She smiled and reached across the space between them to touch his hand. Her fingers were soft and their traces ran across his skin like electric currents. He knew he should pull away but he was disappointed when she leaned back in her chair and folded her hands in her lap.

"Have you made other progress?" she asked after a moment.

"Some," said Max. He told her about the men he had followed from Armand's house and what he had learned of her husband's intelligence activities both before and since the war.

"I knew he was involved in some work for the government, even though he officially left their employ years ago. But we didn't talk about it. Mark kept me from all that; I think he was protecting me. He could be sweet that way, even if in most other ways, he was a terrible husband."

"Why did you stay with him?"

"He was Catholic even though I wasn't. He refused a divorce and I refused to go through the sham of an annulment. Then, of course, there was the money. I had a little of my own but not enough to keep living the way I could with Mark. So, we made... arrangements. Believe it or not, our marriage improved once we knew it was over."

"Much too sophisticated for a Canadian farm boy, I'm afraid."

"I grew up on a Canadian farm, too. You would be surprised what life's demands can teach you."

Max nodded. He was not the boy who left the family farm at eighteen to pursue law at Dalhousie, nor even the young man who quit three years later to fight for King and Country. Life had taught him many hard lessons in the six years that followed.

"What will you do now?" Sarah leaned forward. A stray breeze from the window rustled the hem of her skirt and carried the faint musk of her perfume to him.

Max was suddenly, almost painfully, aware that he too had leaned forward in his chair so that now their faces, their mouths, were less than a foot apart. He wanted to close that distance and, he thought, so did she. Instead, he rose suddenly, turning as he did so, as if something had caught his eye through the window. He followed the impulse and stepped to the window, pulling aside the lace curtain to look at the street below, to look at anything other than Sarah's face. At his client's face, he reminded himself, a recent widow with other commitments. It all seemed too complicated.

"Armand is at the centre of this. If he wasn't involved himself, he knows who was. I can get nothing more by skulking around. I'll confront him, see if I can force him to reveal what he knows." Max shrugged. "It might work."

"A man of action, after all," said Sarah.

He turned but the moment, if there had been a moment, had passed. Sarah smiled sadly and looked back at her hands.

"If you see Denis, ask him if he can't come see me. I know it's difficult for him but..." her voice broke slightly, "...I get so lonely."

"I'll pass that on to him," said Max, stiffly.

"I'm sorry," she said.

"For what?"

She looked at him again as if considering what to say, what apology she needed to make for his bad behavior. She shook her head and smiled.

"I appreciate what you're doing for me. Despite your doubts."

"I have no doubts. About your innocence."

She was still laughing when he left the room.

Eleven – Tuesday, June 2nd, 1920

The wicket door of Armand's Marais home was shut and bolted from the inside when Max arrived early the next morning. Max pulled the heavy rope and heard the distant toll of a bell. A few minutes later, a cadaverous manservant in a worn black suit arrived and took Max's card, shutting the door behind him. He was about to ring again when the small door opened again, this time by Pierre Armand himself. The servant stood on the steps in front of the double doors, his arms folded and a grim expression on his face.

"What do you think, coming here to my private residence?" Armand said. "I do not conduct business here."

"I thought you did."

"You are mistaken. If you want to see me, make an appointment at my office like a civilized person."

"Who said I was civilized?"

Armand snorted. "You think to intimidate me? I could have the police here in five minutes. And if that isn't enough, I have friends who are far less civilized than you."

"Yes, I saw you at the Camelots' march a few days ago."

"What of it..."

"Or perhaps you were thinking of Tourangeau and Giamatti. They're your friends, too."

Armand started at that and glanced past Max, as if he were afraid his neighbours might be listening. "Step inside," he said, moving to one side.

Max looked past Armand at the elderly servant. No threat there, he thought, but it's hard to say who might be past those double doors. Still, nothing ventured...

Armand shut the door behind Max, although he didn't bolt it again. "No need for you to sully my carpets with your dirty boots. What do you think you know about these men?"

"That they came here a few days ago and each came away with a briefcase, containing... well, who can say but them and you? Tourangeau used to be muscle for Andre Bucard, when the Black Cross was still a going concern. Giamatti is the more interesting of the two, at least according to Captain Gereau of the Prefecture. Well-connected to all sorts of people back in Italy."

"What of it? In business, you can't always be too particular who you deal with. None of my dealings with them are the least bit criminal."

"Or traitorous?"

"You go too far, Mr. Anderson."

"Is that what happened with Mark St. John? Did he go too far? Is that why he was killed?"

"Surely you're not suggesting I had anything to do with that? Mark and I were partners; we were friends."

"It's not me making the suggestions. I've had several people do it for me. But forget Giamatti for a moment. Tell me about the Russians."

"I have nothing to do with Russia – that was Mark's foolish obsession."

"Now I know you're lying to me – I've got a very credible witness who has seen you with our friends from Petrograd. And if you are lying to me about that, you're probably lying to me about other things."

Armand snorted. "A logical fallacy. My business dealings are of no concern of yours."

"Unless they have something to do with St. John's death. Then, everything you do is of concern to me."

"I think it is time you left."

"You haven't answered my question about Giamatti."

"You should ask him yourself," said Armand, swinging the wicket door open and making a gesture that contained more than a suggestion to leave.

"I intend to."

"I shall be interested in seeing how he answers you." The tone in Armand's voice sent a slight frisson along Max's spine, the same tingle he used to feel right before charging out of the trenches in the fields around Amiens.

§

It was a short walk to the hotel where Giamatti was staying. Alain, the bell hop, was on duty but Max didn't want to risk the young man's job by asking for him directly; hotel managers frowned on having their guests spied on, except by official members of the Prefecture. He found a spot where he could watch the back door without being observed and waited until Alain took a smoke break.

"I thought we were meeting after my shift," said Alain, glancing nervously at the kitchen door.

"This will only take a minute," Max said, slipping him a twenty franc note. "Is Giamatti here?"

"Yes. He's always here in the morning – I took him his breakfast about thirty minutes ago. But he goes out at ten every day except Sunday. A job maybe."

"Good work, Alain. Anything else? Visitors?"

"None that I've seen. Except for one night, there was a girl. You know. One of those. Like in Pigalle."

Pigalle or Pig Alley as visiting soldiers used to call it during the war, was the main but not sole red-light district in Paris. It wasn't far from Max's new apartment, though it wasn't an area he had frequented often. He gave the boy another ten to keep him interested and went across the street to a café to wait for Giamatti's appearance.

The Italian appeared at the door of the hotel at precisely ten o'clock, turned left into the street and started at a brisk pace away along Bretagne toward Reaumur. Max followed at a discrete distance. Giamatti kept glancing from side to side and Max fell back a few more paces. When Giamatti paused to buy a package of cigarettes at a sidewalk stall, Max suspected he had been spotted. When the Italian reversed direction and walked directly to the doorway he had ducked into, there could be no doubt.

"I don't like it when people follow me, Mr. Anderson," said Giamatti. "If you want to ask me a question you should knock on my door and ask it." Up close, he looked older; flecks of grey colored the dark curls of his hair and lines carved deep around his prominent nose and full mouth. The white line of a scar jagged from above his right eye to below this earlobe, clearly visible against his olive skin. His smile came and went like the sun on a cloudy day; when it appeared, white and even, it knocked five years off his age.

Max shifted from side to side. The door behind him was closed and bolted, the interior of the shop dark. He didn't like being pinned with no easy route out, except past Giamatti, or through him. The Italian was shorter than Max by several inches but as broad; his wrists were thick where they emerged from his jacket and his hands large and knobbed. Max suspected the other man had seen more fights at close quarters than he had.

"You know my name." Max wondered at that. Armand had seemed genuinely surprised to be confronted with Giamatti's name.

"Sure," Giamatti said, his upper lip curling. "Pierre called and said you'd be by." Max must have looked puzzled because Giamatti added. "The telephone. Ever hear of it?"

Telephones were common now in most American and many European cities, but Parisians had proven strangely resistant to their charms. Businesses sometimes had them and the police had recently installed the devices in their stations, but they were still rare in hotels, even more so in private homes.

"Mr. Armand is full of surprises."

"You don't know the half of it," said Giamatti. He offered Max one of his cigarettes; when he refused, he lit one of his own. "Let's walk. I've got places to be. You can ask your questions while we stroll."

Giamatti set off in his original direction, pausing to let Max join him. If he was still upset at being tailed, he didn't show it. They walked in silence for half a block, almost like friends before Giamatti broke the silence.

"Do you like Paris, Signor Anderson?"

"Well enough. It suits my current temperament."

Giamatti laughed, a throaty chortle of genuine amusement. "Sounds like you were born here. Me, I find it too orderly. You know, all these straight streets like the spokes of a wheel, all those buildings with the same design."

"Baron Haussmann was nothing if not consistent. But there are quartiers that retain their own character."

"It's not Rome. Been there?"

"Not yet. Maybe in the fall."

"Now that's a city – everything piled on top of each other like layers of a cake. Ancient, medieval, modern, side by side, sometimes in the same building." Giamatti laughed again. It was a good laugh – which, of course, told nothing of the man who made it. "I should get a job with the City Fathers. You got questions. Ask them quick. We'll be parting company in a few minutes."

"Mark St. John. Did you know him?"

"Met him a few times; didn't know him. Didn't like the way he died. I know people in Sicily died like that."

"So?"

"So this isn't Sicily. Something like that happens, it makes people ask questions, makes people suspect an Italian connection."

"The police suspect St. John's wife."

"There is that. But the police aren't the only ones who ask questions." Giamatti draped his arm across Max's shoulders and squeezed his arm hard. "Am I right?"

Max pulled away; Giamatti didn't resist but grinned sideways at him. No amusement there.

"I don't figure the wife for this. Not unless she's from Sicily. Or she has a friend from there. Or a friend who knows how things are there and wants to divert attention elsewhere."

Max had wondered the same thing. Whoever had killed Mark St. John had done so with deliberation. They must have had a reason for so elaborate a death. Fontaine had arrested Sarah St. John because it was the easy choice – the spouse was always the first suspect and often the right one. But he had been unable to hold her. Surely the influence of an opposition politician – even a rising star like Jourdain – wouldn't have held much sway if Fontaine had a real case. Maybe Max needed to look farther afield.

"You do business with Armand?"

"A lot of people do business with Pierre. He's useful. Well connected and clever, too. And his heart is in the right place, if you know what I mean."

"With the Action Française."

"It doesn't stop there. The Bolsheviks operate on an international scale; we must as well. They almost took Germany, you know, last year, uprisings in Kiel, Berlin and Düsseldorf. Only Soviet hubris and good luck saved the day. And the men of the Free Corps, of course. The Reds had their chance, ours is coming." Giamatti spoke with the conviction of a true believer.

Ginger Buchan should hear this, thought Max. He's always going on about the Red Terror but the other side was no better. The uprisings in Germany had started peacefully enough but it had ended with machine guns on the Brandenburg gate and Germans killing Germans. A hundred or a thousand depending on whose story you believed. And the Spartacus leaders, Liebnicht and Luxembourg, gunned down like dogs by so-called "rogue" elements.

"What's his connection with the Russians?"

"What else? Money. Though where it came from is anyone's guess. Last question."

"Who do you think killed St. John?"

"*Who* is the easy question. Once you know *why*, who will be obvious. The method makes it look like honour was involved. Revenge for some transgression or betrayal but I'd discount that. Money, politics or a combination of the two. Or maybe Mark St. John found something out about someone that made him too dangerous to live. A secret. That's what I'd be looking for."

"You seem remarkably open," said Max. Giamatti was too easy to like.

"Why not?" Giamatti said, shrugging broadly. "I know I didn't do it. I don't think any of my friends did it either, though nothing is certain. You seem like a decent fellow. I don't want you to get into any trouble you can't handle. A word of advice. Italian business is Italian business. It has nothing to do with you or with this St. John business. Keep that in mind and you'll be all right. Forget it and... well, let's say what happens won't be personal. But it won't be fun. And you may not live to regret it."

Giamatti stuck out his hand and, when Max took it, pulled him into an embrace that lasted several seconds longer than Max was comfortable with. When he released him, Giamatti smiled broadly up into Max's face, turned and walked away, whistling a tune Max had last heard at the Opera house.

§

The family seeking their lost grandchild had responded to his telegram along with the small deposit he had requested and Max had spent the afternoon filling out forms at the Prefecture, requesting information from the central files. His initial inquiries among the boy's friends had provided no clue as to his current whereabouts but several suggestions for further inquiries.

It was nearly dusk as he made his way from Clichy toward Le Coq Bleu. He was halfway up the long stair that separated the lower half of Rue Drebec from the upper when four men stepped from an open doorway and surrounded him on the landing. They were dressed in the shabby pants and jackets of tradesmen but didn't wear the rough boots typical of that class. Their shoes weren't stylish but had been recently polished, men who were down on their luck but still remembered more prosperous days and careers.

Even with caps pulled low and the lower half of their faces wrapped in thick scarves, a style Max was beginning to dislike, he was sure he had never met any of them before. Two had dark eyes, another, hazel; the fourths were piercing blue. If they had any other distinguishing features, Max didn't notice; he was too busy dodging fists.

The two closest made a grab for his arms.

Max turned sideways, slipping past their grasping hands. He ducked a flailing fist and shot a hard blow of his own to an exposed mid-section. He darted for the stairs; an assailant blocked the way.

The tight space made it hard to avoid the punches and kicks and Max took several hard blows to his chest and shins. He slipped past one lunging body, turned and pounded the man's kidneys as Kid O'Brien had taught him. The man's knees buckled; he lurched into another of the gang, sending them both tumbling on the steep stairs.

A string of invective, in clear, if provincial, French and another, vaguely familiar, language followed.

The largest caught Max in a bear hug. The final assailant – hazel eyes – closed, his fists flailing on Max's chest and shoulders, scraping against his bobbing head.

The man holding him growled in execrable French. "Halt asking questions about things that don't worry you, Yank. Gone things should stay gone."

Max jerked his head back, heard a grunt and a satisfying crunch of cartilage, as the man behind reeled back, dragging Max with him.

Max used the created gap to lift his legs and kick. He caught the man opposite flush in the chest. He lurched back, crashing into the wall.

The bear hug loosened and Max relaxed his arms, slipping through the ring of flesh that held him.

He scrambled away. Too late. A savage kick caught him in the ribs. Air rushed from his lungs. Black spots danced across his vision.

He rolled, lashing out with his own feet. He caught a shin, then a knee. Bought a moment to breathe.

Then hands were grabbing at him. One clawed at his face; Max bit hard on fingers, tasted blood. The hand jerked away.

Max kicked again, felt flesh spasm back from the blow. He rolled onto his knees.

Hazel eyes was still down, on hands and knees, blood streaming from a cut behind his ear. One of the men was gone, tumbled down the stairs or run off but Bear-hug was still on his feet though favoring one leg.

The fourth one was unscathed, standing one step below the landing, knife in hand, uncertainty in his blue eyes. He nodded at

Bear-hug and they both moved forward, cautious now. Max had proved more than they expected.

Shouts from the top of the stairs decided it. Bear-hug growled a sentence or two; the other barked a reply. *Russian*, thought Max. Or something like it. Hazel eyes lurched to his feet.

The two others grabbed him and, supporting his still swaying steps between them, went down the stairs into the night.

Max slumped back onto his haunches, fighting blurred vision and nausea. Henri, a truncheon in his fist, swam into view. Two of the bar regulars slipped their hands under his arms, gently hoisted him to his feet and helped him up the stairs.

Twelve – Thursday-Saturday, June 4-6th, 1920

Max spent the night in Yesim's spare room in the small apartment above the bar. It was late morning when he awoke. Whatever Henri had given him to kill the pain in his ribs and face had worked. His side ached but he could get out of bed and wash himself without too much difficulty. He made his way down the narrow metal stairs with only occasional twinges in his metal-reinforced leg.

Henri fussed over the bandages and sticking plasters he had applied the night before, replacing several with fresh squares of gauze. Yesim busied himself at the bar, pouring steaming garlic soup into a bowl. Garlic was Yesim's cure for whatever troubled you, from cuts to flu to troubles of the heart.

"You'll never get a wife," said Henri, "if you keep adding scars to that face of yours."

"Who says I want a wife?" asked Max. He was still embarrassed by his improper thoughts about Sarah St. John.

"All men want a wife," said Henri. "They never know it until it's too late."

"I never had a wife," interrupted Yesim from the bar. "And look at me."

"He makes my case," said Henri, laughing gently at his old friend.

Yesim plunked the bowl of soup in front of Max, along with a fresh baguette and a few thin slices of hard cheese.

"I don't think it will scar," said Yesim, gazing appraisingly at Max's wounds. "Much. Besides a woman would be a fool not to be charmed by our young friend. He has money, that charming Canadian accent of his, and did you see the way he handled that gang of apaches?"

"No," said Henri. "And neither did you."

"I saw the blood they were washing off the stairs this morning," said Yesim. "A lot more than Max shed, I'll tell you."

Max let them talk. His mouth was still sore from the fight; he may have bitten his own lip as well as his assailant's fingers. Besides, he had better things to do than talk. The soup was sweet, the way garlic gets when it is well roasted and the cheese was sharp and tasted faintly of port. The sound of their banter soothed him.

The bowl was soon empty and Max didn't turn down a refill when Yesim offered it. Henri perched on the seat across the table, his face creased with worry.

"Who were those men?" he asked.

"Not professionals," said Max. He'd had his share of fights with professionals; he didn't usually do so well. "They were trying to make up in numbers what they lacked in skill."

"That doesn't answer the question. The streets of Paris are full of eager amateurs these days. For many, the war isn't over yet."

"People keep reminding me. Some of them were foreign, I think, though one swore at me in very idiomatic French. I'll clearly need more lessons when you have the time."

Henri laughed, which was Max's intent. Henri had worries of his own these days; he didn't need any of Max's.

"Immigrants falling on hard times?"

"Maybe," said Max. "They certainly were dressed the part. Except for their shoes. They were fairly new. Stylish too. Like in the better shops on Les Champs. Two of them might have been Russians. From the sounds of it."

"You've picked up another language?" asked Yesim, returning with more soup and a replenished plate of cheese, now augmented with black olives.

"French is enough of a challenge. But it sounded like things I heard at the Restaurant Petrograd. It's worth looking into."

"Are you sure, Max?" asked Henri, the worry returning to his eyes. "You may have given better than you got but it was still a bad beating."

"I'm fine," said Max, pushing back his chair. Black dots swam across the window and he had to put his hands flat on the table for support. "Maybe you're right."

"Do you want to stay here?" asked Yesim. "My home is your home."

"No," said Max. "I'll take a cab to my office and send a few messages from there. It takes time to arrange to meet people."

"Then you'll go home?" asked Henri.

"No," said Max. "Then I'm going to see about getting a telephone."

"This detective business must pay better than I thought," muttered Yesim.

"I might get one for this place, too. And Chez Jake. Don't worry, Yesim, I'll pay for it out of my share of the profits."

"What profits?" said Henri, smirking.

"What do we need with such a contraption?" asked Yesim, trying to sound unenthusiastic.

"It's the coming thing, Yesim. Pretty soon we won't know how we got along without one."

Henri snorted but Yesim nodded thoughtfully, already considering the possibilities.

§

Getting a phone proved more complicated than it sounded. There were several different companies that served the Montmartre area and it was difficult to decipher their competing claims. Max finally decided on the one that had the most subscribers; a telephone was of little use if you couldn't reach anyone.

He had sent messages to both Ginger Buchan and Joseph Asper to arrange rendezvous. Buchan responded within the hour suggesting a late breakfast near the American Embassy on Saturday; Asper had not responded by the time Max left his office at Chez Jake to inquire about the telephone. It was late afternoon before he finally limped home to his bed.

He awoke the next day, feeling sore but considerably more energetic. He had eaten little the night before and now his stomach craved more than his usual breakfast of fruit pastries and coffee. There was a restaurant on Raspail that was run by an expatriate couple from Oxford; it catered to English tourists. It was a lengthy walk but the weather had turned overnight and the morning was warm and sunny.

Max ordered a full English breakfast, poached eggs on an English muffin with a rasher of bacon and a serving of brown beans. Cold toast served with hard butter and a pot of marmalade rounded out the meal. He ordered a pot of tea rather than trying his luck with the dubious looking coffee.

Over breakfast he wrote up his notes from the last few days. In particular, he tried to recall any significant details about his assailants that might help him identify them if he met them again. The clothes were undoubtedly a disguise, obtained from one of the many used clothing stores that filled the back streets of St. Denis, just over the hill from Montmartre. They had probably been discarded within minutes. The shoes, however, were almost certainly their own and Max jotted down colors and styles – one black in smooth leather, two dark brown, one smooth and the other in the style known as

Beau Brummel, the final pair brown and white with intricate stitching across the sharply pointed toe.

As for the rest, it seemed that the men were mostly young, judging from the way they moved, and athletic, if untrained in the martial arts. Two had been roughly Max's height, though neither was as broad. Blue-eyes was a few inches shorter but quite thick through the chest. Bear-hug was by far the biggest, two or three inches taller than Max and perhaps thirty pounds heavier. He was also, thought Max, older than the other three; his face above the scarf had been haggard, his eyes puffy and lined. Now he likely had a broken nose to improve his looks. If he or any of the others had been sporting beards or mustaches, the scarves had kept them well hidden. Max was about to close his book when he remembered a final detail. The man with the knife had thick brows that almost joined into a single black line.

His notes complete, Max turned his attention to the pile of newspapers kept on a shelf near the back of the café. The tea had grown cold and bitter, so he ordered a fresh pot. There were copies of several London papers, all several days old, as well as the English language Herald, published in Paris. Max no longer avoided the English press, as he had when he first came to Paris, but they held little of relevance to his current concerns. Instead, he picked up the early editions of Les Temps and L'Humanité.

They had nothing to say about the St. John murder; the story had grown old in the eyes of the press. Besides neither paper was much interested in the lurid details of crime. They left that to Paris Soir and the other yellow journals. If the connection to Jordaine was ever revealed, of course, both would blare it from the front page, if from very different angles.

Les Temps had a front-page story about the imminent signing of the Peace Treaty between the Allies and Hungary in Trianon, which left only the Ottoman Empire officially at war. It reminded him that he had still not heard from Joseph Asper. That was curious; Asper was cash-strapped and would be eager to peddle whatever he had found for francs. Perhaps there was a message at his office over Chez Jake.

L'Humanité seemed mostly taken up with the visit of Socialist leaders to Moscow. Cachin had written a lengthy letter describing the accomplishments of the new Soviet regime in generally glowing terms. It was a far cry from the lurid reports of the "Red Terror" that had filled the Parisian papers, even the left-leaning ones, during the first half of 1919. Then, of course, all of France had been gripped by the fear that Bolshevik-inspired uprisings in Kiel, Berlin and Munich would lead to a collapse of social order in Germany and a resumption of the horrors of war. The crushing of the Sparticists in the spring of the year, followed soon after by the collapse of the short-lived Hungarian Soviet had quelled those fears, though Conservative papers periodically ran stories of fresh atrocities, both in Russia and in the current fighting between the Soviets and the newly independent Poland.

The day had turned from warm to hot and Max removed his jacket and loosened his collar for the walk to his office. He took a circuitous route, walking along Barrière Blanche, so he could pause to look over the wall at the small rectangle of stone that marked the grave of his friend, Havel Barzani, in the absurdly crowded Montmartre Cemetery. It had been over a year since his death, but the memory of his friend still tugged at his heart.

Asper had been to the office after Max left the day before. He had left no note but had told Jake he would return no later than Monday if "everything goes according to plan." Jake thought he had seemed nervous and a little bit furtive. Max laughed and said: "It's his natural state."

The man seeking his brother had replied with a short letter, providing the details Max had requested and a hundred francs in tattered five- and ten-franc notes. Max determined he would return the money no matter how his investigation turned out. There was also a request from a previous client to undertake another investigation; items had been disappearing from his warehouse in southern Paris and he wanted Max to find out which if any of his four employees was responsible. Never turn down repeat business, his father used to say, so Max put a reply in the mail accepting the job and promising to get on it in the next day or two.

Max had occasionally hired an agent or two to help with a case but now that business was burgeoning maybe it was time that he hired someone on a full-time basis. For some reason, Pierre Roget came to mind. The man had worked for a notorious criminal but had, so he said, reformed, and he certainly was good in a tight spot. Besides, he had wanted to talk to Roget about Jourdain. Might as well kill two birds with a single toss.

After a quick lunch in the kitchen with Jake – a thick lamb and potato stew served with polenta – Max took the Metro a few stops to the 17th arrondissement. He walked along Daru until he reached the address of Irina Pavlovna's apartment. He had planned to leave her a message before heading over to the Petrograd on the off-chance Asper was there. Instead, he was ushered into her third-floor apartment by a young maid servant who couldn't stop giggling from behind the hand covering her mouth. She pushed open the salon doors and nodded for Max to enter. Irina Pavlovna rose from her seat by the window where she had been conversing with an older couple. A third man, older still but with the straight posture of a soldier, was standing some feet away beside a small brick fireplace. The girl erupted in a fresh round of giggles.

"That will be all, Maria," said Pavlovna sternly. The girl flushed and scurried down the hall into the back of the apartment.

Although it was barely past two, the countess was in full evening wear, her long hair piled on top of her head in an elaborate coiffure supported by several bejewelled pins and clips. Max wondered if she ever appeared in casual dress.

"Max. darling!" Pavlovna grasped his shoulders and kissed him on both cheeks like they were long separated relatives. "So good to see you again. Do you know Baron Denidov and the Countess Solikov? This is my Canadian friend, Max Anderson."

Denidov crossed the wide salon. He was portly and dressed in an expensive, if somewhat dated, black evening jacket with wide lapels. A cluster of military decorations adorned his left breast and he had the firm grip and frank open gaze that typified many military men. Max judged him to be about sixty, his thinning hair and full beard white, although his round reddish face was only faintly lined.

"Sergei Davidovitch Denidov, at your service. And this is my sister, The Countess Katrina Isabella Solikoff."

Countess Solikov nodded at the mention of her name but showed no interest in moving from the circle of ornate chairs that dominated the far end of the salon. She was much younger than her brother, not yet forty, Max guessed, her skin pale and almost translucent, her lips, thin and colorless. Even her blue eyes were pale, but her hair, which she wore in thick ringlets, was a deep golden color.

Max glanced at the other man, who still stood aloof, only his eyes moving as he followed Denidov's every move.

"Yes, of course, my..." Denidov paused as if searching for the right term, "...valet. Ivany Federov."

No middle name, Max noted. Federov might well have been a batman; he certainly held himself with an upright military posture. Still, his grey wide-set eyes spoke of deep intelligence and a faintly amused, slightly sardonic smile played on his lips. His age was less easy to judge; his thin aesthetic face was deeply lined but his thick hair was black without even a trace of gray at the temples.

"To what do I owe this pleasure?" asked Pavlovna.

"I'm sorry to disturb you," said Max. "I can come back when you aren't occupied."

"Nonsense. Sergei and Katrina are old friends. We have no secrets between us. They know all about Mark."

"Terrible business," said Denidov, frowning.

"I've really told you all I know about the matter," said Pavlovna.

"Still, I have a few questions. About that. And other things."

"Things?"

"I was attacked yesterday. On Rue Drebec."

Countess Solikoff gasped, her hand flying to her mouth. Federov poured a glass of water from a pitcher on the mantle and brought it to her.

"I wondered about the marks on your face," said Pavlovna. "But why tell me?"

"I believe that two of the men were Russian. At least they spoke a language similar to what I've heard in the Restaurant Petrograd."

"To the untrained ear..." Pavlovna shrugged.

"Surely you are not suggesting Irina had anything to do with this?" asked Denidov.

"No. Of course not." It was, Max realized, poor planning on his part. Pavlovna might well have sent those men after him, though her motive for doing so was unclear. Still, it did no good to make unsubstantiated claims – not when he still needed answers to more important questions.

Federov, who had returned to his place by the fireplace, came to his rescue.

"Perhaps Mr. Anderson was hoping we might be of assistance in locating the men who attacked him. The Russian enclave has grown over the last year but it is still, as they say in America, small beans. There are one or two establishments in the 15th where such men might be found."

"I wouldn't know about that," said Denidov. He didn't seem to want to meet his valet's eyes.

"Anything you can tell me would be helpful," said Max.

Federov nodded at the Countess Solikov. "Perhaps privately."

"Ivany is a great help to us all. Now if there is nothing else." Pavlovna reached for a bell cord that would recall the maid servant.

"I have one or two questions – but, as I say, I can return when it is more convenient."

"Questions are seldom convenient. We may as well be comfortable," said Pavlovna, gesturing to the circle of chairs. "Ivany, ask Maria to bring some refreshments."

Federov didn't quite click his heels before turning to obey. Countess Sokilov rose and followed him out without a word.

"My sister is a delicate woman. She dislikes talk that might remind her of our unpleasant departure from Mother Russia." Denidov resumed his seat in the largest of the chairs, brown leather cushions and heavy legs and arms of carved dark wood, more like a primitive throne than salon furniture.

Pavlovna sat with her back to the window. The afternoon light surrounded her head in a golden nimbus and made her features indistinct.

Federov returned with a large silver tray, containing a samovar of tea and a plate of delicate petit fours. There was also a bottle of chilled vodka and three shot glasses. The older man served the other three and then returned to his position next to the fireplace.

"Won't you join us?" asked Max.

Federov looked embarrassed; his head gave an almost imperceptible shake.

"You'll have plenty of time to talk to Ivany at the appropriate time." She ignored the steaming teacup and lifted the glass of vodka to her lips, sipping it delicately.

Denidov was not nearly so delicate, downing the liquor in a single swallow. He reached for the bottle to refill his glass but then thought better of it. He leaned back in his chair and balanced the cup and saucer on his expansive belly.

"I hope you don't mind," said Denidov. "We Russians have grown suspicious of men with questions." He seemed to find his remark so funny that his laughter threatened to send the tea sloshing onto his jacket.

"That's fine," said Max, ignoring both the vodka and the tea. "Did you know Mark St. John, Baron Denidov?"

"I met him once or twice but I can't claim to have known him well."

"That seems to be a common assessment."

"Mark had the ability," said Pavlovna, "to charm without revealing much of himself to those he was charming. I'm not sure how well I knew him myself."

"But I thought you and he were..." Max still hesitated to say it. Especially in front of other men.

Pavlovna showed no such reluctance.

"Lovers? What of it? Marc was a secretive man by nature, paranoid by training. He doled out details like a miser spending pennies; each nugget fetched the greatest return possible."

"What kind of secrets did St. John have?"

"Dangerous ones," said Pavlovna. "That should be obvious enough."

"Then you think he was killed for a secret."

"I don't know," said Pavlovna, her voice breaking slightly.

Was it real emotion, wondered Max, *or an elaborate act?* He didn't trust the woman, despite being all too aware of her charms.

"Can't you see you're upsetting Irina?" asked Denidov. "Perhaps it is time you left."

"One more thing," said Max, rising. "I suspect St. John was giving you money..."

Denidov flushed and started to get up; Pavlovna held up a restraining hand.

"Not..." Max shook his head, frustrated at his own clumsiness. "To support your cause – whether to help General Wrangel in Russia or simply aid your friends and allies to escape the clutches of Trotsky and the Red Terror. By some accounts, it was a lot of money." Which could explain the variations in the estimates of Pavlovna's own wealth. "Where did the money come from? St. John's own funds? He was reputed to be comfortable but hardly wealthy. From some other source? His wife? His business partners?"

"He was an agent of the American government," said Denidov. "Only the Americans have money nowadays."

Max didn't even bother to look at the aging aristocrat. *Denidov doesn't matter*, he thought, *he's nothing but protective covering.* Pavlovna was the power in the room. Max spared a glance at Federov. His brows were drawn together and his lips pursed. He's as interested in the answer to this question as I am.

"I never asked," said Pavlovna. "It was enough that he had it."

"Was it wise?" asked Max. "Taking money when you didn't know where it came from? St. John was known to associate with criminals."

"Crime is relative. The greatest crimes in history are being committed in the streets of Moscow and on the steppes of the Ukraine. I would take money from Satan himself to stop it. What is theft, what is extortion, what is the trade in drugs to me? If Mark committed crimes, it was for the greater good."

"I've heard anarchists make the same argument," said Max. "And didn't Bolsheviks rob banks to fund their revolution?"

"That was for the greater evil," said Denidov. "Now it is time for you to go. Ivany."

Federov didn't stir until Pavlovna nodded her agreement. He came to stand beside Max's chair. It wasn't clear what he could do against a younger fitter man, but his grim expression showed he meant to try. Max retrieved his hat from the side table and stood.

"Perhaps we can talk again at another time."

Pavlovna nodded again. "Perhaps next week."

"I'm part owner of a jazz club, Chez Jake. Perhaps you'll let me take you to dinner there. Baron, you and your sister are welcome to join us." It would be an opportunity to question them on his own turf, away from threatening valets and giggling maids. It would be interesting to see if Smitty, the club's bouncer, recognized any of them.

"An intriguing invitation," said Pavlovna. "I'll check my agenda and send you a note in a few days."

Federov followed Max into the hall, closing the salon doors behind him. Max took out his journal and pen to write down the addresses of the places Federov had mentioned.

"Not here," said Federov. "I need to pick up tobacco for the Baron. We could walk together."

The older man seemed a different person by the time they hit the street. His gait lost its military precision and his face relaxed into a gentle smile. He offered Max a cigarette from a battered brass holder, and then lit one himself with a matching lighter. He stood for a moment, his face lifted to the sun, before exhaling a cloud of smoke.

"Lady Pavlovna does not allow smoking in her apartments. Unless you have the rank of Count or higher."

"I understand her reluctance."

Federov shrugged his indifference and started along the narrow sidewalk to Courcelles, a broad boulevard that led to Parc Monceau. Cafés and shops, many now catering to Russian clientele, lined both sides of the street. Federov took a seat in the Bar Russe on the sidewalk beside the nearest tobacconist.

"Buy me a vodka," said Federov.

Max raised his brows but complied, ordering vodka for Federov and a glass of white wine for himself.

"Are you always so assertive?" asked Max.

"Isn't that how it's done? The detective plies his informants with drink and then pays for the information?"

"I should introduce you to my friend, Henri. I think you have similar tastes in popular literature."

"In any case, you can keep your money. I'm happy to assist my mas... my employer, Baron Denidov."

"Have you been with him long?"

"Since we were both children. It's no secret, I suppose. I was born a serf. The Baron's family owned mine. That changed after the revolution of '05, when the last of us were freed, in theory at least. I could have gone anywhere I liked after that – but where was I to go? I was already well over forty and knew no other life. The Baron was a decent man. He seldom beat his servants and treated his serfs as a kind of people, not property. A liberal by Russian standards. I became his valet. He had to pay me, but on the other hand he could now charge me for my room and board. When the Bolsheviks drove his family from their home, I chose to go with them."

"Are they as bad as the press says?"

"They are fanatics. Like all fanatics, they pursue their vision with relentless fury. They've killed thousands for no better reason than they had a small holding or ran a shop or a café like this one. Or been a member of a more moderate socialist party. The Bolsheviks are barely human. Monsters with an endless appetite for blood."

Max had no response that would be useful. In one way, he agreed with Federov. He had seen things done in the trenches that still haunted him. All were done for the noblest of reasons. But he had also seen acts of great bravery and kindness, sometimes in defiance of orders. It was those he tried to think of when he awoke sweating in the night.

He had no doubt the Red Terror was real but he had no doubt either that atrocities had been committed on both sides. The western powers had not abandoned the White cause because of the wishes of the generals at home. Wartime censorship still prevailed but there were hints in some papers of mutinies by men sick of fighting. But it was reports of reprehensible actions by their erstwhile allies that had provoked most of the withdrawals. That line of discussion was unlikely to loosen the tongue of Ivany Federov.

"You said you knew of some places in the 15th where the men who attacked me might be found."

Federov nodded and signalled for another drink. He was clearly making up for lost opportunities in Pavlovna's apartment.

"Some Russians came to Paris with money, but most did not." His face darkened. "Some who came with money frittered it away on drink or games of chance. Jobs are scarce, a convenient excuse for a certain class of men. There are bars that cater to that type. They can drink cheaply and blame others for their fate. If you wanted to find a ruffian or two, it's where you might start looking." Federov wrote two addresses in Max's journal. After a moment's thought he added a third.

"They weren't skilled fighters."

"The best have already been employed as agents for the Cheka or bodyguards for Russian nobles worried about the Cheka. What's left... well, they have the advantage of coming cheap."

"The Cheka are the Bolshevik secret police?"

"Yes. Men who learned their trade at the hands of the Okrhana, the Tsar's secret police." Federov might hate the Bolsheviks but he had no illusions about the society they had overthrown.

"Then there *are* Soviet agents operating in Paris."

"Not as many as the Baron or his sister thinks, but more than a few. I know of at least one. Gennady Sidorov was also a servant of the Denidov family, one who was more than eager to join the revolution. I'm told he has risen fast and is now here in Paris."

"Told by whom?"

"I'm not at liberty to say. But he is in a position to know."

"Ginger Buchan?" Max guessed. Buchan's work at the American Embassy and his obsession with the Bolsheviks made him a likely candidate.

Federov flushed and looked away. "I... I don't believe I know that gentleman."

Whatever else Denidov's valet might be, he was a lousy liar. Federov downed the last of his vodka and rose to go.

"The Baron will be wanting his tobacco," he said. "Thank you for the drink. I must reciprocate someday."

Max watched Federov walk past the tobacconist next door to one farther down the block. If the vodka had had any effect, it didn't show in his posture or gait.

§

La Brassiere Russulka made Le Coq Bleu look like an upscale establishment. Dark, even in the late afternoon sun, its zinc bar could barely be seen for the collected grime, though compared to the sawdust covered floor, it was practically spotless. The men hunched along its length didn't seem to mind. They clutched tumblers of vodka in meaty fists, mumbling to their neighbour or simply staring blearily at their distorted reflections in the mirror behind the bar.

Tables along one wall were crowded with men, some already insensate with drink, others glaring angrily through dirt-streaked windows at more affluent passers-by. There were no women, even the servers being men. A few customers were eating, some sort of lumpy goulash served in earthenware bowls with slabs of dark bread, but most were satisfied to take their nourishment from bottles. None looked up as Max pushed his way past them and took the lone vacant stool.

The other two bars on Federov's list had proven dead ends. The first he had visited, the one Federov had added as an afterthought, was not far from the Ternes Metro station and had, at one time, been moderately prosperous. Its décor still reflected its former status and it was obvious that the owners, a middle-aged couple with harried expressions, were doing their best to maintain it despite the decline in their clientele, a mixture of young men and neatly-dressed older couples. Most of the men vaguely resembled the dark-eyed ones who had attacked him, but none had their specific features or any marks of recent fighting. Max's inquiries, which implied an offer of questionable employment, were met with stony silence or grumbled curses, until the male proprietor asked him to leave. These men might be on their way to the bottom but they weren't there yet.

The second bar was a few blocks away and several rungs down the social ladder. The few women here were as shabby and despairing as the men. Most of the men here had no compunction about hiring themselves out as "bodyguards," but few had actually done so. In any case, none resembled those who had beset Max the day before. Still, the way some of them had looked at Max made him glad he had chosen to retrieve his five-shot Kolb from his office before investigating Federov's leads.

Max had been in a lot of bars in the last five years but none like La Russulka. Down a narrow alleyway, its small, hand painted sign barely visible above the door, this was not a place people came to by accident. Certainly, no one came here to meet a friend or to enjoy a quiet drink or a meal after work.

This was a place to drink until you fell over, a place for fierce arguments and low plots. Men came here when they had no place else to go. Most were of Max's age; at least half were veterans of the war, scars of past battles worn on their limbs and faces without pride or honour. They were society's cast-offs. A few were French; most weren't. Some, like those who had attacked him, had seen better days as evidenced by their once-stylish suits and shoes; most would never see them again.

Max had little doubt these men would hire themselves out for a few francs and do whatever their employer asked of them. From the appraising looks on a few faces, at least a few were willing to act without any other encouragement than the opportunity to take what they could lay their hands on. Max shifted on his stool so he had easier access to the gun weighing down his jacket pocket.

"You're either lost or stupid or looking for trouble," said the man behind the bar, dropping a glass of murky looking liquor in front of him. "Five francs."

Max dropped a twenty on the bar. "I'm not looking for trouble but I am looking for information."

The bartender swept up the bill but didn't offer any change. "Go to the library." Those within earshot grunted their appreciation and shifted on their chairs to watch the show.

"I'm told this is a good place to find men who hate Bolsheviks and are willing to do something about it."

"For twenty francs," said the bartender, "they'd be willing to tug on Lenin's beard. Or the Tsar's for that matter."

"And what would they do for fifty francs?"

"Kill you if you're not careful, young gentleman," sighed a grey-haired man on the next stool. "Look around. These men have nothing to look forward to but their next drink."

"Why didn't you say so?" Max dropped three more twenties on the bar. "Drinks all around."

The barman shrugged, tucked the bills into his pocket and brought out a large bottle of vodka from under the bar. A ragged cheer rolled through the bar, even among those who didn't know what they were cheering for yet.

"You're only delaying trouble," said the older man, "not preventing it. A drink will only make them thirsty for more."

"No doubt," said Max. "But delay may be good enough. My name is Max."

"Like the old emperor. I'm Carmine." He took his hand off his glass long enough to shake Max's. "Maybe I have the information you're looking for. I'm here most days."

Max had little doubt that was true. Carmine's face was puffy; the veins in his nose distended from long years of heavy drinking. His hand, when he extended it, shook slightly. Still, the light of intelligence shone in his dark green eyes.

"A few days ago, a young man, shorter than me with piercing blue eyes may have come here looking to hire some men for a job."

"It happens," said Carmine, stretching out his hand again. Max pressed a twenty into his palm. "I seem to recall this gentleman. Blue eyes, a long straight nose above thin lips, hair short and black, perhaps thirty. He was well dressed, better than you even. It caused quite a stir. He had to talk fast not to be robbed on the spot. He hired three men, I think. All Russians."

"Sounds right. Did this man have a name?"

"None that I heard."

"What about the Russians?"

"Russians always have more names than you can remember," Carmine said, laughing at his own joke. "One of them comes here often, a big man named Ivan, though I haven't seen him since. The other two, who knows? Toughs, though not from a tough background, I think. Aristocrats without any real skills other than whoring and brawling. And speaking French?"

"French?"

"Yes, Ivan and the others all speak French, more than I can say for most of the men who come here. The man hiring them was French – from somewhere down south, I'd say by his accent."

A Frenchman, thought Max, how does that fit into the pattern? Was the attack meant to drive him off the case or had it been a decoy, to make him suspect the Russians when the real culprit was French? Armand's work or Michel Tourangeau's or someone else all together?

Max looked around the bar. Most of the men had turned away, satisfied to have a fresh drink in their hands. A savage hunger twisted the faces of those who were still looking his way. *It's time to go*, thought Max.

He fixed a grim expression on his own face and slipped his hand into his jacket pocket, pressing the barrel of his gun against the fabric. A dozen men watched him move the length of the bar to the door but none thought it worth their while to challenge him.

§

Max spent the evening and most of the next day, setting his cases in motion and trying to track down Roget. He had moved from the hotel where he had been staying at the end of May and it took several visits to find an assistant manager willing, for a hundred francs, to give Max his forwarding address. *If this keeps up*, thought Max, *I won't be able to* afford *to hire an assistant.*

As it turned out, Roget's new accommodation, a single small room in a boarding house on Véron, was only a few blocks from Max's apartment. Roget was out Friday evening when Max called, but the concierge, an elderly woman in a grey shawl, promised to pass on a message in the morning. Max undertook to drop by after his breakfast with Buchan.

Ginger Buchan was already seated at a window table of the café on Boulevard des Italiens where they had agreed to meet, drinking coffee and smoking one of his ever-present American cigarettes. He stubbed it out as Max approached and waved to the waiter who immediately delivered a large carafe of coffee and another cup.

"Are we having real breakfast," asked Buchan, "or the desert tray they prefer in France?"

Max smiled. Ever since he had known the young American diplomat, Buchan had complained about the sugary confections the French started their day with, though Max had never actually seen him turn one down.

"Depends on who's paying," said Max. By all rights, he should pay – it was his invitation – but the St. John investigation had been expensive so far and, despite the promises of Sarah St. John and Denis Jourdain, he had yet to see any money.

"I'm not that hungry anyway," Buchan countered. Turning to the waiter, he said. "A continental. For two. He's paying."

"Another cut to the expense account, Ginger?"

"They figure, with the recent devaluation of the franc, we should be able to stretch our dollars further." Whatever the financial limitations placed on the embassy, Buchan, as usual, looked like a million in any currency, in a black morning coat with silk trimmed lapels. His shirt was of the most recent Parisian style with attached collar, white with thin vertical stripes of pale green. He wore a tie of darker green that matched his eyes and complemented his longish red hair. "I suppose I shouldn't complain. If the Senate had its way, they'd reduce the staff to a part time ambassador and downstairs maid."

The waiter brought a large basket of baked goods. A pyramid of butter squares, surrounded by eight pots of assorted jams and jellies, completed the selection. Buchan looked dubiously at the basket before selecting a croissant and a flaky square of toasted brioche. Max took the second croissant and a pair of pear tarts.

Max refilled their cups with steaming coffee and the two ate in companionable silence for several minutes. When the back of their hunger was broken, Max said, "I was speaking to a friend of yours the other day. Ivany Federov."

Buchan pursed his lips and adopted a thoughtful look as if he were trying to place the name.

"It's okay, Ginger. You don't have to admit it. Why don't you tell me about a Russian named Genaddy Sidorov instead?"

"Have you met him?"

"Not yet, but I intend to as soon as I can find him. I was hoping you could help me."

"Why the sudden interest in Bolsheviks? I thought you didn't take sides in the great debate."

"It's looking less and less like a debate every day. More like mobs in the street than any civilized discourse. I don't take sides, but I don't ignore them either." Max repeated what he had heard of Mark St. John's vehement campaign against the Reds and the danger some people thought it might have put him in. There were few people in Paris Max trusted more than Ginger Buchan.

"Interesting. I developed the same theory myself. The Reds killed St. John because of his financial support of Pavlovna and her gang of brigands but made it look like he was killed by Italian mobsters. But it doesn't quite ring true. St. John was a cautious man, and a dangerous one in his own right. I can't see him lowering his guard if he sniffed a Bolshevik."

"It's a starting place. Right now, everyone seems a likely suspect, even my client, who hasn't been entirely honest with me. If I can eliminate one theory, maybe it will make the right one stand out."

"Fair enough," said Buchan, fishing another piece of brioche out of the basket. "Like most of the new men in Russia, we don't know a lot about Sidorov. There was a Sidorov who went to prison for a few years after the 1905 revolution. My 'friend' says he's pretty sure it was Gennady, a troublesome former serf who had been kicked off the Denidov estate that year, which would make him about forty now. A Genery Sidorov led a mutiny of sailors in the dying days of Russia's involvement in the war; he could be the same man or not. Sidorov is a common enough name. In any case, he became a Commissar in the Cheka and according to all reports is still in Moscow. Except, my 'friend' claims to have seen him in Paris. And I've got intelligence that a G. Sidorov has registered with the Prefecture as a refugee from the Ukraine."

"He's required to leave an address and inform the police if he moves."

"Spies are notoriously unreliable and the Prefecture is swamped. Thousands of people are flowing into Paris from across eastern Europe and both sides of the Mediterranean. If they don't catch them in a general sweep or in the act of breaking the law, they pretty much ignore them."

"You must have some ideas."

"I have lots of ideas. It's facts that are in short supply."

"Why would someone like Sidorov be in Paris?"

"To keep track of the White supporters for one. General Wrangel isn't out of the fight yet, despite his abandonment by the west. Not that he didn't deserve to be abandoned. They call him a general but he's more like a warlord. The French are keeping quiet about the mutinies in the south, but I'm told the soldiers couldn't stomach the massacres, mostly of Jews, he perpetrated in some of the villages. People like Denidov portray themselves as liberals, but all they really want is their land back. For me, Wrangel is the lesser of two evils. Barely."

"Would he do anything more than spy on them?"

"That's the question, isn't it? Is he here to kill the enemies of the proletariat? That would make him a prime suspect in St. John's murder. To tell you the truth, I'd be surprised. Not that he's above murder but I understand he practices it on a grander scale. There are several villages in the Ukraine that disappeared shortly after a visit by Sidorov and his men. If he really is this commissar, would they waste him on two-bit conspirators in Paris?"

"What else then?"

"Yevgeny Miller and Baratov are secretly in Paris as we speak, trying to raise funds. Meanwhile, Blum and Denis Jourdain have raised the warning flag about getting too close to the new Third International. Sidorov could be here to 'persuade' reluctant Socialists to take the next step with threats, money or both. Lenin hates capitalists but he hates social democrats and centrist socialists even more."

"I can't see the French embracing Bolshevism. They may believe in equality and fraternity but they love their liberty."

"Many do," agreed Buchan. "But not all. The Action Française wouldn't have fifty thousand members if they did."

"I suppose."

"If I were betting, say fifty francs, I'd agree with you. The Bolsheviks won't take over the socialist party but they may split it down the middle. That would send shivers of delight up the spine of the ruling coalition. There is nothing better for a government than a divided opposition."

"And nothing improves the prospects of an ambitious politician than the departure of his chief rivals to another camp," said Max. "Two socialist parties would double the chances of advancement."

"It all depends," said Buchan. "Is Denis Jourdain the kind of man who would rather rule in Spain than serve in Rome?"

"Given what happened to Julius Caesar, it might be the wisest choice."

§

Roget was sitting on the step of his boarding house when Max arrived, his face tilted up into the warm June sun.

"I had almost given up on you," he said, rising. "My stomach says it's too late for breakfast. How about lunch? My cousin has a new place on Junot. I'm sure he'll give you a deal."

Max shrugged. His breakfast with Buchan had been cut short by a messenger from the Embassy. A sandwich and maybe a bowl of soup might carry him until supper at Chez Jake tonight.

The Café Provençal was a modest establishment at the corner of Junot and Girardon but the aromas wafting from its small kitchen were anything but timid. The improvement of rail services to the south of France during and after the war had vastly improved the range of foods available in Parisian markets. In the last year, regional cuisines had become all the rage and Roget's cousin, a native of Marseille, had capitalized on their popularity.

Flaneurs, those who endlessly strolled the streets of Paris seeking new experiences, had already discovered the place and all the best seats, any on the sidewalk or by the broad front windows were already taken. However, Roget's cousin found them a spot in the second tier where they could still have a partial view of passersby dressed in their finest weekend attire.

The plat du jour consisted of a choice of a hot basil and bean soup "pistou" or chickpea bread slathered in an olive and caper tapenade, followed by either a seafood bouillabaisse with several types of fish and pieces of crab seasoned with fennel, sage and thyme in a cognac-infused broth or a braised chicken breast with a lavender cream sauce.

It's a good thing I've booked an extra session with Kid O'Brien tomorrow, thought Max as he selected the tapenade and fish stew. Roget ordered the same along with a bottle of the "second best" bottle of white burgundy in the cellar. He was very generous with other people's money.

Roget turned down Max's offer of employment over the main course, hinting that he expected other opportunities would soon occupy his time and elevate his station in life.

"Political opportunities?" asked Max.

"I'm in the process of making myself indispensable to the Socialist party," said Roget, with no hint of arrogance in his voice.

"Doing what?"

"Whatever needs to be done," said Roget.

Max wasn't sure he liked the sound of that. Roget had a chequered past – military police during the war, enforcer for a drug dealer after. He drew the line at murder but not at much else. Given the increasing violence of politics in France, would even that moral line hold?

"Which side of the socialist movement will you be indispensable to?"

"Side? Oh, don't believe all that talk of dissension in the ranks. Rumours put out by the government or their agents in the police."

"Then the Bolsheviks don't worry you?"

"I'm a man of action, Max," said Roget, almost gently. "I hate the Camelots; I hate the current government. Jourdain is the future of the left, the future of France. Where he leads, I'll follow."

"And does he know that?"

"We've spoken. He knows talent when he sees it. He's already asked me to do a few things. Top secret, of course. And no money. Yet. I think he's testing me." Roget slurped the last of the fish broth from his bowl and sighed with satisfaction. "I know I tricked you into more lunch than you planned. I'll pay you back as soon as I'm flush."

"I don't mind. The food here is good." *Yesim comes from Marseilles*, thought Max, *maybe I can get him to serve this at Le Coq Bleu.*

"Then let's finish with a calisson and coffee. Almond cookies with melon confit," said Roget.

"Why not?" Max looked at Roget across the table. The man looked genuinely happy, maybe for the first time in a year. Politics had never appealed to Max, even before he had seen its results in the trenches of northern France, but he could understand the appeal of belonging to something bigger than oneself. He hoped it would not lead to Roget's ruin.

Thirteen – Sunday June 7th, 1920

Kid O'Brien was closed Sunday mornings out of deference to his Catholic neighbours but had no qualms of renting it out for private lessons on occasion. Americans who had flooded into Paris in the wake of Prohibition at home and deflated currencies abroad were more than willing to shell out for a place to work off the excesses of Saturday night under the watchful eye of a former champion.

A group of them were talking and working the bags in one corner of the large room when Max arrived, their flat nasal accents producing a steady but not unpleasant drone. He had a few cobwebs to clean from his own head. The band from New York had been hot. Max had stayed for the third set and drunk more wine that was his custom.

"You've been fighting," O'Brien said, gripping Max's chin in one hand and turning his face from side to side.

"There were only four of them," said Max.

O'Brien's eyes widened slightly but he didn't say anything, just handed him a skipping rope and pointed to an empty mat. Ten minutes with the rope, followed by ten more pounding a bag left Max slightly winded, his face and arms dripping with sweat. A couple of the Americans were in the ring, swinging wildly at each other, while the others looked on. Kid O'Brien perched on the edge of the canvas, alternating shouted instructions with muttered curses.

"Come here, Max," O'Brien said at last. "Let's show them how this is done."

Max ducked between the ropes and shuffled around the ring, shadow boxing while O'Brien recruited a timekeeper.

"Three three-minute rounds," said O'Brien. They usually only went two minutes at a time, but the Kid clearly wanted to make a point to his new clients, though Max wasn't certain what it was.

"Usual rules," asked Max. Anything but a deliberate low blow.

O'Brien grinned savagely and tapped Max's gloves with his own. They retreated to their corners and came out fast at the sound of the bell.

O'Brien was eager. He met Max more than halfway across the square of canvas. A flurry of left jabs and then he tried to step inside. Max glided left, countering with a one-two combination that O'Brien slipped.

The Kid stepped in again but Max kept moving. His ribs were still sore from the fight and O'Brien was deadly if he got you pinned. O'Brien tried his luck again. Max leaned forward to meet him, catching his opponent with a hard right to the face. O'Brien covered, taking several blows to his gloves.

Max dropped his guard to go after the Kid's exposed mid-section. O'Brien grunted, countered with a left-right-left combination that drove Max back to the ropes. As O'Brien tried to close again, Max countered with a couple of right jabs and a left hook. No real damage done but it got Max off the ropes and back in the centre of the ring.

O'Brien danced on the balls of his feet, moving from right to left, feinting a couple of punches, trying to draw Max in. Max followed him slowly, conserving his energy, throwing a few jabs to keep the Kid honest. The older man had great stamina and quickness and he always could take a punch, but Max hit harder.

Three minutes in a boxing ring can seem like an eternity. Max was breathing hard now, his mouth gaping. The gloves on the end of his arms felt like ten-pound weights. O'Brien was still bouncing, his breathing steady but a red welt had started to rise over his left eye.

The Kid feinted again then danced in with a combo. Max blocked most of it with his forearms. A short left hook snuck through. Max jerked back. O'Brien tried to follow. Max threw a wild right, then a left, no better than the Americans now. The Kid ducked and answered with a series of body blows. He pushed Max steadily back to the ropes.

The bell sounded. O'Brien got in one more shot then stepped away. Max kept his guard up until his opponent had turned for his corner, then staggered back to his. One of the Americans, a burly young man with a square jaw and dark mustache offered him a cup of water. Max drank half of it and poured the rest over his head.

"Watch the left jab," the American said. "It stings but if you can slip it, you have a clear shot at his midriff. Work the body. The head will follow."

Max nodded. The Kid always told him he tried too hard for the knock-out punch. "A lot of boxers ain't got any brains – but they all got stomachs and lungs."

"And work on that left eye." The American dabbed at his face with a towel. It came away streaked with blood. "Nothing but a cut lip."

The bell sounded again. Max pushed himself up, his legs leaden and his ribs throbbing. The first round had almost emptied him, but he was determined to last two more.

If O'Brien felt the effects of the fight, he didn't show it. He danced and circled, looking for an opening. Max dropped his right and the Kid took the bait. He stepped in and jabbed hard with his left, trying to set Max up for the right cross.

Max took a jab but ducked under the second. He drove his right hand into his opponent's sternum. O'Brien's breath pounded out of him. He stepped back; Max followed. O'Brien's punches slipped off his arms and the side of his head. Max kept working the body, solid blows to ribs and belly. O'Brien threw his arms around Max and held him until someone in the crowd yelled break.

They both stepped back, Max wary of one of O'Brien's tricks. O'Brien's face was red and his breath ragged. He circled slowly to his right, keeping Max at bay with jabs, until he recovered. He grinned again, though less savagely, and gestured at Max with his glove to keep it coming.

O'Brien still danced, though some of the spring had gone out of his step. He shifted his tactics, fewer jabs, more lunging combinations, designed to keep Max off balance and on the defensive. Max kept his feet planted, moving only when necessary. He tried several times to close but the Kid drove him back or slipped to one side.

O'Brien was landing a lot more punches now; three or four for every one Max threw. None of them hurt but the sheer number was starting to take their toll. The bell sounded and they returned to their corners.

"He's fighting a war of attrition," said the American.

"Like the trenches," muttered Max between swollen lips.

The other man nodded knowingly. Max wondered if his new friend had served anytime in the trenches himself. Probably not. He didn't have that haunted look.

The bell came all too quickly.

Max circled to his left, waiting for O'Brien to make the first move. The other man seemed willing to wait, feinting forward to drive up Max's guard, then dropping back again. Some of the Americans started to hoot their displeasure, as if they had paid to see a prize fight.

Max's legs felt better as he continued to move; O'Brien gestured him again to bring it on. *He's looking to finish me*, thought Max. *Get me while I'm moving and off balance.*

Instead, Max echoed the Kid's gesture, shuffling his feet in an imitation of O'Brien's first round dance. O'Brien's face darkened. The welt above his eye oozed blood through a thick layer of ointment.

Max took a step forward. O'Brien lunged to meet him, unleashing a flurry of blows. Max planted his feet, protecting his face with his gloves, his elbows tucked in to save his ribs. Six, eight, twelve punches rained on his arms. A couple snuck through, a wild haymaker from the left that banged Max's ear and left his head ringing, a hard straight right to his upper chest.

Max rocked back on his heels, dropping his guard. When O'Brien followed, Max stepped past his guard and threw a combination – left, right, left, right – into his midriff. O'Brien stumbled back. Max followed, throwing everything he had. Most missed but it was enough to keep O'Brien off-balance.

Then he was on the ropes. When he tried to slide right, Max punished him with hook to the ribs. He tried for a clinch, but Max pulled back. Hard jabs to the face drove O'Brien back again, his gloves covering his eyes.

Max stepped close. A hard left uppercut caught O'Brien flush on the chin. O'Brien stared through his gloves into Max's face. Then his eyes rolled back and his knees buckled. Max stepped back as O'Brien slumped to one knee, head down, arms dangling by his side.

The Americans were yelling now. At O'Brien to get up. At Max to finish him. Max turned his head to acknowledge the cheers. O'Brien lunged from the canvas, throwing all his weight and energy into a smashing right hand.

As Max knew he would. He stepped back and O'Brien stumbled past him. Max's fist caught him at the point where the jaw meets the ear. O'Brien was unconscious before he hit the mat.

The Americans were stunned into silence. Max stripped off his gloves and knelt beside his trainer, rolling him over on his back. O'Brien's eyes flickered open.

"What..." he mumbled. Max lifted O'Brien's head and dribbled water into his mouth.

"Never lower your guard until you're sure your opponent is finished," Max said.

O'Brien grinned, a little lopsidedly. "I got nothing left to teach you," he said.

§

After ensuring O'Brien had suffered no ill effects from the fight, Max headed up the hill to Le Coq Bleu. The iconic neon rooster was dark, but Max used his passkey to let himself in. Henri and Yesim were sitting at the table at the back halfway through a bottle of Bordeaux.

"I was about to serve lunch without you," said Yesim, getting up and going into the small kitchen.

"Don't tell me you were attacked again," said Henri, as Max stepped closer.

"Kid O'Brien was giving a boxing lesson to a bunch of Yanks," said Max, "and he was using me as the blackboard."

"I'll have to speak to him," said Henri.

"Don't worry," said Max. "The lesson ended with the teacher flat on his back." Max felt a faint flush of pride at his victory. O'Brien might be ten years his senior but he was as tough a man as Max had ever met.

Yesim brought back a tray with three bowls of thick potato soup and a platter of sliced sausage, cheese and assorted olives and pickled onions. He went back to the bar for another glass and a second bottle of red.

"Any luck finding the men who attacked you?" asked Henri.

"I'm not sure," said Max describing his encounters with the Russians and his trips to the bars in the 17th arrondissement. "The men who attacked me were Russian but the one who hired them wasn't."

"Doesn't mean much," said Yesim. "He could have been working for anyone. Loyalty comes cheap these days."

"Sometimes, though not always." He described his need for an assistant and Roget's surprising refusal of sure work in hopes a possible future reward. "I don't know who else to ask."

"It's not the kind of thing you can advertise in the local papers," said Yesim. "But I'm willing to ask around."

"I'd be happy to help," said Henri. "As long as it doesn't involve getting beaten up."

Max should have known his friends would leap to his rescue. "I'll think about it," he said, more from kindness than any serious intent. Henri was smart and a hard worker, but Max was reluctant to put either of his friends at risk.

Talk shifted to the news of the day and the gossip that seemed to be a staple of life in Montmartre. An hour had passed and they were still lingering over the last of the wine when there was a rap at the shuttered front door. Max leaned against the window; a boy in a messenger's jacket shuffled from one foot to the other, an envelope clutched in one hand.

The message was from Andre Bucard. *Meet me at the usual place today at 1500.*

It was already nearly two but Max decided to stop at his apartment to brush the smell of wine off his breath and change into something suitable for Saint-Germain-l'Auxerrois. The Metro was crowded and slow and it was a few minutes after the hour when Max hurried up to the wide double doors of the ancient church. Bucard, alone for a change, was waiting on the steps.

"Walk with me," Bucard said, gesturing toward the Quai that stretched along the Seine.

They walked for several minutes without speaking. The morning sun had given way to a low overcast and the river reflected the grey of the sky. Bucard seemed lost in thought but Max made no effort to break his silence. Bucard had asked to see him and would tell him why in his own time.

Bucard's steps slowed and at last he stopped to sit on a bench near the statue of Henri IV, an unsurprising choice, given his political leanings. When Max had joined him, Bucard turned and studied his face.

"I was impressed with you last year," said Bucard.

"You compared me to Don Quixote," said Max.

"Is that such a bad thing?" Bucard asked. "Tilting at windmills is a fine occupation. I've tilted at a few myself."

"I suppose," Max said. Bucard had taken positions even his fellow conservatives found hard to swallow, welcoming syndicalists, Jews and even Algerians into his organization, the Black Cross, before it fell spectacularly apart in a series of well-publicized and highly acrimonious meetings over the previous winter. "A Frenchman is a Frenchman" had become his motto, though the definition only included those who ascribed to his rigid view of a properly ordered society led by a dictator with a clear head, a sound heart and a firm hand. Whether Bucard himself had aspired to provide that leadership was never clear.

"Quixote displayed an intense loyalty to his principles and his friends," said Bucard, "a characteristic I observed in you as well."

Bucard looked across the Pont Neuf at Île de la Cité, his expression sad, his shoulders slightly stooped. "Loyalty is a difficult quality to find when times are hard."

"Michel?" asked Max.

"Perceptive as always. Michel's departure was a great disappointment to me. I had thought... well, it doesn't matter what I thought."

"Maybe he no longer shared your values," said Max.

"In Michel's case it was not so much a question of values as of price."

"I see," said Max. Michel Tourangeau had never seemed more than a thug to Max, the type of man who attached themselves to others in hope of advancement they could not otherwise earn. Bucard, apparently, saw other qualities in him. It must have been disappointing to find his loyalty could be bought with mere money. "Pierre Armand is a rich man."

"Indeed," said Bucard. "But Armand was not the agent of Michel's... seduction. Have you heard of a man called Jean Martel?"

That's right, thought Max, *Gereau told me that.* Jean Martel, not Armand, was Michel Tongereau's new political idol. "A deputy in the Bloc National."

"Among other things. A deal maker. A blackmailer. A traitor to every cause but his own betterment. Everything that keeps France from achieving its true greatness. Yet, he is well regarded in conservative circles."

The contempt in Bucard's voice was palpable. It had always puzzled Max how fiercely ideologues derided their own compatriots, like ancient zealots burning each other over the minutiae of Biblical exegesis.

Now that he was talking, he couldn't stop, spilling his bitterness at Tourangeau's betrayal and Martel's role in it. "It all began last year, before the overwhelming victory of the Bloc National in the elections. Then, we were all one big happy family. The conservative parties were happy to use the AF and groups like the Black Cross to intimidate unionists and break up socialist meetings. Martel came to us with money and promises of support. Always, the implication that once the election was won, the victors would abolish the Republic and restore the monarchy as a first step towards the construction of a proper French state. Even I was completely taken in."

Several passersby had stopped to stare. Bucard's voice boomed off the stone wall that separated the walkway from the river. He seemed oblivious to the attention he was drawing.

"And Michel Tourangeau found a new hero," said Max. Bucard swiveled to glare at Max, his handsome face flushed, his blue eyes fierce.

"Tourangeau's new hero is money," said Bucard, his voice more controlled. The flaneurs lost interest and moved on. "That was the damage Martel did. He turned a man who knew the value of a cause into one who valued nothing but money."

"I find it hard to believe someone could change so completely. Perhaps he had never been honest with you."

"If you're trying to comfort me, you're doing a very poor job. In any case, what is done is done. Michel had made his decision."

"Is this what you wanted to tell me?" Max had hoped for something more substantial, more useful.

"In part," said Bucard. "I needed you to understand how Martel works. He was very close to Mark St. John."

"That's the first I've heard of it."

"I'm not surprised," said Bucard, his anger faded like a summer storm. "They went to great lengths to keep their relationship a secret. Clandestine meetings, coded letters and the like. I stumbled on it and questioned Martel closely on why he was close to what was obviously an American spy. He laughed at me. Said it was only business and if I knew the details, I most likely would approve. I never learned more than that. Then St. John was murdered. But by that time, of course, Martel and the rest of his cronies in the Bloc National wanted nothing to do with me or the Black Cross. Michel left, and, soon after, the seeds of dissent Martel so carefully sowed took root and destroyed us from within."

A new player can change everything. Martel had found his relationship to Bucard and the Black Cross inconvenient and so destroyed the organization. Had his relationship with Mark St. John become equally inconvenient, leading directly or indirectly to his death?

Bucard apparently had nothing more to add. He rose and extended his hand for Max to shake. Max watched him go, wondering what his motive had been to tell Max this piece of information now. Bucard's star may have dimmed but Max doubted his ambitions had. He wanted to drag Martel into this investigation. Was it merely revenge for what had happened with Tourangeau or did he have some deeper motive, some longer plan?

Max looked across the bridge to the Left Bank. It had been some days since he had spoken to Erich Harvey. He'd likely be at one of the outdoor cafés on St. Germaine this time of day, if his reputation could be relied on. Max only hoped he hadn't already had too many brandies to be coherent.

§

Harvey was sitting under an umbrella at the Brassiere Lipp. The remains of lunch and a half-finished beer were spread on the table in front of him while he scribbled in his ever-present notebook.

"Hello, boss," said Harvey. "I was wondering when I would see you again."

"Do you have something for me?"

"Maybe." Harvey caught the eye of a nearby waiter. "Two pastis, if you please."

"A little early in the day for that, don't you think?" According to Henri, one should only drink the potent anise liqueur when you have nothing left to do but sleep.

"Depends on what time you got up. I've been up since four."

"Why?"

Harvey took a sip of the liquor and made a face. "It's a vicious circle."

"I'll take your word for it," said Max, pushing his glass across the table.

Harvey shrugged. "Have a beer at least – I hate to drink alone."

Max glanced at the half empty glass already sitting in front of Harvey but didn't comment. He had friends who didn't count beer or wine as drinking. He gestured to the waiter and pointed at Hervey's glass.

Harvey said nothing until the glass of beer had been delivered and Max took his first sip.

"Armand is connected to St. John's death, though not in the way I originally thought," Harvey said. "Pavlovna is mixed up in it, too."

"I can't see the connection. St. John was giving her money. Was Armand a partisan for the Whites as well?"

"Yes, but he didn't know it at the time."

"So, Mark St. John was stealing from him."

Harvey shook his head. "That's one interpretation but I think it's more complicated than that. St. John was using Armand to steal money from an Italian named Jacopo Giamatti. Using Armand as a shield against possible reprisals."

"It doesn't seem to have worked. I've met Giamatti. He claims he had nothing to do with it. That someone else pulled the trigger and tried to make it look like a gang execution."

"He would say that, wouldn't he?"

"I suppose."

"Giamatti is not exactly what he appears to be," said Harvey.

"Who is?"

Harvey finished the first pastis and eyed the second speculatively. Max pushed it closer to him.

"Did he tell you of his connections to Mussolini?"

"No, but I've heard of them."

"Mussolini is a man to watch,' said Harvey.

"I've heard him dismissed as a two-bit demagogue."

"They used to say the same thing about Lenin. We're living in the age of demagogues." Harvey raised the glass to his lips but set it down without drinking. He leaned across the table and lowered his voice. "The War settled nothing, you know. All it did was upset the old order without putting a new one in place. The German peace is unworkable. Austria has finally fallen in on itself and the Treaty of Trianon has crippled Hungary, freeing the Serbs, Croats and Bulgarians to tear each other's throats out. Wait until you see what happens when they finally deal with the Ottomans."

"The League of Nations..."

"Without the Americans, the League is dead in the water. America doesn't want to carry the burden of Empire."

"What does this have to do with Mark St. John's murder?" Max couldn't do anything about the fate of Europe but he could solve one killing, couldn't he?

"Damned if I know. But I do know that Italian money disappeared from a deposit box in a bank in Marseilles. Eight days after that, Mark St. John was killed. Did Giamatti kill him? I don't know but it certainly points at him. But if he did, why? Because it was Mafia money or because it was fascista cash? Or both? Italian politics! They're worse than the French."

"It's a tenuous link."

"I thought so too," said Harvey. "Except, two days before Mark died, a boat left the port of Brindisi bound for the Crimean. A boat full of guns Armand had acquired for Baron Denidov and paid for with Italian lire."

"That seems too short a time to make that kind of arrangements."

"The cargo had been sitting in a warehouse for nearly a month. Armand was merely waiting to be paid."

"Did Armand know where the money came from?"

"You'd have to ask him that." Harvey cleared his throat and wouldn't quite meet Max's gaze.

"I suppose this information wasn't free," said Max.

"Five hundred francs would cover my expenses and time. And keep me looking for more."

"Three hundred now," said Max. "And three hundred more if and when you get me something that actually links any of these characters to the death of St. John."

"But it's clear Giamatti..." sputtered Harvey.

"It's not clear at all. You said so yourself. Giamatti may or may not have known it was St. John who took the money – if it was his money in that box – and his motives aren't clear. If he saw funding the Whites as a blow against the Bolsheviks, who can say if the money was actually stolen? He may be playing a double game himself. Denidov is linked to Pavlovna but that doesn't mean he was linked to St. John. He claimed to hardly know him. And Armand, is he a knowing conspirator, a willing dupe or something else altogether? Your information is useful but hardly conclusive. All I have now are more questions."

Max slipped three hundred francs from the dwindling reserve in his billfold and slid them across to Harvey.

"Don't suppose you can cover lunch, too?" Harvey's voice cracked slightly, and Max nodded. The American downed the last of his pastis and rose unsteadily. The francs had disappeared from the table, scooped up with the rest of Harvey's papers. Max watched him weave his way down St. Germaine to wherever he called home. *Not every American in Paris has money*, thought Max. *And it's a hard place to be poor.*

Fourteen – Monday June 8th, 1920

Max returned to his apartment after a morning of largely fruitless inquiries into the whereabouts of the missing grandson. The boy, Gaston, might not be actively avoiding Max but he wasn't making it easy to be found either. Ferdinand LePêcheur was sitting on the floor outside the door when he arrived. He wasn't wearing his uniform, though his black pants and white shirt were crisp, his boots polished and his blue jacket old but spotlessly clean. Only the crumpled cap on his head seemed out of place.

"I showed the concierge my badge and she let me up, though not in," said LePêcheur.

"I think you need to have a Captain's rank before she'll do that," said Max. He held out his hand and pulled the gendarme to his feet. "I take it this isn't an official visit."

"No," said LePêcheur. "It's my day off."

"Then let me take your coat and hat and get you a beer."

"Most kind," said LePêcheur, smiling, "Though I must warn you, without my hat, I'm little better than a crook."

It took a moment for Max to understand the joke – without the circumflex accent, sometimes called a "chapeau," LePêcheur changed from a fisherman to a thief. When he did, he almost couldn't stop laughing.

"It's not that funny," said LePêcheur, taking the beer bottle from Max's hand before he dropped it.

"No, but..." Max sputtered. He lowered himself into the chair opposite LePêcheur. The laughter stopped as suddenly as it had begun. "It's... I think this case is starting to get to me."

"The St. John murder? Then perhaps my visit has come at a poor time. What I have to tell you isn't likely to make you feel any better."

"What is it? Has Fontaine come up with new evidence?"

"Quite the contrary," said LePêcheur. "He seems to have lost interest in it completely."

"I thought they called him 'the bulldog.'"

"We call him a lot of things, though 'bulldog' is a new one on me," said LePêcheur, smiling again. "I think someone has told him to leave it alone."

"Does that mean the charges against Sarah St. John have been dropped?"

"Not exactly. But the court date has been delayed again. And Fontaine has pulled everyone off the active investigation."

Jourdain was able to get the initial delay and arrange for house arrest, thought Max. Was he behind these latest developments?

"I've seen this before," said LePêcheur. "It's political. Someone in the government has put a word in his ear. Fontaine doesn't care if he advances his career by a successful conviction or through political favour."

"You're sure it's a government official."

"Without doubt. Fontaine knows which way the bread is buttered. Someone high up though probably not a Minister. Too risky if it comes out."

"A fixer. Someone like Jean Martel?"

"I've heard that name a lot around the Prefecture," said LePêcheur. "Though I can't say for sure. You need to be careful, Mr. Anderson. When the government takes an interest in a criminal case, it's usually wise for investigators to find something else of interest to investigate."

"I thought the Prefecture of Police was incorruptible."

"But of course. But that doesn't mean they're stupid about it."

§

The logical place to look for a Deputy was the legislature that faced the Place de la Concorde, the vast open plaza next to the Tuileries gardens. Max took the Metro to Concorde, climbing the narrow stairs that led up to the Rue de Rivoli, emerging from the dim stairwell into the shimmering light. The scent of flowers wafted over the wall separating the street from the gardens, a sharp contrast to the acrid mix of gasoline fumes and urine from the street.

Max took a few steps from the entranceway to the edge of the square. The cloudless sky formed a pale blue dome, echoing the shape of the Invalides that hulked on the far side of the river. Max stood for a moment letting his eyes adjust, watching the chaotic mix of pedestrians, bicycles, horse-drawn carriages and motorcars stream past. From where he stood, the great obelisk that had been a gift to the Emperor, aligned almost perfectly with the Eiffel Tower, rising from the Champs de Mars on the far side of the Seine. He waited until a white gloved gendarme brought the traffic to a halt before crossing to stand beside one of the massive fountains where statues of Neptune and his attendant nymphs spewed gouts of foaming water into a wide basin.

Max sat on the edge of the fountain and considered the best way to approach Martel. The man had no reason to want to talk to him, especially if he were involved somehow in the murder of Mark St. John. Nor did Max have any way to force the deputy to speak to him. Gereau, even if they were still on speaking terms, would be of no use in this case. The captain might be high up in the political branch of the Prefecture, but he had often made it clear that he avoided dealing with actual politicians as much as he could.

Perhaps Jourdain could provide an introduction, thought Max. He and Martel were from opposite sides of the political spectrum but Henri had told him that there had always been a certain collegiality among those who were elected to the legislature. They dined in the same clubs, traveled on the same rail cars, worked together on committees; they might insult each other across the aisles of the assembly but, in the back halls and meeting rooms, far from the eyes of press and public, they retained cordiality, even friendship. Max wondered if that were still true after the fractures the war had created in society. Could men with radically different values still treat each other as mere adversaries rather than mortal enemies?

In any case, Max was reluctant to call on Jordain. There was something duplicitous about the man. He didn't like the way he treated Sarah. He protected his lover but would not risk his reputation by visiting her. Whatever his feelings for her, they were clandestine, unacknowledged. And what about his wife? Did she know and, if she did, how did she feel about it? Did she feel it was a fair exchange for her own bourgeois comfort and the privileges of being the wife of a man of import?

"Max?"

He almost didn't recognize the man standing in front of him. Despite the heat of the day, Asper had on a heavy jacket, its collar pulled up to meet a cloth cap pulled low over his brow. What little of his face was showing was red and blotchy, the skin around his eyes puffy and bruised. Max shifted on the stone bench and Asper crumpled into the open spot.

"I've been looking for you," said Max.

"I heard," said Asper. "I thought if you couldn't find me, then neither could anyone else."

"You look awful."

"Thanks. Too little sleep; too much vodka."

"Do you want to go somewhere? Get some food?" Max felt genuinely concerned. Asper looked on the verge of collapse, his shoulders slumped like that of an old man, his voice little more than a cracked whisper.

Asper's eyes darted from side to side, fixing on one person, then another as if he feared someone might suddenly leap upon him. Finally, he shook his head. "I'll eat later I suppose. If you find what I have to say useful."

It was as private as any café, hundreds of people – businessmen, government officials, shoppers and tourists – all rushing or sauntering by, lost in their own thoughts, their own private missions. "Can you walk?" he asked.

Asper nodded. He grunted as he rose but, once they were moving, seemed to regain some semblance of his old nervous energy. Max led the way past a cluster of Americans, gawking at the obelisk, past another fountain, towards the broad walkway that bordered the Quai des Tuileries. Asper leaned close, his shoulder almost brushing Max's as he talked steadily in a low monotone.

"You asked me to find out more about Irina Pavlovna. I have done that. At some cost to myself. Financially and otherwise. I have lost all my affection for Paris."

Max was strangely moved. He could not imagine losing his love of Paris. It was the home he had lost, the community he had always craved.

"Pavlovna is loved, hated and feared. Often at the same time. She has two goals that drive her. The destruction of the Bolshevik regime in Moscow and, failing that, the creation of a Russian diaspora as a bulwark against their spread westward. The Cheka have sent two assassins to kill her. Neither has ever been seen again. Though parts of them have."

Asper leaned against the retaining wall and gazed out at the Seine, though whether to collect his thoughts or regain his strength was unclear.

"She is indiscriminate in who she helps. If they oppose Lenin, she welcomes them with open arms. There are at least three former members of the Okrhana, the Tsar's secret police, in her employ. These are not policemen; they are murderers, torturers, worse. She doesn't care. She finds a way to get them here, finds ways to keep them safe. And she brooks no opposition. Any talk of compromise or negotiation is met with a knock on the door in the middle of the night and a car-ride from which you are fortunate to return. It's as if Ivan the Terrible had been recreated as a woman."

"Surely the Prefecture doesn't stand for that," said Max. "They keep a file on everyone who comes to the city. It's not as if the Russians can go to their embassy and complain of police harassment and intimidation."

"What's true of you and me is not true for the Russians," said Asper. "There are plenty in the government and in the Prefecture who oppose the Bolsheviks. I think Pavlovna has files of her own. She has mixed in the upper echelons of French society for a long time. She undoubtedly has secrets to use against any that question her methods. Besides, the French police have never cared much what foreigners do to each other as long as it stays out of the public eye. It's not as if she's killing Socialist politicians in the street – though from what I've heard she's furious that Frossard had gone to Moscow to take lessons at Lenin's knee."

Max was surprised at how little shock he felt at Asper's words. Pavlovna was at war; a soldier in the struggle between Whites and Reds. Max had been in the trenches, knew that actions during war could not be measured with the same moral standard as during peacetime. He had killed men in battle, men who in another life might have been friends. He felt no guilt for his actions, only regret that his country had put him in that place where such actions were not only necessary but were deemed good. He even felt a certain admiration for her, a woman who was as much of a warrior as any who had fought in the fields of France. He had felt it the first time he had met her, that he was in the presence of a great tigress, a force of nature both beautiful and fearsome. Now he understood why.

"Where did Mark St. John fit into all of this?" asked Max.

"I'm not sure," said Asper. "He supported her cause no doubt. With money and influence at the very least. Rumour has it that he was a big talker, always going on about 'justifiable force,' but always shied away from its actual application."

Like half the generals in the war, thought Max.

"Maybe he finally had enough," said Asper. "Maybe when it came down to it, he decided the ends don't really justify the means and she – or, more likely, one of the madmen who work for her – decided to make an example of him."

"It's possible, but it doesn't sound much like either of them."

"Don't be so sure," said Asper. He had removed his jacket and cap but sweat still ran down his face. "Maybe we could stop for a drink."

They crossed the street to a nondescript brasserie. Max ordered a lager, Asper, a large brandy. He was quenching a different thirst. His hand shook as he lifted the glass to his lips.

"There's something else," he said. "There was an Englishman. Lock or Long, something like that. In Zurich. He had a similar relationship with Pavlovna as St. John. If you know what I mean."

Max nodded. Pavlovna did "it," not only because it pleased her but because it was useful to her; it bound men to her, blinded them to her faults and made them do things to which they might not otherwise agree. He had experienced the same thing himself once.

"Something happened – no one I talked with seemed exactly clear. Was he spying on the Cheka and they found him out or had he been subverted to the Red cause and turned against her? I've heard both versions. What is striking is the way he died. Shot in the back of the head and left naked in a public park. Not propped up on a bench but the similarity is obvious."

Asper's shoulders rose and he leaned back in his chair. It was as if revealing this last horror had lifted a burden from his spirit. He finished his brandy and Max signalled the waiter for another. Asper had earned it. He smiled gratefully and for a moment Max saw the eager young student, pacifist and patriot Asper had been before the War had taken it all away from him. He reached across and placed his hand on Asper's arm.

"Are you afraid, Joseph?" he asked.

Tears welled in Asper's eyes and, for a long moment, his lips quivered as he tried to speak. He nodded, then, "There's something more. It's gone mad in Germany. And Hungary. Other places. When the Freicorps and the Sparticists aren't fighting in the streets, they are gunning down syndicalists and generals, politicians of all stripes, men with reputations. Men like me. It's coming to Paris too. I can feel it." His voice broke off in a sob.

"How much would it take to get you out of Paris for a while? To someplace you can feel safe."

"I don't know. A thousand francs?" Asper sounded as if he were asking for the moon.

Max emptied his bill fold. "Here's twenty two hundred. Think of it as advance – for when you're feeling better. It's all I have on me so you'll have to cover the bill."

Asper smiled at that, though a tear still trickled down his cheek. "I can't thank you enough. You may have saved my life."

Max had no answer to that. He feared Asper's life was already beyond saving but if a few thousand francs could produce a miracle, it seemed an easy bargain. He patted Asper's arm once more and then left him to his brandy and his thoughts. He doubted he would ever see him again.

§

He was no closer to solving the problem of finding Martel, let alone speaking to him. Somehow what Asper had told him made him more certain than ever that approaching the politician would be difficult, perhaps impossible for someone like him. Perhaps there was another way but if there was, he couldn't think of it.

He strolled back the way he and Asper had come. The day had grown hot, the sun beating down mercilessly on the stone covered streets and walkways. Even the faint breeze from the river seemed warm. He stood in the light spray from one of the fountains, gazing through the heat shimmers rising from the plaza at the massive stone edifice of the Chamber of Deputies.

"Nothing ventured, nothing gained," he muttered.

As expected, Secretary Martel was far too busy to fit him into his schedule today, or the next day, or the day after that, or the following week. "Perhaps you could come back on the twentieth-fifth; he has some time then." Martel's assistant could barely keep the contempt from his voice.

Jourdain's advisor was more polite but of little more help. "Deputies are so busy at this time of year, so much to do before the summer makes the city unliveable, you know. Perhaps on Thursday?" It wasn't much but Max took the appointment, carefully noting the time and location down in his journal.

Perhaps it's time I visited Sarah again, he thought. *At least I know exactly where to find her. And she is technically my client, so I suppose I should let her know what I've discovered. As little as it is.*

§

Sarah St. John was pathetically eager to see him. It had been almost a week since they had spoken and, as near as he could tell, she had had no other visitors since then. He doubted if the dour looking police matron had provided much comfort or even conversation. *Perhaps*, he thought, *I could arrange for someone to drop by*, though he couldn't see either Yesim or Henri perched on one of the delicate chairs of the Hotel Grand, sipping tea and making polite conversation. Perhaps a woman would be better, though he realized he hardly knew any women other than Irina Pavlovna and Jacqueline Grand, neither suitable companions.

"I'm sure you can leave us alone, Maria," Sarah said. "Mr. Anderson has Captain Gereau's trust."

Max wondered if that was still true and saw his doubt reflected on the face of the heavy-set matron. Still, she took up her place in the next room with the connecting doors slid almost shut.

"Have you spoken to Denis?" Sarah asked as soon as they were alone. They were sitting, as before, in chairs facing each other, near the window and as far from the matron as possible. The space between them remained uncomfortably narrow.

"Not since I last spoke to you. Though we have an appointment on Thursday morning. I'll ask him to come see you then."

She turned her head and looked through the gauze curtains at the street below. When she turned back her expression was unreadable.

"Are you any closer to proving my innocence?" she asked.

Max noted she was no longer asking if he had found her husband's killer. He wondered whether she had given up hope or no longer cared. He recounted the events of the last six days, his encounter with Giamatti and what he had learned of St. John's involvement with the White Russians.

"As you suspected, Armand is connected in every aspect of your husband's activities here in Paris," he concluded. "It seems doubtful he was unconnected to his death."

"You should confront him. Make him confess."

"I doubt if that would work. Armand must have grown up learning how to stand up to men bigger than himself. He wouldn't be physically intimidated by me and he's not stupid. Stupid men don't become that rich or that influential."

"That hasn't always been my experience," said Sarah, "but in the case of Pierre Armand, I think you are right. If I learned anything from Mark, it's that you should never underestimate your opponents."

"For now, I have no proof," said Max. "Until I do, or until I have no other avenues to pursue, I think I'll leave him be. Maybe he'll grow complacent, make a mistake."

"Maybe," said Sarah, though she sounded dubious. She leaned into him, the way she did when she was engaged. Her face was slightly flushed and her eyes bright, staring straight into his. He had to resist touching her. "What can I do to help?"

"Did Mark know a man named Jean Martel?"

"Oh, of course, we dined at Jean and Angeline's house several times. Mark liked him – called him a mover and shaker – but I found him slippery. More of a huckster than an honest broker."

"Do you know him well enough to arrange an introduction?"

"I liked Angeline. We're not friends," she glanced around room, "obviously not, but I could send her a note. It might work. Though I'm not on anyone's social calendar these days. Surely you don't think Jean was involved in what happened to Mark."

"It seems unlikely. But he is connected to several people who are on my list of suspects. He may have information that will help sort it out."

"Surely he would have gone to the police."

"Of course, if he knew it was relevant. But if all you have is a few pieces of the jigsaw it is difficult to know what puzzle they fit into."

"I suppose. I'll try to convey the urgency to Angeline without alarming her. But I can tell there is something else you wanted to ask."

Max felt his face flush. *Am I that easy to read*, he wondered. "Who knew of your affair with Denis Jourdain?"

"You mean, did my husband know?"

"Yes, I suppose that is what I mean."

"He knew we had a brief dalliance before the war. At least, I told him it was brief when he confronted me with it. I also told him it was over."

"How did he react?"

"Angry at first. As if my transgression somehow outweighed all of his. Then he became amused, almost derisive. 'You only picked a socialist to annoy me,' he said, as if all my desire only existed in relation to him. Mark was a supreme egoist. I think that was the moment I finally stopped loving him."

"Not when you began your affair with Jourdain?" asked Max.

"No. Denis was kind and charming but he was also ambitious, and he was married with a child and another on the way. Living with Mark was the loneliest thing I ever did. I don't suppose that makes sense to you, does it?"

Max shook his head. What could he offer? His own experiences were limited, insignificant, though he still bore the wounds of them. He knew nothing of love.

"You can love more than one person, you know," she said. "It's happened to me. More than once. But it doesn't last. At least, I've never found it does."

"Did Jourdain know your husband knew?"

"I never told him. But he's not stupid."

"Being a detective would be so much easier if fewer people were 'not stupid.'"

Sarah laughed, leaning back in her chair. The moment of intimacy broke. Max remembered he was talking to his client, a widow, if not a grieving one, ten years his elder, who needed his help, not his solicitude.

"If you can send that note, it would help advance the case. I'll ask Jourdain to visit you."

"I understand his situation. I'm sorry."

"For what?"

Sarah smiled at him sadly. "You're a good man, Max. Better than you know."

For the second time that day, Max found he had no answer in response. He bowed slightly and took his leave.

Fifteen – Tuesday to Friday, June 9-12th, 1920

A note arrived from Irina Pavlovna accepting his invitation to dine at Chez Jake on Friday night at nine. Baron Denidov and his sister would come as well, though there was no mention of Federov. With his meeting with Jourdain not until Thursday and no clear path to Martel, Max spent the next two days dealing with his other cases.

The elusive grandson remained so; Max was beginning to suspect that someone, perhaps the boy himself, was actively keeping him out of reach. He sent a telegram to the family's lawyer, seeking more details of the circumstances of the inheritance, notably if anyone stood to gain if the boy didn't surface.

The missing brother, Geoffrey Monsot, proved less difficult to track. It was a story all too typical in France; he had been the youngest son of three, working a small farm in the south of the country. He had enlisted in the army in 1915 to earn exemptions for his two older brothers who were needed to produce food vital to the war effort. Monsot had fought valiantly from all accounts, winning several medals for bravery while rising to the rank of sergeant. He had been wounded twice, at the Marne in 1916 and again in the push to Amiens, the same battle that had ended Max's war. His sacrifice had not been in vain; both of his brothers had been spared military service, though the oldest had died in the influenza outbreak in the winter of 1919. He had survived the war where a million of his comrades had not, but like one in four French men, he would carry its marks to his grave.

Monsot had failed to return home after his release from hospital. He had quarrelled with his father during his last leave, seriously enough to cause a complete rupture. Now that the father, too, had died, the surviving brother wanted nothing more than to be reunited with the last of his family.

Max knew that not all wounds were limited to the body. His own struggles with fear and paralysis had haunted him for years. Even now, nearly two years from the trenches, images would flash before his eyes, overwhelming his senses and freezing him into immobility. If Monsot had suffered similar trauma, shame and fear might have kept him away.

There were homes all over Paris who cared for men who no longer could care for themselves. Some, like that occupied by Colonel Ledux, were more like hotels than hospitals. Others were little better than warehouses, filled with broken men dependent on meager pensions and the charity of strangers.

Monsot was living in one of those. He had lost his left arm and much of the left side of his face, which was now covered in a leather mask. His voice had been reduced to a whisper that made him difficult to understand but his remaining eye was bright and alert.

"You say my father is dead?" Monsot asked.

"I'm sorry, yes."

"Don't be sorry. He was a son of a bitch. But I would have liked to see him again. If only to tell him that." Monsot looked away. "And Stephen wants me to come home to the farm."

"He paid me to find you," said Max.

"Things must be doing well on the farm."

Max remembered the tattered bills Stephen Monsot had sent him. "I think he wants his brother back."

"Like this? I doubt it."

"I'd give anything to see my brother again. I wouldn't care about anything else."

"Your brother dead?" asked Monsot.

"Yes," said Max. It wasn't literally true but Max's Uncle George had turned the whole family against him so thoroughly that it might as well be.

"Sorry. I suppose I could go for a visit. If it doesn't work out, there's always a place for me here. Don't suppose he sent train fare?"

"He provided a hundred francs for expenses. It should get you home, with enough left over for a meal or two." It was as good a way to refund the money as any.

Max waited while Monsot gathered together his meagre belongings and said his goodbyes to his few friends and to the sisters who had cared for him. He took him by cab to the Gare Saint-Lazare and watched as a heavy-set porter helped him on the train. A quick telegram informed Stephen Monsot of his brother's arrival time. *All cases should be that easy to solve,* thought Max.

Since he was already in the south, Max dropped in on the warehouse of the client who feared his employees were stealing from him. A few brief conversations later and Max was pretty sure he knew who the guilty parties were – two cousins who had recently moved to Paris from Tours. He spent the night wedged into a doorway near the back entrance of the warehouse and, by morning, he had gathered enough evidence to have both the cousins and their fence, a "respectable" competitor of his client, arrested. It was nearly supper by the time all the paperwork was completed at the Prefecture and Max satisfied himself with a sandwich before tumbling into bed for a well-earned rest.

§

On Thursday morning, Max made his way to Jourdain's office near the Chamber of Deputies. The smiling young man at the reception had been replaced by a scowling Pierre Roget, looking uncomfortable in a morning suit.

"I have an appointment," Max said.

Roget made a sham of glancing at the ledger in front of him. "It's been changed. The deputy has other commitments now. Come back next Thursday."

The morning papers had announced that the Chamber had almost finished its work and would adjourn on Tuesday. Jourdain would undoubtedly retreat to the comforts of his country home for the duration of the summer. Paris was beautiful in the summer but the heat was unbearable after the end of June and the sweet perfume of flowering plants barely hid the stench of urine in the streets.

"Jourdain has an interest in what I have to say."

"Mr. Jourdain's only interest is the future of France."

Roget came from behind the desk. He might have put on a suit but his posture was still that of a street fighter, arms loose, hands half curled into fists.

"I know the kind of messes you get involved in. A future prime minister can't afford to be tainted."

Max braced himself for a fight. Roget seemed determined to evict him; Max was equally determined to stay. It might well have come to blows if Jourdain hadn't burst into the antechamber from the hall. His face was flushed and sheened with sweat and he was slightly breathless.

"I'm sorry," said Roget. "I told him you had –"

"It's all right, Roget," interrupted Jourdain. "I have a few minutes. I can spend them with Mr. Anderson."

Roget looked disappointed but he resumed his seat. Jourdain patted him on the shoulder on the way into his office and Roget smiled like a boy receiving a treat.

Jourdain waved Max to a wingback leather chair. He crossed to a low hutch against the far wall. "Do you want coffee? It's from this morning but it should still be hot."

He mixed steaming coffee with warm milk from two silver urns, adding sugar to Max's but not his own. Despite Roget's insistence and his own harried look when he arrived, Jourdain gave the appearance of having all the time in the world. He didn't say anything further until he was seated opposite Max in a matching chair, the tray of coffee on the table between them.

"You've seen Sarah?" he asked. Max nodded. "How is she?"

"Lonely."

"I'll try to see her next week."

"You should do more than try."

"Yes." Jourdain took a sudden interest in his fingernails, as if his manicure wasn't perfect.

"What was your relationship with Mark St. John?"

"I would think that was obvious. I was a rival for his wife's affections."

"She told me she had lost all affection for her husband."

"Yet she remained with him."

"Women often have little choice in these matters. Even in modern times." Max tried the coffee; it was bitter and he added another lump of sugar. "Was St. John aware of your relationship with his wife?"

"Yes. Or, at least, he knew there had been one before the war."

"Did she tell you that?" She had said she hadn't. Max wondered if Jourdain would contradict her.

"No. He did. He came to see me before they left for America. He was quite insulting."

"To her or to you."

"Both," said Jourdain. "I think he found it galling that his wife would find comfort in the arms of a socialist. As if that had anything to do with anything. Americans are odd that way."

"Did he know that the relationship hadn't ended?"

"Who can say? I never saw him again. I knew he had been back to Paris, of course, but we don't travel in the same circles."

"No. I suppose not. Still, you must have discussed him with Sarah."

Jourdain laughed. "My dear Mr. Anderson, I assure you we had better things to talk about, better things to do, during the brief time we had together."

"It must have been a shock when he was murdered. Did you talk about him then?"

"I was surprised, yes, but not shocked. Mark St. John had plenty of enemies."

"I thought you were convinced he was killed by his business partner."

"Armand was involved," said Jourdain. He stood abruptly and went to look out his window at the Seine. "I'm sure of that. The how eludes me. He might have been the trigger but not the agent of St. John's death. Mark was playing a dangerous game."

"Helping the White cause in Russia."

"You've been busy. I mentioned that St. John disliked my politics. That was before the war, before the Bolsheviks had their little revolution. After, I'm told, his hatred of the left – all of it, not just its radical cousin – became fanatical. Not surprising, I suppose. America is at war with itself."

"I don't see –"

Jourdain spun around. The light from the window haloed his face, making his features difficult to read but there was no mistaking the passion in his voice. "The Red Terror! The men who own the newspapers and the politicians they fund and support, they use the

Bolsheviks as an excuse to roll back all the gains working men made during the war. They imprison anyone who tries to organize, anyone who opposed the war, anyone who fights for the rights of immigrants or even their own Negros. Mark St. John was one of those. I don't know if his views were genuine or merely a tool to defend the interests of his class. But unlike the mass of St. John's fellow citizens who pursue their ends through peaceful means, the Russian Communists truly are dangerous. They make war – physically and metaphorically – on any who get in their way."

"Including the bourgeois left, I'm told."

"Yes, I think they hate democratic socialists most of all."

"Is that why Roget is now guarding your office door?"

"He's a good man in a fight."

"I can attest to that. Then you think it possible the Cheka might have been involved?"

"It's possible. Their agents are everywhere. You might be surprised how deeply they've penetrated French society. They have many converts, even in my own party."

"I'm told the party may split in two. Where will your loyalties lie?"

"The stories of division are overblown by the conservative press but the risk is real. I am a Frenchman, Mr. Anderson, and I am a democrat. I adhere to the principles of our revolution. Liberty is as important to me as brotherhood and equality. I find the idea of dictatorship, even that of the proletariat, appalling."

"Why didn't you tell me this before? Has something changed?"

"I have learned certain things. From those in the party more sympathetic to Moscow. They've given me reason to think Mark St. John was killed by foreign operatives."

"Why not go to the police? It wouldn't connect you to Sarah St. John. Your reputation would remain intact." Max tried not to let his anger at Jourdain's shabby treatment of his mistress creep into his voice.

"The police are no friends of the left. The current Prefect is bad enough; Jean Chiappe, who many say will soon take his place, is worse. I will not jeopardize my colleagues, my friends, by turning to them."

Max stood. He had nothing left to say to Jourdain. He didn't know what he thought of the public figure, but he was coming to hate the private man.

"Go see Sarah," he said.

§

Max walked back to his office. He had not gone to O'Brien's gymnasium since Sunday, uncertain of the reception he might receive after their fight. The morning was still cool along the river though that would not last. When he reached the Trocadero, he climbed the long steps up to the plaza and stood for a while gazing over the city. The river was calm; it had not rained in several days and the water was slow-moving and clear. Sunlight sparkled along its length and the barges seemed to glide on a ribbon of light.

From here, the Eiffel Tower dominated the city, an elongated tower of steel rising high above the flat plain of the Champs du Mars, its peak as high as the Basilica on Montmartre. Max had not yet ascended the long stairs; he had never liked tall buildings and he wondered if, even two years after his wounds, his leg was strong enough for such a climb. To the left, he saw the bulk of Notre Dame, made famous by the Victor Hugo novel. *Am I like Quasimodo*, Max thought, *a broken man always doomed to love unattainable women?*

The melancholy of youth, Henri would call it. "Wait until you are old to be sad, Max. That's what I'm going to do." His friend had lost both his wife and his only daughter and, at seventy, still had to work as a railway porter four days a week to make ends meet. Yet, he seldom went a day without laughing or making a kind gesture "to one worse off than me."

Rejuvenated, Max strolled along the Champs-Élysées, its broad sidewalks filled with window-shoppers and students making their way to the Arch, before turning to climb the hill to Clignancourt and Chez Jake.

Jacopo Giamatti and Michel Tourangeau were sitting at a table just inside the front door, picking at a plate of charcuterie and drinking beer. Smitty hovered a few feet away, his muscular arms folded across his barrel chest and a fierce expression on his dark face. Giamatti stood when he saw Max but Tourangeau remained sitting.

"Join us," said Giammatti. "The beer is good."

"I know," said Max. "I bring it in from Alsace."

"Nothing like a German lager," said Giamatti.

"French," growled Tourangeau.

Giamatti laughed gently. "Of course – the whole point of the war."

"You didn't come here to discuss the changing provenance of beer."

"No," said Giamatti, "but I'm willing to share one before we discuss business. In private." He glanced pointedly at Smitty but the big man didn't budge.

"I'm not thirsty," said Max, though the long walk had left him parched. These were not men he wanted to share a drink with. "Let's go up to my office."

The office was small; the desk and two chairs nearly filled it. Max took one and Giamatti the other, so they faced each other across the narrow oak desk. Tourangeau leaned against the wall by the window, his bulk looming in the space like a small mountain. He had taken out a small knife and was cleaning his nails with it. The threat was obvious and Max felt under the desk for the small button that would ring a bell in the kitchen. Smitty and likely half the kitchen staff would be up the stairs in a moment if he needed them.

And if either of them was carrying a gun, Max had the answer to that, too, in the top drawer of his desk.

"What do you want?' he asked.

"See, what did I tell you, Michel?" said Giamatti. "A very direct approach. I sometimes think we could learn from these Americans."

"He's Canadian," said Tourangeau, smirking. "I can be direct if needs arise. Right, Mr. Anderson?"

"I'm waiting."

"I like you, Max," said Giamatti. "Michel maybe not so much. He's from Tours."

"What does that have to do with anything?

"The men you had arrested yesterday were from Tours. They're a close-knit bunch up that way."

"A lot of people come from Tours. I didn't realize they were your friends."

"Would it have made a difference?" asked Giamatti.

"No."

"He's a warrior, Michel, no doubt about it."

"The cemeteries are full of warriors."

"If you came here to threaten me," said Max, "get on with it. I've got work to do."

Tourangeau took a step toward the desk, the knife clutched in one meaty fist. Giamatti raised his hand, placatingly, and Tourangeau stepped back.

"Michel is an emotional man. A useful trait at times. It seems inevitable that our paths will continue to cross. We have shared interests whether we like it or not. Financial, political, maybe even social. These little conflicts are bound to arise. It doesn't have to be that way."

"Go on."

"I'm prepared to pay you, what do they call it, a retainer? An emolument as the French would say. A little bit of money every week or so."

"And what would I have to do for this emolument?"

"Keep us informed. Me, Michel, someone we assign. Let us know the cases you're working on and we'll let you know of the potential for conflict."

"And then I drop the case?"

"I know you would never do that," said Giamatti. "But you might delay solving it for a day or two."

"The other thing," said Tourangeau.

"What other thing?"

Giamatti cleared his throat. "This is a delicate thing. We're concerned about Pierre Armand."

"Join the club. People keep telling me he killed Mark St. John."

"Yeah, that," said Tourangeau. "We don't care about that."

Max raised his eyebrows.

"If he did or didn't, that's your business. Our only interest is in why. Money has gone missing. Italian money. Armand seems to have a good story. We'd like to know if it's true."

"Why don't you ask him?"

"He might not take it right," said Tourangeau. "Coming from us."

"What if he both killed St. John and stole your money?" asked Max.

"We can live with that," said Giamatti. "As long as he doesn't."

"And if it's only the money?"

"Then that becomes our problem," said Tourangeau, making a slashing motion with the knife.

Max shook his head. He knew the rough justice practiced by the gangs of the city. Men were killed for the slightest transgression of the so-called code of honour. It wasn't always a quick death; it was seldom a painless one. There were those who claimed the state shouldn't be allowed to take a man's life, even for murder or treason. Max didn't know. He had seen too many men die meaningless deaths to think there was anything sacred about life. Yet, he had vowed after the war not to take another life. If he turned Armand over to these men, he might as well be wielding the knife himself.

"I think you gentlemen better go."

Tourangeau spat on the floor and shoved the knife in his pocket. *He knows there are men with bigger knives in the kitchen below,* thought Max, *and he is not ready yet to measure himself against Smitty.*

"I told you this was a waste of time," Tourangeau said.

"Not at all," said Giamatti. "A good soldier always takes the measure of his foe. Well, don't say we didn't warn you, Mr. Anderson. The next men to pay you a call may not be as reasonable as Michel and me."

§

Max spent Friday in another futile search for Gaston Deschamps, the runaway boy who would lose out on a sizable trust fund if he didn't take up his duties at the family estate by his twenty-first birthday, only a few weeks hence. Max had never understood the need some men felt to control their sons and grandsons after their death, but it was far more common than not. According to the lawyer, Patrice Fumoleau, the money would go back to the estate and would gradually be doled out to a dozen cousins, a motive but not a strong one for keeping him away. Max was sure the lawyer wasn't telling all he knew but, then, that was what lawyers were supposed to do: keep family secrets.

Chez Jake was half full when Max arrived a little after seven. A few tables of laughing young men and women were clustered near the stage – holdovers from the lunch crowd, Max guessed, from the range of glasses and bottles that littered the table. A single musician, one of the Montmartre locals, was doodling on a piano, showing an occasional flourish that would silence the audience before slipping back beneath the rising gabble of voices.

Four or five black men lounged at the bar, watching the pianist and talking in low voices or nodding their heads at a particularly nice bit of jazzing around. Jake called Max over and introduced him as his "silent partner." The musicians, recently arrived from Chicago, laughed and slapped Max on the back as if the idea of a silent white man was the funniest thing they had ever heard. Max laughed too and chatted with them for a while about the differences between Chicago and New York jazz which changed the laughter into genuine smiles.

After a bit, Max went back into the kitchen to talk to LeBeouf, the newly acquired master chef. He had asked him to add some Russian dishes to the evening menu. LeBeouf had frowned but promised to do his best and gone off muttering something about peasants and paprika. The kitchen was redolent with the smell of roasting meat and vegetables and the tang of cinnamon and sour cream. Dishes full of steaming dumplings and thick meaty stew looked vaguely like those served at the Petrograd but were delicate and aromatic instead of heavy or oppressive.

The bar, too, had been transformed at his request. There were six varieties of vodka on ice, each from a different region of Russia and each, so the barman insisted, with their own unique bouquet and flavour.

Jake had reserved one of his special tables, located in nooks to the right of the stage where customers could see and hear the musicians but still carry on a private conversation, away from the eyes and ears of the other patrons. Satisfied that everything was as ready as it could be, Max retreated to his office to write up his notes from the day's investigations and change into the tuxedo he kept in a closet for special occasions.

He was knotting his tie for the third time when Jake rapped at his door to announce the arrival of Pavlovna and her party.

"Let me do that for you, boss, you're making a hash of it."

Max stood still as Jake adjusted the tie and snugged it around his neck. "There," he said, "you look as fine as one of those Long Island millionaires everyone talks about."

Jake's own suit was the latest Paris cut, broad shoulders and thin lapels, made of black wool shot through with blacker silk. His white shirt gleamed and his high collar was cinched with a red silk cravat.

"Next to you," said Max, "I look like a Bowery bum."

"I do my best. A man has to look how he wants to be seen."

Pavlovna was already seated. Denidov and his sister, Countess Solikov, were there as were two others, a man and a woman, Max had not met. There was no sign of Federov. If he were elsewhere in the bar, he was well hidden. Pavlovna patted the seat next to hers.

"You remember Baron Denidov and Katrina? And these are my dear friends, General Gregor Leo Chersky and his wife, the Lady Ivana Petrova Chersky."

Chersky was in his fifties but fit with a military bearing. He compensated for his receding hairline by sporting a thick white mustache that drooped over his lip. Lady Chersky was twenty years younger with rosy cheeks and a substantial bosom, which her dress did little to hide.

The Russians made their usual show of it, the men rising to click heels and kiss cheeks, the women demurely extending their hands for Max to kiss. Even after all this time in Paris, such elaborate greetings came off as stagey to Max, who grew up with the dour Scots and phlegmatic Yorkshire men of northern Nova Scotia, where a brief nod and a firm grip came across as effusive.

When they were seated, Max gestured to the waiter Jake had assigned for their exclusive use. He arrived moments later with a tray of glasses and three bottles of vodka in silver ice buckets.

"My God," said Denidov, holding up one stubby bottle that had a few blades of yellow grass floating in it, "I haven't seen this since I left St. Petersburg. All we need now is a card game and I'll be in heaven."

Denidov poured a round for the men, as well as Pavlovna; the other women declined. The four of them downed it in a single drink as seemed to be the custom, and Denidov poured another set of drinks from a different bottle. This one, apparently, was for sipping and Max was surprised to find that it did, in fact, have a slightly different flavour than the first.

"This is your club?" Chersky asked.

"No," said Max, "this is Jake's club. I'm merely a junior partner."

"But surely," said Lady Chersky, "you don't let a..." She searched for the proper word. "A... run your club... I mean..."

"A what?" said Max. "A gentleman?" He made no effort to keep the contempt from his voice. Lady Chersky blushed and dropped her gaze.

"We live in a different world," said her husband. "Everything has been turned on its head."

"Not as much as you think," said Max. "Money still runs the place; the only change is who has it."

"Lions or foxes, General, lions or foxes," said Denidov. "It makes little difference to the sheep they rule."

Pavlovna laughed. "Always the philosopher, Sergei." She leaned toward Max and put her hand on his forearm. The smell of her, rosewater and lilacs, wafted over him, enwrapping him. He was again struck by the sheer power of her presence, forgetting for an instant that they were at a table with others, or in a public place at all.

"I leave philosophy to the Bolsheviks," said Denidov, breaking the spell. "We should have closed the universities years ago. We wouldn't be in this position now."

"We should have done a lot of things years ago," said Chersky. "The question is: what are we going to do now?"

"I'm sure Max didn't invite us here to discuss Russian politics," said Pavlovna. She leaned away, her fingers trailing down Max's arm and across the back of his hand, sending a shiver up his arm and across the top of his head. "What did you invite us here for, Max?"

"A few drinks, a little supper, some music," said Max. "And, of course, the pleasure of your company." Solikov laughed and put her hand to her mouth. Lady Chersky still wouldn't meet his eye; she was not used to being rebuked for expressing her sense of superiority.

"Tell me, Max, I can call you Max?" said Denidov.

"We're all friends here, Sergei."

Denidov frowned at the reciprocity of familiarity, but continued. "How did your adventures in the17th go? Was Federov able to direct you to the villains who attacked you?"

"They were Russians, or three of them were, that much is certain. Bullies for hire. But they were working for a Frenchman."

Denidov's frown deepened. "You spoke to these men?"

"Not directly," said Max. "Or at least not yet. Nonetheless, I'm certain of my facts. I even have a few names." Max shifted his gaze from Denidov to Chersky to Pavlovna. None showed any expression of concern at this revelation.

"I'm sure it will prove unrelated to Mark's death," said Pavlovna.

"Still," said Chersky, nodding gravely, "I'm sure someone is trying to send you a message."

Max had little doubt of that but he was beginning to question who and what. Conversation died as the waiter arrived with the first course, a hot vegetable puree, flavoured with vodka, pepper and nutmeg and served with the thick dollop of sour cream in the middle.

After several spoonfuls, Chersky looked up from the bowl. "Nothing like mother made," he said.

Max frowned until Lady Chersky took pity on him. "His mother was a terrible cook."

Conversation rose and fell, inconsequential or amusing, as they finished supper, black cavier on thin slices of dark bread followed by lamb stew, heavily flavored with paprika – along with several bottles of excellent Bordeaux. The band played a tight fast set that drew the Cherskys to the dance floor. Even Denidov escorted his sister to the front of the stage for a turn. Pavlovna declined Max's half-hearted offer. When they were alone, she leaned over and kissed him on the mouth. Her lips were soft and warm against his and for an instant he felt the tip of her tongue brush his mouth. She leaned away and laughed softly.

"You liked that," she said.

Max had, though he felt uncomfortable admitting it. If Sarah was ten years older than him, Irina Pavlovna was nearly old enough to be his mother. Yet there was something powerful about her, so certain in her womanhood and in its effect on men. Had Mark St. John been so enthralled with her that he had been willing to take any risk to help her, even if it put his life in danger? Max could believe it was true.

"I like men," Pavlovna said. "I especially like young virile men. But I'm not good for them. I use them up. But you're a rare breed, Max. I don't think I want to be responsible for ruining you."

"Thanks, I suppose." Maybe it was the wine or the heat of the club, but Max felt disappointed there would be no more kisses nor any of what came after kisses.

The music ended and the other Russians returned to the table. Denidov was red faced and panting after a single dance; Chersky was cool despite three or four. Both women were smiling and relaxed.

The waiter arrived with dessert, a thick chocolate pate with raspberry coulis and crème fraiche, and coffee and tea in silver urns. He placed a bottle of Armagnac, a tray of snifters and humidor of cigars on a side table.

"The detective business must pay better than I thought," said Chernsky, selecting a fat Cuban. "Perhaps I should go into it."

"I doubt if you would like it, Gregor," said Denidov. "Criminals are not much better than serfs."

The conversation continued in a desultory manner until half the bottle was gone and several cigars were smoked. Russian aristocrats, it seemed, could talk endlessly about nothing and Max gathered little from it other than that good vodka was hard to find in Paris and the Bolsheviks were the spawn of Satan. Max barely touched his own cognac.

"Have any of you ever been to Zurich?" he finally asked of no one in particular.

"We've all been to Zurich," said Pavlovna into the sudden silence. "Why do you ask?"

"I heard that an Englishman had been murdered there. His death sounded remarkably like that of Mark St. John."

Denidov and Chernsky exchanged a glance, the latter chewing at the ends of the mustache, perhaps as way of not blurting out his thoughts.

"Andrew Locke," said Pavlovna. "He was murdered by the Cheka."

"Are you sure of that?"

"Have you heard differently?" Denidov's face was redder than usual, though his voice was calm.

"I heard there was some uncertainty as to who killed him."

"I am certain," said Pavlovna.

"Were you close?" asked Max, not sure if he wanted to know the answer.

"I think it's time to go," said Countess Solikov. "I feel ill."

Pavlovna made no effort to hide her contempt. "Take her home, Sergei. This is no place for weaklings. Take Ivana too. Gregor can see me home."

Lady Chernsky looked as suddenly ill as Solikov claimed. *She's distressed*, thought Max, *at the thought of leaving her husband in the company of Pavlovna.* A mask fell over her expression as she nodded and accompanied Denidov and his sister. General Chernsky shifted his seat so that he and Pavlovna flanked Max, both of them leaning in closely. The expression on Chernsky's face had lost any hint of friendliness. Smitty took a few steps from the front door but Max shook his head and he retreated.

"Andrew had his own reason for hating the Reds," said Pavlovna. "We found common cause in the struggle against terrorism. If you are asking if I bedded him, I'll leave that to your own imagination."

"What happened?"

"It was a few months ago," said Chernsky. "Irina was already here in Paris. I had left Kiev a few days earlier with an urgent message from General Wrangel to supporters in the West. I stopped in Zurich for reasons that do not concern you. Locke came to see me at my hotel. He was excited, almost ecstatic. He claimed that he had infiltrated the local Bolsheviks –Lenin had lived for a time in Zurich and converted many locals – and uncovered plans that would deal a real blow to the Red army. I, of course, demanded them at once. 'I don't have them yet,' he claimed but would have them the next morning if I could meet him at a certain hotel with a sum of cash. I put him off for a day – though I in fact had the money in my room, again none of your concern why – so I could check my own sources. I never saw him again. His body was discovered in a public park three days later. You can draw your own conclusions."

It was clear to Max what conclusions Chernsky wanted him to draw. The Bolsheviks had discovered Locke's duplicity and had him murdered by agents of the Cheka. Those same agents had followed Chernsky to Paris and, when they discovered Mark St. John providing funds to Pavlovna, murdered him using the same methods. It was a very neat package. Far too neat as far as Max was concerned.

"You said you wanted to check your own sources? What did they tell you?"

"What?"

"Did they confirm that Locke had done what he claimed, that he had acquired Red plans?"

Pavlovna saw the trap as soon as Chernsky opened his mouth to reply. She shot him a frantic glance but it was too late.

"I didn't bother once Locke was dead. The plans, if there were any, were gone."

"But you only put off Locke to the second day. You must have intended to discover his fidelity by then. His body only appeared the day after that."

"I... I..." Chernsky closed his mouth with a snap, his previously calm demeanour collapsing in confusion.

"It's all right, Gregor," said Pavlovna, reaching past Max to pat the General's arm. "Locke had gone over to the Reds. He intended to kill Gregor and steal our gold. When Gregor's sources discovered his treachery, they took matters into their own hands. No one was more shocked than he at the violence of their response. Isn't that right, Gregor?"

Chernsky nodded and turned away.

"Why didn't you tell me that in the first place? Why such a clumsy lie?"

"Gregor was caught off guard. He had no time to concoct an elegant one. If you thought us involved in Locke's death, how could I persuade you we were innocent in Mark's?"

"I'm not sure you can. If not you, then who?"

"It's obvious. The Cheka. They really are diabolical. What better way to implicate us, then to copy our methods?"

Pavlovna's face was calm, almost serene. She had all but admitted that Chernsky had ordered or perhaps even carried out Andrew Locke's murder in Zurich. Max remembered the look of distress on

Lady Cherensky's face as she left. Irina Pavlovna had the same hold on Gregor Chernsky as she had had on Mark St. John, the same hold she might have had on him if she had not, for some reason, decided not to "ruin" him. Max suppressed a shudder. Giamatti was right. Discover the why of St. John's death and the who was obvious. If Mark St. John had betrayed Pavlovna, then there was no question she had killed him. But if he hadn't, who did that leave? The Cheka? Armand? Giamatti? Or someone as yet unknown?

He needed to know why Mark St. John had been killed. That would tell him who and how. But the motive, like everything else, remained hidden in the shadows.

Sixteen – Saturday to Sunday, June 13-14th, 1920

By the time Max rolled out of bed it was mid-morning. He had stayed at the club until nearly two, long after Pavlovna and Chernsky took their leave. He had finished most of the bottle of Armagnac, his thoughts as convoluted and insistent as the syncopations of the Chicago quartet. Jake had finally poured him into a cab. How he had made it to his bed was as much a mystery as St. John's murder.

Max forced himself to eat day-old brioche, toasted but unbuttered. It seemed to settle his stomach, though not the throbbing in his head, so he pulled on yesterday's clothes and walked down the street to the Luxe for coffee and a more substantial breakfast.

The late morning newspapers were full of reports on the assassination of Essad Pasha, a renegade general who claimed to be the legitimate ruler of Albania. He had been largely ignored at the peace Conference but as negotiations with the Ottoman Empire dragged on, someone had gunned him down as he left his mansion in the Marais, early that morning. Police commentators were divided; some blamed "foreign agitators" while others laid the responsibility at the feet of local anarchists.

Max was finishing his second espresso when he spotted LePêcheur, in full uniform, complete with brand new Sergeant's stripes, approaching the door of his *pension*.

"I'm over here, Ferdinand."

LePêcheur turned at the sound of his voice and fixed a stern expression on his face.

"Mr. Anderson," he said, with only a slight waver in his voice. "I've been ordered to escort you to the Prefecture for questions."

"Has Fontaine had another brainstorm?"

"I now report to Captain Gereau. Will you accompany me?"

"With pleasure," said Max, though his thoughts were far from pleasant.

§

Gereau was in his usual position behind his desk on the fourth floor of the Prefecture, half hidden by piles of paper and stacks of bulging files. He gestured for Max to take a seat and asked LePêcheur to wait outside. The new sergeant looked relieved to be excused from the coming interrogation. Gereau shuffled papers from one stack to another for a few moments before clearing his throat and staring across the desk at Max, who was doing his best to look untroubled by the sudden summons.

"Mr. Anderson."

Max had hoped Gereau had planned a reconciliation. The formality dashed those hopes.

"Captain Gereau." Max tried to match Gereau's serious gaze with one of his own. The left side Gereau's mustache twitched.

"You've read the papers, I presume."

"About the assassination? I know nothing about Albanian politics."

"Who does?" Gereau leaned back, the fingers of his left hand drumming on the one bare surface of his desk. "You know about anarchists."

"I've had anarchy explained to me but I don't pretend to understand it."

"I leave the theory for the academics," said Gereau. "I should have been more precise. You know a few anarchists."

"A few," Max acknowledged.

"The Jacques, for example."

Max wondered if Jacque Court had ended his self-imposed exile. "You know that I've met them."

"Recently?"

"No." Not technically a lie. He had only met with one of them.

"What about Yesim?"

"Yesim?"

"Don't play stupid with me. You aren't very good at it. Yesim Coriveau. Your business partner. We have a file this thick on him." Gereau held his thumb and finger two inches apart.

"Oh, that's nothing. You should see the file he has on you."

Gereau slammed the desk with the palm of his left hand, the report as loud as a pistol in the small room. LePêcheur called in alarm from the hall.

"Damn it, Max, do you want me to take you down to the cells for this questioning?"

"And do you want me to turn rat on my best friend? Yesim talks the black flag but he's too busy trying to make a living to do anything about it. He doesn't even subscribe to their papers anymore. What is it with you and anarchists, anyway? They don't all adhere to illegalism or even violence. There are worse radicals in Paris than the anarchists."

"Anarchists are enemies of the Republic. They always have been and always will be. Their methods may differ but their goals are the same."

"The Action Française is an enemy of the Republic, too. They want to bring back the King."

Gereau grinned without humour, showing a broad expanse of yellowing teeth. "Not all these files are on anarchists."

"What about the other theory – that this Essad Pasha was gunned down by one of his own people or some other foreigner with a score to settle or a mysterious cause to advance?"

"That's Fontaine's theory."

"Maybe for once in his life, he's right."

Gereau snorted. "Has hell frozen over?"

"Do you remember Joseph Asper?" Gereau nodded. "He was afraid of something, something that would cause France to dissolve into the same kind of violence as Germany. It's only been a couple of months since French troops had to enter the Ruhr to stop Germans from killing each other."

"To stop a Bolshevik revolution. There's a difference between France and Germany."

"What's that?"

"We won the war. You claim to have no idea where the Jacques are holed up?"

"I swear I don't." *Again, not a lie,* thought Max. Jacqueline had left him a way to contact her and she knew exactly where he lived. But as to where she, or her fat friend, was hiding, he had no idea. As long as Gereau doesn't think to ask the right question...

Gereau glared at him. Max tried to look innocent. Gereau choose to believe that he was.

"Asper? I suppose you don't know where he is, either?"

"Not in Paris."

"The last time I saw Asper he could barely buy a Metro ticket. How did he leave Paris?"

"I loaned him the money." Gereau glared at him again and Max shrugged. "He had done some work for me."

Gereau sighed. "One of these days, you'll try my patience too far. Tell me, Max, why do I like you?"

It was a surprise to Max. He couldn't help smiling. "My boyish charm?"

"That must be it. Any luck with the St. John case?"

"I've finally figured out what it is I don't know."

"Really? Then you should have it solved in another week or two."

Max appreciated the vote of confidence. He only hoped it wasn't misplaced.

§

Max was about to return to his apartment when he had a sudden thought. The Hall of Records was only a block away and was still open for a few more hours. The clerks were starting to tidy up their desks by the time Max found what he was looking for, the name of the trustee for the Deschamps estate, P. Fumoleau.

Max scribbled out an advertisement and put it in the classifieds of several of the more popular papers. *It worked for Sherlock Holmes,* he thought, *why not for me?*

By the time he returned home, it was nearly six. As he approached his door, a grimy young boy in shabby clothes, emerged from a doorway and plucked at his sleeve.

"Can you help a veteran in distress, kind sir?"

"You're too young to be a-" Max recognized the smile through the layers of grime. "Jacqueline?"

"There's a police agent watching us," she said in a low voice. "Send me on my way. I'll come back when it's dark. If I can?"

Max shook his head vehemently. "Of course," he said. In a louder voice, "Be off with you, scoundrel!" He raised his hand as if to strike her and Jacqueline scuttled away.

Max went up to his apartment but left again almost at once to buy bread, wine and a roasted chicken from the local boulangerie. If Jacqueline was on the run, she would be hungry.

Light still lingered in the western sky when Max heard a soft tap on his apartment door. Jacqueline had washed her face and changed her clothes though she still wore a man's jacket and pants. Max supposed it was easier for a young man to walk alone in this neighbourhood than a woman of any age. A thin stage mustache and cloth cap that covered her hair completed the masquerade.

"Are all anarchists masters of disguise?" Max asked after he had closed the door.

"I trained for a year at the Comedie Française," said Jacqueline. "They kicked me out for organizing a union."

She pulled the hat from her head, letting her dark hair tumble past her ears, and entered the tiny water closet, emerging a few minutes later without the mustache. Max had laid out a small supper and opened a half bottle of burgundy. From the way she attacked the chicken, it was clear she hadn't eaten all day. The food was nearly gone and the bottle empty before she looked up.

"I'd have another glass of wine if you have it," she said.

Max retrieved another half bottle from his stock below the sink and drew the cork. After he poured them both another glass they retreated to the more comfortable chairs at the other end of the room. Jacqueline took the one farthest from the window.

"The police were particularly aggressive in their sweeps today," she said. "The safe house where I was staying wasn't, though, lucky for me, they didn't know about the emergency exit. I came out on the far side of their cordon – my friends weren't so lucky."

"Gereau even had me down at the Prefecture asking about anarchists."

Jacqueline looked at him over the rim of her glass. "Lying to the police is a dangerous game."

"I didn't lie," said Max. Jacqueline shifted in her chair, her body tensing. "But I didn't tell him anything either. You're safe here."

Jacqueline smiled. "I feel perfectly safe."

There was something in the way she said it that made Max feel insecure. He was acutely aware that this was the first time in over a year that he had been truly alone with a woman. The sky was dark but neon lights from the street below flickered an abstract pattern of red and blue across the ceiling. Jacqueline's face was a rosy oval in the dimness.

"It's late," he said. "You must be tired."

"I haven't finished my wine yet," she said, holding out her glass.

Max refilled their glasses and settled back on the sofa that would soon be his bed. "What does Gereau have against anarchists?"

"He's a policeman from a long line of policemen."

"There must be more to it than that."

"The black flag now competes with the Red and the symbols of the far right. But before the war, it was the only real thorn in the side of the Republic. If a bomb was tossed or a politician or policeman gunned down in the street, you could be pretty sure it was an anarchist, or at least someone who claimed to be one. They weren't all as flashy as Bonnot and his gang or as relentlessly violent as Libertad. I heard Gereau's brother was seriously wounded in one such attack and had to retire to Brittany."

It might explain Gereau's obsession, thought Max.

"And have you ever tossed a bomb?"

"Not every anarchist believes in violence. It is in the nature of anarchists to differ with each other. I wouldn't know which end of a bomb to light."

"And what do you believe in?"

"I am an adherent of Broutchoux's thinking."

"And what did Broutchoux think?"

"Let me show you."

Jacqueline set her wine glass on the floor and stood and front of him. She had shed her jacket after dinner and now began to loosen the buttons of her shirt.

"What are you-"

"Shhh." Jacqueline leaned forward and pressed her mouth against his. Her mouth opened and she nibbled at his lips until he responded. Their tongues twined together for several long moments. When she leaned away, the shirt fell to the floor. Her breasts were outlined against the thin silk chemise that was her only undergarment.

She took his hand and pulled him up and toward the open bedroom door.

"We can't," he said. Heat flushed from his face to his knees.

Her other hand brushed down his chest, past his waist. "We obviously can," she said, her hand squeezing his stiffening manhood.

He nodded dumbly and followed her in the bedroom. They tumbled on the bed. Max fumbled at buckles and fasteners, but Jacqueline's fingers were more adept. Freed from the constraints of their garments they become imprisoned in the tangle of their limbs.

Long lingering kisses became quicker and more frantic; hands clutched at shoulders and thighs and caressed faces and breasts. Fingers stroked and probed; Jacqueline's breath gasped hot against his neck and chest as he entered her.

They moved against each other, faster now, then slower, and fast again, shifting from top to bottom and back. Across the courtyard a light flashed on and glimmered tendrils across their bodies through the small window. Jacqueline's face was flushed and damp, her eyes black and glittering. She pulled him down and thrust her tongue into his mouth in rhythm to his own movements.

She gasped and stiffened, lifting her hips to meet him. He followed on, head thrown back, teeth gritted against his own cries.

They rolled apart, his hand resting on her still heaving belly, her fingers tangled in his hair. They lay in silence, listening to the thudding of their hearts, watching the faint sparkle of neon on the ceiling. As their breath slowed, they lay together on their sides, touching and kissing without speaking, until their passion took them again.

"I think I like the way this Broutchoux thinks," he said at last.

Jacqueline laughter tinkled against him. "The doctrine of free love is a well-developed tenet of anarchist thought."

"When has love ever been free?"

If she had an answer to that, she didn't make it.

When he awoke, the bed beside him was empty. The smell of frying ham and the clatter of dishes wafted from the next room.

Max staggered to the water closet. When he came out, Jacqueline was putting plates on the small table. She was wearing one of his shirts and, as near as he could tell, nothing else. The shirt flapped as she moved, revealing tantalizing glimpses of her smooth thighs and the curve of her buttocks.

"Hungry?" she asked, pouring two large mugs of steaming coffee.

"Famished," he said. In addition to thick slices of country ham, the plates were piled with heaps of fluffy scrambled eggs, fried potatoes, slices of toasted brioche slathered with butter and heaped with marmalade.

"I thought you might be, after last night."

Max shivered at the memory. "An English breakfast?"

"I worked in a café near the front during the war. We served a lot of Tommies."

Jacqueline sat across from him and they ate mostly in silence. When they both reached for the salt, she laughed and tangled her fingers in his. She poured more coffee and they sat at the table until the morning sun had crawled across the floor and begun to ascend the wall.

"They have someone for the assassination," she said. "I heard the vendors bawling the news before you woke up."

"Who?"

"I don't know. I didn't want to open the window and ask in case it was someone I knew."

Max went down and brought back several papers. They all had variations of the same story. An Albanian school teacher, Avri Rustemi, had turned himself in. He was not an anarchist at all but a liberal democrat, determined that the old regime must never return to his homeland. A magistrate had decided that foreigners killing foreigners was of no concern to the French courts – a popular if legally dubious decision. Rustemi was already on a train back to Tirana, where he would undoubtedly be hailed as a hero.

"That should get Gereau off your back," said Max. "Though you're welcome to stay here if you've no place else to go."

Jacqueline smiled and slid onto the sofa beside him, draping her arm across his shoulders, her legs stretched out onto the table in front of them. He pulled her closer, but she put her hand on his chest and looked up into his face.

"I don't think you understand, Max."

"Understand what?"

"Gereau will never leave me alone. He'll never be happy until Paris is empty of anarchists. He might as well wish the Seine to be empty of fish."

"I can handle Gereau."

"I doubt that, Max, though I am sure you would be very gallant in trying. Besides, that's not why I can't stay."

"No?" Max didn't think he liked the way the conversation was going.

"Free love, Max. Two words of equal weight. We made love because we both wanted to. We may well want to again. But I have no claim on you and you have none on me. If I stay now, you might think otherwise and I might let you. Then, later, one of us would wind up hurt."

"So you might as well get it over with, is that it?"

"You know better than that, Max. This isn't real. Not yet at least. And neither of us will be hurt – much – if we end it now."

Max did know. He had been hurt before and it had felt nothing like this. He hardly knew this woman, though something told him he wanted to get to know her. With Sarah and Irina, he had felt drawn, like an animal walking into a trap. He had felt nothing like that with Jacqueline; there was no cage waiting for him here. Yet, he almost wished there were.

"Not end it," said Max. "That sounds too final. Farewell instead of good-bye."

"I can live with that,"

"Where will you go?"

"Away from Paris. For a week or two, until the latest sweep is over. It's better you don't know where."

Jacqueline stood and walked to the bedroom. She paused at the door and looked back at Max. "Don't look so forlorn, Max. You'll see me again. I promise. In the meantime, surely you're not going to send me packing without a proper 'farewell.'"

§

A note from Sarah had arrived late in the day. Martel had agreed to meet him after church on Sunday at the Café de la Paix, across from the Opera Garnier. He was well known there, and the concierge would guide Max to his table if he arrived after two.

Max arrived a few minutes past the hour and was directed to a booth near the back of the restaurant. Martel, still dressed for church, observed him closely as he approached and Max returned the favour.

The politician was of middle age, middle height and medium build, handsome in a non-descript way. His hair was dark and cut short, though not unstylishly so. His eyes were dark and gave the impression that little escaped his gaze. His smile was genuine though not particularly warm. Max could well imagine that this was the face of a go-between, a deal maker who left nothing of himself in the deal.

Martel stood as Max crossed the last few metres, removing a thin leather glove to extend his hand. He knew North Americans well and did not offer the Gallic kiss in greeting.

"You are Sarah's friend?"

"Yes. Max Anderson. Thank you for seeing me."

Martel gestured to the waiter who brought a tray of sherry and cheese.

"I had a few minutes to spare. Angeline wanted to see Sarah. It was convenient to wait here." Le Grand was less than a block from where they were sitting.

"You chose not to go yourself."

"I don't know her well. My dealings were with her husband."

"Did you have a lot of dealings with Mark St, John?"

"I didn't kill him if that's what you're asking." Martel smiled as he said it, whether because he thought it was funny or he thought Max should.

"Not yet," said Max. smiling back.

"He was always looking for money. I sometimes could point him in the right direction."

"Did you know what he wanted it for?"

"To give to that Russian witch, Pavlovna. What he got in return..." Martel shrugged broadly. "Money is the great lubricant."

"I thought money was the root of all evil."

"A misquote. It is the desire of money that leads to evil. Personally, I suspect it is the lack of money that is mostly to blame. People will do almost anything to get it – no matter what the socialists think."

"Do you lack for money?"

"Seldom and never for long."

"Did you point St. John at Armand?"

"Pierre? No, Mark knew him from years ago. I suggested ways their relationship might be more... profitable."

"For both of them?"

"Armand is, if you will excuse the word, a prick. He has no real principles."

"That troubles you?"

"As a matter of fact, it does. I know what people think of me. That I'm nothing but a broker willing to bend in the wind if it gets a deal done. I'm not ashamed of that. We live in precarious times. We are beset by ideologues, willing to sacrifice anything to advance their cause. The only altar I sacrifice at is France herself. I would make any deal to ensure my country is not destroyed. Armand doesn't care about that. As long as he gets paid, all is right with the world."

Max had nothing to say to that. He had heard much the same from every politician he had ever met. Patriotism was a useful cover for self-interest.

"I've heard that St. John stole money from Armand."

"I doubt that. If Mark stole from Pierre, it wasn't Pierre's money in the first place."

"I've heard that too."

"I bet you have." Martel checked his pocket watch. "Angeline will be here soon. We are going to a recital; all the important people will be there. Impress me."

"I doubt I could do that. Do you have any idea who killed Mark St. John?"

"That information would be worth a lot of money to someone."

"Who?"

"The killer, of course."

"Isn't France served when justice is done?"

"Nonsense. What good did Zola do? Justice for Dreyfus humiliated half the general staff. It ruined men who might have saved a hundred thousand in the war."

"If you know something..."

"Then, I'll reveal it to my best advantage."

"Sarah St. John is innocent. If you can-"

"Innocent? What a naïve young man you are. Pay the bill, won't you?"

§

Nothing about his encounter with Martel made Max happy, least of all paying the inflated tab. Martel and his wife had eaten a sumptuous lunch before Max arrived. By the time he reached Le Coq Bleu, he had worked off most of his anger. He had also worked up an appetite. It had been a long time since his meagre breakfast of croissants and steamed milk.

The bar was almost empty, not unusual for Sunday afternoon. Max sometimes wondered why Yesim even bothered to stay open. *No place else to go I suppose, he has no more friends in the city than I do.* Henri was there, of course, sipping wine and reading one of the cheap detective novels he favoured, while Yesim busied himself restocking the bar and serving the one table of truck drivers, celebrating the end of their shift. Henri looked up from his book as Max slid into the chair opposite.

"You look upset," said Henri, his brows furrowed with concern.

"I haven't eaten. You know how I get."

Henri leapt up before Max could stop him, returning a few moments later with a basket of sandwiches from behind the bar and another wine glass. Max nodded gratefully as Henri poured him a generous serving. He found a croissant stuffed with egg salad and added a ham and cheese layered between two slices of seedy dark bread.

Henri waited until Max had finished the first before speaking again. "Any progress with your case?"

"Cases," corrected Max, describing the warehouse heist and the aftermath of solving it. "I also found the missing soldier; he should be re-united with his brother by now. And I think I know what's going on with the wayward grandson. It's the lawyer."

"I thought it was the lawyer who hired you to find the boy."

"Exactly. It's perfect cover. He sends me to look for the boy and all the time he's the one responsible for keeping him on the move."

"But why?"

"When the grandson fails to make an appearance, the inheritance reverts to the estate, which he manages. He'll have plenty of time to drain it dry – if he hasn't already done so."

"Hard to prove," said Henri.

"I don't need to prove it. I simply need to find the boy before the deadline passes. If I've gauged it right, he'll come looking for me."

"But what about the other case, the important one?" For Henri, if there wasn't a death involved, it was hardly worth the time to solve it. "Any leads on who hired those thugs to attack you?"

"That's one of several things that don't seem to add up. I was attacked by Russians but the leader was French. Why would Pavlovna and her gang hire a Frenchman to be the go-between to their own people?"

"You can never tell with foreigners," said Henri.

"Careful," said Yesim, who had joined them at the table. "You're starting to tread on my turf." He poured himself a tumbler of wine from the carafe and made a face. "I really need to start serving better wine."

"It does the job," said Henri. "And after the third swallow you hardly notice the taste."

"Jean Martel bothers me," said Max. "He may only have been toying with me but I got the distinct impression he knows or suspects who killed Mark St. John."

"Get Gereau to take him in for questioning," said Yesim. "The flics have ways of getting people to talk. Trust me on that."

"As if the Prefecture would lay their hands on Deputy Martel," said Henri. "He's not Cabinet material but he has dirt on anyone who is."

"Since when do you follow politics?" asked Yesim. "I mean, recent politics."

Henri would, at the drop of a sou, happily recount his adventures during the Paris commune or relate some juicy scandal from the Belle Epoch, but seldom spoke of more recent events.

"Politicians make me sick," said Henri. "One should always pay attention to one's health."

In the last two years, Max had learned much from Henri about the language and about the history and values of Paris. He had come to respect his opinions deeply.

"What did you hear about Martel?" he asked.

"This and that. You learn a lot working the train stations and hotels. People talk as if we weren't even there. If you keep your eyes down and your mouth shut, they'll say almost anything. Look interested, and that's another story. Martel is a professional politician. I don't think he's done anything else in his life. Served as a page while still in school, worked for a Minister as soon as he left university, ran for office at the first opportunity. He's already served more than twenty years and he's not yet fifty."

"Yet he never rose to real power," said Max.

"Don't kid yourself," said Henri. "He wields a lot of influence. The man trades in secrets and scandals. It has made him powerful, and it has made him rich. Though I'm told his wife spends it as fast as he brings it in."

"Behind every great man..." Yesim said.

"He said he advised St. John how to make his relationship with Pierre Armand more profitable," said Max. "If the plan backfired, that might have led to St. John being murdered, either by Armand or by the Italians."

"Then everything still points at Armand," said Yesim.

"So it seems." There was something Max was missing; he was sure of it. If the motive was money, then Armand or his Italian friends were almost certainly behind the killing; if it were politics, St. John's great obsession, then the finger pointed at the Russians, though whether White or Red was unclear. And if it were love? Could Fontaine be right? Could Sarah St. John have killed her husband? And where did the gang who attacked him on the stairs come in?

The three workmen had finished their drinks and stood to go. Yesim scurried to their table to ensure they had left enough for the bill. From the smile on his face, it was clear they had left far more than enough. He locked the door behind them and turned off the neon rooster.

"I'd like to get a little sleep before the evening crowd," he said when he returned to the table.

"Isn't Alice coming in?" asked Henri.

"I caught her with her hand in the cash drawer," said Yesim. "You can't trust anyone these days."

"Too bad," said Henri. "I liked her. I'll come back and give you a hand."

"You aren't working at the station tonight?" asked Max.

Henri frowned. "They say I'm too old. I only get a couple of shifts a week."

It was Max's turn to frown. "If that offer to help me still stands..."

"I won't take your money for nothing," said Henri.

"I wouldn't offer it. Talk to your colleagues. Anything you can find out about Martel's relationship to Armand, to St. John, to the Russians. It would help."

"It would be my pleasure. We can talk about salary later."

Max laughed. He knew Henri would earn whatever he was paid. "But stay away from Martel himself. And especially avoid the Russians."

"Don't worry about that," said Henri. "I'm not eager to gather any new scars."

Max repressed a shudder. "I hope I don't live to regret this."

Seventeen – Tuesday, June 17th, 1920

Max woke up Monday morning determined to focus his full attention on the murder of Mark St. John, but the day seemed to get away from him, the way days in Paris often did. After an hour at the gymnasium working the weights and the bags – Kid O'Brien was too "busy" to spar with him – he dropped by his office.

Jake was waiting for him with a stack of paperwork and a list of concerns, mostly about a new Sergeant of police in the district who seemed to think their licences weren't in order. Max knew a few hundred francs would make the problem go away but it was a bad precedent and would only lead to other demands further down the road. The gendarme wouldn't have tried it on a citizen but considered foreigners fair game. A few words to the man's superiors at the Prefecture sufficed to correct his opinions but cost Max the rest of the morning.

There had been no answers to his advertisements, so Max had a few handbills printed up and posted in the neighbourhoods Gaston Deschamps seemed to frequent. He finished making arrangements to have telephones installed in his office and both of the bars and ran a few more necessary errands before heading for Le Coq Bleu for an early supper.

The few sidewalk tables were already full of customers and several of the ones near the windows were also occupied. There was a new woman, Suzanne, behind the bar helping out. She wasn't much to look at, dumpy and sour-faced, but seemed competent. *We can only hope she's honest, too*, thought Max. Yesim was too busy to talk for more than a few minutes. Henri had been in briefly and promised a full report the next day. Max ate quickly before heading back to his apartment to read before heading off to his bed – a bed that somehow seemed too big.

§

The next morning, Max headed back to the fifteenth arrondissement. None of the bars he had visited before were open that early, but the cafés of the district were doing a brisk trade. Several seemed to cater to the Russian crowd, with signs in the Cyrillic alphabet augmenting those in French. At the third one he tried, the owner pointed him to a table in the back, where a solitary man sat sipping tea and reading from a leather-bound book.

He did not look like the kind of man who could order the murder of entire villages. If he was forty, then life had been kind to him, leaving few lines of worry or hardship on his thin handsome face. His hair was black and slicked to his head; a pencil mustache drew a line across his upper lip.

His dark eyes glistened and his sensitive mouth trembled as he read. The hands holding the book were graceful. His limbs were long and relaxed and Max estimated he would be several inches taller than him if he were standing. He was wearing a pale grey suit and had a red silk scarf draped casually around his neck.

"Gennady Sidorov," said Max.

The head came up slowly, showing no alarm. Sidorov smiled, nodded and gestured Max to sit.

"And you are Max Anderson. I've been wanting to meet you." His voice was strained, as if he were about to cry.

"I'm easy enough to find." How did Sidorov know who he was?

Sidorov nodded. He placed a silk ribbon in the book and sat it on the table. He poured Max a cup of tea and topped up his own. He cleared his throat.

"You must excuse me," Sidorov said, his voice calmer. "Turgenev is such a beautiful writer. It always affects me like this."

"Is it required reading for Commissars of the Cheka?"

The Russian laughed. "Ah, you Americans are so direct. It's refreshing."

"Canadian," Max corrected, more from habit than because he thought it mattered. He thought of himself as Parisian now.

"A thousand acres of snow. Isn't that what Voltaire called it?"

"I bow to your greater knowledge," said Max. Why did every Russian he met have to approach things in a spiral? "As I said, I'm easy to find. I take it you know what I want."

"I've made inquiries. Don't look so surprised. Russians have grown very sensitive over the years to strangers asking questions of them. The Okhrana taught us well."

"I understand the Cheka has adopted their methods."

"Not at all. The Cheka is far more thorough and determined. But, of course, only the enemies of the people need be concerned."

"I understand that is a fairly large category."

"It's getting smaller every day."

"Was Mark St. John an enemy of the people?"

"Undoubtedly. If he had lived, I might have had to arrange his death." Sidorov smiled gently and waved to the waiter. "They make excellent sirniki – cheese pancakes – here. Try them with sour cream and preserves."

"I'm not sure -"

"Please. I'm flouting tradition. In Russia we say: eat breakfast alone, share dinner with your friends but serve supper to your enemies."

"Why not?" Many people believed that sharing food created an obligation between them. Max wasn't one of them but maybe Sidorov was. Besides he had eaten nothing but a stale croissant and a piece of hard cheese before leaving his apartment.

"We are not monsters, Max. Never mind what Pavlovna and her band of parasites tell you. They are not monsters either, merely relics of an era that has passed away. They are dead but their bodies are still twitching. It makes them dangerous."

"They say you're the dangerous one."

"I would expect nothing else. We are both governed by the infallible laws of history. Capitalism is through. Communism will follow as surely as day follows night. Though as our friend, Trotsky, likes to say, nothing of value is achieved except in struggle."

"The civil war is nothing but a necessary evil?"

"Like the Great War that spawned it. You were in the trenches. You must have seen how natural communism is to real men. Or were you one of those who couldn't bend low enough for the aristocrats and officers who sent millions to their deaths in the name of profit?"

"It's a little early in the day for speeches, don't you think?"

Sidorov laughed. "That's why we eat breakfast alone. Russians really aren't fit company until noon."

The waiter arrived with their food and a large urn of coffee. The pancakes were thick and well-browned, with the cheese mixed into the dough, lending it a rich slightly smoky flavour. Max followed Sidorov's lead and piled his high with sour cream and jam, enjoying the contrast of sour and sweet. Lightly spiced sausages and a melange of fried potatoes and onions finished off the meal. The coffee was strong and hot. Sidorov took his black but Max added a healthy dollop of cream to his.

They ate mostly in silence. Max suspected Sidorov would have preferred to read his book but was too polite to do so.

"If you didn't kill St. John, who did?" Max asked as he wiped up the last of the cream and jam with a final morsel of sirniki.

"I will not bow to cliché and blame the Whites, though I'm sure they weren't nearly so delicate. Have you heard of a man named Andrew Locke?"

"Yes. He was killed in a similar way in Zurich. General Chernsky all but admitted to the crime."

"Really?" Sidorov looked puzzled.

"They claimed you killed St. John using the same method in order to cast suspicion on them."

This time Sidorov guffawed, drawing stares from neighbouring tables.

"How beautiful! Like a plot from Dostoyevsky. Admit to one crime in order to prove your innocence in another. The logic is so twisted; it has the ring of truth. Someone may well have copied Locke's murder, but it wasn't me. I swear on my father's grave."

"Then who?"

"Someone with an intimate knowledge of our struggle, who knew enough of Locke's murder to copy it."

"Who could that be, other than Pavlovna and yourself?"

"I'm afraid I haven't been clear. I knew of Locke's death, that's all. And I've never been to Zurich. The Cheka operates in compartments. Only Dzerzhinsky, the head in Moscow, knows what every cell is doing. If someone found out the details of this murder, it had to come from the other side. You need to ask yourself who in Paris has ties to the Whites."

Max shook his head. It made no sense. As near as he could tell, the Russians stuck to themselves, though surely there were sympathizers to their cause that Max knew nothing about. Harvey had mentioned no-one in his reports.

Asper, of course, had some ties to the Russian community, but Max doubted he had the stomach or the skill to arrange St. John's murder. Federov had implied he was working for the American embassy and Ginger Buchan hadn't denied it. Colonel Ledux had insinuated that the Americans may have decided St. John's activities ran counter to their interests, but Max couldn't believe his friend Buchan was somehow involved.

"You seem like a smart young man, someone who can tell the winning side when he sees it. You know these Whites better than I. I can pay you well for any information on their activities."

"I thought their defeat was inevitable."

"It is. But think of the lives that can be saved if they meet their fate earlier rather than later. I can pay you in gold. Untraceable. And for now, still valuable."

Max wanted to tell Sidorov what to do with his gold. *But I may need to talk to him again*, thought Max. *He might not be so easy to find if I reject him outright.*

"I'll consider your offer. How can I reach you again?"

Sidorov removed a card from his billfold and slid it across the table. "I keep a mailbox at this hotel. I check it twice a day. Suggest a location and a time and I'll meet you within the day."

§

Max walked over to Parc Monceau, a green haven between the 17th and 8th arrondissements. He bought a flavored ice at one of the many stands that clustered near the park's entrance and listened to the music from the small carousel. The laughter of the children as they rode the colorful animals lifted his spirits.

He strolled beside the large pond with its faux Roman colonnade until he reached the monument that marked the first successful parachute landing. He found it hard to imagine that someone would willingly jump from the basket of a hot air balloon, trusting his life to the strength of a canopy of silk and the vagaries of the wind.

Was he truly any closer to solving the murder of Mark St. John? The two Russian factions each accused the other while everyone else pointed their finger at Pierre Armand.

I've been sloppy, Max thought, *allowed my feelings for Sarah St. John and Irina Pavlovna to cloud my judgment – to distract me from the investigation. I see that now – I suppose I have Jacqueline to thank for that. So many threads to this case, it's hard to hold them all in my hands. The ones I've dropped could be the ones that lead me to the killer.*

He sat on a bench, the same one he had stopped at several weeks before, and took out his journal. His notes were a jumble; he needed to give some order to them.

Mark St. John had been murdered during the second week of May and his naked body dumped in the Luxembourg gardens.

At about the same time, another man, Paul Ponant, had also been shot and his body, and the car that contained it, had been dumped in the Seine. He had forgotten about Ponant. The only connection were the date and the similarity of the wounds but, still, it was a lead he should have followed up.

Sarah St. John had arrived in Paris a few days before her husband's death – ostensibly to meet with Denis Jourdain and resume their love affair. Why, after so many years? And which of them had taken the initiative? Did it matter? Was it simply a convenient cover to murder her husband? If so, had Jourdain been involved?

St. John had a business relationship with Pierre Armand. They may have shared political views as well. In any case Armand was connected to the Camelots du roi and, therefore, Paul Ponant.

Someone had stolen money from Jacopo Giamatti, who was either an Italian gangster or a fascista or both. He was connected to Michel Tourangeau, a man with close ties to the French right. They both were linked to Armand but claimed to think he was a thief. Was it Armand or St. John who stole the money? The French deputy,

Martel, implied it was St. John. He also implied he knew who the killer was.

St. John was linked to Irina Pavlovna. He had certainly shared her bed, but their relationship was far from romantic. He had supplied money to support her cause. Its source was unclear but likely came from the Italians. Armand, too, had a link to the Russians, having sold arms to Denidov.

The White Russians had killed Andrew Locke in Zurich. The method mirrored St. John's death. They accused the Cheka agent, Sidorov. His accusations were more subtle. Only someone who knew the details of Locke's murder could have copied it. Fedorov might have told Buchan. The alternative would be someone with connections to the highest levels of the new Bolshevik government.

A Frenchman had hired the group of Russians that attacked him. Was their motive to kill him or scare him off? Or simply distract him from the obvious answer?

Mark St. John had been murdered for a reason. Love, money or politics. If he knew the motive, he would know the killer. Perhaps he had been going about this the wrong way. Instead of trying to find proof for one particular motive, he should try to find proof that would eliminate the other two.

Everyone said Armand was the key. He knows about the money and he almost certainly knows about Ponant. It was time he paid the little businessman another visit.

§

Max decided to stop at his apartment to retrieve the 5-shot revolver he kept in the bottom of his sock drawer. Armand wasn't likely to pose a threat but he seemed to have ready access to those who might. Max doubted he could shoot someone but Armand – or his cronies – couldn't know that.

Jacopo Giamatti called to him from the café across the street when Max emerged, the familiar weight of the revolver weighing down his jacket pocket. Max ducked behind a lumbering delivery van and joined the Italian. Giamatti was drinking a pastis and Max ordered a small beer to be sociable.

"Have you spoken to our friend, Armand, yet?"

"I was on my way when you called me over," said Max.

"No hurry. He's coming in on the last train from Marseilles tonight."

"You're well informed."

"That's what they pay me for."

"Where's your friend, Tourangeau?"

Giamatti looked sour and ordered another pastis. "Michel's affections are exchangeable for cash. I haven't seen him since the last time we spoke."

That didn't sound right to Max. He had no doubt Tourangeau was untrustworthy; his behavior toward Bucard had demonstrated that. But why would he disappear now?

"Are you sure it was Armand who stole your money?" asked Max.

"Who else could have...?" Giamatti's voice trailed off. He laughed. "Brilliant tactics. Sow discord among your enemies."

"Armand is rich. Why would he steal from you?"

"Some people can't resist." Nonetheless, he looked thoughtful. "Do you have any other likely suspects?"

"Mark St. John gave a lot of money to Irina Pavlovna. No one can say for sure where it came from."

"Sure. Armand steals our money and gives it to his friend, St. John. He turns it over to the Russians."

"Who then use the money to buy weapons from Armand. A nice tight circle."

"Exactly."

"Except... who then had a motive to kill St. John? Not the White Russians, not Armand. They both need St. John. For protective cover if nothing else."

"The Bolsheviks. The Whites have their bodyguards. It might be easier to cut the conduit then go after them."

Max took a sip of his beer and watched Giamatti over the rim of the glass. The Italian turned away, not willing to meet Max's eyes. The alternative was obvious. Armand, too, was well protected by his own people and by the French police. "Cutting the conduit" might be a tactic Giamatti's bosses, whoever they were, would approve. That could explain Ponant's involvement and subsequent death.

"Did you know a man called Paul Ponant?"

"I know a lot of people," said Giamatti. He signalled the waiter for a third pastis. "Bring me a tray of charcuterie while you're at it."

"He was a Camelot du Roi. He was shot the same way as St. John."

"That guy. I read about that in the papers."

"The car he was in wound up in the Seine. There's not much left to look at after things have been in the river for ten days."

"I don't like the direction this conversation is going. I already told you I had nothing to do with this St. John's death. And I didn't know this Ponant from nothing."

"Tourangeau might know something. Maybe you could ask him if you see him again."

"Yeah. You never answered my question – about other suspects. Who else might have stolen our money?"

Giamatti isn't a fool, thought Max. *But neither am I. As long as I think St. John might have been killed over money, I'll keep my counsel. Too many innocents could be hurt if I'm wrong.*

"I was... fishing. But I'll be certain to ask Armand when I see him." Max finished his beer and threw a couple of francs on the table. He didn't want to be beholden to this man for anything.

"Tell me how that works out," said Giamatti. "Michel being gone changes nothing. Muscle is easy to find."

§

Freed from tracking down Armand – he would surprise him at home in the morning – Max walked over to Chez Jake. The troublesome police sergeant had been reassigned to another district; his replacement was drinking coffee with Jake and Smitty. There were smiles all around. The day's mail was mostly routine. Only two items were of any interest.

Jacqueline was in Marseilles. She had seen Joseph Asper though they hadn't spoken. "He's living the high life with your money. I never trusted that snake; neither should you." She went on to report that the Action Française was particularly active in the city; their vigilantes had a freer hand than in Paris. Most of her anarchist friends were urging her to return to the relative safety of Paris. Max, for one, hoped she would heed their advice.

Her final bit of news was the most interesting, if least understandable. Pierre Armand had been publicly disowned by his brother who claimed he was "wasting the family fortune" on reprehensible "political adventures." Given that the brother, Gregoire, was high up in the local wing of the Camelots, it was confusing what Armand's actions entailed.

A handwritten note from "Gaston D" offered to meet Max at a café in the 4th arrondissement on Wednesday the 24th in order to collect "the reward" offered. He would he said, "be sitting outside and wearing a white carnation in his lapel." Max's poster campaign had finally had an effect, though the delay would certainly cut it close.

Max dashed off a quick note to Jacqueline thanking her for the news and urging her swift return to Paris. On his way out of the bar, he asked Smitty if he could accompany him to his rendezvous with Deschamps. If his suspicions were correct, he might need a little extra muscle. He then headed over to Le Coq Bleu to grab some supper and to hear what Henri had to report.

"Thank God you've come," said Yesim, when Max came through the door. "Henri was supposed to come by to help me at lunch. He didn't show up. When I sent to his house to see if he was well, his neighbour told the boy, they saw him get into a black sedan last night. He never came home."

Eighteen – Wednesday to Friday, June 17-19th, 1920

Henri still had not made an appearance the next morning, which had dawned gray and cool and gotten worse as the day progressed. Max had checked all his usual haunts – a couple of restaurants near Gare du Nord that he frequented when he wanted a break from Yesim's cooking and a social club where some of his old cronies hung out playing dominoes or cards. No-one had seen him for several days. More ominously, he hadn't reported for his morning shift at the train station.

Max filled out a report and dropped it at the Prefecture.

"Henri hasn't missed a day of work in fifteen years," Max told LePêcheur, when the desk sergeant seemed unconcerned. "Something must have happened to him."

LePêcheur promised him he would look into the matter himself and come by Le Coq Bleu at the end of his shift to let them know what he had discovered. Reassured, Max headed for Armand's place in the Marais to conduct his own line of inquiry.

Armand was enjoying a late breakfast when his man ushered Max into the dining room. Despite his early annoyance about being disturbed at home, he was polite, even welcoming.

"I wondered when I might see you again," said Armand, after Max had taken a seat and the manservant had served him coffee and an assortment of pastries. "That will be all, Caron."

Caron nodded and backed out of the room, his icy glare never once leaving Max's face.

"Don't mind Caron," said Armand. "He's been with the family for years. He'd glare at me if he thought he could get away with it."

"I understand you've had a bit of a disagreement with your family."

"You are well informed. My brother has strong views and is more than happy to express them to anyone who will listen. His opinions are seldom backed up by facts. As for his understanding of business and wealth creation, if our father had been like Gregoire, there would have been no family fortune to waste."

"I take it he doesn't approve of your dealings with Baron Denidov."

"I really should consider employing you," said Armand, looking genuinely amused. "Gregoire would be thrilled about it if he knew. What bothers him is that I'm equally happy selling arms to the Bolsheviks or any other cash customer."

"Does it matter where the cash comes from?"

"I didn't steal Jacopo's money."

"Did Mark St. John?"

"How would I know? Though it would certainly explain his death if he did. Mark had sources of his own."

"He wasn't a rich man."

"No, but he knew plenty who were. Both here and in America. Until a few months ago, every allied country except Italy had troops fighting the Bolsheviks or supporting those who were. If Mark St. John wanted to funnel money from America to the Whites, do you think anyone in the American Embassy would stop him? I'd be surprised if they weren't bringing it over themselves in diplomatic pouches."

Armnd was now the third person to suggest the American government might be directly involved in St. John's schemes, and therefore, his death. *Maybe it's time I had another chat with Ginger Buchan.* Time to switch gears.

"Did you know Paul Ponant?"

"I knew of him, enough to know his body was hauled out of the Seine. Is he connected to this?"

"Perhaps. I think he helped move St. John's body to the park and was rewarded with a bullet in the head."

"It fits. I made some inquiries. Ponant disappeared the day before St. John's body was found. He was considered... unreliable by the high command."

"Because of his previous anarchist leanings?"

"There was that. Many thought he still had connections on the left. A few thought he might be a police agent. They all thought he was too in love with the cane and the knife. Violence can be addictive."

Armand's hand hovered over the remaining pastries before selecting a thick slice of brioche. He dropped a spoonful of raspberry jam in the middle and then carefully spread it with the back of the spoon until it formed a thin layer across the entire surface. He took a bite and chewed it slowly before putting the rest on his plate.

"He had a girlfriend. Not French. American. She lives in the 8th, near Parc Monceau. She works as a dresser in one of the Grands Magasins. I have both addresses if you want to speak to her."

"You're being very helpful."

"Why not? Mark was my partner. My friend in many respects. If I didn't kill him, I would want him avenged. And if I did, wouldn't I do whatever it took to send you looking elsewhere?"

"I couldn't have put it better myself," said Max.

§

Clouds hung close over the city, trapping the oppressive heat. The Metro was even hotter, but Max couldn't waste time walking the dozen blocks to the Place Concorde. None of the handful of reasons he could imagine for Henri's absence suggested good news. Yesim and a few of the regulars were checking the hospitals but had turned up nothing yet. LePêcheur would put out the word to the "swallows" who patrolled the streets but there were simply too many narrow ways and dark spaces, even in modern Paris, for them to search them all. Max still held out hope that Henri was alive, a victim of kidnapping rather than murder.

Max was almost certain that Henri had been taken to get at him. The question was, by whom? Martel seemed the most likely suspect. Henri had been making inquiries about him. Perhaps he had found something so serious, so illegal, that Martel had decided to handle things himself rather than risk calling in his allies in the Prefecture. He shuddered to think what a man like Martel might do if he were too afraid to rely on the law.

Giamatti and Tourangeau, acting together or alone, were his second choice. They had both threatened him, with little result. They may have decided it would be more effective to threaten his friends. At least, then, Henri would still be alive. A dead hostage was of little use.

Given his previous difficulties, Max was surprised to find Martel at his office in the Chamber of Deputies and available to see him.

"I am a public figure," he said when they were both settled in his oak-panelled office. Max had refused an offer of brandy but Martel hadn't denied himself. "My life is an open book. I assure you nothing your elderly assistant could have turned up from the porters or concierges of Paris would give me any concern."

"A hidden mistress, perhaps?"

"My mistress is discreet but hardly hidden. For a French politician not to have a mistress would be far more suspicious. I would immediately be suspected of unnatural practices."

"A deal gone wrong."

"You are stabbing in the dark. Mr. Anderson, I can see you are worried about your friend. It's admirable I'm sure, but perhaps you should have thought of that before you placed an old man in harm's way."

Nothing makes you madder than the truth, thought Max, clenching his jaw to hold back a response.

"When did your friend go missing?" asked Martel.

"Monday afternoon or early evening." The eyewitnesses, as usual, differed in their accounts.

"There you have it then," said Martel, smiling. "I wasn't even in the city."

"And you have proof of that?"

"I'm hardly required to account for myself to every adventurer who wanders in off the street. But there is no harm in it. I was at the country estate of Denis Jourdain from Sunday evening until late last night."

"Jourdain? You didn't mention that on Sunday."

"Don't be stupid. We are not friends, nor confidants. Besides, I only received Denis' invitation after I arrived home."

"What did you discuss?"

"Really, Mr. Anderson. You are growing tiresome." Martel lifted the receiver of the telephone on his desk and mumbled a few words. A few seconds later, Martel's assistant, backed by a stout man in the uniform of the congressional guard, appeared to show Max out.

As they walked down the corridor to the main exit, a commotion in a side hall drew Max's attention. In the brief instant it took to pass the entrance, he saw Denis Jourdain, shaking his fist in the face of Gennady Sidorov.

§

The brief encounter with Martel left Max uneasy and restless. His absence from Paris only indicated he had not been personally involved in Henri's disappearance. A man like Martel would have countless associates, endless favours he could call in at a moment's notice. His explanation had been glib, his alibi too easy to check to be false.

It was odd that it should be Jourdain who provided that alibi, though, on second thought, why wouldn't a go-between be involved in deals that crossed party lines? For all the public bluster, most politicians were pragmatists. As an avowed moderate, Jourdain might well be willing to cut deals with the centrists in the Bloc National if it would protect his flank from the more radical elements of his own party.

He needed a new perspective, a different way of looking at recent events. Perhaps a man who couldn't see at all could give it to him.

Colonel Ledux received Max in the same room as before; it was undoubtedly his office and command centre, whatever other purpose it might serve. He was seated in the same wingback chair, a cigarette in one hand and a glass of sherry in the other. A crystal decanter and a second glass were on the table next to the brass cigarette case.

"Help yourself. It will help settle your lunch."

"I haven't eaten yet."

"Then it will improve your appetite. I dislike drinking alone."

Max poured himself an ounce or two; when he had tasted it, he wished he had poured more. "It's very good."

"It's older than half the men I commanded during the war. I import it by the barrel from Jerez. I take it you haven't found Mark's killer yet."

"I'm not sure I'm closer than when last we spoke."

"What has the American embassy told you about Mark St. John?"

"Nothing extraordinary." *That was true enough,* thought Max, *but only because I haven't had the nerve to ask hard questions.*

"I suppose not." Ledux crossed and uncrossed his legs, took a long drag on his cigarette. Smoke drifted from his nose and curled in lazy ringlets around his face and hair.

"I don't think the Russians did it," said Max. "At least not Irina Pavlovna or her crowd. I'm not so sure about the Bolsheviks. The Whites had nothing to gain by Mark's death – he was unlikely to betray them and was providing cash for their operations. I'm inclined to think that Pierre Armand wasn't directly involved either – though I wouldn't risk my own money in a wager."

"Armand would sell his mother for a few francs, but you may be right. Who are your suspects? Leave no one out."

"In order of likelihood: a couple of gangsters, one Italian, one French, who thought Mark had stolen gang money; a Bolshevik spy who opposed his helping the White cause; Armand, if Mark was stealing from him; Pavlovna if she thought Mark was a turncoat; and an unknown American agent for unknown reasons, though that seems unlikely. Mark stopped working for the American government more than five years ago."

"Don't be so sure."

"Then there's Jean Martel."

"Martel? The deputy? What involvement could he have in Mark's death?"

"He was a friend of Mark's, though it seems it was a friendship of convenience for both of them. Martel claims he advised Mark how to make his relationship with Armand 'more profitable.' Even if he didn't do it, it's possible he knows who did."

"But named no names."

"The information would be too valuable to give away, he said, without admitting he had it."

"That sounds like Martel. I know him slightly. We travelled in similar circles, when I travelled at all." Ledux stubbed out the remains of his cigarette and lit another. He made a circling motion with his hand and Max poured them another glass of the excellent sherry. "He was notorious for being able to close deals no one else could even propose. They say his files on the rich and powerful rival the Prefecture of Police."

"Blackmail."

"In politics, it's referred to as bargaining chips." Ledux's chortle ended in a fit of coughing. He recovered and wiped his mouth with the sleeve of his jacket. "I took gas during the war. Never been the same since."

"I shouldn't impose on you like this," said Max, rising.

"No, sit down. I... I don't get many visitors these days."

No one wanted to be reminded of the War. Ledux had nothing left except his memories. He wore them on his breast and in the blankness of his gaze. Fame, family, money – none could protect you from being relegated to the past. Max settled back and took another sip of sherry.

"Haven't you forgotten the most likely suspect of them all? Sarah St. John?"

"I haven't forgotten her. But she is my client. I wouldn't be working for her if I thought she was guilty."

"Are you sure? Sarah is a lovely woman."

Max was glad Ledux couldn't see the flush that was heating his face. "She's ten years older than me."

"Of course," said Ledux. "Still, a jealous woman or a possessive lover."

"Jourdain?"

"Why not?"

"I don't get that sense from him. Frankly, he seems like a cold fish."

"He's passionate enough about the damned working class. Have you heard him speak?"

"Once."

"What do you want from me?" asked Ledux. "I see hardly anyone. I can't go out. I have the nurse read the morning paper. Otherwise, I am a relic in a museum."

"You knew St. John from before. Any insight you could provide might be the key to the whole thing."

Ledux leaned back in his chair, his eyes closed and his fingers steepled in front of him. After a few minutes, he said, "Mark was still in love with Sarah."

"How do you know that?"

"He told me. Right in this very room. He came to see me a few days before his death."

"What?"

"He swore me to secrecy. It is painful to me to break that promise."

"Why would Mark St. John confess his love for his wife to you?"

Ledux shook his head. "That was incidental to the discussion. He had come to seek my advice. We had known each other for nearly fifteen years – had maintained a correspondence until my... injury... made it too difficult. I knew as much about Russia as anyone in Paris. I was stationed in St. Petersburg before the 1905 revolution and again after I returned from America. I knew them all, Tsar Nicholas, Tsereteli, the Menshevik leader, Lenin and his cronies. He wanted my advice on how far he could trust Irina Pavlovna."

"What did you suggest?"

"I suggested that he stop dealing with Russians. Have you ever heard of nesting dolls?"

Max nodded. He had seen them in the shops around the Petrograd, brightly painted wooden dolls that opened to reveal ever smaller replicas within.

"It is the perfect expression of the Russian character," said Ledux. "Whenever you think you have reached past their façade, all you find is another façade. They consider their souls far too precious to reveal to strangers or, perhaps, even to themselves. Even now, after the great revolution, Russians haven't changed. Mark my words, these Commissars will prove no different than the Barons and Tsars they have replaced. I told him that and quite a bit more, things that I would rather not repeat to you, unless absolutely necessary. I'm afraid I was quite harsh in the end."

"I take it Mark didn't take your advice."

"No. Though I think he took it to heart. It was when he was leaving that he mentioned Sarah. I said, half in jest, that Irina Pavlovna was a dangerous woman to love. He laughed, a cold bitter laugh. 'We may share a cause, even occasionally a bed, but there's nothing more to it than that. There never could be. Despite everything, I still love my wife. But there's no future there. I made sure of that a long time ago.' Those were the last words he ever spoke to me."

"Did your conversation touch on a man named Sidorov?"

"Not directly. Mark had heard the Bolsheviks were growing interested in Pavlovna's operation and had dispatched a man to investigate. I knew Sidorov from some of my few remaining contacts at military intelligence; he was reported to be on his way here via Vienna. He was not someone who would come all the way to Paris to spy on a few dissolute aristocrats."

"Why else?"

"No-one seemed to know. But I would guess it has something to do with the current flirtation between Moscow and the Socialist Party."

§

Yesim had not returned to Le Coq Bleu and Suzanne had no word of his whereabouts or his search for their friend, Henri. Max ate an early supper in the hopes that Yesim, or better yet, Henri, might turn up but, after an hour, he gave up and headed over to his office. Jake said "he knew some people who knew some people" that might be able to help. Max didn't want to know the details – some of Jake's contacts were not too healthy to know – but asked him to do what he could.

The next day Max went in search of Isabelle Grassie, Ponant's American girlfriend. The floor manager at the Galleries LaFayette looked down his considerable nose at Max's business card before announcing in clipped tones that Mademoiselle Grassie had failed to make an appearance for her last three shifts and was at risk of dismissal if she missed another.

The concierge at Grassie's rooming house, a bottle-blonde of middle years, ran her eyes over Max's body before granting him what he was sure she thought was a winsome smile.

"Isabelle is in and out so often, I can't keep track," she said. "But you're welcome to wait for her in my apartment."

"Try to remember: when did you see her last?"

The woman rolled her eyes upward, the way people do when they're trying to recover an unimportant detail. "It was three, no, four days ago. She came tearing down the stairs, almost knocked me over while I was mopping the step and climbed into the back of one of those automobiles. It was grey or silver and long."

"And she hasn't been back?"

"How should I know? She keeps odd hours and I have a life of my own. Her rent is paid until the end of the month. Does she owe you money? Or are you one of those men who can't leave their exes alone?"

"Neither. Miss Grassie is a key witness in a case I'm investigating."

The concierge took a step back, blocking the narrow doorway to the house. "Are you a police officer?"

"A private detective," said Max.

"Like in Leroux's novels?"

"Yeah," said Max, flinching at the comparison. Leroux was one of Henri's favorites, a sensational and occasionally brilliant writer of lurid crime stories.

"I've never met a detective before," she said. The smile was back.

"Maybe I could take a look at her room?"

"Why not? If she knows something important..." The concierge turned sideways, leaving barely enough room for Max to squeeze past her, his chest brushing her ample bosom. Her eau de toilette was floral, but her breath smelled faintly of garlic.

"Well come on then," she said, patting his rear in encouragement, "Her room is on the third floor."

Max led the way up the narrow stairway with the concierge close on his heels, chattering amiably about the decline in the morality of Parisians since the arrival of American tourists *en masse*. It wasn't clear if she approved or disapproved.

"That's her, at the end of the hall on the left," said the woman, pulling a ring of keys from her pocket. "Odd. It's ajar. What a careless girl."

"No," said Max. "The lock's been broken. Stay here."

"Gladly." The woman stepped back, clutching the keys in her hand like a weapon.

The door swung easily on its hinges. The lock had been solid; the doorframe less so. Splinters of wood were scattered in front of the door where a jimmy had pried apart the mechanism. That they were still there after three or four days and the fact no one had reported what must have been a noisy operation told him all he needed to know about the rooming house and the kind of people who lived there.

The small room beyond was a shambles. The narrow bed had been turned over and the mattress slashed open. Drawers were ripped from the small dresser and their contents scattered across the bare wood floor. The dresser itself, along with the small night table, was pushed over. Broken glass sparkled in the pale sunlight.

Dresses from the closet were piled in a heap to one side of the narrow curtain that separated it from the room and several pairs of shoes were pushed into a jumble to one side. The searchers had even pried up a few of the floorboards and pulled the small gas heater away from the wall. At least they hadn't broken the gas pipe; there would be nothing left to investigate if they had.

There was no way to know what they had been searching for or whether they had found it. It might have nothing to do with the murder of Ponant or St. John but Max doubted it. On Sunday or Monday, the girl had gotten into a car and been driven away. She hadn't been seen since. The same thing had happened to Henri. It was all too much of a coincidence for there to be nothing behind it.

Nineteen – Saturday and Sunday, June 20-21st, 1920

Max spent all of Friday going over the same ground Yesim and his cronies had already covered. It was no use. No one had seen Henri since he climbed into the back of a car outside his house. A few of the porters repeated what they had told his friend. Martel was right; there was little scandalous or surprising in any of their gossip. Certainly nothing that pointed to the politician as anything more than what he appeared: a sharp operator with an eye to his own advantage.

Yet Max was almost certain that Martel was involved in Henri's disappearance or knew who was. The girl was a puzzle. Who besides Armand knew she had been Ponant's paramour? In any case, his body had been fished out of the Seine weeks ago. Why had she disappeared now? If the two kidnappings, as Max now thought of them, were connected, what was the link?

The one useful bit of information was Martel's Parisian address, a small house on a side street not far from the Place de la Concorde. Saturday morning, Max found a café where he could see the gated entrance of the building half a block away. He was finishing his second coffee when a long grey sedan stopped in front of the gate, which swung open to allow access. The gate did not close again, signalling either that Martel would soon depart again or that he was expecting visitors.

The car that had taken the girl had been grey, if the concierge was to be believed, though witnesses to Henri's disappearance had agreed that car had been black, though they had disagreed on almost every other detail.

Max waited another twenty minutes before paying his bill and sauntering down the street to the still open gates. The grey car was pulled over to one side and a uniformed chauffeur leaned against the driver's door, smoking a thin cigarette. The man glanced at Max as he passed but made no effort to speak to him or bar his way.

Martel answered the door himself. He was dressed in a dark morning suit, a maroon cravat tied loosely about his throat.

"Oh, it's you."

"You were expecting someone else."

"I still am. This isn't a good time."

"I won't take long."

Martel frowned and glanced at the driver. Max heard the scrap of his boot on stone and the faint creak of metal as the man stood away from the car. Max's shoulders tensed but he didn't shift his gaze from Martel's face. If there was an attack it would start with a signal from the politician.

"Very well," said Martel, assuming his practiced and artificial smile. "Ask your questions."

"Do you know Isabelle Grassie?"

"I know who you mean."

Max had expected a flat denial; Martel's response left him momentarily speechless.

"Don't look so surprised. I make it my business to know every transient who passes through Paris."

"I find that hard to..."

Martel laughed. "It's the kind of answer you deserve, showing up at my private residence and asking stupid questions. I had lunch with

Pierre Armand yesterday. He told me he had sent you on a wild goose chase. Though perhaps the goose proved tame after all."

"She was seen getting into a car on Sunday or Monday. She hasn't been seen since. Someone broke into her apartment and tore it apart. What they were looking for, and whether they found it, is uncertain."

"Why ask me about her? I was barely aware of Ponant; I never heard of the girlfriend until Armand mentioned her yesterday."

"The car she got into was a long grey sedan," Max jerked his head in the direction of the car, "like that one."

"It might well have been exactly like that one – it was part of a custom lot produced by Citreön. I believe there are seven others like it in Paris. Not to mention the hundreds of other grey cars rumbling over the cobblestones of the city. And as you may recall, I was out of town on Sunday and Monday."

"And did you drive to Jourdain's country house?"

"What?"

"Did you take this car to see your colleague?"

Martel's face blanked and his eyes focussed on a point over Max's shoulder. This time Max did turn but whatever or whoever Martel had been staring at through the open gateway was now gone. When Max turned back, the smile was back on Martel's face.

"As a matter of fact, no. The roads in that part of France are still terrible. I took the train. Jourdain sent a carriage to pick me up. The car was here. Feel free to question Francis before you go. Now, if you will excuse me."

Martel didn't wait for Max's reply before closing the door in his face. Francis, of course, had nothing to add.

§

Max took the Metro to the Marais and walked from the station to the hotel where Giamatti had been staying. Max doubted the Italian was still in residence but it was the only lead he had. Giamatti, on the other hand, seemed to know the location of all of Max's hangouts. The need for operatives was becoming increasingly apparent, if he were to continue in the detective business.

Max was in too much of a hurry to wait for his informant, Alain the bell hop, to make an appearance in the back. Instead, he went straight to the front desk, slid a twenty franc note across the counter to the assistant manager. The bill disappeared into the man's waistcoat and he spoke into a cone attached by a tube to the wall. A few seconds later, Alain appeared from a room in the back.

"Five minutes," said the manager. Alain nodded and followed Max onto the street.

"Mr. Giamatti checked out a few days ago," said Alain before Max could ask. "I got a copy of his forwarding address when Mr. LeBoeuf wasn't watching."

Alain was taking to the detective business like a swallow to a cliffside, thought Max. *I may not need to look far for operatives after all.* He examined the slip of paper. Giamatti had come up in the world; he was now ensconced at Le Meurice, one of the finest hotels on the Rue de Rivoli. It was also, coincidentally or not, the favorite watering hole of Andre Bucard.

Max peeled another twenty from the roll in his pocket and then added ten more. "I don't suppose you know anyone who works at Le Meurice."

"My second cousin, Jean-Jacques, works in the kitchen, but he knows everyone from the manager on down. Monsieur Giamatti has a suite on the third floor overlooking the Tuileries. He isn't there much but, when he is, he's usually in the company of a big tough-looking Frenchman."

Michel or his replacement, thought Max, handing over another twenty. Alain's eyes almost popped out of his head. *It's probably the most money he's ever had in his hand at one time*, thought Max.

"Good work, Alain."

Max dropped into Le Meurice but, according to the front desk, Giamatti was not currently at the hotel. They refused to say when he had left or speculate when he might return. The assistant manager merely sneered at the fifty-franc note Max slid across the desk. He wasn't prepared to see what it would take to break through his code of silence. Besides, he had better and cheaper informants a twenty-minute walk across the Pont Royal.

Harvey was at his usual place at a sidewalk table of one of the dozen cafés that littered the Boulevard St. Germain. Max sometimes wondered how they all kept in business, though he supposed the recent influx of Americans had helped the balance sheets of most of them. The old journalist was sober, at least by the liberal standards Harvey sat for himself, but he still had most of a bottle of red wine sitting in front of him so that condition wasn't likely to last.

"Celebrating?" asked Max as he slipped into a seat opposite. The wine was a better vintage than Harvey usually drank.

Harvey smiled wanly. "Sold a piece to the New Yorker about the American renaissance in Paris. Thought I'd treat myself before the landlord stopped by for the back rent." He signalled the waiter for a second glass.

The wine was good, full bodied without being too tannic. It left a velvet aftertaste on the back of his tongue. Max nodded his appreciation and took a second sip.

"My friend, Henri La Chance, has disappeared. He was looking into the background of the deputy, Martel, and I suspect he was kidnapped. Martel has an alibi but I'm sure he has agents who could operate on his behalf."

"Martel has nothing to hide," said Harvey. "Believe me I've looked. I always thought a man that connected had to have skeletons in his closet. He doesn't seem to have a closet."

"A life like an open book? I suppose if you have no secrets, you can't be blackmailed."

"Oh, Martel has plenty of secrets. They just aren't his own, if you catch my drift."

"The secret to his success as a go-between."

"A go-between, a fixer, a man who makes problems go away."

"And gets paid well for his efforts? I've seen his house and car."

Harvey looked sour and poured himself another glass of wine. "His family has business interests in Brittany, factories that survived the war and have prospered since. Whether that's the source of his income or simply a front is difficult to tell. The Prefecture is notorious for turning a blind eye to deputies' private affairs."

"You have your doubts about Martel's innocence."

"Never confuse transparency for honesty," said Harvey. "The man is a villain. He places his party first and himself second. Everything else – the people, the state – come in a distant third. I have no doubt Martel would commit the vilest crimes if it suited his interests. All I said is there is no evidence that he ever has. His life, as you say, is an open book, but it may still be a work of fiction."

"Then he may have been involved in Henri's kidnapping after all."

Harvey shook his head. "I doubt it. Unless your friend is a better investigator than either of us."

Henri is smart and he certainly knows the city, but I doubt he could have uncovered anything that would threaten Martel.

"Is Pierre Armand married?"

Harvey seemed taken aback by the sudden change of direction. He consulted one of his notebooks before replying. "A widower. His wife died eight years ago. He hasn't remarried, though I'm sure he could find someone if he wanted. He may be short on inches but he's not short of funds. Money is a tremendous aphrodisiac. Why?"

"I'm not sure. Everyone involved in this case seems to have both wife and mistress; I wondered why Armand is the exception."

Harvey looked as if he had something to say but thought better of it. He finished his glass of wine and poured another. *At this rate*, thought Max, *Harvey won't make it through lunch let alone the afternoon.*

"Did you find out anything more about Armand's relationship with the Russians?"

"Have you met Gennady Sidorov?" When Max nodded, Harvey added, "So have I, though I can't say I enjoyed the experience. He's all smiles and Russian affability, but there is something ugly underneath."

Max didn't disagree. Sidorov claimed to have come to Paris after St. John was killed, but Max wasn't sure. The Paris police were world-renowned for their system of tracking immigrants, but even the finest net could miss a fish or two. "What does Sidorov have to do with Armand?"

"The new Soviet government is sitting on a pile of Tsarist gold. But gold doesn't win wars and they are fighting on numerous fronts. Armand is an arms dealer."

"He hates the Bolsheviks."

"Yes, and I'm sure selling to them is a terrible strain, but gold is a tremendous soother for the nerves."

Every time I turn around, someone presents me with a new theory. Harvey drained his glass and, after a half-hearted offer of a refill to Max, emptied the rest of the bottle. He sat the dead soldier between them and gazed at it mournfully. Max made no move to buy another.

"Are you suggesting Sidorov had something to do with Henri's disappearance?"

Harvey looked thoughtful. "In a way. I told you Martel had nothing to hide. But what about the people whose secrets he holds? If Armand were selling guns to the Soviets, he wouldn't want it widely known. And Sidorov wouldn't want the deal soured."

"But that doesn't explain the disappearance of Isabelle Grassie."

"Who?"

Max quickly explained her possible connection to St. John's murder. Including what Martel had said about it being a "wild goose chase."

"If she was Ponant's girl friend, maybe she knew who killed him, who killed St. John."

"But why wait so long to go after her?"

"Maybe she didn't know she knew and only figured it out when she was going through his things. Or maybe she was scared and only worked up her nerve to try blackmail after she figured she was safe." Harvey rocked his glass back and forth on the teble.

"I suppose. Though why did Armand send me to find her now, at the moment of her disappearance. It seems too big a coincidence to be real."

"Ask him."

That was the problem with this case, thought Max. It was all a matter of conjecture and accusation. He said, she said, they said. Everyone had a theory, but no one seemed to have any concrete evidence. The gun that killed St. John and Ponant, assuming it was the same one, had long since disappeared, probably at the bottom of the Seine. There were no objective witnesses, no notebooks full of incriminating evidence, no hidden letters, no telltale clues. If he were going to solve this case, someone would have to slip up. Or someone would have to confess. But how do you make someone do that?

"You were going to give me some more money," said Harvey softly.

"For what? What you have wouldn't even pass for a rumour."

"I was holding this back. For next time. But..."

"Go on."

"I have a friend in the Socialist party, several in fact. They tell me that Sidorov has been holding meetings with some of the left caucus, men who want to align themselves with Lenin's new Socialist International. He and Jourdain had a run-in."

"I saw them arguing at the Chamber of Deputies."

"It wasn't the only time. Jourdain apparently broke in on Sidorov and some of his fellow deputies. Sidorov said something in Russian that made Jourdain go pale. No one knows what it was, but my informant says it included the name St. John. My guess is it was a threat – get out unless you want what St. John got. Something like that."

A slip up? Perhaps. It wasn't much but it was something. Max gave Harvey another three hundred francs.

"Don't drink it all in one place."

§

Max left a note at the hotel where Sidorov kept a mailbox before heading to the Russian quarter to try his luck in the many bars and cafés that Russians frequented. Even if he failed to find Sidorov, perhaps he would run into Pavlovna or some of the other Whites. He had questions for them, none urgent, but all worth asking.

First time lucky, Max found Sidorov at the same restaurant as before, lingering over coffee and a book, a thick tome with yellowing pages and green leather cover.

"More Turgenev?" asked Max, sliding into the chair opposite the Russian.

"No. The great apologist, Tolstoy." Sidorov slipped a bookmark between the pages and set the book down. "Comrade Trotsky recommends him as a window into the bourgeois soul, but I find it slow going. Turgid and convoluted."

"Perhaps that's what Comrade Trotsky meant."

Sidorov frowned, a deep crease forming between his brows. Then he laughed and nodded. "A joke. Yes. That would be in Lev's character."

"Trotsky is a hero of yours? You've mentioned him before."

"Have I? Perhaps I should be more careful. It can be dangerous to have heroes in Moscow." Sidorov gestured at his coffee cup and, when Max nodded, signalled the waiter for more. "How goes your investigation?"

"You were heard threatening Denis Jourdain."

"I'm sure you've been misinformed."

"My source was reliable. They say you mentioned Mark St. John."

"Why would I do that? I didn't know St. John. He died before I came to Paris. Besides, Jourdain is a friend of mine."

Another fact that needed checking. Buchan said that a G. Sidorov had registered with the Prefecture but hadn't mentioned a date.

"I saw you arguing with him at the Chamber of Deputies."

"People often make that mistake. We were not arguing; we were having a heated discussion. Nothing personal, merely a difference of opinion."

"Over the Socialist International?"

"What else?"

"Do you know Pierre Armand?

"Should I?"

"If you're in Paris to buy guns, as my sources suggest, you should."

"I'm a very busy man. It's a wonder I can find time to read and drink coffee with amusing young Canadians."

The waiter brought their coffee, thick dark espresso, with small chunks of crystallized sugar on the plate beside them. Max dropped a piece into the murky liquid. The spoon tinkled musically against the cup as he stirred.

"I did not kill Mark St. John. I don't know who did, although I suspect it had something to do with Pavlovna. I don't say that because she is a White but because she is Pavlovna. The woman is like a tiger. Beautiful, fierce and casually dangerous."

"Why should I believe you?"

Sidorov shrugged. "Because Captain Gereau believes me. I know you know him. The Paris Police do a remarkable job at keeping track of immigrants. I'm told people come from around the world to study their methods. Even Scotland Yard consults them on the matter, and you know how much it must pain the English to do that. I told you I wasn't here when St. John was killed. Not quite true. I was here, answering questions in the cells beneath the Prefecture. Not a pleasant experience when you have no embassy to call if things get out of hand. Not pleasant, but useful. It gives me the perfect alibi for St. John's murder. As for the rest, I don't care whether you believe me. Pavlovna's days are numbered. She will be punished soon, if not for that crime, then another. Now, if you'll excuse me, Tolstoy calls."

Sidorov opened the heavy book and held it so that it hid his face. Max would get nothing more out of him, but at least he had gotten something. One name removed from the list of suspects. He had no doubt Sidorov was telling the truth; it was too easy a thing to verify. His accusation against Pavlovna had been pro forma; it neither increased nor decreased the likelihood of her guilt.

Max thought of seeking her out but decided he'd had enough of Russians for one day. Instead, he headed back to Le Coq Bleu to see if Yesim had heard anything more of Henri's whereabouts.

The lights were out and the door locked. Max let himself in and found Yesim in the back corner of the bar nursing a brandy and staring at nothing. Max felt a painful lump start to form in his stomach as he took a seat beside his friend.

"Have you heard something?"

"No," said Yesim. He gestured at the empty bar. "I can't face it today. I'll make up your share of the lost revenues."

"He's my friend, too," said Max, resting his hand on Yesim's shoulder. "I'm sure he's all right."

"Yes. I think somehow I'd know if he were dead."

It was the first time either of them had spoken of that possibility out loud.

"I'm worried though," said Yesim, a faint smile appearing on his lips. "Henri has such a temper. What might he do if he gets the chance?"

Twenty – Monday to Tuesday, June 22-23rd, 1920

Max woke to the sound of someone pounding on his apartment door. It was barely six but already the streets of Paris were flooded with sunlight, a promise of heat to come. A bellboy from the Grand Hotel shifted nervously from foot to foot until Max had read the note from Sarah St. John and scribbled a reply. Max pressed a franc into the boy's hand and sent him scurrying back to the hotel with a promise to be there by seven if not before.

He showered quickly and donned his best morning suit and was on the street in less than fifteen minutes, his hair still damp and his stomach grumbling in complaint. He bought a pastry from a stand outside the Metro station and ate it on the train as it carried him to the stop at L'Opéra. It would have to do until he had time for a proper breakfast.

The police matron answered the door at the first knock and ushered him into the sitting room, a worried expression on her usually blank face. Sarah was pacing, clasping and unclasping her hands. Dark circles bruised her eyes and strands of hair had escaped her coiffure to dangle along her cheekbones. It did nothing to diminish her beauty.

"Oh, Max, I'm so glad you could come."

Max took her arm and guided her to the chair by the window. She looked up at him gratefully, her lips curved and slightly parted.

Her perfume mingled with the pleasant spice smell of her body; he guessed she was still wearing yesterday's clothes, had not, in fact, slept or eaten since the night before.

"Your letter didn't say much. Only that the matter couldn't wait."

"Fontaine is coming today. To take me back to jail."

"Are you sure?"

"Yes. Oh, I don't know. You know what he's like, all hints and veiled threats." Sarah slumped in the chair and, for a moment, Max thought she might faint.

"We should have breakfast," said Max. "You can tell me all about it and I'll see what can be done. Then you can get some sleep while I go to the Prefecture to see if there is any substance to his threats."

"All right," she said. "You must think I'm a hysterical woman. Working myself into a frenzy because of the idle words of a stupid policeman."

"I think you're a woman put under a terrible strain. Your husband has been murdered. Whether you loved him is irrelevant; it must have been a shock. This is a comfortable enough cage, but it is still a cage. None of the men you've relied on have been much use to you. Not me, in any case."

"Denis is doing what he can."

Max wondered if that were true. He had gotten Sarah moved from a cell to this room but, other than that, he had been absent. Sarah deserved better than that. He asked the matron to order them an English breakfast; she looked relieved to be doing something for her charge.

Sarah agreed to lie down until breakfast arrived, though Max doubted she would sleep, given her state of mind. He used the time to write notes to Yesim and Harvey, asking them to renew the search for Henri. Martel had no secrets, but what about those whose secrets were the stock and trade of Martel's business? It might be worth questioning Henri's contacts again to see if he had learned anything about them. Roget, too, had been a friend of Henri, though whether he would act on his behalf was an open question. Still, nothing ventured, nothing gained.

Sidorov had an alibi, but was the man working alone? Ginger Buchan would know if anyone did. The man had a busy schedule and wasn't always keen to see Max, despite their friendship, but it was worth trying to set up a meeting. Despite Sidorov's accusation and the lingering question of who had hired Russian thugs to attack him, Max was more and more disinclined to think Pavlovna or her cronies had killed Mark St. John. Yet, somehow, he knew that Russia was the key to the death. It was like the feeling he used to get in the trenches when they were waiting for a German attack or for orders to make one of their own. He always knew when the moment was approaching. Maybe that was why he had survived when so many others hadn't. He needed to talk to her again, and this time he wouldn't put up with her evasions.

But if the Russians weren't directly involved, then what was the connection? Armand was working both sides of the street. St. John might have confronted him about it. But the murder seemed too premeditated to have arisen from a confrontation. Giamatti's motive was much clearer. St. John had stolen his money. The murder was an execution. But where did Ponant come in? Giamatti had Michel to help him; a third person only complicated matters. Had Ponant been a witness instead of an accomplice? Despite his protestations of innocence, Giamatti now seemed the most likely candidate.

No matter how he turned it over in his mind, it always came back to those two. Yet, what if money weren't the motive? According to Ledux, St. John still loved his wife. Could this be a crime of passion? Had Jourdain killed Mark to keep Sarah from returning to her husband? It seemed doubtful. A man who loved a woman that much surely wouldn't abandon her to her fate.

Ledux also claimed St. John was still an agent of the Americans. Max had heard there was no honour among thieves but was there any love lost between spies? Could someone from the Embassy have been involved in St. John's death? Had he crossed some invisible line that made him *persona non grata* with his superiors? Max shuddered. Murder made you question everyone.

Sarah came out of her bedroom when the waiter arrived with their food. She claimed not to have slept but she looked fresher and steadier on her feet. The Grand, only a block or two from the financial district, was accustomed to catering to the needs of foreigners who expected more than a few croissants at breakfast. Scrambled eggs, ham and sausages, piles of toast, kept slightly warm under a white napkin, plus fruit, pastries and preserves all ensured no appetite was left unsatisfied. The coffee and steamed milk were hot and there was even ice water.

They both ate without speaking until the worst of their hunger was blunted. When Max looked up from his food, Sarah was leaning on her elbows, her face cupped in her hands, smiling.

"What?"

"It's good to see someone who enjoys their food," she said. "It's like being back on the farm, watching my brothers eat."

Max forced a smile and took another drink of coffee, as much to hide his expression as anything. *Sarah is your client,* he told himself, *and ten years your elder.* Still, a man doesn't like to be told by a beautiful woman that he reminds her of her brother. He thought, then, of the last time he had seen Jacqueline and wondered what Sarah would look like dressed in nothing but a man's shirt. His face flushed and he stammered the first thing that came to his mind.

"J-Jourdain doesn't enjoy his food?"

"Denis' appetites are more... restrained," she said, looking away.

"Do you know when Fontaine is coming?"

Sarah sighed and got up from the table, as though she regretted the abrupt return to business.

"Sometime today. As I said, he was vague."

"Maybe it was a bluff. I have contacts at the Prefecture. I can see what they have to say." He needed to talk to LePêcheur in any case – to see if his swallows had heard anything of Henri's disappearance. "I... I should go."

"Yes," said Sarah, her back to him. "I suppose you should."

"I'll come back when I have news."

"Please. I'd like that." Her shoulders trembled and she raised one hand to her mouth. Max took a step toward her, his hands lifting of their own volition to reach for her. He shook his head and turned to the door.

"Until then," he said, but she didn't respond. *What am I feeling,* he wondered, *pity or love? More importantly, what are* you *feeling? About me? About Jourdain?*

§

LePêcheur was already at his desk outside Gereau's office when Max arrived. No light shone from under the captain's door and, for that, Max was grateful.

"I'm not disturbing you, am I?"

LePêcheur gestured at the stack of files in front of him. "I thought getting a promotion would make my life more exciting, not less. Gereau is a stickler for paperwork. What can I do for you?"

"Any news on Henri Compte?

"I was going to ask you the same question," said LePêcheur. "It's as if he disappeared off the face of the earth. If I do get news, you'll be the first to know."

"Thanks. It's not the main reason I came. My client, Sarah St. John, thinks Fontaine is going to have her re-arrested."

"She never stopped being under arrest, but I suppose you mean taken back to the cells. I heard that, too."

"Has he something new?"

"Maybe a new judge? One less likely to listen to the entreaties of a politician?"

"No new evidence?"

"If he had, I would have heard of it. Fontaine is nothing if not indiscrete. If he had found proof of her guilt, she would already be in prison and he would be bragging about it to anyone who would listen. No, I think he's trying to pressure her into a confession."

"She can't confess to something she didn't do."

"You might be surprised. People will do strange things when the only company they have are lowlifes and rats."

"They have lowlifes in the cells?" Max said.

LePêcheur laughed. "Someone has to keep the rats company."

"Can I put my client's mind at rest?"

"There are no guarantees, but I think she'll be at the Grand a little while longer."

§

Sarah was sitting in the wingback chair by the window staring out at the street below. The breakfast dishes had been removed, although a samovar of tea stood on a low table beside the chair. The matron nodded at him and took up her station outside the drawing room, pulling the door closed behind her.

"Fontaine is bluffing."

"Are you certain? He seemed so pleased with himself."

"I think sometimes he convinces himself of his own imaginings. The captain is connected, not competent."

Sarah smiled. "I've been a terrible host. Would you care for tea?"

"I'm afraid I had my fill of it in the trenches."

"Of course," she said. She gasped softly and her eyes welled.

"What is it?" Max knelt beside her chair and took her hands. She leaned against him, resting her head against his shoulder. Her breath shuddered against his cheek and her body trembled. "Do you need something?"

"I don't know," she sighed. "I don't know what I need."

She leaned away far enough that she could look into his face. She stroked his cheek, her fingers gliding along the faint scar that ran from below his eye to his jawline. She bent towards him and their lips touched. Max moved into the kiss, hungry for the taste of her mouth.

"No," she said, pulling away. "I'm sorry."

Max felt hot and slightly dizzy. "I'm the one who should apologize. You're..." He didn't know how to finish the sentence. His blood pulsed in his temples. He forced himself to stand.

"Weak is what Mark would have said. Maybe I am."

"Mark still loved you." Max regretted the words as soon as he spoke them.

"What?" Sarah's face went white. "You couldn't know that."

"He told a man named Ledux, right before he died."

"Ledux? The blind colonel? Why would Mark tell him that?"

"I don't know. They had formed a bond. From their time working together before the war."

"The Great Game. I didn't know that about Ledux but it makes sense."

"He also said he had wrecked it all. He blamed himself for what happened in your marriage."

"Why are you telling me this?" Sarah had turned away to stare out the window again. Her voice was strained; Max thought she might be crying again. *Why was he telling her? To make her feel guilty? To wring a confession from her? Did he, despite all his protestations, still think she might be linked to her husband's murder?*

"Maybe it's never too late for someone to apologize. Maybe Mark would have wanted you to know he was sorry for what he did to you."

"An apology from beyond the grave? It's sweet of you to think so," said Sarah. "But you didn't know Mark. If he told Ledux that, it was because he wanted something from him. Mark never wasted a secret and if he still loved me, it was the deepest secret he ever had."

Her voice was no longer strained but hard and cold. Whatever emotion she felt now, it was neither sadness nor guilt.

§

Max lingered in a doorway across from the office building on Boulevard d'Opera until he saw Pierre Armand return from lunch. Armand was still in the outer office, giving instructions to his assistant, when Max arrived.

"Does Mr. Anderson have an appointment?" Armand snapped.

"There's nothing in the book, Mr. Armand."

"I'm here to talk about Isabelle Grassie," said Max.

"That's all right," said Armand to the assistant. "I remember making the arrangements myself. Step into my office, Max."

"Do you want coffee, Mr. Armand?"

"No, our business won't take long."

Armand closed the door behind them and crossed to his desk, waving Max into the chair opposite.

"Well, what is it? I expect a client in fifteen minutes. A paying client."

"He may have to wait," said Max. He leaned back in his chair and crossed his legs.

"You aren't the police."

"No. If I were, you would be at the Prefecture, answering questions about why you are selling arms to the Soviets. French troops have left Russia for now but that could change."

"Unlikely," said Armand. "Besides, who says I'm selling arms to the Soviets? That ship from Vieste wasn't bound for Red hands."

"No, but you know what Paris is like. Rumours abound. Perhaps I should hang around and meet this paying customer of yours."

"My clients are my business," said Armand. "I can assure you that nothing I do can be proved illegal. Besides, you said you were here to talk about Isabelle Grassie, not Genady Sidorov."

"Then you do know Sidorov?"

"You said..." Armand flushed. "I shouldn't drink wine at lunch; it makes me careless."

"Grassie is missing," said Max. He's off balance. I should see if I can keep him there. "She was kidnapped. In much the same way and at roughly the same time as my friend, Henri. Maybe by the same person."

"Isabelle kidnapped?" Armand looked down at his desk as if he might find her there. "I'm sure you're mistaken. I understand she's a bit flighty."

"That's what you told Jean Martel when you saw him, isn't it?"

"Martel?" Armand's voice had risen half an octave. "Yes, yes, we had drinks a few days ago and he asked about her – if I knew where she was. I gave him the same information I gave you. But I said she might not still be there, that she was flighty."

"Why would Martel ask about her? Did he know her?"

"Well, he must have. Martel is well connected across the right. He will have heard that Ponant's death is connected somehow to that of the American."

One of them is lying, thought Max. His story disagrees with Martel's on almost every point. Even though Martel had the reputation as a consummate liar, it was Armand who seemed on shaky ground, making things up as he went along. The question was, why?

"Jacopo Giamatti asked me to find out if you stole his money."

"We've established that Mark St. John was the thief."

"You suggested that, yes." Time for a bluff. "But everyone I've talked to says Marc hadn't been in Italy for months. How could he have taken money from a safe in Genoa?"

"I… he could have taken the night train. He would be back before anyone knew he was gone."

"The voice of experience?"

"Are you accusing me of stealing?"

"Denidov got the money to pay for that shipment of arms somewhere."

"The Baron is fabulously wealthy. He was simply waiting on his banker." Armand moved his pen set from one side of the desk to the other and then moved it back.

"The Baron seems dependent on the generosity of Irina Pavlovna."

"I thought the general view was that Mark St. John was supplying Pavlovna with funds. That he stole the money from the Italians."

"People keep telling me that, but why not cut out the middleman? I've got witnesses that put you together with the Russians. You hand Denidov the money and he hands it back a few days later. After he's talked to his 'banker.' Very neat."

"You have no proof. Idle speculation." Armand seemed intent on rearranging the items on his desk, squaring the blotter, adjusting the position of the wooden telephone box. Sweat sheened his brow.

Max waved at the line of cabinets that covered one wall. "In my experience, people can't resist keeping records. They don't trust their memory or their business partners; they want a record of their own brilliance, saved for posterity, or they are natural born clerks or packrats. If not in those cabinets, somewhere there are documents linking you to Denidov, linking you to the Reds. That is if rumours linking you to the Ottomans during the war are to be believed and, in your case, I'm certain they are."

"What does it matter? You don't have those documents. You have no proof."

"I don't need proof. A word in the ear of Captain Gereau and he'll start to look. Things have a way of being found when enough people start to look for them. A word in the ear of Giamatti and he won't need the documents. With a theory to pursue, he'll find you."

"It would be my death sentence."

"In the army, we shot traitors."

Armand blanched and stopped moving things on his desk. Max slipped the revolver out of his pocket. Armand may not have killed Mark St. John but that didn't mean he wouldn't kill him if he got the chance.

"Keep your hands where I can see them, Armand."

Armand shuddered like a dog when it's wet. He placed his hands flat on his blotter. His hands were small and pale. They trembled slightly and he pressed down on the desk to stop them.

"Giamatti is staying at Le Meurice. I'm sure they have telephones there. Shall we call him?"

"No, I... What do you want from me?"

"The truth."

"The truth is many things to many people."

"Can the philosophy. You know what I want." Max felt the heat rise in his face, the return of the old anger. This time it wasn't paralyzing, it was liberating. He showed Armand the gun. "Spill it."

"All right. What choice do I have? Even if you're not prepared to kill me yourself, you won't lift a hand to stop someone else, unless I cooperate, right?"

Max nodded. "Go on."

"I'm a businessman. I do what it takes to make a profit. What do I care who buys the things I sell? Is it more moral for an Italian to shoot a Turk than the other way around?"

"It is to the Italian."

"Perhaps. I leave these quibbles to the priests and politicians. I have a a large extended family to support. I employ thousands..."

Max slammed his hand on the desk, making Armand jump. "I don't need your goddamn justifications. I need the truth."

"Yes." Armand took the handkerchief from his breast pocket and mopped his brow. "St. John had nothing to do with Giamatti's money, which Jacopo would have soon discovered if someone hadn't shot Mark."

"This hardly convinces me of your innocence."

"Nonetheless. The money was taken by... an associate."

"Michel Tourangeau," said Max. It was a wild guess but it felt right. It explained Tourangeau's sudden departure from Giamatti's company.

Armand's eyes widened. "Yes, Michel was an old friend from the Action Française. He had grown disillusioned with Andre Bucard and came to me, looking for new opportunities. I persuaded him that Giamatti was nothing but a gangster pretending to be a partisan. He obtained the money and passed it on to Denidov. The rest you know."

"That seems to let you and the Russians off the hook for St. John's murder, though not Giamatti. If you're telling the truth."

"I have copies of Michel's train ticket and hotel bill. I'd be prepared to show them to you – before I send them to Jacopo."

"Putting the blame for the theft squarely on Michel's shoulders."

Armand shrugged and looked more relaxed. "Who is there to gainsay it now that Michel has fled to America?"

"You say St. John had nothing to do with your deal with Denidov? What about the other Russians? Pavlovna or the Reds? What was his relationship to her?"

"I only know what I hear whispered in the bistros of the seventeenth arrondissement. Pavlovna is a woman of prodigious appetites, like those of her famous great grand dame. As for the Reds, I have had no contact with them, although my secretary tells me a Russian gentleman has been to the office several times without leaving his name."

"What does he look like?"

"Tall, slim, refined looking with black hair and a thin mustache. I think my girl was quite taken with him."

"Gennady Sidorov. A spy, a bloodthirsty Commissar or a lonely tourist, depending on who you ask. A Red, for sure, whatever else he is."

"To me, he is a potential customer."

"One who will happily cheat you. Based on his politics it's almost obligatory."

Armand smiled. "I'll take that as good advice."

He's back in familiar territory, thought Max. *He's no good to me there.*

"There's still the question of Ponant."

"I thought he was killed by the same person who killed St. John," said Armand.

"The link is tenuous. No-one has connected the two men or their murders. Both shot, yes, probably on the same day or close to it."

"There's more to it than that," said Armand. The sheen of sweat had returned. The man has a tell, Max thought. Stealing doesn't prick his conscience but violence does – or personal danger. "Ponant was known for his violent tendencies. He had been heard bragging about some secret mission, one that would change the face of France. Then there was the money."

"Money always seems to come into it," said Max.

"Being a Camelot can be a full-time job but it doesn't pay like one. And it's expensive – they all like to look like toffs. I heard he was suddenly flush with cash."

"For someone who claimed to hardly know the man, you seem a fount of information."

"One hears. I'm not unconnected."

"Isabelle Grassie." An educated guess, this time. "She's your connection to Ponant."

Armand looked away. His hands, still pressed against the desk blotter, twitched. *He has a gun in his desk drawer.*

"Go ahead. You could claim self-defence. Or I could. You took the girl, didn't you?"

"I didn't take her," said Armand, the tremor shifting to his voice. "She came willingly. You can ask her yourself, if you like. She's at my house in the Marais."

"Did your affair start before or after Ponant's murder?"

"Before." Armand was barely audible.

"He was jealous and you killed him."

"It wasn't like that. Isabelle had broken with him – several weeks before his death. He knew nothing of us. I had met her at a rally last Christmas. It was..." Armand smiled softly, "surprising."

"I didn't take you for the romantic type."

"Neither did I. We saw each other a few times. Then it became more serious. She had grown tired of Ponant's rantings, his boastings. He had been taking money from her but once he had money of his own... I don't think either of them was heartbroken."

"Why keep it secret? You didn't even have a wife to protect."

"I have children. My family is very traditional. Isabelle is a Protestant, quite devout in her own way. Conversion and, therefore, marriage are out of the question. We were both quite happy with the arrangement. And, once Ponant was killed... neither of us relished being interrogated at the Prefecture. As you say, our relationship would appear suspicious."

"It still is. Grassie was taken the same day as my friend, Henri. In much the same manner."

"Coincidences happen. I've told you all I know. I am guilty of stealing Giamatti's money, although I'm certain it was ill-gotten in the first place. I did not kidnap your friend nor kill Paul Ponant. I am still of the view he was involved in the death of Mark St. John – his mysterious mission and the money both suggest that – and paid for his crime with his life. My instincts, and yours I suspect, tell me Martel either is involved in all three crimes or knows who was. If not Martel, someone with whom he deals. The Russians were a particular interest of St. John. Martel's main interests are domestic but, in this case, I think, St. John's death has international implications."

"Why?"

"When we had lunch, I was talking about how difficult it was to manage an international business, so many strings to keep one's hands on. He said, 'Armand, you're not the only spider in Paris.' Then he laughed and changed the subject."

A spider whose web extends from Moscow to Washington, while it lurks in the dark centre of Paris, waiting to catch the unwary. "Paris is full of spiders."

Armand shrugged. "Perhaps."

Max leaned back in his chair and looked across the desk at Armand. The little banker met his gaze without flinching. *He has unburdened himself, like a parishioner at confession*, Max thought, *and feels absolved.*

"I'm satisfied."

"Then I need not worry about police raids in the middle of the night."

"If the police come it won't be because of anything I said. I may need to talk to Mademoiselle Grassie but I'll be discrete. I'll send ahead before I come."

"I have a telephone at my house. The girl out front will tell you the exchange."

Max stood up and slipped his pistol back in his pocket. He didn't offer to shake Armand's hand. He felt dirty enough as it was.

§

Max walked down L'Opéra, heading for La Place de la Concorde. The legislature was meeting overtime in an effort to finish before the summer break. There was a chance that Jourdain would be available and would agree to see him.

His conversation with Armand had left him jumpy. He felt barely competent to investigate the simplest of crimes. Yes, he could find a missing person sometimes, but murder? International conspiracies? It all seemed too much. His shoulders twitched and the skin on the back of his neck crawled. Max turned and locked eyes with a man a few steps behind him.

Before Max could place him, the man swore, a guttural curse that Max was certain was Russian. It was one of the men who had attacked him, the big one. Max stepped to block his way, but the ruffian was quicker. He turned his shoulder and barrelled into Max, knocking him to the ground.

By the time Max regained his feet, the man had rounded the corner and disappeared.

Another coincidence? They were starting to add up, and Max didn't like it. Was the Russian following him? And, if so, on whose behalf?

Max was still mulling that question over when he arrived at Jourdain's office. Roget was sitting behind the reception desk with his feet up. There was no sign of the deputy's usual assistant.

"Is Jourdain here?" asked Max.

Roget nodded. "In the building, at least. He thought you might drop by. Your 'client' sent a note."

"And?"

"He said I should put you in his book for tomorrow morning." Roget made a show of taking a ledger from the desk drawer and flipping through the pages for the correct date. He ran his finger down the page before announcing. "I can give you fifteen minutes at seven or ten at eleven-thirty. Your choice."

"What I have to say may take longer than ten minutes."

"Then I suggest you get up early. Mr. Jourdain is an important man."

"So I've been told."

"You're lucky he has time to see you at all. If it were up to me, you wouldn't get the time of day."

"I thought we were friends, Roget."

Roget grunted and closed the book, sliding it back into its place in the desk. He leaned back in his chair and put his feet back on the desk. There was a small hole in the sole of one shoe.

"Of course. Bosom buddies. But Jourdain is my... boss."

"And you're nothing if not loyal." Sometimes, Max wondered what drove Roget. He had gone straight from the military police to the right hand of Eduard Lachance, a criminal of the first order. Now he had thrown his allegiance behind a rising socialist leader. Given his history, he seemed better suited to belong to the Action Française.

"I'll see you in the morning," said Roget. "Don't be late."

§

Max stopped at Le Coq Bleu on his way to his office. Yesim was behind the bar wiping the zinc surface desultorily. His face was haggard, his eyes bleary from lack of sleep and worry.

"Any word?" asked Max without any real hope.

"No," said Yesim. "It's been over a week and I'm starting to worry."

"I'm sure Henri will be okay."

"No doubt," said Yesim. "But what about Le Coq Bleu? Sales are down ten percent."

Max was no stranger to trench humour. He patted Yesim on the arm and ordered a small brandy. "Someone has to pick up the slack," he said.

"But you never pay."

Max shrugged and sipped his drink. Yesim kept a tally and took it out of Max's share of the profits, on those weeks there were profits. They could only hope the Americans would "discover" the charm of Montmartre soon.

Fortunately, business at Chez Jake was booming. Jazz had become the latest craze for residents and tourists alike. They had already expanded the kitchen twice and Jake was in negotiations with the café next door to knock out a wall and increase the seating area and dance floor. Even with the additional expenditures, Jake presented Max with an envelope of cash every Monday – his share of the previous week's take. This week the bundle was especially thick.

"Best weekend of the year," said Jake. "I'm thinking we should stay open right through August."

"Nobody stays in Paris in August," said Max.

"I don't think they told them that back in Pittsburgh. Americans like to drink every month of the year."

They never mentioned it in the guidebooks but there was little doubt that booze, along with the devaluation of the franc, was one of the main attractions of a Parisian visit. The Americans could be boorish, and often were, but they had money and were more than happy to spend it.

"It's your business," said Max. "I'm nothing but the silent partner."

That was mostly true. Jake insisted he co-sign the cheques and review the contracts. A couple of years of law school had to be useful for something. But Max never interfered in the running of the club and used his negotiating skills, gained from four years under colours, to make sure no one else did either. Max had stumbled into his partnership with Jake but it had worked well for both of them and Max was now proud to call his partner his friend as well.

"Those Russians were here again on Saturday."

"The ones I had dinner with."

"The same, though one of them had his arm in a sling, the red-faced one with the big mustache."

"Denidov?"

"We weren't formally introduced. *She* asked if you could come see her. Didn't say what about."

From the tone in Jake's voice, there was no question the "she" in question was Pavlovna. "Any suggestion as to when?"

"She said at your convenience, but she meant as soon as possible. She left before the others and took the military-looking gent with her."

Which, Max thought, *could mean anything.*

§

Max arrived at Jourdain's office several minutes before seven. Roget was there, reading the morning papers. An empty coffee cup and crumb-strewn plate indicated he had been there for some time.

"I'll announce you," said Roget, without formality. He disappeared behind an oak door and emerged a few minutes later to usher Max into Jourdain's office. "Fifteen minutes."

Jourdain came out from behind his desk to shake Max's hand, refraining from the customary kiss on the cheek in deference to Max's North American sensibilities.

"Always good to see you, Max. What can I do for you?"

"Go see my client for a start. She... misses you."

Jourdain flushed slightly and looked away. "I'm beginning to regret my decision to renew our relationship. It has raised difficult questions with my colleagues. And with my wife."

"I thought it was a secret."

"It is. Up to a point." Jourdain paused, his eyes now fixed on Max's face. "I must seem cold to you."

"It's not what I've come to expect from the French."

Jourdain laughed. "And are all Canadians the same? France is a complex place, Paris, even more so. I doubt foreigners can ever understand it, no matter how long they live here."

"Perhaps you're right. I don't understand your attitude toward Sarah. Mrs. St. John."

"You have no idea what my attitude is toward Sarah." Jordain's voice had gone cold, his expression blank.

"You said you regret..."

"A man may regret having drunk too much brandy; it won't stop him from wanting to taste it again the next night. I appreciate what you are trying to do for Sarah but that doesn't allow you to pry into what are essentially private matters. Is there something else you wanted?"

"What is your business with Martel?"

"We are colleagues in the Chamber."

"Close colleagues? He claims to have been at your country house having dinner the night my friend Henri disappeared." Max would have liked to pursue the issue with Martel himself, but the man had been infuriatingly elusive since their last brief encounter.

"What else does he claim?"

"Martel is a man who knows the value of information."

Jourdain laughed. He went back behind his desk and opened the top drawer, removing a packet of letters. He tossed them on the desk. Even from several feet away, Max recognized Sarah's distinctive slanting cursive.

"You will have noticed I have a new assistant. The last one stole these from my safe and sold them to Martel. He came to my house, the house where my wife and children live, and offered to sell them back to me."

"Nothing like blackmail to bring people together."

"So young and already so cynical."

"What do they say?"

"Go ahead and read them. I'm sure your client won't mind."

Max was tempted. The letters might contain clues that would clear Sarah once and for all. Or prove her guilt. What would he do then? Carry on and try to clear her anyway, or turn her over to Captain Gereau? He picked up the letters and put them in his jacket pocket. Jourdain furrowed his brows but didn't rescind his offer.

"I'm sure Martel knows who killed Mark St. John."

"If he does, he didn't mention it to me. What makes you so certain?"

"Something Pierre Armand told me."

"Armand is a parasite, a blood-sucking tick feeding on the body politic. Someday he will be forcibly removed. By surgery or by fire."

"I thought you were a moderate."

Jordain chuckled. "I am. But men like that make my blood boil. So ready to accuse others of treason when they would sell their own loyalty for a few sou. The Dreyfusards are all alike."

Twenty years later the Dreyfus affair still split France between left and right, republican and monarchist, secularists and Catholics. There were few who were neutral on the issue, none who weren't touched by it.

"And Martel?" Max persisted. Jourdain's outburst made no sense except as an effort to avoid the question, attacking the messenger instead of the message.

"If Martel knows who committed this atrocity he would go to the police."

"Unless he thought someone would pay him to stay silent."

"Jean Martel is a blackmailer and a liar, but even I do not believe he would cover up murder for personal gain." Jordain had resumed his earlier blank expression. Was he hiding something, or simply uncomfortable with the moral implications of the matter at hand? "Whom do you suspect, Max?"

Who don't I? thought Max. Not Armand. Nor the recently departed Michel. Not Sarah, out of loyalty if nothing else. Not Buchan, despite the attempts of several people to point the finger at someone at the Embassy. He had no illusions about the purity of those who engaged in international intrigue. His experiences during the negotiations of the Treaty of Versailles had stripped away the few illusions the war had left him. But if the Americans wanted to dispose of one of their own, it would be less public and more pointed. Not the anarchists, whatever Gereau's personal prejudices claimed. And, somehow, not Martel.

That left Giamatti, Pavlovna. Sidorov and Jordain. There was a one in four chance that the murderer of Mark St. John was standing right in front of him. He felt the weight of the letters in his jacket pocket and wondered if one of them contained his death sentence. If Jordain had killed St. John, he had also killed Ponant and probably taken Henri, though for what reason remained obscure.

"Armand thought there was a foreign connection. Russian, perhaps. Though I still suspect the Italians."

Jourdain nodded. "Progress, then."

Roget stuck his head in the door. "Time's up, Mr. Anderson. Our next appointment is waiting."

§

The sun was already warm on his face as Max strolled across the Seine on the Pont des Artes. It was too early in the day to expect to see Harvey, but Max headed to St. Germaine anyway. Sometimes, though he would seldom admit it, even to himself, he liked to hear English spoken and, these days, one could always hear the chatter of American and British tourists exploring the shops and cafés of the Latin Quarter. He stopped in one for a brioche and an espresso and listened to the voices that almost reminded him of home.

Later he wandered down to Notre Dame and watched the men fishing on the banks of the Seine or working the barges that still carried most of the goods sold in the markets at Les Halles. He bought a couple of cheap editions from one of his favorite booksellers whose stands had lined the left bank since the first days of the Sorbonne and, with his acquisitions tucked under his arms, walked all the way to the Tour Eiffel before turning west and starting the long climb toward home.

There was a grey envelope shoved under the door of his apartment. It was unaddressed, lacking even his name, and unsealed. Inside a single sheet of paper contained a simple message written in block letters. 'FORGET ST. JOHN OR YOUR FRIEND DIES.'

Twenty-One – Wednesday to Thursday, June 24-25, 1920

Messenger boys are faceless behind their uniforms. He had been seen by several people entering the apartment building a few minutes after seven, but no one could give a description beyond the pale blue and gold of his jacket. The company that used those colours claimed no knowledge of the delivery. As he left their office, he spotted Alain, the bellhop who had been so helpful in tracking down Giamatti, wearing a messenger's jacket. He had been fired from the hotel but seemed happy enough in his new position, although not so happy he didn't ask Max if he had more "detecting" work for him to do.

Whoever had made the delivery had either been watching for Max to leave or knew of his appointment with Jourdain. In either case, it led him nowhere. Henri's disappearance was the talk of the streets. Anyone could have made the threat, even if they had nothing to do with the kidnapping.

Max had made arrangements to meet Pavlovna at the Café Petrograd. She was already sitting at a table near the back when he arrived. Her skin was paler than usual, and, for the first time, he noticed the crows' feet gathered at her eyes and the deep lines that formed around her mouth when she frowned. Whatever had happened to Denidov had her worried.

She rose as he approached the table and leaned forward so he could kiss her on each cheek. Her perfume enveloped him in its warm embrace, but beneath it he could smell something cold and bitter and afraid.

"What's happened, Irina?"

"Denidov has been shot."

Max started at that, then remembered what Jake had said about the sling. "But he's all right."

"He'll live. The bullet fractured his upper arm and tore the bicep, but the doctors say he should recover. He puts on a brave face, but I know he's frightened."

"What happened?"

"It was a few days ago. He won't say much, but I gather he was returning home from playing cards in one of the clubs in the 17th when he was accosted by a group of men – Russians. He tried to get away and one of them shot him. It might have been worse, but a pair of gendarmes came around the corner and the men ran away."

"And they say there's never a policeman around when you need one."

"They never say that in Russia." Pavlovna signalled the waiter. "Have you eaten?"

When Max shook his head, Pavlovna ordered breakfast – bellinis and spicy sausages. After the waiter brought two steaming mugs of coffee, she said: "It was the Cheka. I'm sure of that."

"Sidorov?"

"Or one of his minions."

"Have you told the Prefecture?"

"No. We will deal with it ourselves."

Pavlovna's voice shook slightly. This wasn't a problem she could fix with a wry comment and flutter of her long white fingers. Max thought he was seeing the real woman for the first time. It made him like her more but want her less.

"Would you like me to look into it?"

Pavlovna smiled softly, the most genuine expression he had seen on her face. She reached across the table and patted his hand. "You have troubles of your own."

The food arrived then and they didn't speak for a few minutes. The pancakes were thin and crisp, stuffed with sour cream and a syrupy raspberry compote. The fat sausages were well cooked, their peppery spice a pleasant contrast to the sweetness of the fruit.

When the edge of his hunger was blunted, he resumed their conversation where it had left off. "Perhaps you could help me with my troubles."

"You want to know about Mark."

Max nodded, saying nothing, as if a single word might break the spell that had been laid over them.

"You've asked if Mark and I were lovers. In the formal sense we were. We shared a bed. Our passion was real but transitory. It never lasted beyond the moment of release."

Max felt the heat rise from his collar to colour his face. Still, he remained silent.

"Mark was never really there. I never asked where he was, though I knew. Sometimes he would murmur her name. It was strangely exciting." Pavlovna smiled again in the old way, her eyes looking past Max. "We used each other. We each had a greater passion. Russia. Mark hated the Bolsheviks more than I did. For me, it was anger and revenge; for him it was something deeper, more visceral. They were an abomination to him; he hated them with all his soul."

"He gave you money."

Pavlovna frowned and shook her head, not quite in denial. "Not me. I was merely the conduit – to Denidov, to General Wrangel, to agents in the heart of the new regime. He paid for war, for murder, for information. It was the information that killed him."

"What information?"

"He never told me. Whatever it was, he found it immensely funny. Like it was the greatest joke in the world."

"He gave no clue?"

"None. I remember the last time we were together. He was in such a mood, laughing, joking. And when he bedded me, he was there, with me. He kissed me – me – and looked into my eyes the whole time he was on me. It was – disconcerting. I couldn't... it was too real."

Max looked away. The intensity in her face was painful. He had only been with a woman like that once and she had nearly destroyed him. *Why*, he thought, *do I want it so much again*?

"Thirty-six hours later they found him in the Luxembourg gardens, naked with a bullet through his brain."

"You're sure he was killed for what he had discovered and not because of the money?"

"Who can be certain of anything now that the world has been burned to the ground and all we have left are ashes and smoke? The money was dangerous. I didn't ask where it came from, but I knew it was no place good."

"Italian money?"

"You mean Denidov's little scheme with Armand? No. This money came from America, from people who shared Mark's hatred for the Reds. I think he had help, someone in the French government who could fix things at the ports of entry. It was blood money. Illegal money. It's a crime in America to do what Mark was doing."

"Doesn't seem to stop anyone."

"No. Men can always justify what their passion makes them do."

The waiter returned with the coffee pot but Pavlovna shook him off. "Vodka." The waiter raised his eyebrows but Max shrugged and nodded.

They drank the vodka when it came and sat together for a while, not talking. When Pavlovna ordered a second vodka, Max declined. He still had much to do.

On the way to the American Embassy, Max stopped in Gare de l`Est to send a telegram to Marseilles. "Jacqueline. Come home. Max."

§

Buchan ushered Max into his office. His usual smile was absent and he didn`t offer Max a drink or a cigar. The young diplomat looked tired, his face drawn and grey beneath the scattering of freckles. His suit, usually impeccable, was rumpled and a small red stain marked one of the lapels.

"It`s been a long week," said Buchan by way of explanation.

"It`s only Wednesday," said Max.

"Don`t remind me," groaned Buchan.

"Baron Denidov was shot. Not fatal. Thought you`d like to know."

"What makes you think I didn`t know? We don't track people the way the Prefecture does but we pay special attention to the Russians. Denidov is a clown. I suspect he was shot for reasons other than politics."

"What other reasons?"

Buchan shrugged. "He has money troubles."

"Pavlovna is convinced it's the Cheka," said Max.

"She sees Soviet agents behind every tree."

"And you don't?"

Buchan rubbed his hand across his face and leaned back in his large leather chair. After a moment he leapt to his feet and went to his open office door. He peered left and right, then pulled the door shut. A half-empty bottle of bourbon emerged from his desk door along with two smudged tumblers. He poured a couple of fingers in each and pushed one across the desk to Max. Max shrugged and tilted the glass at Buchan. The morning shot of vodka had left him with a slight headache; this was a certain if unfortunate remedy. Max drained half the bourbon in one gulp.

"There are six known Cheka agents in Paris, including Sidorov. We've been tailing him. He's careful not to meet any of the other agents directly but we've been able to identify the go-betweens."

"Did he have something to do with St. John's murder?"

"He was involved, yes, but not directly. He was in Paris on the day St. John was murdered but he was sitting in a cell at the Prefecture, answering Captain Gereau's questions."

"I heard that. I was surprised."

"He stays very busy for a man who's semi-retired. So Sidorov wasn't the trigger man."

"But one of the other Cheka might have done it."

"Possibly. We can't account for the movements of two of them during the time when Mark was shot, but my instincts say no. Have you ever heard the term 'Nackenschuss?'

"Sounds German."

"It is. It's a technique of execution favoured by the Cheka. Victim on his knees, head tilted forward, a single downward shot to the nape of the neck. Instant death with little blood to clean up afterwards. Mark was shot in the back of the head, it's true, but it was hardly neat. You saw the body."

Max nodded, trying not to remember the wreck of St. John's face caused by the exiting bullet.

"If the Cheka were involved, they used local talent. There's no shortage of Parisians eager to commit mayhem for the glorious revolution."

"Or to stop it."

"Everyone thinks the war ended in 1918. You and I know different. I sometimes think the isolationists have it right. Europe will never learn to stop fighting. America should stay the hell out of her affairs."

"Yet, here you still are."

"Yes," said Buchan, offering a small smile. "It's hard to leave Paris."

"Even if the Cheka didn't take a direct hand, you still think St. John's murder was ordered by the Bolsheviks."

Buchan stared into his whisky glass for a long moment, as if the swirling liquid would tell him how much of the truth to reveal and how much must remain concealed. The bourbon made its decision and Buchan set the glass back on the desk, his drink untouched.

"Mark had a long career in the diplomatic corps. But he was more than a diplomat. The same way I am."

Max had always suspected that Buchan operated outside of normal channels. He came and went as he liked and always seemed to have money to throw around, for information and perhaps for other things, too. But it was the first time Buchan had openly admitted to being a spy. Max felt strangely touched by the admission.

"I thought St. John had left public service and returned to business."

"St. John left, yes. He exceeded his authority once too often, ventured too deep into the great game for even the Secretary to continue to tolerate him. President Wilson always disliked spies, even after the War persuaded him of their necessity. High level complaints were made – from the British mostly – about Mark's 'attitude,' and, on at least two occasions, his methods. Mark officially retired and returned to his father's business. Unofficially, he still worked for American interests. And if you repeat that elsewhere, I'll swear I never even met you."

"I think we're a few lunches past making that claim stick."

"This isn't funny, Max. Unless you understand that, I really can't see you again."

"I'm sorry," said Max. "St. John was still working for the... some secret service."

"Yes," said Buchan, "though not The Secret Service. I've never known for sure which one. Officially, there's only the Black Chamber but they deal mainly in reading other people's mail. But we all know there are groups within the War department and, now, the State department who have 'special' assignments. All I know is he didn't work for mine."

"I'm not sure what you're getting at. Did the Bolsheviks order Mark's death or didn't they?"

"I'm operating in the dark here, Max," said Buchan. "The Ambassador asked me if Sarah St. John would be going to trial soon. Not if, but when. I think they've washed their hands of the whole affair. There are only two reasons why they would do that."

"They think Sarah did it, or hired it done."

"That's the most obvious conclusion. But why not simply say so? Why come to me? No, I think the Ambassador is under pressure to make all this go away."

"Pressure from whom?"

"I don't know. My instincts are screaming that this has something to do with the Reds, but I can't see the connection. Hugh Wallace is not our most distinguished Ambassador, but I can't see him under the influence of Moscow." Buchan stopped pacing long enough to drain his whiskey glass. "I told you Mark had fallen out of favour with State. He might still have been working for them or for one of the divisions in Justice that worry about foreign revolutionaries in America. I suspect he got his money from some 'independent' group, like the National Security Association. Lord knows they have no shortage of it with backers like Morgan and Rockefeller."

"You're suggesting American millionaires were funding Mark St. John to support the Whites in Russia? I thought that was illegal."

"It is, if it could be proven. But I think the money he was giving to Pavlovna was a cover. No-one seriously thinks the Whites are going to bring back Russia, even most of them. Mark had a real hate on for the Reds. It went way beyond politics. I suspect whoever was giving him money – and he wasn't a pauper himself, no matter what you may have heard – didn't ask a lot of questions. I don't think you have any idea how close we came to losing Germany to the Sparticists and Hungary to Bela Kun. If certain things hadn't been done, certain key people not eliminated, all of eastern Europe could now be flying a red flag."

"Then the Bolsheviks, whether in Russia or here in Paris, would have a good reason to kill him."

"If they knew he was involved. It's not called a secret service for nothing. He was open in his support for Pavlovna to hide what else he was doing. Even if they suspected, getting to Mark wouldn't have been an easy thing. He was careful and used agents, both to do his dirty work and to protect him from harm."

"Then what happened?"

"Mark made a mistake. He trusted the wrong person or underestimated someone he was dealing with. For some reason, he let his guard down and it cost him his life."

§

Max had almost forgotten his rendezvous with Gaston Deschamps, the missing grandson, would have forgotten it if Smitty had not shown up at his apartment to accompany him. Together they took the Metro to Bastille and walked the short distance to Bofinger, a brasserie that claimed to have been the first to sell draft beer in the city. The weather was fine and the outside tables were full, though the interior was only three-quarters full. There were two men with white carnations but one of them was nearly sixty.

Max looked along the street and then back toward the central square, with its golden "Spirit of Liberty" atop the July column.

It was only a few blocks from the place where he had first met Jacqueline in the days when she was still masquerading as Jacques Grand; he wondered if she would respond to his request to return to Paris.

Satisfied that none of the men lounging around the monument or at the other nearby cafés were members of the gang of Russians who had attacked him in Montmartre, Max stationed Smitty a few doors away while he approached the thin-faced young man sitting alone, nursing a beer and glancing nervously around.

"Gaston Deschamps," said Max, sliding into the chair opposite. The boy jumped – he had been looking the other way – and almost spilled his beer.

"Y-yes," he stammered. He had a thin mustache that drooped over his lip and made him look much younger than his nearly twenty-one years. *The French*, thought Max, *will serve liquor to anyone.*

Max extended his right hand across the table while signaling the waiter with his left that he wanted the same. "I'm Max Anderson. I put up the posters."

"You're American," said Deschamps. "I thought..." he shrugged and didn't elaborate on his thoughts.

"Canadian, not that it matters." The waiter brought Max a tall glass of amber colored ale and a plate of olives and pickled onions. The balance between bitter and sour was almost perfect and Max could see why it was the most popular place on the street.

"You mentioned a reward. Though I wasn't sure for what."

"An inheritance, in fact. Your grandfather died."

"Really? When?"

"A couple of months ago. You're the main beneficiary."

"You're joking. The old man hated me."

"Perhaps, but blood runs thicker than water. There is a catch. You have to claim the estate by your birthday."

"That's in three days," sputtered Deschamps.

"There's a train in the morning."

"I don't believe you."

"About the train or about the inheritance?"

"About all of it. This is a trick. You're working for the old bastard. Or you're a police agent." Deschamps made to get up. Max squeezed his wrist until the boy grimaced and sat back down.

"That's Fumoleau's doing, isn't it?"

"What?"

"The family lawyer had to make a show of looking for you, so he hired the least well-known detective in Paris to do it. Then he was in touch. He has been in regular communication, hasn't he?"

"He sends me some money and... he told me the old man, my grandfather, had reported some things missing from the house and accused me of taking them. Fumoleau said the police were looking for me. Why would he do that?"

"Because he's the estate trustee. With you out of the picture he'd be free to bleed it dry. Your cousins would eventually get their inheritance, what was left of it."

"Grandpapa is truly gone?" Deschamps sniffed and for a moment Max thought he might actually shed a tear. *Funny how the thought of an inheritance brings out the finest sentiments. Only one more puzzle to clear up.*

"Is Patrice Fumoleau young? With blue eyes and a long thin nose?"

"Patrice? No, he's at least fifty and fat, his nose swollen from too much port. But his son, René, he would fit the description."

The mystery of the Russian gang was solved. They, at least, had nothing to do with St. John's murder. They had been hired by Fumoleau to make doubly sure Gaston Deschamps would not be found in time. Max wasn't sure if it brought him closer to an answer but, somehow, the path toward one seemed clearer.

§

Max stopped at Le Coq Bleu for a quick supper with Yesim, who seemed more and more despondent with each passing day. "No news is good news," Max told him but Yesim merely grunted and turned back to his brandy. Back home, he called the Hotel Meurice to see if Andre Bucard was in residence. He was, and Max left a message that he would stop by the restaurant for breakfast at nine. Bucard would either be there, or he wouldn't; he was not a man you could meet with if he didn't want to talk.

The restaurant, dimly lit even on a sunny morning, was over half full when Max arrived a few minutes late, though none of the tables near Bucard's booth were occupied. His bodyguards, David and Michel's replacement, a thick-set man with a shaved head and a heavy black beard, made sure of that. Max nodded at David and slid onto the dark leather-covered bench across from Bucard.

If the disbanding of the Black Cross, announced with great fanfare by the Minister of the Interior a few days before, troubled Bucard, it didn't show in his handsome face or the square set of his broad shoulders, but Max had met the man often enough to know he was troubled. Bucard was a man of considerable appetites but the tray of breakfast pastries was untouched.

"Sorry I'm late," said Max. "There was some hold up on the Metro."

"Wildcat strike," said Bucard. "The unions won't be happy until they destroy this country."

"I thought Action Française supported the right to organize."

The AF supports a lot of foolish things. Besides there is a difference between a syndicat and a union." The word Bucard used for the latter was quite vulgar in French. Max was surprised; Bucard took pride in his refinement.

The waiter brought them both lattes; Bucard was silent until he left. Max selected two pastries from the plate and slathered them with butter and preserves. Bucard broke off a piece of croissant and dabbed it with jam.

"Michel Tourangeau has sailed for America," Max said.

Bucard raised his eyebrows and nodded as if that explained everything. "Michel was a great disappointment to me."

"Because he went to work for Martel?"

"No," said Bucard. "I sent him to work for Martel. I don't trust that little weasel. But Michel was corrupted."

"Power does that to men."

Bucard smiled bitterly, the irony clearly not lost on him.

"Power and money, too. I blame Armand as much as Martel. Martel passed Michel on to him once he was done."

"They have ties?"

"The way a puppet has ties to his puppeteer," said Bucard.

"But which is which?"

"Armand is a simple man, a clever banker, but a simple man. He has no understanding of the forces that operate all around him. He thinks the world runs on money."

"Doesn't it? I thought the official line is that Jewish money caused the war."

"Money is a necessary lubricant, like the oil I put in my car, but power is a more subtle currency. From where does it come? Signor Mussolini has no money of his own, yet power clings to him."

"You admire him."

"He will change Italy. Men like him will change Europe."

Men like Bucard crave recognition, thought Max, *demand the adulation of the masses*. Despite his natural charisma and his old family money, it had never come to Bucard the way he wanted, the way it came so easily to Martel, who lacked Bucard's natural advantages. Michel's betrayal must have been exceptionally bitter. "Men like you," he said.

Bucard shrugged with a slight smile.

"It was Armand who sent Michel to America," said Max.

"Yes, yes," said Bucard, waving his hand dismissively. "To cover up the theft of the Italian's money. But Martel was the one behind it all. He connected Armand to Denidov. That's what he does, make connections. All part of some larger scheme."

"What scheme?"

"I don't know," said Bucard. "But the ship..."

"What ship?"

"The one carrying arms to the Whites. It sank in the Adriatic. All hands lost. A great tragedy to the Tsarist cause."

"You're saying Martel had the ship sunk?"

Bucard laughed. "Nothing quite so direct. But he knew about its route. And he may have let it slip. Or traded it for something else. Martel collects facts like some men collect coins or mistresses, not because they're useful or even desirable, but merely to have them."

"He seems more pragmatic than that," said Max.

"Yes, Martel is the great pragmatist. He hasn't an ideal worthy of the name. He wants to be the power behind the throne and doesn't care a whit who is sitting on it."

"But to what end?" Somehow every time he eliminated a suspect, someone else thrust them back into the picture.

"If I knew that, I would take action. I am not short on resources of my own." Bucard didn't look at the men who guarded him, but Max knew what he meant. Bucard's adherents were, for the most part fanatically loyal. Michel Tourangeau would be wise to stay in America. "Now, if there is nothing else."

"One last thing," said Max. "I originally thought that Michel was involved in Mark St. John's death, working for Giamatti."

"For a minute, I thought you were going to accuse me of murder again. That's becoming a bad habit."

"I won't let it happen again." *Until I have proof,* he thought. "I'm almost certain it was a political killing. But I can't figure out the politics."

"I'm not as connected as I used to be," said Bucard. "You've met Colonel Ledux? Then you know he and St. John were close. I had a drink with the Colonel a few days ago. He seemed angry. It had something to do with Martel. He wouldn't say what it was, but I think it had to do with St. John's death."

§

Ledux was no more open with Max than he had been with Bucard. After fifteen frustrating minutes of small talk, Max asked him point blank if Martel had been involved in St. John's murder. "Implicated but not involved." was all the blind man would say before going silent. When it became clear he would say nothing more, Max got up to leave. He barely heard Ledux's whisper as he went: *France's interests rise above those of a man.*

Max had no doubt that Martel was the key to the whole sordid mess – the murder of St. John, the treason of Armand, the theft of the Italian money, the betrayal of the White Russian cause in the Adriatic Sea. He was almost certainly linked to the kidnapping of his friend, Henri, if kidnapping was all that was involved.

The man had managed to avoid Max at every turn, absent from his legislative office or, if there, unavailable and unassailable behind well-guarded doors. Max had dropped by his Paris house on Aguesseau, but Martel never seemed to be home, or so his manservant, Francis, claimed. In desperation, he had hired Alain to watch the place whenever he was off duty.

As Max walked up Lepic to his apartment, the young man, who had been sitting on the front step of the building, leapt up and hurried down the street to meet him.

"Martel," said Alain. "He's having lunch right now at Mollard's near St. Lazare."

The St. Lazare train station was one of largest in the city with links to western France and the Atlantic seaports. If St. John's American backers were newly arrived in town, Mollard's might be a convenient place for a fixer like Martel to meet them.

The restaurant was packed when Max arrived. He pushed his way past the short line-up, despite the protests of the maitre d', moving from one ornate dining room to the next. The interior was typical Art Nouveau with pastel colored marble columns, frosted multi-colored lamps and tile mosaics depicting pastoral scenes. The hum of conversation rose and fell amid the clinking of metal and glass. Martel was sitting at a large table nestled into a semi-private alcove.

Martel spotted Max as he crossed the room. He leaned over to say something to the man next to him, who quickly rose without looking in Max's direction and ducked out another exit. He had shaved his mustache, but Max was almost certain it was Gennady Sidorov.

"This is a private meeting, Mr. Anderson," said Martel, rising and coming around the table to intercept him. Max scanned the faces of the four other men at the table, who did their best not to meet his eyes. He was sure he had seen one or two of them before in the restaurants of the Russian quarter.

"I've a few questions for you. It won't take long."

"Make an appointment with my assistant."

"I've tried that," said Max. "He never seems to be able to fit me in."

"Do I need to have the manager call the police?" asked Martel.

"Go ahead," said Max. The men behind stirred in their seats, and Max wondered briefly if they were going to take the law into their own hands, but no-one stood up. "Though I'm not sure your lunch companions would appreciate their presence."

Martel pasted on a smile and took Max be the elbow, leading him away a few paces. "Make it quick."

"Were you blackmailing Jourdain?"

"Did he say I was?"

Martel was a master at avoidance, there was no doubt about that. Max felt his stomach clench and it wasn't from the enticing smells wafting from the kitchen.

"What about?"

"Politicians are vulnerable on so many fronts; he was having an affair."

"Weren't you the one who told me it was considered bad form for a politician not to have a mistress?"

"Was it? I can't remember."

Martel was still holding his arm and now Max shook it free and stepped closer until his face was only inches from Martel's. The politician didn't flinch or try to step away.

"Henri was asking questions about you at my request. Then he disappeared."

"Your friend was an old man."

"Is an old man," said Max. "Unless you know something you're not telling me."

"I know many things I'm not telling you," said Martel. "My business doesn't concern you."

"It does if it involves my friend. Did you take him? Did you kill him?"

"Don't be stupid." Martel turned away. "The waiters are bringing our food."

"They say nothing happens in Paris that Martel doesn't know about," said Max, through clenched teeth. "You know what happened to Mark St. John. And you know what happened to Henri."

When Martel turned back, his smile was genuine but not attractive. "Mark St. John was murdered by person or persons unknown. Though I suspect your client knows well enough. As for your friend, Henri, it was you who sent him into danger. You used him as a pawn in a game of kings. Pawns are disposable, Mr. Anderson. Surely you know that."

Max did know. He'd spent long enough in the trenches of France to know the value politicians put on pawns.

"I'll take a man like Henri over all the kings and bishops in France."

"That is the difference between you and me," said Martel. "You cling to old-fashioned values while the world moves on. The new order will have little place for men like you or your drinking companions."

Max knew there was no point of arguing; he was sick of words. Martel either didn't know what happened to Henri or, knowing, didn't care.

"You won't win." The words barely escaped through his clenched teeth. Max was surprised Martel even heard them.

"I have won," said Martel. "You just can't see it yet."

Max stepped forward, turning and dropping his shoulder as he did. Martel's face registered confusion, then shock, his hands coming up in a gesture barely remembered from school yard brawls. Max's fist connected with Martel's jaw, snapping his head back. Max's second punch, aimed for the midriff, caught his shoulder instead, as Martel's knees buckled and he crashed to the floor.

Max stood over the fallen politician, his fists cocked, the blood burning in his face and lungs. A woman's cry punctuated the silence. Martel's companions pushed back their chairs and leapt to their feet. Max stared them into immobility. Martel stirred at his feet, trying and failing to rise onto his elbows.

"Nothing happens in Paris," Max said. "If you don't know what happened to Henri, find out."

"Or what?" The words burbled through the blood in Martel's mouth. "You'll kill me?"

"Yes," said Max. "I'll kill you."

Twenty-Two – Saturday, June 2nd2, 1920

Max had reached the street before the gendarmes arrived in force, but the helpful maître d' pointed him out before he could get to the Metro entrance. Max knew better than to resist arrest when the swallows laid their hands on him; he'd be lucky to avoid a beating as it was. One couldn't assault a prominent politician in a busy restaurant without consequence, both formal and informal.

His treatment proved less severe than his last bout with Kid O'Brien and, if he could have slept, he would have had few complaints other than the constant shouting of his fellow inmates, the inedible food and the bugs that seemed to infest every corner of the cell. By the time, he was hauled before a magistrate late on Friday afternoon, Yesim had shown up with his lawyer, a clever young man whose enthusiasm made up for his lack of experience.

It helped that Martel had refused to testify or even provide much of a statement. The judge released him with a warning and a substantial fine; Max would be on short rations for a few weeks. Yesim insisted on treating him to supper, despite Max's protests. He suspected Yesim was proud to have a friend who punched prominent politicians.

After two bottles of wine and four courses, including an amazing duck confit served with wild mushroom and brandy sauce topped with sliced almonds, Yesim sprang for a taxi to take Max back to his apartment. Yesim half carried Max up the stairs and made him strip off his clothes in the outer hall, 'to avoid unpleasant house guests,' before shoving him into the shower and then to bed. Max never heard him leave.

§

Though the sun was pouring through the window across his still naked body, it seemed as if only moments had passed. Yesim's presence at the foot of his bed only confused him more. Had he never left?

Yesim's face was contorted as if he couldn't decide what emotion was in control, anger, fear, sorrow or joy.

"Henri?" Max asked. Yesim nodded. "Not...?" Max left the question unspoken.

"No," said Yesim, joy for the moment lighting up his eyes. "Not dead, but..."

"But what?"

"You should get dressed," said Yesim. "The police will be here soon."

"The police? Why?"

"Martel. He's dead. Shot in the face."

Max bolted upright; all trace of sleep gone now. He looked around for his clothes and then remembered Yesim had shoved them in a sack to take to the cleaners. Yesim tossed him trousers, socks and underpants from the small dresser against the wall and then rooted in the closet for a shirt.

"And Henri?" asked Max as he pulled on his clothes.

"He was there, unconscious in the next room. He had a gun in his hand. They've taken him to the hospital. Under guard."

Max was still buttoning his shirt and looking for his shoes when Captain Fontaine came through the door of the apartment.

"I thought it was police procedure to knock before kicking down the door," said Yesim.

Fontaine scowled but didn't respond. He put his hand on Max's shoulder.

"You're arresting me?" asked Max.

"If you like. You threatened to kill the man. I have several witnesses who will say so in court."

"We both know I didn't do it."

"A judge might be convinced otherwise," said Fontaine. He glanced pointedly at Yesim. "Why don't we go someplace where we can talk? In private."

Max nodded. He had nothing to lose by talking to Fontaine and he might even be able to pry some information out of him. He turned to Yesim. "Go see about Henri."

"He's under arrest. No visitors allowed," said Fontaine.

"I just want to see he's all right," said Yesim. When Fontaine shook his head, Yesim added. "He saved my life in the flood."

Fontaine grunted. Those who had been in the flood of 1910 shared a camaraderie that extended past other divisions. "You can see him, but don't talk to him. Tell LePêcheur I sent you."

Fontaine might be human after all, thought Max. Once Yesim had left, Fontaine sent the gendarme who had accompanied him across the street for coffee and pastries. He sat at the table and opened a window before lighting one of his dark cigarettes.

"See, I remembered: you don't like smoke."

Max dropped the plate Fontaine had ruined on his last visit on the table and took a seat as far from the captain as the small room allowed.

"How is Henri?"

"The doctors say he will live. At least until his execution."

"Henri didn't kill Martel."

"The murder weapon was in his hand. He was found in the next room."

"That doesn't mean he pulled the trigger."

"No, but there is no way to prove he didn't."

"He was unconscious."

"He had a bruise on his forehead—"

"It's hard to shoot someone after you've been knocked out."

"But," Fontaine continued, "the doctors say he was drugged. So, it could have been self-inflicted. He shoots Martel, then takes something."

"If you think Henri did it, why are you talking to me?"

Fontaine took a long drag on his cigarette, then turned his head to blow the smoke through the window. "It doesn't make sense," he said.

Max bit back a retort. "Which part of it?"

"Henri Compte is known to us," said Fontaine. "He was not always the brandy-soaked old man you know."

Henri's father and brother had both been killed in 1871 when the Paris Commune was crushed by the French army. Henry was no anarchist – he left that side of the political spectrum to Yesim – but he made no secret of his contempt for the Prefecture. Still, as far as Max knew he had never been in trouble with the police.

"If he's known to the police..."

Fontaine shrugged. "I didn't say what he was known for. My witnesses tell me you did more than threaten Martel. You said he knew something of the murder of Mark St. John. That interests me. It is suggestive."

"Of what?"

"That whoever killed St. John killed Martel."

"I came to the same conclusion," said Max. "Which eliminates my client."

"You might think that," said Fontaine. "Except that for several hours last night, Sarah St. John's... companion was incapacitated. While Jean Martel was being shot, I cannot confirm that she was in her room in the Hotel Grand."

"What?"

"She claims to have been asleep. She also claims she had no visitors. But that is a lie. We know that at least two people went to her door. But we don't know who they were. I want you to find out."

"Why would I do that?"

"Someone has to lose their head for Jean Martel. The people will demand it. More importantly for me, the Prefect will demand it. We have enough evidence to try Henri Compte. He'll do if a better suspect doesn't come along."

§

Yesim reported that Henri was comfortable but drifting in and out of sleep when he saw him. LePêcheur had let him stand by the bed for a few minutes, long enough to assure himself that Henri was on the road to recovery.

"I'm still worried," said Yesim. "I told him he was an old fool who didn't know when to back down. He merely smiled and nodded. I hope that blow on his head hasn't permanently addled his brains."

Fontaine hadn't explicitly forbidden Max from seeing Henri but then Max hadn't asked. LePêcheur was chatting to one of the women at the nursing station when Max arrived; two gendarmes farther down the hall stood outside a closed door.

"I wondered when you would show up, Max," said LePêcheur.

"Can I see him?"

"See him, yes. Talk to him? No. My orders are pretty clear."

"Where was Martel shot?"

"He, and your friend, were found in an empty suite of offices on the fourth floor of the Banque Lyonnaise."

Two floors above Pierre Armand's offices. Max doubted that was a coincidence. Either Armand was connected, or someone wanted to make it look that way. He wondered if Fontaine had made the connection yet.

"Any witnesses?"

"At eight o'clock on a Friday night? Even usurers take the weekend off. No-one admits to hearing a shot."

Max would check on that himself; Parisians' natural urge to gossip often failed them around police uniforms. LePêcheur shooed the swallows away from the door and followed Max into the tiny hospital room. Henri was propped up in the narrow bed, his spectacles perched on his nose, reading one of several newspapers spread across the coverings. A breeze from the open, but barred, window stirred the papers as they entered. Henri looked up. He was pale and looked his seventy years; his rumpled white hair failed to hide the ugly bruise across his forehead.

"I quit," said Henri. "This detective business is too tough."

Max glanced at LePêcheur who shrugged his shoulders and went to look out the window.

"What do you remember?" asked Max.

"Nothing more than I've already told Fontaine. I came out of my house, on my way to follow up a couple of possibilities, people from Martel's home town who might know something about his history. A car pulled up and someone asked me how to get to Parc Monceau. I leaned into tell them they must be holding their map upside down; they were that lost. Someone put something over my face and the next thing I knew I was tied to a bed with a bag over my head."

"Did you recognize them?"

He shook his head. "I never saw a face and their voices were muffled because of the bag. When they took mine off to let me eat, they had on ones of their own. There were three or maybe four of them. They all spoke French, but they weren't all Frenchmen. A German maybe. I really don't know. I'm not good at this sort of thing."

Henri looked miserable and Max patted him on the shoulder. "I tried to find you."

"I know," said Henri. "They moved me a few times."

"Any idea why they took you?"

"No," said Henri. "They asked me a few questions about what I was doing for you, why you were interested in Martel and so on. They never mentioned the other thing, the murder of that American, but I heard them arguing."

"About what?"

"About whether to kill me for one thing. I had some rough moments, but it soon became clear that the one in charge – he was French for sure and well educated too – had something in mind." He pointed at the headlines: *Prominent politician murdered. Railway porter arrested.* "Now I know what."

"I know you didn't do it," said Max.

"Good," said Henri. "I'm glad someone does."

"What do you mean?" said LePêcheur, turning from the window.

"It was... I remember... being moved again. But not like before. There was no bag over my head, but my vision was blurred. Two of us riding up in an elevator. He had to lead me by the arm, like I was drunk. There was a man, and shouting. A gun went off. Then I had a gun in my hand. The next thing I remember was the police standing over me."

"We got a call," said LePêcheur. "At the Prefecture. Just an address and the report of a shot. It took the desk sergeant an hour to send anyone over. He'll be back on the beat on Monday. There was no sign of anyone but Martel and Henri. And no witnesses to say there ever had been."

§

It was nearly one by the time Max reached the Banque Lyonnaise building. The tellers were shutting down their windows and the security guards were preparing to roll the iron grill across the main entrance as soon as the last of the customers left. The offices on the floors above that kept Saturday hours were rapidly emptying. Two gendarmes stood idly near the main entrance, occasionally stopping one of the office workers, usually a giggling young woman, to ask a question or two.

Max watched until the stream slowed to a trickle. He hadn't spotted either Armand or the woman who worked in his outer office. Either they didn't work Saturdays or else Armand had chosen not to risk coming in. If Max wanted to check his alibi, he would have to drop by his house in the Marais. It would give him a chance to question Isabelle Grassie as well, though he doubted she had much to add.

He was about to head back to his apartment – anything to avoid the meeting with Sarah St. John – when he did spot someone he knew. Jacopo Giamatti emerged from a café and was walking towards him. The Italian's eyes were fixed on the building across the street, and he didn't notice Max until he spoke.

"Jacopo," said Max. Giamatti jumped at the sound. "Armand's not there."

"You should be more careful. Some people react badly to surprises." He shook himself to readjust his jacket. "Armand left about an hour and half ago. I've been waiting to see if he came back."

"Why didn't you grab him when he left?"

"I don't grab people, Max. What do you think I am? Armand came out of the building and got into a black sedan. He was gone before I could get up from my table."

"Was he forced?"

"I don't think so. He came out of the building, looked down the street and the sedan pulled up beside him. He got in easy as anything. They might have been pointing a gun at him, but he was smiling – the way a crocodile does right after it's bitten down on something tasty."

"You still think Armand stole your money."

"Who else?"

"Michel Tourangeau has gone to America."

Giamatti spat a long string of Italian. Some of the words were close enough to their French equivalent that Max caught the essence.

"There is no shortage of Italians in America," said Giamatti. "Michel may wish he'd gone someplace else."

"You seem quick enough to shift the blame," said Max.

"I found some things in his room that made me wonder."

Planted by Armand's agents, thought Max. "Where were you last night?"

"Martel's murder? I was having dinner at the Italian Embassy. I was there from five until after midnight. I no more killed him than I did St. John."

"I don't think you did kill St. John," said Max. All along, he had been sure the murder had something to do with money. Now he wasn't so sure. Now he was looking at other motives. Giamatti had started walking. Max called after him. "Which way did the sedan go?"

"Down L'Opéra toward the City."

Not much help there, thought Max. He was driven away from the Grand Hotel but not toward anywhere in particular.

§

Max could feel the answer tickling the back of his brain; he was missing something, some clue that would tie everything together. Whoever had killed St. John had almost certainly killed twice more – Ponant and now Martel. There was no reason to think he, or she, would stop at that. Henri's kidnapping may have merely been meant to distract Max, his framing for Martel's death, a convenience. The next few days would tell; either he would catch the killer, or the killer would catch up with him.

He decided to return to his apartment to retrieve his gun. This time, he'd take the Webley. More stopping power.

Jacqueline was waiting for him when he arrived, sitting on the bed sorting through a stack of letters: Sarah's love notes to Jourdain.

"How did you get in?"

"I made a copy of your keys the last time I was here," said Jacqueline, matter-of-factly. "This is pretty steamy stuff. I thought Sarah was your client."

"She is. Those weren't written to me."

"Really? 'I lose myself in your eyes, your lips, in the secrets of your heart.' It sounds like something someone would write to you."

"No-one would write—"

"I might." Jacqueline dropped the letters on the bed and slid to her feet in front of him. She draped her hands around his neck. "I missed you."

"I missed you—" Jacqueline's mouth on his wiped his thoughts of whatever else he might have said. After, while they were picking up the letters from where they had scattered on the floor, he said, "Are you back to stay?"

"I'm here now. Why isn't that enough?"

"It is," said Max, though it wasn't how he felt.

"We've gotten these out of order," said Jacqueline, dumping the letters on the bed.

"It doesn't matter. I don't think they're important."

"No, that's not it. You're too much of a gentleman to pry into her secrets. These letters are from the murdered man's wife to her lover. If the Prefecture had them, they'd be going through them word by word, looking for a clue to the murder. How did you get them?"

"Jourdain gave them to me."

"Why would he do that?"

"I don't think he meant to. Jean Martel had stolen them to blackmail him. He offered to let me read them to see how foolish that was. I don't think he expected me to take them, but he didn't object when I did."

"How could he? You would instantly have suspected he was hiding something. You wouldn't have stopped hounding him until you found out what it was. It's how the cops do it, you know. Decide who did it and then chase them until they find the evidence."

"Or make it up. A lot of innocent people wind up charged with crimes they didn't commit."

"True, but it seems more efficient than simply flailing around. Where did you learn to be a detective anyway?"

"I didn't. It just happened."

"Hmm." Jacqueline looked down at the letters she had spread on the kitchen table while they talked. "These are the last three – written after she came to Paris. See, they're on hotel stationary. The tone is different, too. Half of the earlier letters start with 'Dear Denis;' the rest, with 'Ma Cherie.' These three are different – 'mon amoureux secrets.'"

"My secret love."

"I don't think so. Her French is very good, but that phrase doesn't really mean anything. But 'mon amoureux des secrets' would mean 'a lover of secrets.'"

"A pet name, maybe. Something she called him by accident once and it stuck."

"Maybe – but the rest is incriminating. She hardly mentions her husband in the letters she wrote from America but here he is, and here, and here, too." She pointed to the last letters. "'If Mark were to find out, he would be furious, even violent.' Violence always begets violence."

"But Mark knew about Jourdain. Their marriage had become one of convenience. Or perhaps, one like those your friend describes: free love."

Jacqueline frowned and turned away. "The heart doesn't always find the head's prescriptions."

Max went into the bedroom and unlocked the top drawer of his dresser. He slipped the Webley into its shoulder holster and put it on, covering it with a leather jacket.

"Where are you going?" asked Jacqueline. Max thought he detected the slightest tremor in her voice.

"It's time I talked to my client and found out what the hell is going on."

§

Unlike at Le Meurice, the concierge at the Grand Hotel was easily moved to talk by a fifty franc note. The matron attending Madame St. John took ill shortly before eighteen hundred and was taken to the nursing station in the basement. She remained there for the night – though a replacement was called and arrived about four hours later. This merely confirmed what Fontaine had told him.

Madame had two visitors – both foreign gentlemen. Neither provided their names. The first came a few minutes after the matron took ill, while both the concierge and the desk captain were busy dealing with her and calling the Prefecture as they had been instructed. The man approached a bellhop who showed him to the suite. His description was sketchy – an Englishman he thought because his French was so bad, with red hair and a freckled complexion. He was very well dressed. He knocked on the door. It had opened by the time the bellhop was back in the elevator, but the boy couldn't attest as to whether he was granted admittance.

Not English, thought Max, *American. Ginger Buchan.*

The second man arrived a couple of hours later, although no-one had noticed the exact time. He was dressed in a heavy overcoat and hat, with a scarf around his face, despite the mildness of the evening. "It was strange," said the concierge, "but not unusual. Le Grand is popular with eastern nobility careful of their privacy."

"He was Russian?" asked Max.

"Possibly," said the man. "His accent was... confused. He might even have been a Frenchman trying to sound like a Russian."

§

Sarah's new matron eyed him suspiciously until Max showed her Fontaine's card. She ushered him into the salon where he met with Sarah. She was already there, sitting in her usual seat. She didn't rise to greet him, instead staring out the window with her back to him.

"Sarah, we need to talk. I know who killed your husband."

"I thought you might finally figure it out. Why didn't you bring Captain Fontaine with you?"

"What?"

"Are you saying you didn't come here to accuse me? That's almost amusing."

"Sarah. Don't do anything foolish."

"That's all I've done since I arrived in Paris. Foolish things. It has to stop before anyone else gets hurt. Before you get hurt Max. I killed Mark. I didn't pull the trigger. That odious little man, Ponant, did that. But I was there. I helped move the body. I drove the car."

"The two of you couldn't have done that by yourselves." He had refused to think of it before, but he had always known it was a possibility.

"There was a second man, a thug Ponant had found. A man most amenable to violence. For a thousand francs he was willing to take care of Ponant and then disappear. You'll never find him. I never even learned his name."

"Why?"

"He was going to destroy Denis – not only kill him, but destroy everything he believed in, everything he was striving to bring about. My husband was a cold man. He had no sense of justice, only a hatred of change. Denis represented a new hope and Marc couldn't stand that."

"Not jealousy, then."

"Envy, but not jealousy."

"And Martel? Why kill Martel?"

Sarah still hadn't turned to look at him but her shoulders had tightened at the mention of the politician's name.

"Martel? I—well, why not? He sent me a note. When Emma fell ill, I slipped out of the hotel in the confusion. The office where he was killed is only a few blocks from here."

Max glanced around the room. A newspaper was tumbled in a heap on the floor. She could have read of Martel's murder.

"So, you walked there, shot him, and returned without being seen?"

"Yes."

"And the gun?"

"I left it there. That unfortunate porter must have wandered in and found it."

"And did this all happen before or after Ginger Buchan came to see you? He was seen entering this apartment." Not quite true but she wouldn't know that for sure.

"Buchan? Oh, yes, he came by. A courtesy call from the Embassy. Belated but still welcome. He only stayed a few minutes. I practically followed on his heels."

"And your second visitor?"

"No one else came to see me," Sarah said, quickly. "I mean, someone knocked on the door, but I had already gone to bed. I didn't answer. I was... distraught."

"Yes. Shooting someone in the face would do that to you."

Sarah caught her breath, a soft choking sob. "I'm glad you understand. Tell Captain Fointaine I'm ready to make a full confession."

Max thought the story almost rang true. She could have walked to the office and back in a few minutes. Henri's kidnappers might have arrived later. Perhaps the kidnapping had nothing to do with

St. John's death at all. Perhaps they panicked when they discovered their – boss? – was dead. Even the motive for killing St. John was believable, more consistent with what he knew of the dead man. Yes, it all hung together, except for one thing. Where did she get the gun to shoot Martel? The police wouldn't have let her bring it with her and she'd had no visitors. Except Max. Max and Ginger Buchan.

"Have you told this... story to anyone else?"

"No."

"Don't. I'll bring Fontaine here, when he's ready to listen to you."

§

Gereau was in his office at the Prefecture; sometimes Max thought he never left it.

"So have you solved it yet?" Gereau asked, leaning back in his chair until it groaned in protest.

I think I know who did it," said Max, "and I have an inkling as to why."

"Care to make a semi-retired captain's day?"

"It's all speculation," said Max, wishing he felt as certain as he sounded "I have no proof. Nothing that would stand up in court."

"You might be surprised what counts for proof these days. Fontaine has transferred your friend from the hospital to a cell in the basement. He's pushing for a quick trial."

"He knows Henri didn't do it."

"Look at it from his perspective. He has future promotions to think of, not to mention his pension. You better find your proof pretty quick. He intends to try him on three counts of murder."

"St. John, Ponant and Martel."

"Clears the docket with a single trial. You have to admit it's tidy."

"He has no proof to link the three."

"Ah, but he does." Gereau shuffled through the files on his desk before pulling out a thin red folder. Max reached for it but Gereau shook his head. "You can't have it. I'm not supposed to have it."

"Well."

"They had to take it completely apart, but they finally found a bullet in our waterlogged car, lodged under a floor board. Our experts think it was the one which killed Ponant. More importantly, they claim it was fired from the same gun as the one that did Martel."

"They can do that?"

"It's all the rage. We've known for two decades that guns leave marks on bullets but Locard down in Lyon has made a science of it. I accept it as true."

"What about St. John?"

"No bullet was recovered but the wounds were consistent with a gun of the same caliber. Not rock solid but sufficient for a judge."

"What about motive? Opportunity?"

"No doubt of the latter in Martel's case. Motive? Revenge, perhaps, for being kidnapped. A good lawyer could get him off. Can Henri afford a good lawyer?"

"No, but I can."

§

He had dealt with a few lawyers since moving to Paris, though none to whom he wished to entrust the fate of his friend. *Jacqueline will know,* he thought. Although she herself had avoided prosecution for her anarchist views, she must know plenty who hadn't. There was little chance of finding a lawyer in town this late on a Saturday, but he supposed those who defended radicals might keep an irregular schedule.

Jacqueline was out when he returned home but there was a note on the kitchen table from Colonel Ledux, urging him to come to his apartment to discuss the death of Jean Martel.

Ledux met him at the door and led the way to the living room. Even though the space must be intimately familiar to him, Max was still amazed at how well he traversed it without the benefit of sight.

"Have they arrested Armand yet for Martel's murder?" Ledux was not a man to waste time with peasantries.

"No, they've arrested a railway porter."

"Your friend, Henri."

For a man who never left his quarters, Ledux was remarkably well informed. The Colonel waved at the sideboard, an invitation to pour them both a drink. Max remembered the Colonel preferred sherry; he needed something stronger and chose an Armagnac. It was, like the sherry, exceptional.

"I've satisfied myself that Armand had nothing to do with St. John's death," said Max.

"Who said anything about Mark? It is Martel I'm concerned about."

"The killings are connected."

"Nonsense. Is that Fontaine's latest theory? The man is an idiot."

"I won't argue the point," said Max. "But there is evidence. The gun that killed Martel also killed Ponant. It probably killed St. John, too."

"One gun. One killer. Elegant in its way." Ledux fumbled for a cigarette from the brass case on the table beside his chair. It was the first time Max had seen him stumble. This is not a man who takes well to having his conclusions challenged.

"Why would Armand kill Martel?"

"Armand was an arms dealer."

"I know that," said Max. "He's also a thief. He used stolen money to fund some of his business deals. He covered his tracks very well; I doubt Martel could shake him."

"What about a charge of treason?"

"Selling arms into the Russian conflict may be immoral but a charge of treason might be hard to prove."

Ledux laughed. "That's what Dreyfus thought. Armand sold arms to the Germans during the war, not directly, of course, but even the most circuitous route can be traced."

"You can prove this."

"No." Ledux sipped his sherry; his cigarette burned untouched in the ashtray. They sat in silence for several minutes. Finally, Ledux stirred and turned his face in Max's direction. If he didn't know better, he would think the man was staring at him.

"A man named Federov came to see me."

"Baron Denidov's manservant?"

"You might know him as that. I know him in another capacity. He and I were friends of a sort. In India. Ancient history now. He told me Martel came to Denidov. They had a long conversation. Federov heard little of it but it was enough. Martel wanted money to ensure the supply of arms to the Whites wouldn't be unexpectedly interrupted. Denidov gave him what he had and promised to get more. Then the boat sank. A few days later, Martel was shot. I'll let you draw your own conclusions."

"You think Martel had evidence that would prove Armand was responsible."

"Exactly. A motive for murder. And don't you find it interesting Martel was shot in the same building as Armand has his office?"

Max shook his head. It didn't add up. Despite common belief, criminals seldom return to the scene of the crime. It was too convenient. If Armand did resort to murder – and Max wasn't sure he had it in him – he would hire it done. He certainly wouldn't have it done in his own backyard. Still, there was the matter of the dark sedan. Whose car had Armand gotten into? And where was he now?

"You've given me a lot to think about," he said.

§

A police van stood in front of Pavlovna's building when Max arrived. A gendarme was leaning against it chatting with curious onlookers. The day's light was fading but he recognized several of the men as regulars at the local Russian cafés.

Max hesitated but then squared his shoulders and crossed the street. He went through the open grill as if he had every right and up the stairs to Pavlovna's suite. Another gendarme stood guard outside her door and barred the way when Max tried to enter.

"Captain Gereau sent for me," said Max. It was a reasonable gamble – Gereau was in charge of expatriates and arresting a descendent of Catherine the Great, no matter how tenuous the bloodline, wasn't a job for a lesser officer. The gendarme stepped aside.

Pavlovna was sitting in an ornate wingback chair, her back straight. The fire had returned to her expression and whatever doubt had afflicted her during their last meeting had fled. Gereau was standing over her, his arms crossed. He was chewing his mustache to keep from saying what it would likely be too impolitic to say.

At the other end of the room, Denidov was gesticulating with his uninjured arm and sputtering at LePêcheur, who calmly wrote it all down in a small black notebook. There was no sign of Federov.

"What's the matter, Captain?" asked Max.

Gereau spun on his heel and glowered at Max. "What are you doing here?"

"I came to see a man called Federov."

"Funny," said Gereau. "I'd like to see him myself, though I'm told he left the city last night. Somebody – perhaps this Federov, perhaps someone else – shot one of their fellow citizens in a café this afternoon."

"Gennady Sidorov is no citizen of Mother Russia," said Pavlovna. "He is a citizen of hell."

"Not quite," said Gereau. "The wound produced a lot of blood but very little damage. Mr. Sidorov is resting comfortable at his hotel. I've sent an officer to bring him here."

"How dare you bring that pig to my home?" said Pavlovna rising.

"So he can identify his assailant," said Gereau.

"It was Federov," said Denidov. "You said so yourself."

"Reports were mixed," said Gereau. "Eyewitnesses get confused when they're diving under tables. Some even said it was a woman. An unusually tall one." He cast an appraising eye at Pavlovna.

"Yes," said Pavlovna, "I shot him. He deserved to die for what he did to Sergei. I suppose it is fitting that I only wounded him."

Gereau smiled. "Your loyalty is misplaced. Sidorov had nothing to do with the attack on the Baron – if Baron he is. There was a matter of unpaid gambling debts."

Denidov turned red but said nothing. A uniformed officer entered the room and whispered something to Gereux, who swore softly.

"It seems that Mr. Sidorov's wounds were even less serious than I thought. He departed from Gare de L'Est an hour ago. I could have him brought back but I won't. The sooner he leaves France, the better I'll like it."

"But he killed Mark," said Pavlovna.

"I know that he didn't," said Gereau. "We had him in a cell in the Prefecture during the entire period during which the doctors say St. John must have died."

"But he had agency..."

"With all due respect, Madame Pavlovna, Sidorov may be guilty of a lot of things but he's not guilty of everything."

There was something troubling Max. Sarah St. John had had a second visitor the night Martel was murdered. Had it been Sidorov or Federov, both now beyond the reach of his questioning? The matter of Sarah's confession nagged at him. Why had she done it? And what did it have to do with the Russians? Because Max was sure he now knew who had pulled the trigger and killed three men. And he knew the reason for those crimes had its origin not in Paris, but in Moscow.

"I have to go," Max said.

"I didn't invite you," said Gereau. "And I won't keep you."

"But, if Sidorov didn't kill Mark..." said Pavlovna, her voice plaintive. "It must have been... it must have been done for love."

Max nodded. "It was. But love comes in many forms."

§

Max needed to talk to two men to confirm his suspicions. There were others he wanted to see but they could wait. Armand hadn't returned to his house in the Marais though his elderly servant admitted he had been in touch and would return in the morning.

Ginger Buchan had a small apartment not far from the American embassy. Max had never been there before but he knew where it was. The concierge proved remarkably cheap to bribe and a few minutes before midnight he showed Max up to the third floor flat. Max pounded on the door until Buchan, bleary-eyed and in a brocaded dressing gown, answered the door.

"Good Lord, Max, don't you ever sleep?" Buchan said, before admitting him to his bed sitting room.

"Not lately," said Max. "Why did you visit Sarah St. John last night?"

"Courtesy call. She is a citizen by marriage at least."

"After all this time of ignoring her, the Embassy suddenly takes an interest."

"Does anyone know you're here?" Buchan went to the window and peered through a crack in the drapes.

"No," said Max. "Should I have told someone?" A slight shiver went up his back and he was suddenly reminded of the comfortable weight of the Webley under his arm.

"God, no. I happen to like my job. What did Mrs. St. John tell you?"

"What you told her to say – a courtesy call were her exact words. She also told me she killed her husband. And Ponant and Jean Martel for good measure."

"Do you believe her?" asked Buchan.

"What do you think?"

"I think I should kick you out and pretend I've never even heard your name."

"What did you really go to see Sarah about?"

Buchan ran his hand through his thinning red hair. He crossed to an all-purpose cabinet standing against one wall, took out a couple of glasses and splashed a finger of bourbon in one. Max nodded and Buchan poured a second drink. It wasn't as good as the Armangnac.

"I got a cable yesterday. Supposedly from State but I have my doubts. Mark was working on a report before he died. They were asking why we hadn't sent it yet."

"Why hadn't you?"

"Nobody, and I mean nobody, at the Embassy knew anything about it. I checked around but no one seemed to know what it was about. Except Erich Harvey. You know him, right?"

Max nodded and Buchan went on.

"Harvey's not the most reliable of sources. Relies on this," he said, holding up his glass, "for too many of his ideas. But he told me that Mark had dropped some hints about something he had found out, something that would take down politicians and businessmen on both sides of the Atlantic."

"Sounds like something that came out of a bottle."

"Maybe, but the next day Mark was dead. If he had something, it wasn't at his apartment or any of his known hiding places."

"Why go to Sarah?"

"Something Mark said to Harvey – about trusting deceivers to be true to their nature. She was two-timing him."

"But she never saw her husband after she got to Paris."

"So she claimed. So she still claims. Two hours of haranguing her didn't change that."

"Two?"

"I got there about six thirty. The clock in the lobby said eight forty when I left."

Which means Sarah only had twenty minutes between Buchan's departure and the arrival of the mysterious second visitor to walk to the Banque Lyonnaise, kill Martel, and return. It was possible, he supposed, but only barely.

§

Max didn't feel like going home after his conversation with Buchan. Despite the drink, he was too edgy to sleep. Besides, Jacqueline would be there. He had wanted her to return to Paris, but he hadn't expected her to move into his apartment. He wasn't ready to deal with that on top of everything else.

Chez Jake was still hopping; Saturday night in the Jazz quarter operated on a different clock. The usual crowd of regulars were gathered around the bar watching the tourists hog the small dance floor. Roget had been a regular for some months. Now it appeared that, for one night, he was a regular again, drinking silently while others laughed and talked around him.

"Your boss give you the night off?" Max asked. Roget grunted and turned away. Max asked the only question that made sense, if his suspicions were correct. "Did you get what you were sent to get from Pierre Armand?"

Roget twisted on his bar stool, his answer in his hand in the form of a bottle. Max blocked the blow and threw an off-balance punch at Roget's mid-section. It missed; Roget's counter knocked Max to the floor. By the time Max had regained his feet, Roget was pushing past Smitty into the street.

"I'll take that for a no," muttered Max as he gingerly rubbed his jaw.

Twenty-Three – Sunday, June 27th, 1920

Max slept in his office chair, rising early after a fitful night. He grabbed a coffee and a stale sandwich from the kitchen on his way out the door.

Sarah St. John refused to see him. He was still standing at her door when Fontaine arrived.

"I got a message that Mrs. St. John has had a change of heart. She has decided that she killed her husband after all. I'm sure I have you to thank for that. As a show of gratitude, I've released Henri. I even had him driven home in a police car."

"I'm not sure his reputation will ever recover. Then you're still convinced that whoever killed Mark St. John also killed Martel."

"It's the only thing that makes sense."

"For once, Captain, I completely agree."

Jordain was in the lobby when they took Sarah away. He pretended to be there on business, and she never spared him a glance. Jourdain tried to slip away, but Max intercepted him. They walked together along the street to where Jourdain's car, a dark sedan, was parked.

"She didn't do it, Denis," Max said. "The confession is phony."

"How can you be sure?"

"I have a witness who will swear he was with her when Martel was murdered." Max was pretty sure Buchan would deny even being at the Hotel but Jourdain couldn't know that. "I think she confessed to protect you."

"You think I killed those three men?" Jourdain smiled and shook his head. "Why would I do that?"

"I don't know. Sarah thinks you did it because of love."

"I suppose she might think that, assuming you are right and her confession isn't genuine. Sadly, my passion for Sarah has been on the wane – ever since she announced she was returning to Paris."

"Really?"

"Did you really think I had avoided seeing her out of fear for my reputation? I'm a politician, Max. We only like to give good news. I had fond memories of our affair. It flattered me to think she was still obsessed by it. But the reality of it was – unpleasant. I didn't have the heart to tell her."

Max nodded. It fit with his own thinking. Mark St. John's supposed confession of lingering feelings for Sarah, made to men who couldn't help but pass it on, was another level of lying. At the end, St. John was lying to everyone about everything, except for his hatred of Bolsheviks. That was real. Who had come to see Sarah on Friday night after Buchan had left, after Martel had been shot in the face? If he knew that, his suspicions would be confirmed. But there was still the matter of proof.

"What will they do to her?" Max asked.

"Deport her, if she's lucky."

"If she's not?"

"I'll do what I can to keep her from the guillotine."

"You'll be in town then?"

"For a few days, until I can see which way the wind is blowing."

They had arrived at Jourdain's car. Max glanced at the chauffeur. It wasn't Roget.

"Can I drive you somewhere?" Jourdain asked.

"No," said Max. "The Metro's right there."

"Heading home for a well-deserved rest?"

"No," said Max. "I have an appointment with Pierre Armand."

§

Max came out of the Metro station a few blocks from Armand's Marais house at a dead run. The streets of this neighbourhood were tortuous and clogged with pedestrians out for a Sunday stroll. If he was lucky, he would reach Armand before it was too late.

Caron claimed his master hadn't returned, although his eyes kept flickering to the side as he said it. It was all the old man could do to keep from looking over his shoulder.

"Is Isabelle Grassie here?"

"She's indisposed," Caron seemed happy to change the subject.

"If she's here, so is he. Let me see him." A man who finds love late in life doesn't leave it at risk. If Armand was still away, he would have sent for her. Since he hadn't, he was either here or he was already dead.

"He has a visitor."

"A tough guy with a dark complexion and a pencil mustache," Max said.

Caron crumpled and stood aside; relieved perhaps to be disobeying an order he had had no faith in. "They're in the library. Through there."

Max drew the Webley and went through the door. Armand and Roget were sitting at a table, drinking coffee. No guns were visible, though Max suspected there were one or two hidden somewhere. It was that kind of meeting. Two file folders were sitting on the table.

Roget jumped to his feet and reached for the jacket hanging on the back of his chair.

"Keep your hands where I can see them," said Max. Roget didn't look happy but he obliged.

Armand hadn't moved. He couldn't keep his eyes off the gun in Max's hand.

"I'll take those files," Max said.

"There's money in the desk," said Armand. "Why don't you take that instead? These papers are of no interest to you."

"I can always get money. Justice is a rarer commodity."

"Take the money, Max," said Roget. "This stuff is out of your league."

"You don't have a clue what this is about, do you?"

Roget didn't answer, though his eyes flickered from the files to Armand to a point over Max's shoulder. Roget didn't know. He was always the loyal soldier, the unwitting dupe.

"I know who killed St. John," said Max. "And Ponant. And Martel. And I know why. And now, thanks to the two of you, I have the proof."

Armand still hadn't moved, though his hands were twitching. It was only a matter of time before he went for his gun.

"I don't know what you think is in those," Armand started.

"I don't think, I know," said Max. It was hard to concentrate, knowing that in a few moments he would have to shoot someone. It was all a matter of timing. "One of those files contains evidence that prove you sold guns to the Germans in the War."

Roget's eyes widened and his head jerked around. Max was right. He didn't know what the files contained.

"It is all hints and innuendo. It wouldn't stand up in court," said Armand. "No reason to kill anyone for it."

"Maybe not. Still, when the chance to get it back came up, you must have jumped at it."

"How did you figure it out?" asked Armand.

"Martel was known as the great deal maker, the purveyor of information. But I kept thinking of all those file cabinets in your office. You deal in information too. And Mark was your partner, the guy who knew more about your dealings than anyone. That's why he could trust you with that, his secret report."

"Is that what that is?" said Armand. "He told me not to read it. I presumed it would be safer if I didn't."

Roget's eyes flicked to the spot over Max's shoulder again. Maybe it was reflected in his dark eyes, maybe it was the flash of sunlight off metal, maybe it was his instincts that told him the moment had come. Max jerked to the left so the bullet meant for the back of his head, clipped his shoulder instead.

He twisted and raised the Webley toward the shattered window but Armand was quicker. The little gun in his hand went pop, once, twice. There was a yell and the sound of a body hitting the ground outside.

"I hope you didn't kill him," said Max, pointing his pistol at Armand. "I'd like to see him go to trial. I'd like to see you both go to trial. Roget, call Captain Gereau at the Prefecture. There's a telephone on the desk."

Armand carefully put his gun on the table on top of the files, while Max backed over to the window. Caron had Denis Jourdain pinned to the ground with a pitchfork. He was bleeding from a wound in his right shoulder but his eyes were open.

"He's on his way," said Roget. His hands were shaking. *Once again, his heroes have betrayed him*, thought Max.

"What is in that report that would drive Jourdain to murder?" asked Armand. "I really didn't read it. It was in English."

"It's the story of an ambitious politician who planned to take leadership of the Socialist party after the radical wing, always the smallest section, split away. The pendulum always swings; he knew it was only a matter of time before he held the reins of power."

"So?" said Roget. "Jourdain was a centrist. A democrat."

"No," said Max. "Mark St. John met Lenin when he was here in Paris and came to hate him. Denis Jourdain had the opposite reaction. He was a convert. His whole life was directed to the moment he could seize power and declare the French Soviet."

"It would never have worked," said Armand. "Paris would have risen in a minute."

"Probably," said Max. "but you don't change the world by dreaming small dreams."

Twenty-Four – Saturday July 4th, 1920

Max sat in the courtyard of the American Embassy, helping Buchan celebrate his country's birthday. He had managed to keep Ginger out of the spotlight, despite the best efforts of Jordain's high priced lawyers to drag him in. The trial was still going on, although Gereau had assured him that Jourdain's fate was sealed. Armand was cooperating fully in exchange for a shortened sentence. Even Roget was testifying for the prosecution. Sarah St. John had refused to testify, though she had provided Max with a deposition, along with a sizeable cheque.

Buchan had extended the invitation to Henri and Yesim. The pair were enjoying their first taste of American whiskey almost as much as they were enjoying shocking the Ambassador's wife with their outrageous, and largely fabricated, tales of Parisian life.

Buchan had raised his eyebrows slightly when Max arrived with Jacqueline on his arm but had said nothing. Max suspected he knew she was one of the infamous Two Jacques but, if he did, he kept it to himself and played the gracious southern gentleman.

Max watched him dancing with his girlfriend – the word still sounded strange to him – but felt no twinge of jealousy. Despite Jacqui's theories of free love, he had no doubts about her. He wished he could be so certain about himself.

A gentle hand rested on his shoulder and he looked up at Sarah St. John.

"I heard you were staying at the embassy," said Max.

"The Ambassador was kind enough to invite me. He thought it best if I were kept away from the reporters."

"The French papers can be vicious."

"Will they really execute Denis?"

"He may get off. He claims he did it for love. Which is true enough. Love of power."

"I feel such a fool."

"You had bad luck," said Max, unsure what else to say.

"With Mark, with Denis." Sarah watched Buchan dancing with Jacqueline. If Jacqui had seen them talking, she gave no indication. "Why couldn't I have met someone like you?"

"You did."

"Bad luck and then bad timing," said Sarah. "Happiness is elusive, Max. Don't throw yours away by looking for something better. There isn't anything better than right now."

The music had come to an end. Jacqui was laughing. Something she said made Buchan laugh, too. Yesim and Henri joined them. Yesim kissed her on both cheeks. Even his sadness was not immune to her youth, her sheer joy for life.

"Yes," he said. "You're right. There is nothing better than this."

But when he looked for her, Sarah was gone.

Don't miss out!

Visit the website below and you can sign up to receive emails whenever Hayden Trenholm publishes a new book. There's no charge and no obligation.

https://books2read.com/r/B-A-ZSKO-TQHSB

Also by Hayden Trenholm

Max Anderson Mysteries
In the Shadow of Versailles
By Dawn's Early Light

Standalone
Let Me Gather My Thoughts

Watch for more at https://www.haydentrenholm.com/.

About the Author

Hayden Trenholm is an award-winning playwright, novelist and short story writer. His short fiction has appeared in many magazines, including Analog Science Fiction and Fact, and anthologies such as The Sum of Us and Strangers Among Us, and on CBC radio. His first novel, A Circle of Birds, won the 3-Day Novel Writing competition in 1993; it was recently translated and published in French. His trilogy, *The Steele Chronicles*, were each nominated for an Aurora Award. Stealing Home, the third book, was a finalist for the Sunburst Award. Hayden has won five Aurora Awards – three times for short fiction and twice for editing anthologies. He purchased Bundoran Press in 2012 and was its managing editor until the press closed in 2020. He lives with his wife and fellow writer, Liz Westbrook-Trenholm, in Ottawa, having retired in 2017 after 15 years as a policy adviser to the Senator for the Northwest Territories.

Read more at https://www.haydentrenholm.com/.

About the Publisher

House of Straw is an Ottawa based publisher of mysteries and other genre books.

www.ingramcontent.com/pod-product-compliance
Lightning Source LLC
LaVergne TN
LVHW050930080826
845145LV00001B/284

* 9 7 8 1 9 2 7 8 8 1 6 4 4 *